# THE LOVING GAME

At the age of sixteen Patrick Kerr discovered he wasn't who he thought he was. His father is a musician named Cody, who had a one night stand with his mother—and disappeared. Two years later Patrick is still trying to trace his father when he meets Leah, Cody's former sister-in-law, a married woman with a son, Kim, almost as old as Patrick. Leah and Patrick's illicit relationship draws him into her chaotic Norfolk household—and closer to Kim and his wild moneymaking schemes. Frustrated by Leah's refusal to give as much of herself as he demands, Patrick brings the relationship to a head—with terrifying results...

| 0 | 1 | 2 | 3 | 4 | 5 | 6 | 7 | 8 | 9 |
|---|---|---|---|---|---|---|---|---|---|
| 1440 | 361 | 562 092 | 2377 | 594 | 843 | 6386 | 238 6798 | | 959 |
| 750 | 74 | 6232 | | 084 | 535 | | 107 | | 319 |
| 900 | | 532 | | 3404 | 097 | 376 | 36 | | 6489 |
| 490 | 801 | | | | | 260 | 7887 | 30688 | |
| 670 | 791 | | | | | 366 | 351 | | 699 |
| 580 | | | | | | | 9587 | | |
| | | | | | | 7886 | | | |
| | | | | | | 6306 | | | |

# THE LOVING GAME

# The Loving Game

*by*

Sylvia Baker

**Black Satin Romance**
Long Preston, North Yorkshire,
England.

British Library Cataloguing in Publication Data.

Baker, Sylvia
   The loving game.

   A catalogue record for this book is
   available from the British Library

   ISBN 1-86110-027-2

First published in Great Britain by Headline Book Publishing, 1996

Copyright © 1996 by Sylvia Baker

The right of Sylvia Baker to be identified as the author of this work has been asserted by her in accordance with the Copyright, Designs and Patents Act, 1988

Published in Large Print 1997 by arrangement with Headline Book Publishing Ltd., and Judith Murdoch Literary Agency.

Black Satin Romance is an imprint of
Library Magna Books Ltd.
Printed and bound in Great Britain by
T.J. International Ltd., Cornwall, PL28 8RW.

All characters in this publication are fictitious and any resemblance to real persons, living or dead, is purely coincidental

For Dean and Freddie,
with love always.

# Chapter 1

Patrick knew there was something wrong the minute he stepped inside the back door. His sister's coat lay in a crumpled heap on the kitchen table, one arm dragging on the floor. Coats were never flung like this on his mother's kitchen table, let alone left there. And the house was quiet; she'd obviously come without the twins. If ever she brought Emma and Heidi round in the afternoon they'd be waiting for him, running at him to be lifted and swung in the air before he'd hardly had time to get in. And, finally, there was no neatly cut cheese sandwich on top of the fridge.

They were all minor things in themselves, and he was only alerted by them because he was feeling particularly sensitive; even the sudden shower that had soaked him on the way home had felt as though it was aimed at him personally.

He closed the back door as quietly as possible and crept through to the hall. Trust Ginny to come round today; trust something to be wrong today.

'Patrick,' his mother called from the sitting room. 'Can you come in here for a minute?'

'Shit,' he muttered under his breath, debating whether to make out he hadn't heard and dash off upstairs.

'Patrick,' his mother called again.

He put his head round the door. They were standing side by side, his mother and sister, one tall and blonde, the other shorter and grey, but both had the same expression, and he noticed a few telltale streaks of mascara on Ginny's lightly made-up face. It was exactly like that day six months ago when he had been called home from school to be told his father had died.

'Hi, Ginny,' he said, lingering in the doorway. 'What's up?'

She lowered her head just enough to avoid his eyes, and for an awful moment he thought, they know; they know where I've been. Then his mother was saying, 'We've got something to tell you,' and waving an impatient hand at him. 'Come in here. We can't talk with you lounging in the doorway.'

'Can I get changed first?' He stretched out his sweater. 'I'm soaked.'

'All right but don't be long.'

Upstairs, he pulled off his school clothes, dragged on an old pair of jeans, and went straight to the bathroom. First he cleaned his teeth, loading his toothbrush with an extra long squeeze of paste to make sure he took away all traces of the whisky he'd drunk earlier. He didn't like whisky much but it was all they had been able to find worth drinking in her parents' cocktail cabinet. Then he undid the zip of his jeans and began to scrub the remaining felt pen from his stomach. The letters were smudged, some almost obliterated by sweat and the rubbing of his clothes. She'd got the idea from a report she'd read about two Brazilian soap stars who had each been tattooed with the other's name. 'You'll never guess where,' she said. But he had guessed and refused to let her write there, more out of shyness than anything, and she'd had to content herself with his stomach.

After a few seconds of scrubbing, all traces of the felt pen had gone. He zipped up his jeans and went to work on his chest. Most of what she'd written there, tracing a path down between his ribs, he'd wiped off with a wet finger. She hadn't actually finished the whole word; he'd stopped her once he realised what it was. But she'd said it instead, taunting him with it while she threw items of his clothing at him. Useless. That's what she'd called him.

The U was still there like a curving scar between his nipples, and he rubbed at it in a fury of humiliation. But even when his chest was perfectly clean, he felt as though the whole word was emblazoned there, carved in bright red on his pale skin. Bright red was appropriate; scarlet blood for all the deaths he'd died that afternoon, he thought dramatically. The death of his pride, his virginity, and the erotic death of the Elizabethan poets. Leonie would not have understood this last idea; she was as interested in poetry, past or present, as he was in her talk of soap opera stars.

He hung about in the bathroom as long as possible, turning on the shower so they'd think that's what he was doing—just as they thought he'd spent the afternoon playing tennis in the school tournament. To make it look convincing, he filled the basin with water and ducked his head in it, then realised that he'd probably been wet enough already. Why, he thought, frantically mopping up the bathroom floor with the towel, why the hell did they have to pick today to tell him bad news or whatever it was they had to tell him?

When he finally went down, his mother was waiting for him at the bottom of the stairs.

'I was just coming to get you,' she said.

'Is it that important?' he muttered, brushing past her into the sitting room.

'Yes, I'm afraid it is.' He heard her take a deep breath as she came up behind him, and imagined he felt a chilly draught on the back of his damp neck.

Ginny was now hunched in an armchair staring into the empty fireplace but she got up as they came in, and he could see that she had definitely been crying.

'You may wonder why we didn't tell you this before,' his mother began, stopping to cough quietly into her hand. 'But we thought it best to carry on as things were. For...for Dad's sake really.' The phrase sounded awkward somehow but before he had time to dwell on it, she went on, 'Now he's no longer here,' that sounded more like her—not dead, just no longer here, 'we thought you should know.' She turned abruptly on Ginny who had started to sniff and wipe at her eyes. 'For goodness sake, Ginny. If you want me to tell him, keep quiet.'

She was getting irritable. How he hated it

14

when she got irritable. She never lost her temper, and he couldn't remember her ever shouting or smacking him. But those impatient little sighs and the quick frowns of disapproval had been just as effective over the years. She cleared her throat. 'I'm not your mother, Ginny is.'

For a moment he wanted to laugh with relief. Nobody was dead; nothing was drastically wrong; and he wasn't about to get a lecture on the dangers of sex at sixteen. But the laugh didn't materialise, because over the next few seconds he felt as though everything was falling apart. Nothing was what it seemed any longer, his whole life was suddenly changed. He stared at them—and so much explained. The woman who had always looked so much older than his friends' mothers. And Ginny. It felt obscene somehow, like a kind of incest. He remembered how, when he was small, she'd seemed to be in and out of his life. A string of incidents came pouring back to him: disturbances when she'd appeared with toys that were later taken away, or came to pieces in his hands however careful he was; the suffocating attention when she was there, and the vague feeling of being a nuisance when she wasn't. And her wedding day; the embarrassment when she had cried over saying goodbye to him as she went off on her honeymoon. She'd clutched him to her at the last moment and confetti had showered over them both. How many people had known? he wondered.

'I'm sorry, Patrick.' He was still staring at

15

Ginny and she took a step towards him. 'I know it must be a shock, I know we should have told you before.'

It would be so easy to say, it's all right, I always loved you best anyway. But he couldn't because he was filled with such a blaze of resentment towards her. It was all her fault. All the humiliation he'd suffered earlier was her fault. For the whole of his sixteen years they'd deceived him; these two who should have loved him better than anyone had damaged him as surely as if they'd physically abused him.

'I should have known.' He saw them look at one another, and felt his throat tighten up as though a giant fist had gripped it.

Ginny visibly gathered herself, and then came to put an arm round his shoulders. But the gesture was too slow, too clumsy—too late, he thought. He pulled away and ran off upstairs.

It had stopped raining and his room was flooded with sunshine. He dragged the curtains across and threw himself face down on the bed. How could any one day be so awful? And it wasn't only going to be today—there was tomorrow to get through yet, and all the following days.

'Can I come in?' Ginny was knocking at the door. He didn't answer and she pushed it open.

He rolled onto his side away from her and fixed his eyes on his bookshelves opposite. And his tapes, neat and tidy in a plastic holder, not to be played too loud. A rule he obeyed like he obeyed all the others, considerate of his older parents' need for peace and quiet.

'It's been very difficult for me, Patrick,' Ginny was saying. 'Please try and understand.'

Difficult. He wanted to spit the word back at her. She'd just turned his world upside down and that's the best she could think of.

'Larry knows.' She lowered herself carefully onto the end of his bed. 'We thought perhaps you might like to come and live with us...with the twins. Mum won't mind. We've discussed it. She'd like to move nearer to Aunt Cath now she hasn't got Dad.'

Patrick flung himself over and then upright. 'Don't keep saying Mum and Dad. They're your Mum and Dad, not mine.' He wished he hadn't cleaned the whisky from his breath, wished he could breathe it into her face. 'And I don't care where she goes. I don't care what either of you do.'

'I didn't think you'd be so upset,' she said bleakly. 'I thought you'd understand. I was the same age as you are now. I didn't know what to do. You know how difficult it is to talk to...'

'We're not living in the Dark Ages,' he broke in as she hesitated over what word to use, 'you weren't about to be slung out on the streets.'

'It felt like I was,' she said, beginning to cry.

'Tell me then,' he said coldly, feeling the tears stinging at the back of his own eyes. 'Tell me why you didn't just get rid of me?'

'I wouldn't have done that. But I was at school and—'

'Who's my father? That's all I want to know. Who is he?'

17

'He doesn't know anything about you.'

'I didn't ask that, I said who is he?'

'He was Irish. A musician.'

The tears evaporated in a sneer of laughter. 'So that's why you called me Patrick. How appropriate.' He thought of Leonie printing the letters low down across his stomach and then letting him do the same to her. What had felt like one of the sexiest things he'd ever done now felt totally disgusting.

'It was his second name,' Ginny said, sniffing and dabbing at her eyes. 'His first name was Gabriel.'

'Was, was,' Patrick barked at her. 'Doesn't he exist any longer?'

'I didn't mean it like that.' The tears overflowed again. 'But I wasn't seeing him for long.'

'And you never told him about me?'

'No...I couldn't.'

Patrick turned his head away from her. 'Why?'

'It wouldn't have done any good—he wouldn't have wanted to know.'

'Why didn't you just stick me in...stick me in an orphanage. Then nobody would have had to be bothered with me.'

Ginny sobbed into her handkerchief. 'I always wanted to tell you, but Mum kept saying it wasn't the right time. When we moved here she told people you were hers. They supported you—financially I mean. They did love you, Patrick.'

'Does he have a surname?' he asked flatly.

Ginny shook her head. After a few seconds

she whispered, 'I don't know it.'

'Nor where he is now, I don't suppose.'

'No, I've no idea.'

'Do you know anything about him? Or have you conveniently forgotten?' Only by injecting every word with anger could he get the whole sentence out.

'It was a long time ago.'

'You've conveniently forgotten,' he concluded. With every unanswered question he was coming nearer to tears himself, but when Ginny stood up and came to sit closer to him, he shouted at her, 'Leave me alone!'

'But, Patrick, I want us to work things out.'

'Go away!' he shouted.

She reached out a hand to touch him but he jerked his head round to glare at her. Her hand hung in the space between them for a moment, then she drew back. 'Patrick, please,' she said gently. 'I can't go and leave you like this.'

'Like what?' he snarled. 'I'm fine. I'm perfect.' And with that he leapt up and stormed off out.

For over an hour he walked round the streets, stopping only to buy a beefburger because he was starving. He dawdled along eating it, jostled by rush hour crowds, not wanting to go home but not sure where he could go instead. Especially with no money. At one point, tripping and nearly falling as he'd careered down the stairs after leaving Ginny, he'd made up his mind to run away. Leave home, leave school—solve everything in one go. But as he calmed down, the idea seemed less appealing. He'd just passed a couple of kids begging. They

19

were dressed in layers of filthy clothes like a pair of old winos, and one had crusted sores round his mouth. That kind of life, especially when it involved being dirty and hungry, held no attraction for Patrick whatsoever. Materially there wasn't much that he needed and didn't have, but he had plenty of dreams about his future. And they didn't include hanging around the streets or being homeless. He crossed over, dodging between the lines of slow-moving traffic. And anyway, he might have lived in London most of his life but he doubted whether he could survive here away from home.

He crossed again using the underpass. There were more beggars down there sitting with their backs against the wall, so still they looked like part of the graffiti. He hurried on, taking the next exit and coming up, almost without thinking, a short distance from the street where his best friend lived. It was quieter here, the houses rising three and four storeys in long Georgian terraces. Each front door was reached by a little flight of narrow steps, and there was space to park in the road. It was packed with cars now. Everyone home, Patrick thought, and hoped Mansour's family would have finished eating. But even if they hadn't he knew he would still be welcome.

Mansour was surprised to see him and took him straight up to his bedroom. 'Couldn't you wait to tell me about it?' he said, once they were settled down, Mansour lolling on his bed and Patrick sprawled on a giant beanbag.

Patrick frowned at him, wondering how he

20

knew and why he was grinning.

'Don't act dumb, Patrick.' Mansour lobbed a paperback from his bedside table across the room. 'We all know you went off with Leonie this afternoon.'

'Oh, that.' Patrick smiled, realising that he hadn't given it a thought since he'd left the house. 'No, it's not that.'

'I thought that's why you'd come round, to tell me about it.'

'Not really.' For the first time since they'd been friends, Patrick found it hard to confide in Mansour. They had met when they were both twelve in their first term at grammar school, and had clung together like two lost souls, timid and mildly bullied, Patrick because he was the headmaster's son, and Mansour because of his prep school background. And they had stayed friends even though they had both changed beyond all recognition. Patrick had grown taller and cleverer and better looking than Mansour, and most of his year. To a certain extent, he was well aware of the use of these qualities. He lapped up the attention he got from girls and the admiration for being a star on the sports field as well as constantly top of his class. But he was often plagued with self-doubt, and relied heavily on Mansour's quiet confidence and common sense. It was Mansour who had got him through his early teens when the smallest upset could send him into a turmoil of anxiety.

'Well, come on, tell me,' said Mansour. 'Did you go to bed with her?'

'We got into her bed, yeah.'

'And?' Mansour got up to close the door. He had five sisters, all of whom seemed to appear whenever Patrick was there.

'Don't ask me, I've had a terrible afternoon.'

'What happened? Did her parents come home early and catch you?'

Patrick shook his head. 'Worse than that —well, nearly.' He couldn't help smiling at the look of comic expectation on Mansour's face, and what had seemed the most humiliating thing in the whole world lost some of its importance. 'It was all over in about half a second.'

Mansour's jet eyebrows shot upwards and he burst into laughter. 'You know what they call that, don't you?'

'Shut up, you stupid fucker.' Patrick slung the book back at him. 'It's not funny. She'll tell everybody.'

'Probably,' said Mansour, catching the book with one hand. 'What did she do to get you in that state?'

'Never you mind.' Patrick had no intention of telling even Mansour how, as soon as they had got into bed, Leonie had spread her legs and pushed his head down between them. Neither was he going to reveal that this was the furthest he'd ever got with a girl, and when she had knelt over him to put on a condom, encouraging him to handle her breasts, things had nearly finished there and then.

'That'll teach you to dabble with eighteen-year-olds.'

Patrick ignored this; he hadn't come here to talk about Leonie. 'Then I go home and...'

He broke off almost immediately, not sure he wanted to tell Mansour this either.

'And what?' Mansour encouraged, his face growing serious.

'I find out my sister's really my mother.'

'Your sister Georgina? I don't believe it. Is she old enough?'

'Just.'

'What a shock for you.'

'That's putting it mildly.' Patrick was suddenly glad he'd confided in Mansour; all he needed now was sympathy. 'I'm devastated,' he said. 'Completely devastated.'

'Oh, come on,' said Mansour after a few seconds. 'It's not that bad. You'll get used to it.'

There was a longer silence. Patrick's emotions did another U-turn and he wished he hadn't come. Mansour just didn't understand, and it was putting a burden on him to expect him to think of consoling things to say.

'I s'pose I will, eventually,' he said, thinking, that's not the point, although what he wanted to hear he didn't really know himself.

'Did she tell you all about it?' asked Mansour. Patrick shook his head.

'Not even about your real father?'

'He's Irish and called Gabriel Patrick something or other. That's all I know. She doesn't want to talk about it—she said he wouldn't want to know me anyway.'

Mansour smiled with disbelief. 'Every man wants to know his son, Patrick.'

'It's different in your culture.'

'No, no. A son is important in any culture.'

'Well, it doesn't make any difference, I'm never going to meet him.'

'Don't you want to?'

'Of course I fucking want to. But what do you expect me to do?'

'You could try and trace him yourself.'

Patrick usually listened to Mansour's suggestions; his good sense had so often solved problems in the past. But tonight it wasn't good, sensible suggestions he needed; it was to let off steam about everything that had happened today and for someone to tell him it was OK to feel as he did. And that if he wanted to, he could just sit there and bawl his eyes out. But there was no way he could do that with Mansour.

'Have you seen your birth certificate?'

Patrick shrugged. 'No, I don't think so. Anyway what will that tell me that I don't already know? His name won't be on it.'

'I suppose not. But you could find other ways, if you were determined.'

'What do you expect me to do? Stick an advert in the paper—will the Irishman called Gabriel who fucked an under-age schoolgirl called Georgina—' He stopped dead as a little tap came on the door. Mansour leapt up to open it.

The eldest of Mansour's sisters stood there. She smiled shyly at Patrick, looking very demure and pretty in a pink and green sari instead of the school uniform he usually saw her in. He smiled back and she blushed and lowered her eyes. 'Mummy says would you and Patrick like to come down for coffee?' she said. A group of younger sisters gathered behind her as she spoke.

'Yes, we'll be down in a minute,' said Mansour. 'Now off you go, we're having a private conversation.' They giggled together and ran off. Mansour pointed after them. 'And you think you've got woman trouble—what do you think it's like living with that lot?'

'At least you know who's who in your family. I wouldn't mind swapping places with you,' said Patrick.

'And I wouldn't have minded swapping with you this afternoon.'

Patrick knew it was meant to cheer him up and he forced another smile. 'So you think you could have done better, do you?'

'Definitely.'

Normally this sort of conversation would go on and on, the two of them trading insults, trying to outdo each other with witty repartee; and sometimes it deteriorated into mock battles where they pitted their strength against each other like a pair of young lions. But this evening it was different. Patrick hadn't the heart for any of it. And when Mansour suggested they went downstairs to have coffee with his parents, adding a warning to watch his language, Patrick felt that even his best friend was picking fault with him now and decided to go home.

The house was empty. There was a note to say he'd find cold meat and salad in the fridge, and he remembered it was his mother's, or rather his grandmother's—that was going to take a bit of getting used to—bridge night. He slumped down at the kitchen table and ate the cold meat with his fingers, then went straight up to bed. Getting undressed, he purposely thought of Leonie, picturing the sight of her naked body and fantasising how it would be next time he went to bed with a girl. But he felt only mild arousal, not enough to do anything about. For once, thoughts of sex were not uppermost in his mind. He could think only of the father he would never know, and his childhood that should have been so different. It had made him into the person he was, not the person he wanted to be.

A car's headlights lit up his room as it turned into the drive to the garage. There was the sound of the garage door being shut, then locked. Soft footsteps round to the back. She wouldn't come up; he was quite sure of that. Not until she went to bed herself anyway. He had vaguely hoped to find Ginny still here, waiting for him. But of course she had the twins to see to; they were her proper children, he told himself as he settled down to sleep, more unhappy than he'd ever been in his whole life.

## Chapter 2

So here it was at last, this house that he'd been dreaming about for so long. And more or less as he'd pictured it with the great awning of the yew tree shading the front lawn.

Patrick leant his bicycle against the stone gatepost and dragged his T-shirt from his jeans to wipe the sweat from his face. It was far too hot for cycling, especially all those miles from his grandmother's bungalow.

The minutes ticked by. He pretended to be checking his tyres, all the while keeping an eye on the house in case anyone should emerge. He kept a watch up and down the lane as well; they could be out and on their way home. He removed his pump, fiddled with the valve. Nearly ten minutes had gone by and still he couldn't bring himself to do it.

He'd known it would be like this, that he wouldn't have the courage to go and knock on the door, march up and say in a politely confident tone, 'Is Mr Cody in?' Of course there was no guarantee that his father still lived here—the newspaper cutting had been dated nineteen years ago. Reading it, crouched over the box of old exercise books in his grandmother's loft, was the first time he'd felt any sympathy for Ginny. For days afterwards he'd thought of her, not yet sixteen and pregnant, seeing that report in the newspaper, hiding it amongst her books. He'd lain awake at night thinking about it, knowing that she must have lain awake too, sick with worry. He hadn't told her he'd found it, and when he'd watched as the books were consumed in the flames of a bonfire shortly before his grandmother moved, he found himself bitter again, angry that Ginny hadn't remembered it and shown him.

Two and a half years ago his grandmother

had gone back to the Suffolk village where she was born, and Patrick had moved in with Ginny, Larry and the twins. Still he didn't mention the cutting, or his father. And every week that went by, he'd sensed that Ginny relaxed a bit more as if she imagined he'd come to terms with not knowing his father. In fact it was constantly on his mind.

Then one night when Patrick was sitting up late watching television on his own, she had come through from the kitchen before going up to bed, and kissed him goodnight. It was only a quick peck on the cheek, but it was the first time she'd kissed him since he was a little boy and had believed she was his sister. He'd looked up at her and smiled and she'd ruffled his hair.

'This is what I've wanted for years, to have you here,' she said, in the half embarrassed way she had of displaying affection. 'Are you glad you came to live with us?'

He nodded. Adjusting to their changed relationship had been a bumpy ride; moments of closeness like this had been few. He waited only a second before seizing his chance. 'I want to find my father,' he blurted out. 'Will you help me?'

Her face changed; she shook her head as though he'd suggested something completely out of the question. 'No,' she said. 'No, I can't.'

He stared at the television screen, rocked with disappointment.

'It's not a good idea, Patrick.' She perched on

the arm of his chair, her tone more reasonable. 'Not after all this time.'

'That doesn't make any difference, he's still my father.'

'But I've no idea where to start looking. I never knew where he lived.'

He had wanted to mention the cutting then, but the fact that she was lying to him made him clam up with resentment.

'I'm sorry, Patrick, but it's too late now,'

'And whose fault is that?' he'd said. And he'd repeated it, louder until he was shouting at her, letting out everything he'd been bottling up since that day he'd learnt she was his mother. When she began crying he didn't care.

That had been six months ago and neither of them had mentioned it since. Mansour had helped him trace the address. He'd wanted to come sooner but his life was filled with so much at the moment. And if there was one thing his grandmother's upbringing had taught him, it was the ability to wait patiently for something he really wanted.

He looked over the fence at the house again. How different it was from Ginny's semi. Yew Tree House was twice the size, with leaded windows, the upper floor tucked chocolate-box style under the eaves. The whole of the front was covered in shiny dark ivy which had crept right up to the windowsills. Curtains were drawn in all the upstairs windows and there were no cars on the gravelled parking area at the side of the house. There was a new-looking garage but it was closed, giving the impression that nobody was due home. The place looked almost deserted.

After a few more seconds of indecision, he swung onto his bicycle and rode back into the village to find somewhere to buy a cold drink. The only shop was closed for lunch, so he padlocked his bicycle and went into the pub.

He ordered half a pint of lager, and the woman behind the bar smiled pleasantly at him and lingered to mop up spilt beer, polishing away at the same spot. 'That'll cool you down,' she said as he took a first long gulp.

He smiled back at her, pushing the damp hair from his forehead. 'I've been cycling,' he said. 'It's hard work in this heat.'

'I bet.' She came to lean on the bar, her breasts propped on her folded arms and bulging above the scooped neckline of her blouse. 'Obviously keeps you fit though.'

'Yeah,' he nodded, fixing his eyes on her for a moment. She was old enough to be his mother, older even, and didn't appeal to him in the slightest, but the appraisal in her eyes boosted his confidence. It had taken him a long time to feel comfortable with the fact that women found him extremely attractive; even longer to play on it. But if they didn't respond to him at once, his confidence soon ebbed away.

He wiped a hand across his mouth. 'Do you know the people who live at Yew Tree House?'

'Not personally. But I know of them, everybody round here does.'

'I see.' He hesitated for only a second. 'I've

been researching my family tree and I think I may be related to one of them. I didn't want to go knocking on the front door out of the blue, and I couldn't find a phone number for them.'

'You won't,' she said, shifting her position as though she was settling down for some intriguing gossip. 'They're ex-directory. A famous guitarist used to live there. Now what was his name?' She closed her eyes and jiggled her fingers in the air. 'Oh, I can't think.'

'Was it,' he swallowed, 'was it Gabriel Cody?'

'No, nothing like that. He was Spanish. Mike!' she called over her shoulder. Mike, whoever he was, seemed to have disappeared. 'De something or other,' she went on. 'He was on telly and everything. We've only been here six months but people round here remember him. He couldn't read or write, but they say he earned a bomb playing the guitar. Apparently, he lives back in Spain now with the eldest daughter—has done for years. It's the younger two who live in the house now.'

'Do you know their names?'

'There's Tanya,' she counted on her fingers. 'Then Leah. But they don't say it like we do, they say it like a chicken laying eggs—you know, a layer.' She gave a little chuckle and adjusted the front of her blouse. 'It's funny because she's the only one with children.'

Patrick waited. The eldest would be Justina, the dark beauty of the newspaper cutting, who had married his father two months before he was born.

'Do you want another?' the woman said, reaching for his empty glass.

He nodded. 'It's the husband of the eldest daughter I'm interested in.'

'I don't know much about him. They were divorced years ago. Our cleaner remembers him—an Irishman. She said you could hear Justina shouting and screaming at him in the next village. Mind you, they're all a bit like that. The young one, Tanya, she'll end up killing someone the way she tears round these lanes.'

'How old is she?' His head was full now of this family, real live people who had grown older and no longer fitted those static figures in the wedding-day photograph. He wanted to get them in some sort of order in his mind.

'About your age, I suppose. Early twenties?' she said, raising her eyebrows. Patrick nodded. People often thought he was older than eighteen, partly because he was six foot tall. He and Mansour had been able to drink in the London pubs without being questioned since they were sixteen.

'What about the others?'

'I'm not sure. I think Justina must be past forty. And Leah's somewhere in between, I suppose. She's the one to speak to—Leah. They say she's the nicest. She's the prettiest as well.' She wriggled her shoulders at him. 'I don't know about you, but I never think scrawny girls are very attractive, they always look so miserable.'

He was only half listening now, absorbed with the thought that his search was just beginning rather than nearly over.

The woman tapped her fingers on his arm. 'Take the bull by the horns, love. Go and knock on the door.'

'What's her surname—the nice one?'

'Carew. Her husband's supposed to be very nice as well. He's a professor of some kind. Mike!' she called again. This time Mike appeared. 'That Leah Carew's husband, what does he teach?'

'Greek.' His tone was curt. 'Maggie, there's someone wanting the lunch menu.'

She raised her eyes towards the ceiling, picked up a menu from behind the bar and went off towards a couple who had just come in.

Patrick would have liked some food as well but the little money he had wouldn't last very long if he started eating out. His grandmother gave him a cooked breakfast and evening meal, but they never quite filled him.

The woman came back, carrying a tourist brochure of some kind. 'If you can't get any joy at the house, you could try their shop,' she said, folding it over at a page of adverts. She leant close to him and nudged an elbow into his side. 'Here it is. It's only a couple of miles—won't take you long on your bike.'

The advert gave the address and then listed what they sold—a strange mix of bric-a-brac and clothes. But strangest of all was the little italic footnote, starred as being of local interest: 'The premises were originally owned by the Norfolk chemist Drew Fossway, known as Drew the Dream Maker because it was rumoured that

33

he supplied laudanum to Queen Victoria when she was in residence at Sandringham.'

'My husband says that's a load of nonsense,' the woman laughed, leaning closer. 'They've only put it to get people in there. Can you imagine Queen Victoria taking drugs?'

Patrick couldn't be bothered to tell her that he'd read somewhere how fond of chloroform Queen Victoria had become after using it during childbirth. But the mention of laudanum brought to mind Coleridge whose work was still fresh in his mind from his A-levels the week before last.

'They're waiting to order.' Mike stuck his head over her shoulder.

'All right, all right,' she said.

Patrick drained his glass. 'Thanks for all your help.'

'Anytime.' She handed him the brochure. 'Let me know how you get on. Pop in and tell me about it.'

Patrick rode back to Yew Tree House veering between disappointment and relief. But it was certainly easier to go marching up to the front door knowing he would not come face to face with his father. He rang the bell three times but no one came. There was a knocker as well but it was bound with an old sock so he didn't bother to try it. He was tempted to look in the windows but imagined peering through those odd little diamond shapes and finding someone staring back at him. He decided to try the back door—he knew from staying with his Aunt Cath that people did that in the country. But when he investigated, he found the back garden fenced off and a notice saying 'Beware of the Dog' prominently displayed on the gate. Patrick had decided long ago, when he did a paper round, that dogs were not his scene. It would have to be the shop.

Cycling up to the main road between hedges so high and thick that the air was trapped there hot as an oven, he wondered what the speeding Tanya would be like. At the top of the lane, he stopped for a rest in the shade of a bus shelter and pulled out the cutting. She must be the little bridesmaid holding her sister's hand. Age and the dark grainy print of the paper had blurred their features. But not his father's. From the moment the cutting had fallen from Ginny's exercise book, he'd known who it was. It had given him an almost painful shock of excitement to see the likeness. To have black hair and blue eyes in a family of hazel-eyed blondes had never bothered him before, and he could only guess at his father's colouring; but to see himself mirrored in that happy bridegroom's face gave him such an intense feeling of pleasure he'd known immediately he had to find him.

There was no name over the shop, only a double frieze of hand-painted flowers which were so brightly coloured they looked like some kind of festive banner. Squeezed between a sober grey-stuccoed solicitor's on one side and an old-fashioned ironmonger on the other, the shop was hard to miss.

Patrick leant his bike against the wall and

looked in the window. It was jammed with bric-a-brac, which looked as though it had just arrived and needed sorting into a proper window display. The door was propped open and he pushed his way through the jungle of printed T-shirts and Indian cotton garments which hung there, blocking light from the interior of the shop.

It was a relief to be out of the sun and he stood there breathing in the cool, slightly musty air as his eyes adjusted to the dim light. There was someone crouched in a corner sorting through what sounded like bottles. At first Patrick thought it was a girl because of the softness of the profile and the long coils of chestnut hair. When the figure turned, he saw it was a boy of about his own age, maybe a bit younger.

'Hi,' he said, jumping to his feet. 'Can I help, or are you just looking?' He was small but muscular with the smooth moonshaped face of an Oriental, and despite the boy's large eyes, Patrick was reminded of Bruce Lee slicing a hand sideways through the air to chop down an enemy.

'Just looking,' he said quickly.

The boy smiled. 'Help yourself.'

Patrick turned to study a row of books, peering closer to read their titles while he gathered his wits and worked out what he was going to say. There was a section of titles that he recognised, standard reading for the few hippy kids in his class who smoked pot and grew their hair long like this boy. He ran a finger across them: I Ching and Carlos Castenedas. He'd read some of them but they'd never caught his imagination like the romantic poets he'd studied in the sixth form. He pulled one of the books out and flicked through the pages, pretending to read.

The boy had gone back to his bottles and was lining up a row of them on a small table, singing quite loudly as he did so. Patrick glanced round the rest of the shop, and catching sight of his untidy image in a large wall mirror, he began to smooth down his hair. When a girl's voice boomed out, 'Kim, you're not to take those, they're worth money,' he nearly jumped out of his skin.

She had come through from a back room, two steaming mugs in her hands. There was just enough likeness to recognise the little bridesmaid. She was slim and dark with short slicked-back hair and jet black arching eyebrows. 'You didn't tell me we had a customer,' she said, putting the mugs down beside the bottles.

'I've seen to him, don't worry.'

'Anything particular you're after?' She came over, her expression and tone lacking any kind of welcome.

'Actually, I'm looking for someone.' Patrick cleared his throat. 'Gabriel Cody. I believe he was married to your sister.'

The dramatic eyebrows shot up. 'He's long gone. Why do you want him?'

'I'm... I'm tracing my family tree. I think he might be a relative of mine.' Inwardly he cursed himself; why couldn't he just say he's my father

37

and I've been waiting for over two years to find him, so please can you help me?

'Didn't know he had any relatives.' She waited for his response, and he found himself mumbling about the woman in the pub telling him that Justina lived in Spain, and asking if perhaps it would be possible to contact her. The girl gave a snort of laughter. 'Justina would slam down the phone if you mentioned his name.'

After a short, numbed pause, he said, 'Is there anyone else who might know where he is?'

'No idea.'

'Don't be a bitch, Tanya.' The boy got up and came over to them. 'My mother might be able to help you. My father and he were good friends once.'

'Where can I contact her?' Patrick asked, wondering where this boy fitted in to the family; wondering about all of them.

'She's in London for the week but you could phone her.'

'I'll do it for you,' Tanya butted in. 'What's your name?'

'Patrick Kerr.' As she disappeared out to the back room again, he called after her, 'I think he's my father. Can you tell her that?'

She came to a sudden halt and looked over her shoulder. 'Really?' she said as though she found it amusing rather than surprising.

'Is that right?' said Kim, hoisting himself on to the counter. 'Have you only just started looking for him then?'

Patrick started to give the briefest explanation he thought he could get away with but Kim interrupted him before he'd finished.

'Where do you live?'

'London, but I'm staying with my grandmother near Bury St Edmunds.'

'London?' Kim was immediately interested and started to question him, but every time Patrick was halfway through a reply, Kim would interrupt to relate something about himself.

'I often go and stay at Carew's house in Camden,' he was saying while Patrick was two sentences behind, having just pieced together that Kim's mother was Leah Carew, and Kim was her son from a former marriage to a singer. 'It's so boring here. When I leave school, I think I'll go and live there permanently.'

'Are you still at school then?'

'No, he's not,' said Tanya, coming back. 'He's been expelled.' She had another mug in her hand and gave it to Patrick. 'Here, have a cup of tea while you wait. The answerphone's switched on but Leah's probably there. She'll call back in a minute.' She pulled out a stool from behind the counter and pushed it towards him, then perched up beside Kim.

Patrick began to relax. 'What were you expelled for?' he asked.

'Nothing much. And I'm suspended not expelled,' he grinned, pinching Tanya's knee. She slapped him quite hard but he only laughed and jumped down from the counter.

'He poisoned half the school,' she said.

'No I didn't, don't exaggerate.'

39

Patrick looked from one to the other, intrigued to know more.

'I'll tell you,' said Tanya. She pulled Kim in front of her and stared at Patrick over his shoulder. 'He's invented this disgusting brew which he calls a love potion. A few drops and you're consumed with lust for the next person you lay eyes on.' She rested her cheek against Kim's head and ran her hands down his chest and stomach.

'Like Titania and Bottom,' said Patrick, trying not to notice that she had moved her hands down even further.

'Like who?' she burst out, collapsing into laughter.

Kim threw her hands off. 'It's Shakespeare, you ignorant wench.'

She laughed again, her eyes fixed on Patrick. 'Is Cody really your father?' she said.

'I think so.'

'You think so,' she mimicked. Her eyebrows were up again and the corners of her mouth turned down in a mocking way.

'All right, I know he is.' Something about her undermined his confidence. 'Why do you call everyone by their surname?' he asked.

She shrugged, looked as though she was going to laugh at him, then said, 'Because they have such awful Christian names, I suppose.'

Patrick looked at his watch. 'I'll have to go soon. Can you give me the number so I can phone her myself?'

He'd hardly got the words out when the phone rang. Kim made a move to answer it, but Tanya dragged him back by his shirt. 'This is my shop,' she said, flinging him round. 'I'll answer the phone.'

He nearly went sprawling but caught hold of Patrick and staggered upright. 'You cow,' he muttered following after her, but he was laughing. Patrick watched him as he stood there, his elbow on Tanya's shoulder, while she spoke to her sister.

Patrick sipped at his tea. It had a strange fruity taste, and after a couple of mouthfuls he left it. While he strained his ears to catch the muffled conversation going on in the back room, he looked round the shop. His eyes wandered over an array of jewellery made from beads and great whorls of Indian silver, and came to rest on a display of postcards depicting lewd images of naked people in spooky woodland scenes. He took a step forward to get a better look, and heard Tanya say loudly, 'Leah! He's here waiting for an answer.' The next second the receiver was slammed down and Tanya came back in.

'She doesn't know where he is,' she said as though that was that.

'Oh.' Patrick was taken aback. 'But there must be someone who—'

'I've told you what she said.'

'She'll be home next week.' Kim came to join them. 'I'll talk to her. I'd phone my father for you, but I think he and Cody fell out years ago.' He looked at Tanya, then back at Patrick with a little shrug. 'So it's a bit awkward.'

41

Tanya frowned at him. 'The only awkward thing is your mother,' she said.

Patrick remembered what the woman in the pub had told him about Leah being the nicest. 'Perhaps I could phone her myself,' he ventured.

Tanya snatched up one of the postcards and scribbled a number on the back. 'I can only give you the London one,' she said. 'We're ex-directory here—Carew wouldn't like it and he pays the bills.' She handed him the card with a little flourish. 'But don't be surprised if you only get the answerphone.'

'Don't be so mean to him,' said Kim. He turned to Patrick. 'She's always nasty to people she fancies. That's why she's still a virgin at twenty-five.'

Tanya seemed completely unperturbed by the remark. Patrick gave what he thought was a nonchalant smile and looked at his watch again. He imagined telling Mansour about these two.

'I'd better go,' he said. 'Thanks for the number.'

'Come and see us again,' said Kim. 'We'll go for a drink.'

'Yes, why don't you?' said Tanya, putting an arm round Kim's neck. 'How long are you here for?'

'Just a week.'

'Give us a bell and we'll come and pick you up,' said Kim. He selected another of the postcards and scribbled the shop number on it. It showed two naked women sitting on the branch of a tree while a pack of wild dogs snarled at them from below. Patrick glanced at the picture and pocketed both cards. He could hardly wait to tell Mansour about today.

## Chapter 3

Patrick went home the following day. He knew his grandmother was disappointed about him cutting short his visit but all she said was, 'Maybe you'll stay longer next time.' Their relationship had never recovered from that day when she'd revealed the truth about his birth, and after the anger and confusion had subsided, he found the only answer was to treat her with polite but distant respect.

She drove him to the station with hardly a word. He'd left his bike in her shed as he had the use of Larry's at home.

He was halfway out of the car door when she said, 'I'll help you towards a car if you get your grades. I've spoken to Larry and he's going to keep a lookout.'

'Thanks,' Patrick murmured, going to get his holdall from the boot. The offer made little impression on him. In the past there had been rewards for doing well at school, and he knew his grandfather had set up a fund to give him an allowance if he went to university. But always it had been impressed upon him that you had to be a good boy and work hard before you were

43

given anything; nothing, it seemed to him, was given spontaneously, no gift was handed over simply because he was loved.

On the whole, he was glad he had moved in with Ginny and her husband. Larry gave him a few pounds whenever he could afford it. Holiday jobs were hard to get and he'd packed up his paper round while he was studying for his A-levels. And he'd grown very fond of the twins; their company was so uncomplicated, their affection so freely given.

They were in bed when he got home but were tapping at his bedroom door before seven the next morning. He was already awake. He had dreamt of Kim and Tanya. He was at the shop and Tanya had begun caressing him as she'd done Kim. Halfway through the dream, he woke, achingly stiff with desire, and had just finished masturbating when he heard the twins.

'Go away,' he shouted, in a tone of voice that said he didn't mean it, and the next thing he knew they were climbing on to his bed.

He didn't mind; the way they clambered all over him reminded him of Mansour's family who were always hugging and kissing one another.

They wanted him to read to them. Unused to living with small children, it was all he would do with them when he first moved in. They had been slightly in awe of him, and always sat perfectly still and quiet even though he refused to read their children's stories and read only his own books to them.

'Just one page,' he said. 'I'm going to school this morning.'

Last night he had sat up with the telephone directory after everyone else had gone to bed, settling at the kitchen table for what he thought would be the tedious job of tracing Leah Carew's London address. But he had found the name Dr Auberon Carew—along with the number—almost at once.

In the end he read the whole of the 'Ancient Mariner' to the twins, and they sat side by side on his bed hardly moving until he'd finished. They had Ginny's blonde hair and small neat features, two perfect little replicas of her, identical to each other but nothing like him. He stared at them intently for a moment, then shooshed them away so that he could get up.

In the bathroom, he studied himself in the mirror, wondering whether to shave or not. Because he was dark, he'd begun shaving early but had never been bothered with rashes or spots even though his skin was delicately pale. For a moment he thought of Kim with that great hank of long hair and fingered his own, girlishly soft and barely past his ears. His grandmother had always insisted on neat haircuts and he'd obeyed without protest, but now he thought he might grow it longer. He flexed his muscles, well developed from school games and all the cycling and swimming he did.

'You're bloody perfect,' he said, smiling at his reflection and thinking of a girl a year below his who had put out the message that she fancied him. Maybe he would catch her at break this morning. He wasn't going into school specially for this, it was mainly to see Mansour and tell him about his trip to Norfolk. And he just wanted to be in school again. The last two years had been the best in his whole school life. He wasn't sure how it had turned out this way when things had gone so drastically wrong at home; why each miserable moment that he spent angry at Ginny, angry at his grandmother and obsessed with the idea of finding his father was compensated for by success in everything he did at school.

He found Mansour in the sixth form common room with a girl. Patrick joined them and the girl came and sat on his lap. Almost at once the games master appeared and she jumped up.

'Claudia Jones, out of here,' he said. She marched off with a sulky look at the teacher and a backwards smile at Patrick. 'If you two are coming into school, find something better to do with your time than chasing after the girls,' he said.

'She was doing the chasing,' said Patrick.

'We can't help it if they pursue us,' said Mansour.

The games master shook his head and went to get the tennis rackets he'd come for, at the same time spotting a book that lay open on the table. He picked it up, read the title and threw it down again. 'No wonder you lot have got permanent erections,' he said, shaking his head as he left.

Patrick burst out laughing and went to see what the book was. *Story of O,*' he read aloud.

'Mansour, you disgusting little beast. Can I borrow it?'

'It's not mine. Now then, how did you get on?'

Patrick told him all that had happened, ending with how he'd found Leah Carew's London address. 'So I'm going to write to her,' he said.

'Why don't you go and see her?'

'I can't just go there.'

'I would and so would you if you were serious about finding your father.'

'Of course I'm bloody serious about it.'

'Well, don't waste any more time—go and see her.'

Patrick fell silent. It was easy for Mansour to talk; he could always come up with the right thing to say to older people. Patrick was fine with his peers, over-confident at times, and he knew how to turn the charm on if older women showed an interest in him. But remembering the phone call in the shop, and the way Tanya had treated him, the prospect of facing her sister was a bit daunting.

'By the way,' said Mansour. 'I nearly forgot. Can you meet Kirsty tomorrow night? She wants you to go babysitting with her.'

'Yeah?' said Patrick, smiling. Kirsty was the girl he'd been thinking about earlier. He picked up the book and flicked through the pages. But he wasn't reading anything, he was thinking that perhaps he would go and see Leah Carew after all; the worst she could do was to tell him to get lost. He might even go this afternoon.

47

On the Tube, he began to wonder if he was doing the right thing and tried to overcome his nerves by thinking about his date with Kirsty tomorrow. Whatever happened, he had that to cheer him up. He was soon lost in dreams of spending the summer holidays in a steady relationship with regular sex, the high point of which would be a meeting with his father.

The house was in a terrace and similar to Mansour's but not as big and only two-storey. The small front garden had been concreted to provide a parking space, and this was taken up completely by a Volvo estate car with a dog guard and a baby seat. He rang the doorbell and waited, clearing his throat and practising his first sentence. There were two doors, the first a half-glazed door to the porch and then the front door to the house, also glazed but in coloured glass, so that when his ringing was finally answered, all he could see was the outline of a woman. A dog had begun to bark and he took a step back, imagining that it would rush out at him when she opened the porch door. As the front door opened, the barking became loud and furious and he saw the head of a large Alsatian. He heard the woman shout something and the dog stopped barking and disappeared back in the hall. She was in the porch now; he could see her clearly. She looked at him through the glass and stood quite still for a moment as though something about him had upset or even shocked her. For a moment he thought she was going to turn round and go back inside, then she licked her lips, smoothed back a stray wisp of hair and came to open the porch door.

'I'm sorry to bother you but your son gave me your phone number...' The first few words came out exactly as he'd rehearsed, then he ground to a halt, suddenly aware that she didn't look old enough to be Kim's mother, and maybe he had got it all wrong. She was like Kim; she had the same smooth round cheeks and big dark eyes; in fact her eyes and mouth seemed to take up her whole face. Her hair was curly like Kim's as well, though lighter and softer looking and tied in two untidy plaits. Only her long black brows were like Tanya.

'I've come to see... I mean, are you Mrs Carew?'

She gave the smallest nod.

'My name's—'

'I know who you are,' she said, pulling the door open wider. 'You'd better come in.'

He followed her into the hall and through to the kitchen, keeping a wary eye on the dog who had gone to lie under the stairs, head on paws, watching him.

'My sister told you that I've no idea where he is, didn't she?' Her tone was almost accusing.

'Yes, but...the thing is... Kim said you might be able to find out.'

She waited, her eyes fixed on him, her expression slightly hostile, and he wished he hadn't come.

'I just want some help to find out where he is, that's all,' he said.

'How old are you?'

'I'll be nineteen in a couple of months.'

The hostile look faded but the way she stared at him without blinking or looking away made him uncomfortable.

'I've been waiting two years to find him.' It came out in a kind of strangled plea and he saw a little frown form between her eyebrows. The front of her hair was streaked with gold as though she had spent a lot of time in the sun, and close up he could see that she had tiny lines round her eyes. It was her full cheeks and thick lips which made her look so young.

'You're the image of him,' she said suddenly. She looked about to smile but instead she drew in her breath and let out a noisy sigh as though he was causing her a great deal of trouble. She had on a thin summer dress with buttons all the way down the front, and he couldn't help noticing how her breasts strained against the bodice. For a moment his eyes were glued to the buttons, then he quickly looked away.

'He's my father and he doesn't even know I exist,' he muttered.

Her head tipped sympathetically to one side. 'I wish I could help you but we haven't heard from him for years. My sister lives in Spain now, but she wouldn't help anyway. You see...it's difficult. You were born soon after she married him. She couldn't have children, so...well, you can imagine how she'd feel about you.'

So this was going to be a dead end. He didn't know what to do or say. His eyes travelled round the kitchen. It was incredibly untidy. There was dirty crockery and pans covering the worktops, and a table in the middle of the floor was piled with papers, books and a heap of clothes; there were even discarded chocolate wrappers scattered on the floor.

He felt helpless, out of place and was just about to say he'd go, when a baby's cry came crackling through an intercom on the wall. It was hesitant at first, not much more than a whine. Then it broke into a fully fledged yell.

'I won't be a minute.' She dashed off and he noticed that she was barefoot and that the hem of her dress was coming unstitched and hung down at the back. He heard her thump up the stairs, and a couple of minutes later she was back, carrying a small baby.

'I might be able to find out something for you,' she said. 'I've thought of someone who might know where he is.'

'I'd be grateful for any information. Anything.'

'Kim's father, my first husband, he might know.'

He thought she sounded more friendly. 'Kim suggested that,' he said eagerly.

She smiled now, holding the baby against her shoulder and stroking its hair. 'What was he doing?' she said. 'Was he helping Tanya?'

'Yes, I think so.' Patrick remembered that the woman at the pub had said she was the prettiest as well as the nicest. 'Can you get in touch with him—your first husband I mean?'

'I'll try.' The baby was rubbing inexpertly at its eyes and seemed about to cry again. 'I'll call him this evening and see what I can find out

51

for you. I don't have time now, I have to feed the baby.'

'Will you let me know then? Shall I phone you?'

'Come back tomorrow—come earlier, about two. Jo-jo's asleep then.' Her eyes flicked to a clock on the wall.

Patrick sensed she wanted him to go, but he was strangely reluctant to move.

'My husband will be in soon and he doesn't like talking about all this.'

'I'll see you tomorrow then.'

She smiled at him over the baby's shoulder, then led him out to the front door. At the last moment she caught his sleeve. 'I will try and help you. I know how you must feel.'

All the way home he felt good, better than he'd felt for ages.

He was twenty minutes early but she answered the door almost at once as though she had been waiting for him. The dog was shut outside somewhere. How different it was from yesterday; straightaway she was apologetic that she hadn't asked him if it was convenient for him to come back.

'You took me by surprise,' she said. 'I forgot to ask how far away you live.'

'Not very.' He'd come by bus this time and the journey had taken him over half an hour.

'Are you at work?'

'No, I'm still at school—well, I've left really. I've just taken my A-levels.'

'I want Kim to take those,' she said in a sort

of dismissive way as though she had no idea of their importance. 'But I don't think he will, he keeps getting into trouble at school.' She led him into the kitchen again, just as she'd done yesterday but this time she smiled and pointed towards the table. 'Sit down and I'll make you some tea.'

He did as she said and sat there in silence listening to the slip slap of her feet on the tiles as she padded about making the tea. It was hot in the kitchen and he rolled up his sleeves. He'd put on a proper shirt and trousers for a change. She brought the teapot to the table and stirred it with a big spoon.

'It smells the same as what your sister made me,' he said as the aromatic steam spiralled upwards. It was more for something to say than anything else.

'It's Orange Pekoe,' she said. 'My husband gets it. He likes special teas and things.' She sat down opposite him and began to spoon sugar into her cup. When she'd finished, she pushed the bowl across the table to him. 'I couldn't get in touch with Lou, he's abroad,' she said at last. 'He's due back in a few days. I've left a message with his flatmate. You'll have to be patient a bit longer, I'm afraid.' She leant back in her chair, staring straight at him. 'I can't get over how like Cody you are.'

Patrick took a gulp of the tea. It was scalding hot and burnt his tongue, but he swallowed it down.

'You're a bit taller.' She leant forward, her elbows on the table. 'But your face and your colouring are exactly the same—especially your eyes. Didn't Tanya tell you?'

'No.' He grinned, feeling embarrassed. 'I do know what he looks like.' He had brought the newspaper cutting with him and he pulled it from his pocket. 'This is how I traced him to you.'

She took it from him and spread it on the table. 'Oh, so it wasn't your mother who gave you our address?'

'No. She hasn't told me much about him.'

Leah glanced up as though she was going to say something, then she seemed to change her mind and studied the cutting instead. 'Would you like the original photo of this?' she asked suddenly.

Before he could answer, she jumped up and went off upstairs. He could hear her above him. Her footsteps were muffled but he could hear cupboard doors opening and closing. She came back down with an old leatherbound book.

'It's somewhere in here.' She shook it by the spine and two photos fell out. 'Ah, I wondered where this one was.' She held up a photo of herself and a much younger Kim, then passed him the other one. It was so much clearer than the newspaper picture and quite startling to see his father in colour. He studied Justina, comparing her to Ginny and thinking how different they were. Then his eyes wandered to Leah. She was pouting, challenging the camera as though she was refusing to smile; a sulky Lolita, her hair tumbling from the band of rosebuds, and her bridesmaid's dress too tight and childish for her.

'It's a lovely photo, isn't it?' she said, then laughed. 'Except for me. Don't I look awful? It's my husband's favourite photo of me. I can't think why, it's years old and I look so grumpy. I'd just been told off about something or other.'

'Will he mind you giving it to me?'

'He won't know. I gave it to him before we were married. He doesn't look at it now.'

'How long were Justina and...' He hesitated, not sure whether to say, my father, or Cody. 'Were they married?' he finished.

'About ten years.' She had spilt some milk on the table, and she started to draw patterns in it with her finger. She was silent for so long that Patrick began to wonder if she wanted him to leave.

'Will you phone me when you find out anything?' he said. 'Or shall I phone you?'

She looked up, her face blank as though she hadn't heard, then she picked up a pencil and paper from the pile of things on the table. 'I'll phone you. You may have to speak to Lou—we'll see what he knows first. What's your number?'

He told her and she wrote it down, then stabbed her finger in the milk again. 'I'm trying to think of something I can tell you about him,' she said. 'Did you know he's a musician?' He nodded and she went straight on. 'He can play the guitar, the fiddle and,' she bowed her head, tapping it with her fingers as

55

though she was thinking, 'the mandolin, that's the other one.' Her hair was loose today and it fell into her eyes, the sunbleached strands very light against her dark brows. She flung it back. 'That's how Justina met him. Our father plays the Spanish guitar. He used to be famous. Did you know that?'

Patrick thought she was waiting for him to answer but directly he opened his mouth to speak, she began again.

'The thing is,' she started, leaning back and folding her arms under her breasts, 'if you find him, we wouldn't want to have any contact with him.' She had on jeans and a T-shirt today; emblazoned across the front of the T-shirt were the words MAID IN HEAVEN. She saw him looking and lowered her eyes to follow his gaze. 'It's from the shop,' she smiled, then went on in the same breath, 'He caused such a lot of rows.'

'Oh, with the divorce, I suppose.'

'Partly. Patrick, I have to tell you the truth. If I don't, Lou might because they fell out quite badly. Patrick,' she began again after a little pause, 'he had hundreds of women.'

The dog began to bark. She jumped up and went to the window, hissing at it to be quiet. 'You'll wake Jo-jo up,' she said in a loud whisper.

As she pulled the window shut, Patrick heard himself say, in a voice that wasn't much more than a whisper either, 'My mother was just one of many then. He probably won't even remember her.'

'He might.' She quickly poured more tea into his cup, as though this would help to make things all right. 'What's her name?' she asked, sitting opposite him again.

'Georgina.'

'Oh, it's quite like Justina, I bet he will remember. Anyway, it doesn't matter. He'll take one look at you and know who you are, believe me.'

'But I might be one of many as well.'

'Oh no, Patrick, I wouldn't think so. No, I'm sure that's not the case, I'm sure he'll want to meet you.' The earnest look on her face, her eagerness to make amends were just too much. The most awful thing was about to happen. He was going to cry; right here in this kitchen with a woman he hardly knew, he was going to cry. The tears balanced in his eyes and he didn't dare move. If only the dog would bark again, or the baby cry, he might have the chance to sniff them away. He saw her looking at him, and raised the back of his hand to his face, but the movement was like jogging a glass full of water and he quickly bent his head as the tears spilt over.

'I'm sorry. Oh, I'm so sorry,' he heard her say, then there was the scrape of her chair on the tiles and she hurried round the table to him. 'I wish I hadn't told you. I'm sorry.' She put a hand on his back, then her arm right round him. He could feel the softness of her breasts against his shoulder and her breath on his forehead. She gave him a little hug and leant her cheek against his head.

'It'll be all right. We'll find him, I know we will.'

In seconds he was in control of himself again, but she rushed off to get him a tissue and also dashed something in his tea. It came from a thin-necked amber bottle and she held it up to show him.

'My father brings it from Spain. I think they brew it themselves. We put it in everything.' She held the bottle to the light. 'He's coming to stay next week. I hope he remembers to bring us some more.' She sat down again. 'It was so tactless of me, I'm really sorry.'

'It's all right.' He couldn't look at her. 'I feel such a fool.'

'Why? There's nothing wrong in crying.'

'But I'm eighteen.'

'I'm thirty-three and I'm always crying.' He glanced up at her now; she was smiling but her eyes were sad. 'I had three miscarriages before I had Jo-jo, and I cried for weeks, every time. My husband cried too and he's nearly sixty.'

Patrick didn't know what to say; he couldn't imagine Ginny talking like this with someone she hardly knew, especially someone of the opposite sex. But nothing about Leah Carew was remotely like Ginny.

'One time,' she was saying, 'I cried so much that the doctor threatened to slap me if I didn't stop. Can you imagine it? Wanting to slap someone because they're unhappy.' She gave a little laugh. 'The pig—I would have slapped him back.' Patrick laughed too, but her eyes clouded over again. 'My mother died when I was ten, and I know all about crying.'

As if on cue, a small whimper came from the baby listener on the wall. Leah put her finger to her lips. 'He might drop off again,' she whispered as though the baby could hear them. They sat there without speaking. There was a multitude of distant noises going on outside but not a sound in the kitchen except for the loud ticking of the wall clock. Patrick looked up at it.

'Have you got to go?' she said, breaking the silence.

'No,' he answered quickly, but wondered immediately if it was a hint that she wanted him to go. 'Not unless you're busy.'

'No, I've got plenty of time.' She smiled and tipped her chair back on two legs, her hands clasped behind her head. The MAID IN HEAVEN was stretched tightly across her breasts, the dark shadow of her nipples clearly outlined against the thin cotton. 'What are you going to do now that you've left school?'

'Go to university. Cambridge, I hope, if I get the right grades.'

'My husband taught there for a while.' She said it in that vaguely dismissive way she had talked about A-levels. 'He does private lectures now. Greek, would you believe? What are you going to do?'

'English literature.'

'Oh, writers and poets and all that.'

He nodded and pointed to the leatherbound book which still lay on the table. 'He's one of my favourites.'

She swivelled the book round. 'Percy Bysshe Shelley,' she read, pronouncing his middle name wrongly. She pushed the book towards him. 'Here, you can have it.'

'Oh no, I didn't say it for that.'

'Take it. Carew won't mind.'

'But it's probably valuable.'

'It doesn't matter, he loves to help anyone who wants to study.' She picked up the wedding photo, slid it back between the pages and put the book in front of him. 'Jo-jo will probably be really clever.' She'd hardly got the words out when another whimper came through the baby listener. It was followed almost at once by a broken-hearted cry.

Leah jumped up. 'He means it this time,' she said, rushing off upstairs.

When she came back, Patrick was standing up, the book in his hand. 'I'd better go. Are you sure about the book?'

'Course,' she said, more concerned with blowing raspberries against the baby's cheek.

'Well, thanks for—'

'Are you in a hurry?' she butted in.

'No, why?'

'I'll walk down the road with you. I want to get a loaf. Can you hang on while I change Jo-jo's nappy?'

'Yeah, OK.'

She laid the baby on the table amongst the cups and the teapot and all the other things that were strewn there. Patrick pretended to be looking at the book, slowly flicking through the pages, but he was watching her. He saw her pull a pair of little fluffy socks from a clothes basket. She held them against her cheek for a second, then stuffed them down her jeans while she changed the baby. 'Better than any airing cupboard,' she said, pulling them out again and putting them on the baby's feet.

As he walked down the road with Leah, Patrick remembered when the twins were babies, in the days when he'd believed he was their uncle, and how he would have done anything in the world to avoid being seen with Ginny and the pushchair. He told Leah, and she laughed and said it probably wouldn't be all that long before he was married with children himself.

'Doubt it,' he said. 'I won't be able to afford it. Anyway, I want to have a good time before I get married, travel and things like that.'

'Have you got a girl friend?' she asked.

'Nobody special.' It was at that moment he remembered his date with Kirsty that evening.

They were outside the baker's now. 'Could you do something for me?' said Leah.

'Yes of course.'

'Could you stay with Jo-jo a minute while I get my bread? Save me getting him out.' She stooped down to pick up one of the baby's socks that he'd kicked off, and tucked it in the side of the pushchair.

Once she was out of sight, the baby eyed him suspiciously and he felt duty bound to reassure it. He clicked his tongue and its face was immediately wreathed in smiles. He did it again and its legs began to kick up and down. It had lots of dark fluffy hair and great brown eyes. He hadn't much idea about babies but guessed it was only a few months old. He leant on the handle of the pushchair and opened the book she'd given him. The baby whimpered, its lips puckering up, its legs kicking impatiently. He spoke to it this time. 'She won't be long,' he said, jigging the pushchair. The other sock went flying onto the pavement and he rescued it and tried to push it back on. It was dark blue with a white frill on the cuff and very soft. On an impulse, he held it to his nose. It smelt of soap and warm bodies, the same as Leah, the same smell that had filled his nostrils when she had put her arm round him earlier. He screwed it up in his hand and stuffed it in his pocket.

She came out of the shop loaded with bread, and handed him a bag. 'It's a cake for you. Kim says it's impossible to go more than two hours without food. You've gone all afternoon,' she laughed.

'Thank you.' He lingered while she put the bread in the basket under the pushchair.

'Now don't worry, I'll phone you as soon as I find out anything. Good luck with your exams and everything.' And with that she was gone.

He stood there like an idiot for a moment, then began to walk away, but after a few paces he turned and watched her until she was no more than a small speck of denim amongst the other shoppers.

Kirsty was waiting for him outside the hairdressers where she worked after school. He was glad they were going babysitting because he had hardly any money left after all he'd spent on fares; and because he felt like being alone with her.

She was a tall girl with pencil slim legs and feathery white-blonde hair. Most of the boys said she was conceited and stuck up and wasn't worth bothering about. But Patrick had seen her on the tennis courts a couple of weeks ago wearing cut-off denim shorts so tiny they exposed half-moons of perfectly tanned buttock every time she moved, and he'd decided he fancied her more than any other girl in the school. When he heard she felt the same about him, he was secretly delighted but waited for her to make the first move. It was rumoured that she'd had her navel pierced and he'd promised Mansour to find out if it was true.

He hadn't given her a thought all day but seeing her waiting for him, he was excited at the thought of their evening together. Her sister's house, where they were babysitting, was only a short walk away and as soon as they were alone, he began kissing her. It wasn't long before he had her on her back on the sofa, but at this point she tried to push him off.

'What's the matter?' he said, his lips against her throat, his heart pounding.

'Cool down,' she said, lifting his hand from her thigh. 'I don't do it.'

He felt unreasonable anger at her; never had he felt quite so desperate to have sex with a girl.

'Why not?' he whispered, sliding a hand up under her top. She had no bra and barely any breasts but he pushed the top right up and found her nipple with his lips, running his palm across her stomach, until he came to the ring in her navel.

'Don't.' She stopped him again. 'I'vc only just had it done, it's still sore.'

'Is that your favourite word, don't?' He sat up to look down at her.

'I'll do other things. If you want me to.' She put a hand on his zip but he pushed her off.

'I can do that myself,' he said irritably.

She wrenched her top down and sat up, her arms folded tightly across her chest. 'I was told you were really nice,' she said. 'But you're not. You're the same as all the others.'

He felt confused and ashamed; normally he was nice to girls, he rarely acted like this on a first date. Often he'd been out with girls who would do no more than kiss. But tonight that wasn't enough; he felt an overwhelming need to have sex, nothing else would do. He swallowed back his desperation, apologised and started to kiss her again, wondering what he could say to make her change her mind. But soon he was pushing his tongue into her mouth and his hand up her skirt. When she stopped him this time, he got up and left.

# Chapter 4

For the next week he hardly went out at all, sure that if he did he would miss Leah's call. After a few days of waiting, he became obsessed with this idea. Whenever the phone rang, he would rush to answer it before anyone else got there. But it was never her.

When another week had almost gone by with no word, he began to wonder if she'd written his number down wrongly or even lost it in that jumble of things on her kitchen table.

He spent hours lying about in his room listening to tapes, the photo she'd given him propped in front of him. He hadn't shown it to Ginny and didn't intend to. The baby's sock was still in his trouser pocket shoved guiltily away in the wardrobe.

His life seemed to be in a state of suspension; he didn't feel like going anywhere or doing anything. Ginny left him alone for a while, but one morning she came and turfed him out of bed early, saying she wanted to clean his room. And at breakfast, she began questioning him about whether he ought not to go into school.

'I don't have to,' he muttered.

'Well, you ought to get out in the fresh air,' she said. 'You look dreadful.'

'Thanks a lot,' he said, shaking cornflakes into a bowl and spilling half of them over the table because he hadn't opened the packet properly.

She snatched it away from him and tore the top neatly across. 'Well, you do. You look like death warmed up.' He ignored her but knew it was not going to end there. 'You look like those kids who creep around in black clothes and purple lipstick,' she went on, scooping up the mess he'd made.

Larry laughed. 'The Goths, you mean,' he said, folding up the paper he'd been reading and tapping Patrick on the shoulder with it. 'She's right, Patrick, you don't exactly look the picture of health.'

'No wonder,' said Ginny. 'He hasn't been outside the back door for nearly two weeks.'

'Oh, leave him alone, Gin, I expect he's worried about his results.' Patrick slammed down the bottle of milk he'd been about to empty over his cornflakes and got up. He heard his spoon clatter to the floor but walked out without picking it up.

Emma and Heidi had already finished their breakfast and followed him upstairs and into his bedroom, creeping along behind him like two little shadows. When he threw himself on the bed, they clambered up on his pillow and positioned themselves on either side of his head.

After a few minutes' silence, one of them whispered, 'Don't you like Daddy any more?'

He couldn't help smiling. 'Of course I do,' he said. 'Now stop asking silly questions and go and get me a mirror.' They looked at each other, pulling faces as though they were having a silent conversation, then they ran off together and fetched him a hand mirror from the bathroom.

He lay on his back, the mirror held above him, twisting it this way and that to catch his reflection from different angles. Maybe he did look a bit pasty, but not as dreadful as Ginny had said.

The twins were watching him with interest.

'Do you think I'm devastatingly handsome?' he asked them.

They both nodded, their little blonde heads bobbing together.

'And do you think a beautiful woman in her thirties is likely to fall in love with me?'

One of them giggled, a hand to her mouth.

'And do you think she might be bored with her husband and want me to fuck her?'

They rolled together on the pillow as though it was the funniest thing they'd ever heard, but he knew they had no idea what he was talking about. He was about to elaborate when Ginny called them to go to school.

As soon as he had the house to himself, he went to the phone and called Leah's number. A man's voice came deep and clear with an answerphone message and Patrick hung up. He got the number again, clearing his throat to speak when the pips had finished, but once again he put the receiver down without saying a word. It might sound a bit suspicious to say this is Patrick and I'm leaving my number in case you've mislaid it—it would probably be her husband who checked the messages—and he couldn't go into long explanations about who he was. Something simple had suddenly become complicated. He sat there a while on the hall floor, his legs stretched in front of him, the phone on his lap. Then just as suddenly it all became clear. She had gone back to Norfolk and forgotten to take the number with her. Why hadn't he thought of this before? As he was deciding what to do next, Ginny came in the front door.

'You looked settled for the day,' she said, stepping over him.

'It's only a local call. I'll put some money in the box if that's what you're worried about.'

She didn't answer but went through to the kitchen and started to clear up the breakfast things. As soon as she turned on the tap, he phoned his grandmother and asked if he could come and stay again.

'Another local call?' Ginny said, coming to the door. 'Sometimes I think you imagine the bills get paid by magic.'

He got up from the floor. 'I'm going to stay with Gran for a while,' he said. 'Then you won't have to see my dreadful face every day.'

'Whatever's the matter with you, Patrick?' she snapped.

'Nothing.' He swung himself round on the banisters, leaping up the first three stairs in one go. 'Nothing at all.'

He heard her sigh, and she came to the bottom of the stairs.

'Have you got the fare?'

'Just.'

'I can let you have some money on Friday.'

'I'm going tomorrow.'

She sighed again, louder and more impatient. 'How do you propose to manage without money?'

'If you must know, I'm going to ask Gran if she can arrange to let me have some money from my trust fund.' The idea had only come to him that minute, but it suddenly seemed a very good one.

'That money's to see you through university, not to doss about all summer.'

'I'm not dossing about,' he said through clenched teeth, I'm searching for my father, he added silently.

'You ought to think about getting a job for the holidays instead of flitting off up there all the time.'

He turned round. 'I don't know what I'm doing yet, so just leave me alone will you?'

'Patrick,' she began, her voice verging on tears. 'Come down here a minute.'

He ignored her and marched off to his room. A few minutes later he heard her start up the vacuum cleaner.

'Would you like me to pay for you to have a haircut?' said his grandmother as they were eating their first meal together after his arrival. 'I know you don't have much money to spare, and I expect Ginny and Larry find things a bit tight what with the twins at school and everything.'

'No thanks,' he murmured. 'I'm growing it a bit.'

He was surprised when she smiled and said, 'Well you've got such nice hair, Patrick, I'm sure it'll look good however you have it.'

It would have been the ideal moment to bring up the subject of the trust fund, but as so often happened when he was with her, he held back, not sure how to say it. The next morning, the subject of money came up again. He was pumping up the tyres on his bike when she came out and asked if he'd be back for lunch.

'No, I don't think so, thanks.'

She went off again without a word and came back with a five pound note. 'Here you are. Make sure you get yourself something proper to eat.'

It was another surprise. 'Thanks,' he said. 'I'll pay you back.'

'There's no need. Your grandfather left me well provided for.' She gave a little smile. 'Ginny rang me. She said you were wondering about having your allowance paid early. I'll see the solicitor. I'm sure it's possible. It's not a huge amount as you know, but if you're continually short of money you might have second thoughts about university, and we don't want that.'

'Thanks,' he said again, and thought, that's all I ever say to her.

She lingered there, watching him. 'I hope you're going to clean that oil off my patio,' she said.

The shop was crowded with a bunch of teenagers in school uniform. Tanya was sitting on the counter watching them like a hawk but looked round immediately when Patrick came in.

She smiled and waved, but as he edged his way towards her he could see there was something slightly mocking in her expression.

'Kim,' she called out. 'Come and see who's here.'

Kim came through from the back. His face lit up with pleasure. 'Hi, Patrick,' he said. 'Where did you get to? I thought you were coming back to have a drink with us.'

'I was but...I had to go home unexpectedly.'

'Yeah, Mum said you were back home when you phoned her.'

'Phoned her?' he said blankly.

'Phoned her about Cody,' said Kim.

It took only a second for Patrick to realise that Kim didn't know that he'd been to their London house. 'Oh yeah, yeah, of course,' he said quickly to cover the pause, aware that Tanya was watching him.

'So she's going to help you find him, is she?' said Tanya.

'Yeah,' he said again. 'That's what I've come about actually. She's supposed to be phoning me when she finds out anything, but I'm not sure if she's got my number.' He looked round the shop, whistling between his teeth, wondering why Leah hadn't mentioned him going to see her, and trying to act as unconcerned as he could. A girl caught his eye and nudged her friend. They whispered together, looking at him with flirtatious smiles. He was too taken up with other thoughts to respond, and anyway, they all

71

looked so young in their school uniforms.

'Write it down, I'll give it to her,' said Kim. 'But I know she hasn't found out anything yet—Lou's still abroad.' He passed Patrick a pencil and pad. 'Don't worry, she won't forget. She never forgets anything, but she's got her hands full at the moment. My grandfather's staying with us and he expects to be waited on.'

'Hands full?' Tanya sneered. 'He doesn't get up until lunchtime, then your mother pisses off out.'

Kim frowned with annoyance. 'Only because he picks on her all the time—that's the only reason.'

'No it isn't. She'd go out whether he was here or not. She'd go out whoever was here if she wanted to.'

'No she wouldn't, you liar. Anyway, she has to walk the dog.'

Tanya gave a little smirking laugh.

'I hope this isn't going to get violent,' said Patrick.

'Take no notice of her,' said Kim. 'She thinks she's the only one who does any work.'

'I am,' said Tanya. 'You don't do much—you certainly don't earn the money I pay you. All you come in here for is to play around with your chemistry set.' She broke off to serve one of the school kids.

'Chemistry set?' said Patrick. 'Are you interested in chemistry?'

Kim scowled at Tanya's back. 'She'll change her tune when I make my first million.' He

72

turned a smiling face on Patrick. 'You could call me a modern day alchemist, I suppose.'

'What, have you discovered the elixir of life?'

'Don't you take the piss as well. I thought you were educated.'

'Aah,' said Patrick with a click of his fingers as it dawned on him. 'I remember, it's the famous love potion.'

Kim eyed him calmly. 'I'm not an idiot, I've done proper research.'

'Yeah?' said Patrick, pretending to sound impressed. 'Does it work?'

'I haven't perfected it yet.' He gave a disarming smile. 'After that little episode at school, I realised it needed a few minor adjustments.'

Tanya spluttered with laughter in the background, and Patrick couldn't help smiling.

'One girl spewed up in the swimming pool,' said Tanya.

Patrick burst out laughing himself now.

'Don't laugh at him,' said Tanya, 'or he'll stamp his little feet and run to Mummy.' She smiled sweetly and blew a kiss at Kim, but there was a spitefulness about her.

'Where do you do all this experimenting?' said Patrick, deciding he liked Kim far more than he did Tanya.

Kim hesitated before answering, studying Patrick with the same large unblinking eyes as his mother. They gave him a slightly crazy look, making it impossible to know whether he was about to smile or get annoyed. 'I'm not going to show you just so you can take the piss,' he said at last.

'Honest, I won't.' Patrick had no wish to upset him, in fact in the back of his mind there was a vague idea forming that it might be a good idea to cultivate a friendship with him.

'Come on then.' Kim led him out the back, through a lobby with a phone and a sink, and into a narrow room with a low ceiling and stone floor so worn it dipped in the centre. It smelt of age, a mixture of mustiness and damp, and another stronger smell which reminded Patrick of the time next door's tom cat had got into his grandmother's conservatory. He wrinkled his nose, remembering how she had scrubbed and scrubbed with disinfectant, threatening to throw boiling water over the animal if it ever showed its face again.

'I think it's the stuff they used to wash out the bottles with,' said Kim. He took a demijohn from a row lined up along shelves above a pitted and stained wooden worktop, shook it, then sloshed dribbles of it over the floor. The air was immediately saturated with a sweet flowery perfume.

Patrick smiled. 'Transformation.'

'Yeah,' said Kim. 'That's what it's all about—transformation.' He put the demijohn back. 'This is the oldest part of the building. My great-great-grandfather worked in here. He was a chemist, or rather an apothecary.' He waved a hand towards the shelves. 'Some of this stuff was his. No one ever bothered to get rid of it.'

'What the hell do you do with it?' Patrick looked round the room at the laden shelves and tiers of brass-plated wooden cabinets. Some of the bottles were clean and neatly labelled but others were covered with grime, the corks and stoppers festooned with cobwebs.

'You'd be surprised how much of this stuff is being used today.' Kim pulled a sheaf of paper from a drawer and waved it under Patrick's nose. 'I told you I've been doing some research.'

Patrick caught a glimpse of an embossed letter-heading and an advert with a naked couple entwined in a canopied bed, but Kim whipped it away before he could read it.

'Have you ever heard of cantharides?'

Patrick shook his head.

'Spanish fly?'

'Oh yeah. Some kind of aphrodisiac, isn't it?'

'You got it. And mandrake?'

'Whatever are you mixing up here, you crazy little idiot?' said Patrick, picking up a tiny blue bottle shaped like a mushroom.

'Sniff it,' said Kim.

Patrick gingerly removed the glass stopper and held the bottle to his nose. A stench of rotten eggs hit him in the face and he began retching uncontrollably, his eyes streaming. He rammed back the stopper and took great gulps of air. 'You bastard,' he said rubbing at his eyes.

'It won't hurt you, but it's bloody useful if you want to get out of doing something.' Kim picked up another bottle, big-bellied and coloured a sinister darkish purple. 'You'd better not try this,' he smiled.

'Why, is it the deadly love potion?'

'It's one of the ingredients. One sniff will make you extremely randy, and three drops would give you a hard-on for a week.'

Patrick laughed and shook his head. 'No wonder you got kicked out of school. You're a danger to the entire female population.'

'Don't get the wrong impression,' said Kim, looking pleased as though Patrick had just paid him a compliment. 'The love potion isn't just to make someone fancy you, it's to make them fall in love with you. Big difference.'

'Where did you learn all this crap?'

'It's not crap. People are making fortunes out of this kind of stuff.' He reached up to take down a miniature chest of drawers. It looked very old, each drawer marked with tiny copperplate lettering. Patrick read the labels: ambergris, attar... Then Kim was holding out a closed fist to him. 'Here, a present for you.' Patrick was careful this time, but all Kim did was to pass him a handful of thin air. 'Revolutionary condoms,' he said. 'You won't know you're wearing them.'

'You're completely nuts,' Patrick laughed.

'What's all the laughter about?' said Tanya, poking her head round the door.

'Nothing you'd know anything about,' said Kim with a wink at Patrick.

She came in and put both arms round him from behind. 'You mustn't keep secrets from Tanya,' she said. She kissed him on the cheek, as though their earlier cross words had been forgiven.

'I'm going to get some lunch now, so keep an eye on the shop.'

Patrick glanced at his watch.

'Why don't you hang around until she gets back and we'll go for that drink?' said Kim.

'Shall I close up for the lunch hour and we'll all go?' said Tanya, smiling at Patrick over Kim's shoulder.

Patrick hesitated. 'I can't today.' He only had the five pound note, hardly enough for one round, and he guessed these two would have money in abundance. 'I've arranged to go somewhere this afternoon.'

'Another time then,' said Tanya. She still had her arms looped affectionately round Kim and she spoke pleasantly, but Patrick had the feeling she was laughing at him for some reason.

'Yeah, another time,' he agreed. But he didn't want to leave yet; there was something he wanted to find out. He told himself it was silly, that he was going to make a fool of himself, but still he lingered.

Tanya gave Kim a little shake. 'You and I'll go for a drink. I'll go and get the stuff in from outside. You lock up the back.'

'Do you work here every day?' he asked Kim as soon as she'd gone.

'It's only because of my suspension from school.' Kim shrugged and smiled. 'But she pays me now and again, so I don't mind. I'd come here anyway. I'm not allowed to take any of this home. That's Carew, he—'

'Oh, so you don't go out with your mother?' Patrick butted in—Tanya would be back in a minute.

'No, I don't like walking much,' said Kim, unconcerned, fiddling with one of his bottles. 'And she goes for miles.'

'Miles?' Patrick's heart began to beat a little faster. 'What? On her own?'

'No, with my little brother and the dog.'

Tanya called to them.

'Where can you walk miles around here?' Patrick said quickly.

'The pine forests. Hundreds of boring miles of forest.' Kim looked up. 'You are a lucky bastard living in London,' he said.

Patrick smiled. 'I quite like the country actually. You won't forget to give her that number, will you?'

It took him three days to find her; three days of cycling along innumerable forest paths, bumping up and down ruts of hard-baked earth or sinking into sudden unexpected puddles hidden in shady avenues thick with pine needles. How could anyone want to spend every afternoon wandering these lonely tracks with only the swarms of insects for company? Biting, winged things had always been attracted to him and it was while he stopped to scratch at his back, sweating and unbearably itchy, that he saw her.

He had come to a crossroads. All four paths looked identical: long, straight and sun-dappled, stretching for ever between rows of gloomy

78

pines, silent and empty—except for one. Even from the back, he recognised her immediately.

The dog heard him first. It swung round and let out a couple of short barks, the sound echoing amongst the trees and sending a flutter of wood pigeons into the air. She let go of the pushchair and grabbed the dog's collar, turning to look over her shoulder as she hooked on its lead. As Patrick rode up to her, the dog began to bark furiously, straining to get at him. A few yards away, he pulled up.

'Am I safe?' he smiled.

She didn't smile back, just gave the dog a jerk on its collar. It sat down, its eyes on her, waiting for a command. 'She won't hurt you. You startled her, that's all. What are doing up here?'

'I'm staying with my grandmother. She lives near here.' He shrugged, thrown by her lack of welcome. 'I was just cycling around.'

'And you just happened to come up here?'

'Yeah.' He shrugged again; he had to brazen it out. He wondered if Kim had mentioned his visit to the shop, and to play safe he said, 'I went to see Kim a couple of days ago. I expect he told you.'

She smiled now. 'Yes, he did. And I have got your number, I haven't forgotten you, I will phone you,' she reeled off.

Patrick smiled back, relieved.

'I haven't heard from Lou yet,' she went on. 'He's still abroad.' She let the dog off, giving it a gentle swipe with the lead so that it bounded on in front. 'Don't worry, Patrick, the minute I

79

know anything, I'll phone you, I promise. When are you going back home?'

'In a few days probably.' He walked along beside her. 'I thought I'd have a look round here, visit some places, you know...' His voice trailed away. She smiled again but said nothing, and he felt suddenly overcome with something like shyness, though it wasn't exactly that. 'You don't mind if I walk with you, do you?' he said.

'No, of course not,' she replied, but he sensed she was uncomfortable too. She had on a halter neck suntop and shorts; more of her was exposed than covered, and with every stride her breasts moved, bouncing softly beneath the brief top. He tried not to look at her, and concentrated on swatting away the circle of insects that whirred round his head.

'It's a bit lonely up here, isn't it?' he remarked as they came to yet another crossroads in the track. 'Doesn't your husband mind you walking round here on your own?'

'I'm safe enough with Zula.' She suddenly pulled up the pushchair and reached over to take a little bottle from beneath the baby's pillow. 'Here, let me put some of this on you, you're getting eaten alive.'

'What is it?'

'Something Kim mixed up. It's for Jo-jo, the gnats never bother me. Come here and put your head down,' she commanded. He did as she said and she poured a handful of the liquid into her palm and rubbed it over his hair. Standing there with her half-naked body under

80

his nose, he was seized with embarrassment, and closed his eyes. When they walked on, the conversation between them dried up completely. He was almost relieved when a little way further on she said, 'I turn off for home here. If you want to get back on the road, it's straight on.'

With a brief goodbye, he swung onto his bike and rode off, cursing himself for behaving like an idiot. What the hell would she think of him? First he'd invented the ridiculous idea that he'd come across her by accident, and then he'd behaved like a tongue-tied kid. And all this after he'd cried in her kitchen.

The next day he rode to her house and waited at the end of the lane where it merged into a rough track, the only entrance to the forests from this side. Just after two, she appeared, and he cycled straight up beside her, determined to make up for yesterday.

'I thought I might see you,' he said. 'Do you mind if I walk with you again?'

She looked surprised at first, staring at him a moment before answering, just long enough for him to think, she's going to say yes I do mind, go away and stop pestering me. But instead, her face broke into a smile and her head cocked to one side. With a little click of her tongue, she said, 'I know you want me to tell you more about your father, but it's hard to think of things that happened all those years ago. And even though he and Justina lived with us, he was away a lot.'

He pounced on her words. 'I'd be interested in anything,' he said quickly, smiling back at her, relaxed and childishly happy because she'd provided him with an excuse to be with her. Yesterday's awkwardness vanished. He bumped his bike over the cattle grid that divided the lane from the track and then went back to help her with the pushchair.

It was cooler today, and she had a denim shirt over the suntop. That, too, made the atmosphere between them easier; he could look at her without being so acutely conscious of her body. In fact, he made most of the conversation at first. He asked her about her father, and she laughingly told him that he was a tyrant who did nothing but complain and expect them all to wait on him.

'He's getting on for eighty, so I don't suppose he'll change,' she said. 'He never learnt to speak English very well and he's always used that as an excuse to get away with things.' She glanced up. 'But we're supposed to be talking about your father, not mine.'

He dragged his eyes away from her. While talking, she had been leaning over the pushchair handle tickling Jo-jo with a frond of bracken. Patrick had been watching her, taking in every detail of her. Her hair was in plaits, like that first time he'd seen her, and little corkscrew wisps had escaped to dangle round her ears and forehead. She wore no make-up and her skin, although lightly tanned and with a sprinkling of freckles across her nose, had a delicate look as though any pressure on it would leave a print She pointed ahead. 'See that?' she smiled, then caught her bottom lip with her teeth as though

82

she was about to tell him something secret, something she shouldn't. 'Now that reminds me of Cody.'

'What is it?' It looked like a tumbledown hut half submerged beneath the ground.

'It's a hide, for watching birds. Justina and I used to use it as our camp. Once we stayed there for two days and nobody could find us.' She laughed. 'They called the police, and even they couldn't find us. It was our dogs who gave us away in the end. We had three dogs then, and I don't think we'd taken enough food with us because they got fed up and ran off home.'

'Your parents must have been worried to death.'

She shrugged. 'My mother was always going off on tour with my father until she had Tanya. We did what we liked most of the time, specially after she died and Justina had to look after Tanya and me. Then Justina got married.' Her voice trailed away and she tossed the piece of bracken into the undergrowth. 'Oh sorry, I was going to tell you something about Cody.'

'You said the hide reminded you of him,' Patrick prompted.

They were level with it now. Leah stopped. 'Yes. He and Justina used to go there before they were married. My father was very strict in some ways. We used to pretend we were all going for a walk together, but it always ended up with Tanya and me sitting out here on the track and Justina and him in the hide. I knew what they were doing but I never told on her. Cody used to buy me things to keep me quiet.'

'Bribery and corruption,' Patrick joked, but he stared across at the hide doing little sums of time in his head, imagining his father meeting Ginny one day and Justina the next.

'I shouldn't have told you that,' Leah said suddenly. 'It's made you feel horrible.'

'No, no it hasn't.' Patrick shook his head and tried to smile. 'Where did he play his music?' he asked to change the subject.

'All over. In pubs mostly, I think. I never went. It was bad enough being dragged to see our father. We didn't go often, thank God. The worst was when he started singing, it was such a dirge and it seemed to go on for ever.'

'Not exactly chart material?'

'You'd be surprised,' she laughed. 'He sold lots of records.'

'Did my father sing?'

'He wasn't the main singer in the group. He smoked too much, I think it spoilt his voice. He used to sing in the house sometimes, but I didn't like the Irish songs, they were all so sad. He used to sing one called "Pal Of My Cradle Days". It always made me cry. He only had to play the first few notes on his mandolin—it always worked. He used to say to everybody, watch her eyes when I start to play.' She frowned, then stooped to pick up a fir cone to throw for Zula. 'I don't know why he did that, he was usually nice to me.'

Patrick watched the dog go bounding after the cone, skidding to a halt as she caught

84

it, then flopping down on the dusty track to chew at it. This man whom he'd thought about so much, inventing characteristics to make him seem real, was emerging like a shape walking out of the mist. But the odd thing was, he seemed even more of a stranger now.

'Did he like to make people sad then?'

'Just me, I think.' She gave a little shiver and looked away. 'It was just something he did.'

'But didn't Justina mind him making you cry?' he persisted.

'I don't know, I can't remember.' She turned on him, slapping him quite hard with the dog lead. 'Don't make me talk about sad things or I shan't let you come with me again.'

But she did, the next day and the next. He waited for her each afternoon at the end of the lane out of sight of the house. As they parted company on that second day, she'd said she would invite him in for a cup of tea, but couldn't with her father there. 'He'll see the likeness,' she said. 'It'll only start him off. Justina was his favourite and there wasn't a threat left in the world that he didn't make against Cody.' Patrick said it was all right, he understood, but really he had felt disappointed. The more Leah told him, the more he wanted to see inside that house. He felt it would make Gabriel Cody's shadowy figure come properly alive for him.

'Perhaps when he goes home,' she said as

though she sensed his disappointment. 'You look even more like him with your hair a bit longer,' she added, putting out a finger and flicking at it. But in the next breath she said, 'It's a bit awkward with Tanya as well—she has such a sly mind. I don't think we should mention about you coming up here with me.'

And on the fourth day she ended the walks. They were on their way back and had come to the lane. Jo-jo gurgled with laughter as Patrick bumped him up and down over the cattle grid. He'd cottoned on quickly that a sure way of pleasing Leah was to show an interest in the baby.

'He'll sleep well tonight,' he said, as Jo-jo gave a great yawn.

'Oh, he rarely wakes up in the night. Jo-jo's a really good baby. Mind you, he only has to whimper and I feed him.'

Patrick felt a little frisson of excitement. The more he was with her, the more certain words seemed to leap out and stimulate him.

'Tanya says I spoil him, but I can't help it, I love him. I hate it when people leave their babies crying.'

Patrick was reminded of a time way back in his own childhood when he'd fallen down some steps. Ginny had picked him up and was told, 'Put him down, you'll spoil him.' The incident became magnified for a moment; he wanted to tell Leah about it, as he'd told her about so much else. But she had turned away to call the dog, and seemed in a bit of a hurry. Instead he asked, 'OK to come with you tomorrow?'

Her short, 'No, I'm not coming out any more this week,' was like a slap in the face, and he stood there spinning in a little welter of disappointment. 'I must spend some time with my father before he goes back,' she added.

Patrick bent to unlock his bike which he'd left padlocked to the fence. He wanted to say, what about when he's gone back? But how could he? It would be like asking her for a date—a married woman, virtually old enough to be his mother. The padlock clanked against the spokes, and Jo-jo's head shot round, his arm waving up and down. Zula came up and licked at his fingers and then Leah was clipping on the lead.

'You'll be back at home next week, won't you?' she said.

'Yeah.'

'Just so I know where to phone if I hear from Lou.'

'Right.'

'I'll let you know straightaway. Whatever time he phones me,' she added with a little upward movement of her lips.

'Thanks,' he muttered, lingering there, slapping the padlock against his palm.

'And thanks for your company,' she said brightly, already gathering herself to go.

There seemed nothing more to say and he jumped on his bike and rode off down the lane. He heard her call goodbye, but resisted the desire to look back and just raised his arm in an offhand farewell.

# Chapter 5

Leah was worried what people might think. Patrick came to this conclusion in the middle of the night. He had been racking his brains to remember if he'd said or done anything to offend her, and decided the worst he'd done was to look at her a bit too long sometimes. It must be that she thought if anyone saw them together they could get the wrong impression; he remembered what she had said about Tanya's sly mind. It was as simple as that. And he'd acted like a rejected schoolboy, going off without saying goodbye properly. He lay there thinking about it, wishing she could see what he was really like back home with his friends. Never before had he felt such a strong need to impress, and now it was too late. He fell asleep miserable and frustrated, his last thoughts of Ginny and how this was all her fault.

The next morning he was supposed to be going home but he changed his mind the minute he opened his eyes. What I'll do, he told himself as he lay there listening to the sound of his grandmother in the kitchen, I'll hang around here a couple more days, then go and find Leah, and apologise for going off in a huff. He clasped his hands behind his head, trying to ignore the fact that he had woken stiff with desire. The smell of frying was seeping under the door, and he tried to focus all his thoughts on the breakfast he'd soon be eating. But instead he began to think about going home and getting hold of the first willing girl he could find.

'One minute you say you're going home, the next it looks like I've got you here for good,' his grandmother said when he asked if he could stay on for a few days. She said it with one of her measured smiles as if it was a joke, but he knew she was pleased to have him there a little longer.

It was hard to while away time at her bungalow as he did at home. Lying in bed half the morning engrossed in books and thoughts was out of the question; she wanted to make beds and dust and always had a cooked breakfast on the table at eight. On the second day he agreed to go to Cambridge with her. She let him drive her Mini through the traffic, and again brought up the subject of his getting a car of his own. But it went in one ear and out the other, as did much of what she said. And trailing round the town and the colleges with her, adjusting his pace to suit her slower sixty-year-old steps, his mind constantly wandered elsewhere.

'Your grandfather always dreamt that you'd come here,' she said, stopping to look at the label of a plant in one of the quadrangles. She bent to sniff a bloom, and without raising her head said in a quiet but very clear voice, 'He was very upset about Ginny. He hardly spoke to her for months, he was so disappointed. But once you were born...' She twisted her head to look at him now. 'He always wanted a son of his own.'

Patrick avoided her eyes, glancing towards a crowd of foreign students whose loud chatter drowned out her next words. He felt her hand on his arm, but it meant nothing to him. 'You never wanted for anything, Patrick,' she said. 'Some people have different ways of showing they care for you.' Patrick didn't answer, neither did he pay any attention to one of the girls who looked over her shoulder at him. His head was filled with Leah.

He found himself thinking about her again and again. And at night, tossing and turning until the sheets were tangled and his pillow had turned to lead, he let his imagination take him up to the pine forest with her. There was no dog and no baby, and when they came to the hide, it was she who suggested they go in. As soon as they were through the door, he began kissing her, and she was saying, no, no against his lips. He liked to imagine that she resisted him a bit, not so that he had to use any degree of force, but just enough to make him feel in control. And then he'd start to undress her. Sometimes he imagined that she wore only the brief suntop and shorts with nothing underneath, at others that she had on a few layers and there were buttons to undo and straps to unhook. Either way, long before he imagined her standing naked in front of him, he would be masturbating, breathless and choking with stifled pleasure, conscious of those crisp white sheets, and his grandmother only feet away the other side of the bedroom wall.

But the relief he got was purely physical and didn't last. Soon he was fantasising about her again, trying to recall the way she had said things and the way she had smiled at him. He even wondered if she was attracted to him at all. It was possible; she had rarely mentioned her husband. Once she had said that after all the trouble with her divorce and then Justina's, Carew had brought stability and peace to her life. It was one of those times when she had seemed to be talking to herself as much as to him, and Patrick hadn't asked any questions. But he knew that Carew was much older than she was and that he had money. It seemed to spell out that she hadn't married him for love. And from this conclusion it was easy to play with all sorts of possibilities.

The day Patrick decided to go and see her again was hotter than ever. He waited for half an hour in the lane but there was no sign of her. Perhaps she had left early to avoid him. Or maybe she hadn't gone out at all, she really was spending time with her father. Two cars were parked at the house, one the estate car he'd seen in London, the other a year-old Volkswagen Golf which he knew was Leah's. So her husband must be there. The thought made him stupidly jealous; he was already exhausted from the heat and the long ride. Suddenly he longed to be back in London, on his way round to Mansour's and going out for the evening. For a moment he imagined telling Mansour about all this, how he had waited around in the heat for a married woman with two kids for no reason that he could sanely think of.

'Fucking hell,' he muttered, wiping fresh beads of sweat from his forehead. 'Fucking place, fucking sun.' It seemed the last straw when he took out his water bottle and found it empty. The pub was only a short ride away; he could be there before closing time and have an ice-cold lager. He rode off in that direction, and that's when he saw her.

She had come out of the village shop and was bent over the pushchair putting something in the tray underneath. She didn't head towards home but went off down a side turning. Patrick forgot the pub and followed her. He kept his distance, able to remain undetected because she didn't have the dog with her and the lane was very winding with high overgrown hedges. Coming round yet another bend, he heard the sound of running water the other side of the hedge. It made him feel almost tortured with thirst and he went to investigate but found only a cattle trough filling automatically as a row of cows drank there. They took their time, raising their heads between gulps and flicking long tongues round their dripping mouths. Cows were a bit like dogs to him, unpredictable, and he waited until they'd finished before he went and lifted the lid over the pipe outlet to see if he could drink from it. It had a ball cock similar to a toilet cistern, and he worked out that if he pressed it down, water would flow from the pipe. It looked clean but he drank just one scooped handful, enough to ease his thirst.

When he climbed back through the hedge and rode on round the next bend, there was no sign of Leah. He rode a bit faster and came to a humpback bridge over a shallow river. A little further on there were crossroads, and beyond this a dark stretch of pine forest. Another way to get there, he thought. Could she have done this to avoid him? He leant his bike on the parapet of the bridge and stood there, staring down into the water, listening to the sound of crickets in the reeds. Or was it frogs? How boring and incomprehensible and hatefully hot the countryside was.

He snatched up the empty water bottle and scrambled down the steep bank. On either side of the river was a band of sandy coloured mud, and he had to walk on until he found a strip of shingle where he could stand to fill the bottle. He slumped down on a patch of grass and poured the water slowly over his head. It felt like paradise as it trickled down over his shoulders and he lay back and closed his eyes. For a moment he thought the crickets or frogs or whatever they were had started to make a noise like singing; but after listening for a minute, he realised it was music coming from further up the river. He stood up, squinting into the sun, and there she was, on the opposite bank. She was standing ankle deep in the river swinging Jo-jo backwards and forwards so that his feet skimmed the water.

With the music from her radio, she didn't

hear him until he was almost up to her. Her head jerked up; there was surprise, then annoyance.

'Have you followed me?' she said.

'Yeah. I saw you come out of the shop.'

She tucked Jo-jo under one arm and put a hand on her hip. 'I thought you were going home.' There was more exasperation than anger in her tone, and something very provocative about the way she stood there with her dress tucked up way above her knees.

'And I thought you were spending time with your father,' he said.

Her expression changed slowly, as though she couldn't quite believe what she was hearing. The annoyance became an amused smile, then laughter.

'Can I come across?' he said.

'What if I say no?' She laughed again and hoisted Jo-jo more comfortably in her arms. 'Come on then, if you must.'

Patrick took off his trainers and waded into the water. In the middle it came to his knees, soaking his jeans, and he floundered about, his feet entangled in a mass of slimy weed.

'Mind the water snakes,' she called out.

'Where?' He sprang forward, nearly losing his balance as he ran splashing to the bank.

She was laughing again. 'I'm only joking.'

'I hate snakes,' he said, looking cautiously round him. 'Are there really any here?'

'Don't worry, I'll protect you.' She sat down, Jo-jo on her lap. 'We won't let the nasty snakes get him, will we?' she said, cuddling the baby, then wiping his wet feet on her dress.

Patrick sat down beside her. It was like a little sandy cove here, sheltered on both sides by reeds and tall creamy-white flowers which gave off a heavy sweet scent.

'I've left my bike up by the bridge,' he said suddenly. 'Do you think I should go and get it?'

'It'll be all right. Nobody comes down here.'

He looked around; it certainly seemed a very lonely place. 'Where's the dog?' he asked.

'She's on heat.'

'Oh.' He didn't know much about dogs but had heard that expression.

'I can't bring her out or I'd have all the dogs from miles around after her.' She rocked the baby against her shoulder, humming to it in tune with the music. 'When *are* you going home then?' she asked.

'Are you trying to get rid of me?' He drew up his knees and rested his arms and head on them, staring at her sideways.

She didn't answer, but got up and put the baby in his pushchair, adjusted the frilled sunshade and gave him a sip of water from a small bottle. Patrick thought, I've said that wrong, she's getting ready to go. 'I don't mean to pester you,' he said. 'I just wanted to say goodbye properly.'

'What's properly?' she said with a little smile, her head to one side.

She's flirting with me, he thought, his heart racing a little as he imagined how he'd like to say goodbye to her. He watched as she took a bag from the pushchair and pulled out a bar of chocolate, crouching down beside the baby to put tiny pieces of it into his mouth. Jo-jo's lips came pouting out in an exaggerated sucking motion, then his jaws began to work up and down and his eyes grew round. 'You like that, don't you?' she cooed, placing another little speck on his tongue. 'The woman in the shop gave it to him,' she said. 'But he's not really old enough for chocolate.' She turned and held out the bar to Patrick. 'Do you want some?'

It was white and melting and looked revolting.

'No thanks.'

She flopped back down beside him and carefully peeled away the rest of the silver paper, then put the chocolate in her mouth in one lump. Patrick pulled a face.

'I know, I'm disgusting,' she said, a hand to her mouth. 'But I can't resist chocolate.' She licked her fingers clean one by one, then took a deep breath and patted her stomach. 'I shouldn't eat it at all. I was a size ten before I had Jo-jo but I can hardly get into a twelve now—unless it's something loose like this. I've never been this fat before.'

Patrick stared at her again. The dress was a riot of crudely-dyed colour and made of some light, floaty material similar to the ones he'd seen hanging in the doorway of Tanya's shop. It had narrow shoulder straps and a decoration of tiny silver bells at the waist. And she had matching silver bangles on her arm, pushed tight up on the smooth round flesh above her elbow. Her hair was caught up in a ponytail, held in place with childish plastic bobbles.

'I don't think you're fat,' he murmured. 'I think you're perfect.'

She glanced at him. He looked away. After a few seconds she said, 'Patrick, I'm not perfect, and I don't want you following me and saying things like that.'

He stared out across the river; she kicked a little spray of sand over his feet but he wouldn't look at her.

'Come on, you can walk back with me if you like.' She began to gather up her things but he still didn't move. 'Or are you going to sit there and sulk all afternoon?'

'I'm not sulking,' he said. He twisted his head to look up at her. She was standing there adjusting her ponytail, her face caught in the triangle of her raised arms like a beautiful picture. A damp half-moon of sweat stained the fabric of her dress at the armholes, and for the first time he noticed the slick of dark hair in her armpits.

For a second she stared back at him, her arms still above her head, her face serious. Then she dropped down to crouch beside him. 'I think you'd better get back home to one of the hundreds of girl friends I'm sure you've got,' she said, playfully reaching out to pinch his cheek.

He grabbed her hand to stop her, pushing her away at the same time. 'I don't want anyone but you,' he said.

She toppled backwards, clutching at him to save herself, and he went with her, pinning her to the ground, his hands on her shoulders, sliding down the straps of her dress. For a moment she lay still, and he had a high delusory sensation that she wanted him to do this. He buried his face in the swell of her breasts, kissing her damp skin, pressing his nose into the smell and the softness of her. He was aware that she was struggling now, and he lifted himself up a fraction and tried to kiss her on the lips. She twisted her head away, screaming at him to let her go, but he could no longer help himself; his hands had already moved down to her thighs, his fingers gathering up the folds of her skirt. She fought harder but it was a one-sided struggle; he was nearly a foot taller than she was and much stronger, and her dress and underwear were all so flimsy. He could hear her saying no, over and over, desperate and breathless as she fought him, and he wanted to stop. But it was too late, he'd found the thick coarse hair between her legs and nothing in the world could have dragged him off her. He hardly had time to undo his zip and was nowhere near getting inside her when he was overtaken by an orgasm so intense it felt as though it would go on for ever.

A great burning silence seemed to settle over them like a heavy blanket. He raised his head, then let it fall against her shoulder. Sounds drifted back: the rustling of the reeds and the soft whirr of some insect's wings, and then tiny sucking noises from the pushchair. He pushed his face into her neck and whispered that he loved her, that he'd loved her every minute that he'd been walking up in the woods with her, and before. She didn't move, but he could feel her breathing beneath him, panting as though she was about to suffocate. He lifted his weight from her and in that same instant both her hands came up, clawing at his face and raining blows against his head. He twisted away, arms raised to protect himself, but still she lashed at him. He rolled over on the ground, his eyes closed, aware that his face was bleeding. She was screaming and shouting at him, 'How dare you! How dare you!' and he felt her bare foot punch against his forehead. He went to sit up, and she kicked sand at him, then snatched up handfuls of it and showered it over his head. 'I've tried to help you,' she screamed. 'I've tried to be nice to you.'

The baby started to cry and she ran to it, lifting it from the pushchair. Patrick stood up and went towards her.

'Get away from me,' she said on a long angry sob. 'Get away.'

There was nothing he could say; nothing to justify what he'd done. He grabbed his trainers and ran into the river.

'Don't ever come back,' she screamed after him.

He made the far bank, cutting through the reeds, soaked and muddy and not caring if there were a thousand snakes curled there. He wanted to die.

# Chapter 6

As Patrick unpacked the last of his things, he came across the photo that Leah had given him. The only reason he'd brought it with him was because he thought Ginny might find it if he left it at home. He pushed it under a pile of books; he had decided to abandon the search for his father.

It was two weeks since that afternoon by the river. He'd gone home and written an impassioned letter of apology to Leah, scribbling down two pages of his feelings for her, trying to explain why he'd done what he had. She'd answered with a brief, curt phone call telling him never to write to her again, or to try and contact her in any way. He had spent the next few days in a snarling black mood and a rampage of late nights. The chance of this room at Cambridge had come just in time. He knew he was pushing Ginny to breaking point, but he couldn't help it, and even when he had reduced her to tears, he'd walked off, telling himself it was all her fault anyway.

This room would be a new start, he decided. It was only slightly bigger than his bedroom at home, and there was more crammed into it, with a washbasin and table and chairs as well as the bedroom furniture. But he could do what he liked here, be as quiet and private as he wanted, or do some entertaining. He thought of the three girls in the large ground-floor flat below: second-year students and all quite attractive in different ways. They had already offered to take him for a drink and show him round. He was musing over the delights of being taken out by all three of them when there was a knock at the door.

He smiled to himself and rubbed his hands together. Then in a sudden streak of vanity, he shouted, 'Hang on,' and dashed over to his little mirror. There was no time to do anything about the gaunt unshaven stranger who stared back at him, and anyway he quite liked him—dissolute and world-weary rather than miserable and scruffy, he decided. Nevertheless, he smoothed down his hair as he went to open the door.

It was Leah. Shock gave way to a rush of embarrassment, and he stood there like an idiot, a hand still stroking away at his hair.

'Can I come in?' she said.

'Yeah, course.' He stepped back. It was on his lips to add, if you trust me, but she was smiling, and he was suddenly filled with a great sparkle of illogical happiness.

'Your mother told me where to find you.' She looked round. 'It's a nice room.'

It didn't matter that it wasn't a particularly nice room, or that she seemed very subdued, nothing like the Leah who had teased him about snakes and sucked chocolate from her fingers. She was here, and it was obvious she was no longer angry with him.

'I might not stay here,' he said.

101

'Oh. I thought you'd moved in ready to go to university.'

'No, I haven't got my results yet. A friend of mine had the room but she's just moved in with her boy friend.' He rushed over to clear some books from the only easy chair, dropping most of them on the floor. 'Have a seat,' he said. 'Do you want some coffee? There's a kitchen downstairs. Or tea if you like.'

She shook her head and perched on the edge of the chair, neat and tidy in a little jacket and matching skirt. 'So you're not staying here?'

He started to babble on again, explaining about halls of residence, but he could see she was only half listening, and he ground to a halt midway through a sentence.

'Patrick,' she said quietly, arranging her hands in her lap. 'Sit down, I've got something to tell you.'

He stepped back without looking round, feeling for the table and the straight-backed chair beside it. 'He doesn't want to see me. That's it, isn't it? You've found him and he doesn't want to see me.' His decision not to search for his father any more evaporated with the disappointment of this realisation. But she was shaking her head, and in a ray of light from the window he could see that her eyes were shiny with tears.

'I'm sorry, Patrick, but your father's dead.'

'Oh.' He turned to rest his elbows on the table and began to chew at his little fingernail.

'It was two years ago. A car accident.' Her voice was soft and slightly tremulous. 'Lou

102

thinks it may have been suicide. There was no one else involved and nothing wrong with the car. Cody had just been through his third divorce. That's all he could find out.' She paused. 'Oh, Patrick, I'm sorry,'

He heard her get up and come over to him; he could see the edge of her jacket out of the corner of his eye. 'Don't worry, I'm not about to burst into tears,' he said, staring at the wall. 'I don't make a habit of it.' The news hurt more because of that surge of happinesss only minutes ago. He heard her sigh, and he felt sorry for his bitter tone. She must have made the journey specially to tell him. 'Thanks for coming to tell me, anyway,' he said.

'I was worried...after everything else... I just wanted to make sure you were told...' she paused again, 'gently.'

'What did my mother say?'

'I didn't tell her. I was going to but she got upset. She said she wished you'd never started looking for him. She said it's altered you and made you unhappy and depressed. I think she blames me. She said she didn't want the past raked up. I told her I'd write to you with the information I had, and she finally agreed to give me your address.'

'Were you going to write and tell me then?'

'No, I only said that.' Her hand came out as though she was going to touch him, but she drew it back and folded her arms. 'I had to come and tell you, after she said about you being so unhappy.'

'Thanks.' He pressed his forehead into his

103

palms. 'I'm really sorry for what I did. And I'm sorry about the letter. I feel so bad about it.' He couldn't remember everything he had written, but some phrases like, 'I don't expect even a million apologies will make you forgive me' and 'If your husband comes after me I shall have to tell him that I did it because I love you, and I shall go on loving you even though you probably hate me now' were impossible to forget.

'Don't worry about it any more. I've forgiven you. And, Patrick.'

He swivelled his head round in his hands. 'What?'

'I don't hate you, and I'm sorry that I've had to bring you such bad news. I know how much you wanted to meet him, and I'm sure he would have wanted to see you too.'

'If only my mother had told me the truth before.'

'You must go home and talk to her about it. Be sad together.'.

'She won't care.'

'Oh, Patrick, of course she will.' Leah reached out again, and this time she stroked his hair. 'You look tired.' She hoisted herself up on the table and leant her head down to his. 'Poor Patrick, you're having such an awful time, aren't you?' Her voice had the soft cooing tone she used when she spoke to the baby. It felt as though she was just a hairs-breadth away from folding her arms round him and rocking him against her. He closed his eyes, caught in a little whirl of self-pity and longing. 'Poor Patrick,' she said again and it took only the gentlest pressure of her hand before he laid his head in her lap. She carried on stroking his hair. 'You've still got a mark where I scratched you,' she said, rubbing a finger against his jaw.

'I deserved it. I'm sorry. I don't know how—'

'Shh, we'll blame the dog—you wouldn't have done it if she'd been there.' She drummed her fingers jokily against his cheek now, and went to lift his head away, but he slipped his arms very carefully round her waist. Just as carefully she removed them.

He looked up at her. 'If you weren't married, would it make any difference?'

She cut him off, taking his face between her hands, her thumbs pressed over his lips. 'You only want me because of the connection with your father, and it's only causing you more heartache.'

'That's not the reason. I meant what I said in that letter.'

'Stop it, Patrick, stop it.' She took him by the shoulders and gave him a little shake, then almost immediately she gathered him up in her arms, pulling his head against her shoulder. 'I know it's my fault as well, I know that.' She leant back to hold his face in front of her again as though she couldn't make up her mind what to do. 'I knew how you felt.'

He wasn't sure who made the next move, only that he was standing up and kissing her, and she had her arms round his neck. And he knew that in some precarious and exhilarating way everything depended on the next few seconds. He drew back so that he could see her face, wanting her to say it was all right. 'I didn't mean this to happen,' she whispered. But she was eager, twisting in his arms and opening her mouth as he began to kiss her again. He was soon violently aroused, moving his hands over her body as though he had to touch every part of her. Again and again he ran his hands over her breasts, but every time she pulled him away. The last time, she took hold of his wrists and dragged his hands down to her lap and held them there. When she let go, he pushed up her skirt, and she made no attempt to stop him. Her legs were bare, her skin very warm. 'Maid in heaven,' he murmured, remembering her T-shirt. 'You were made in heaven.' She laughed very softly and reached down and caressed him through the thickness of his jeans. He caught his breath. The next minute she was tugging at his zip.

'I can't do it,' she whispered. He did it for her, enclosing both her hands for a moment. She had funny rough little hands. He lifted them up and kissed them, pressing them against his lips in a fever of excitement, sure she was going to let him have sex with her right here on this table. But she pushed at his chest. 'Not here,' she said, reaching down to touch him again. He looked towards the bed; it seemed a mile away, he didn't want this moment interrupted. 'Patrick,' she purred, stroking away with those rough little fingers, 'I'm uncomfortable here.' He hooked an arm under her knees and carried her to the bed. 'Wait, wait,' she said, holding him off as she unbuttoned her jacket. She shrugged it off, then began to unbutton her blouse. He was immediately kneeling in front of her, pulling it from her shoulders. She laughed at him to slow down, shoving him away with both hands, then standing up on the bed to take off her skirt.

He stood up himself and tore off his own clothes, watching her while he did it. He was surprised to see she wore very plain white underwear.

'Don't stare at me,' she said. 'Or I'll get dressed again.'

'I won't let you.' He caught her round the legs, and they rolled together on the narrow bed, ending up against the wall. Dizzy with arousal, he pulled her against him, sliding his hands round to unhook her bra.

'No, don't.'

'Why?'

'Just don't.' She twisted away to stretch flat on her back and pulled his hand between her legs.

He knew what to do; he'd been out with girls who would go no further than mutual masturbation, and he'd grown good at it, finding that if they became aroused enough, they would give in to full sex. But with Leah it was all so different. She was demanding and wild, noisier and more exciting than any girl he'd ever known or imagined. When she rolled over and took hold of him using both her hands, it was only seconds before he was seized with an orgasm as intense as he'd had that day by the river.

He lay there on his side, his face in her hair, an arm round her waist, and listened to her breathing grow quiet. She sighed and smiled to herself, stretching like a contented cat. But Patrick felt vaguely disappointed. He hadn't come as quickly as this since that first disastrous experience when he was sixteen. The gnawing ache of not being quite satisfied grew. It was like zipping down a slide as a child, then wanting to do it all over again. He fidgeted against her. The remains of his erection stirred a little, and Leah caught hold of him by the hair and pulled his head closer to her.

'I like it that you're so excited by me,' she said, taking his bottom lip between her teeth.

'You didn't like me by the river,' he murmured, reassured enough to mention it.

'That was then, this is now.'

'What does that mean?'

She gave a gruff little sigh as though something had momentarily troubled her, then suddenly raised her head, listening. 'Whatever's that?'

Patrick propped himself on an elbow and listened too. 'Oh, it's a violin. It's the girl downstairs.'

'It's beautiful.'

'You're beautiful.'

She smiled. 'Am I?'

'Yeah, very.'

They lay face to face, gently biting and kissing each other. Patrick's confidence grew. This wasn't going to end with this one afternoon; he suddenly hugged her tight with the certainty of it, glad he'd got this room and happy in a way he'd never been before. She moved against him, gripping his buttocks with both hands and squeezing with her rough little fingers.

'Do you like me doing that?' she asked.

He laughed self-consciously. 'I like everything you do.'

'And this,' she said, sliding her hands round to his groin. 'You like this, don't you?'

'Yeah,' he said weakly, smiling against her cheek.

'I know what you want to do most.'

'Do you?' he murmured. He tried to push her onto her back but she resisted.

'Don't be in such a hurry,' she scolded, hooking an arm round his neck and opening her mouth to kiss him. The kiss became heated, like a battle of lips and tongues, and in the middle of it he slipped his arms round to her back and unhooked her bra. She let him do it this time but still pulled his hands away when he tried to fondle her breasts. But the feel of them, hot and swollen against the bare skin of his chest, provided that last inch of stimulation, and he took hold of her shoulders and forced her down.

'Wait,' she said sharply.

He let out an impatient throaty sigh and looked down at her with half-closed eyes. 'Please, Leah, don't stop me.'

'Condom,' she mouthed at him.

'But I thought...' He screwed up his face at her. 'I thought being married you'd be on the pill.'

She shook her head. 'No, I don't need it while I'm breastfeeding. It's not that.'

'I've always been careful. I haven't got anything.'

'Just do it, Patrick.' He didn't want to, but she folded both hands between her legs and looked defiantly at him. 'Or you'd better go and play with yourself.' He laughed in disbelief and went to pull at her wrists because she was smiling slightly. But she hit out at him. 'I mean it. And I'll do more than scratch you in a minute.' There was something playful in her tone, but looking down at her naked body, her hands held between her legs and her big dark nipples sticking up towards him, he didn't feel like playing about; he wanted only to be on top of her and in her, and he hopped off the bed and over to the cupboard.

It was over far too quickly again. One minute he was kneeling between her spread thighs, tenderly stroking her stomach, the next he was plunging up and down on her as though his life depended on it. And in the last seconds, when it felt as though he was going to be lost for ever in the sheer pleasure of it, he heard Leah say his name, felt her clutch at him and say she loved him. It sounded as though she said it over and over, but when he finally raised his head to look at her, she was silent, her mouth closed, her eyes closed, and her arms and hair spread out like someone drowned.

He kissed her gently on the lips but it was like kissing a doll; not even an eyelash moved. 'Leah?' he whispered, but she didn't answer. He shifted his weight, worried that he was becoming too heavy for her; there was little room in the single bed to lie properly beside her. The sweat grew cool and uncomfortable

110

between them, and his limbs became cramped, but still she didn't move. He didn't think she was sleeping. 'Leah?' he said anxiously, kissing her lightly on her neck. 'Leah, speak to me, please. What's the matter?'

She opened her eyes and wrapped her arms briefly round him, then wriggled free of him to sit up. 'I have to go,' she said, drawing the duvet round her.

'Don't go yet.'

'I have to.'

'I don't want you to go,' he said, trying to hold her.

'Patrick, let go of me.' He let go and watched as she gathered up her clothes, then went to sit on the end of the bed, her back to him.

'When will I see you again?' he asked as she began to get dressed.

She shrugged.

'Leah, what's the matter? What have I done?'

'It's not you, it's me.' She put both hands over her face. 'I shouldn't have let this happen.' He scrambled down beside her but she quickly stood up and pulled on her skirt. 'I feel so ashamed. I came here to tell you your father's dead, and then I do this.'

'Ashamed?' He repeated the word as though it was the most hurtful thing she could possibly have said. 'Is that how you feel about me?'

'I'm sorry, I didn't mean it in that way.' Her hands flew to her face again. 'I mean it about myself.'

'So you regret what's happened?'

111

'I'm married. I've never been unfaithful to him before.'

'Well, you have now,' he said, feeling a great stab of resentment towards this man he had never seen or even thought much about until this moment.

'Please, Patrick, don't let's part like this.' She came and stroked his shoulder and tilted his chin with a finger. 'Come on, you started this, you know. I like you, I like you a lot, but you know as well as I do it can't go on.'

'You like me, do you?' He stretched back on the bed, hands clasped behind his head, and stared up at the ceiling. 'Bit of a comedown from what you were saying a little while ago. But I suppose that was just in the heat of the moment—like all of it. You change like the wind.' He raised his head to look at her but she turned away, and he sensed fleeting embarrassment, as though his nakedness bothered her now she was dressed. He settled back, oddly confident. 'Or does it just depend what mood you're in?'

'I have to go,' she said firmly without looking at him. 'I've left Jo-jo with Tanya. I've never done that before.' Her voice faltered. 'And I've been gone such a long time.' He saw her fold her arms and drop her head, and knew she was crying. All desire to hurt her vanished. But he hesitated, not sure what to do, how she would react if he went and put his arms round her. And in that moment's hesitation she ran to the door and left.

He heard her all the way down the uncarpeted

stairs. The violin music had been playing until this moment, short little practice pieces one after the other. Now it stopped as though the player also listened. Patrick went to the window, wondering if Leah had left her car in one of the parking spaces behind the house. But no, she wasn't there; she probably didn't even know about the car park. He felt cheated, as though he could have called to her and she would have come back.

There was a fly buzzing against the glass, and he took a swipe at it. It fell upside down on the sill, defenceless and buzzing hysterically, and he hadn't the heart to kill it. The violin started up again. He thought of his father playing that song Leah had told him about, but couldn't remember the title, only that it was very sad and had made her cry.

## Chapter 7

Walking round the town half an hour later, the name of the song came to him—'Pal Of My Cradle Days'. He had a sudden urge to know the words of it and went and looked through some Irish music tapes in a record shop. There were quite a few and he skipped through the titles not really expecting to find it. And then there it was, sung by a woman. He read it again, stupidly happy, but when he took it to the counter, he discovered that he hadn't got enough money. He left the shop in a flurry of embarrassment, and went and bought chips and a can of lager instead.

When he got back, there was a note on his door. 'A woman phoned you. She will call back at six.' It was ten to and he went straight back down and sat on the stairs. The phone was in the hall; whoever happened to hear it, answered it. Ginny and Mansour both had the number and so did Ruth, the girl who had put him on to the room. It would be one of them, probably Ginny because he had promised to call her and hadn't. But when finally the phone began to ring, he leapt up, his heart racing, and his 'Hello?' came out on a sharp expectant note.

'I was worried about you. I know you must be thinking about your father.'

'Oh, Leah.' He cleared his throat. 'I thought it was my mother.'

'I'm sorry, I should have left my name.'

'It's OK.' He caught hold of his bottom lip, squeezing it between finger and thumb.

'I just wanted to know you were all right. Have you got someone you can talk to?'

Two girls came into the hall, laughing together, and banged on one of the ground-floor doors.

'It's so noisy here.' Patrick put a hand to his ear, his forehead against the wall. 'Give me your number, let me call you back from somewhere else.'

'No, I can't...' Her voice was drowned out by a burst of loud music as the door opened. The girls disappeared inside and it grew quiet again.

'You're the only one I want to talk to.' He shifted round with his back against the wall. 'Let me come and meet you, like we used to.'

'Patrick, you know we can't do that.'

'Then why have you bothered to phone me?'

'I told you, I was worried about you. I thought about you all the way home. I feel sad about Cody, but I know you must feel ten times worse. Patrick, are you there?' she asked when he didn't answer.

He turned to the wall again, thumped his clenched fist lightly against it, then sank down on his haunches. 'Please, Leah, can we meet just once more?' He heard her sigh, then someone called her name. It sounded like Tanya, but he wasn't sure. 'Please,' he said again. 'I just want to talk to you.'

'I have to go. I'll phone you in a couple of days.'

'Leah, don't cut me off.'

'Ssh,' she said.

'I'll meet you anywhere you say. Leah, please.'

'I'll come to you,' she said. 'Not to your room—and it's the last time, I mean it.'

'Tomorrow. Come tomorrow.'

Her voice had dropped to little more than a whisper, and he heard her stifle a laugh. 'The day after,' she said, and he was almost laughing himself.

'There's a parking space behind the house, I'll meet you there. Any time. I'll wait for you all day.'

'Eleven,' she said. A door slammed and someone was calling her again, a man this time.

'I have to go,' she whispered, and the line went dead.

He was in the car park waiting for her well before eleven, leaning against the back wall of the house, tapping his palms against the sun-warmed bricks in a fidget of impatience. Through hour after hour of thinking about her, going over and over all that had happened, what she'd said and how she'd said it, he'd come to the conclusion that he'd been nothing more than an interlude of excitement in a boring marriage. Today she would wind their relationship down to how it had been on that first day he'd met her and go home with a clear conscience. 'That's how it's going to be,' he'd said aloud to himself in the dark last night. 'Get that in your skull and stop being such a fucking idiot.'

The moment he saw her, all sensible intentions vanished. She had the baby with her, and the first thought that leapt into his head was that she might stay longer with no excuse to get back in a hurry.

'Have you brought him along as protection from me?' Patrick joked, trying to sound light-hearted.

'You've got a short memory,' Leah said, smiling over her shoulder as she leant into the back seat to lift Jo-jo out.

Patrick watched as she fiddled with the straps of the car seat. Her small waist and rounded hips were emphasised by the tight jeans and wide belt she wore. The urge to wrap his arms round her and press his face into the curve of

116

her back overwhelmed him. When she turned round, the baby in her arms, and smiled at him again, he was paralysed with longing for her.

'Can you give me a hand?' she said.

'What? Oh, the pushchair, sorry.' He went and got it out for her but couldn't fathom how to unfold it.

'You brainy people are all the same,' she laughed, and did it with one hand.

They walked up through the town. It was her suggestion, and she who did most of the talking. She didn't mention Cody, but chattered on about a dog she'd had once who was so devoted to her it insisted on sleeping in her bed. 'It used to crawl under the bedclothes and sleep by my feet,' she laughed. 'Luckily it was only a Jack Russell. I might get Jo-jo one like it when he starts walking.' Almost without pausing, she said, 'I don't regret what happened. I feel guilty but I don't regret it.' She glanced up at him and her face changed. 'You look nice today, Patrick,' she smiled. 'New shirt?' She often talked like this in fits and starts, veering from one thing to another and sometimes making quite ridiculous statements. But this was too obvious, too jerky even for her.

'No—it's just one I haven't worn much.' It was nearly new; he'd spent ages getting ready that morning, preening himself in front of the bathroom mirror until he had the girls from downstairs hammering on the door. 'Leah,' he said hoarsely. 'Come back with me.'

She shook her head. 'You know I can't. We've both got too much to lose. I came today so that

117

we can be friends, like we were before...so that we can part happily. I was awake half the night worrying about you.' He put his arm round her shoulders and came to a halt, but she shook her head again and walked on a few paces without him. And in the few seconds that they became separated, he heard someone call his name. As he turned, two fat arms encircled him.

'Patrick, darling, we've been looking for you. How do you like the room?'

'Hi, Ruth, Carl.' He smiled at the girl and nodded at the man standing beside her. 'It's great. I was going to come round and see you.'

'So you say. Come round later.'

'I can't, I...' He looked towards Leah who had stopped a few feet ahead. 'I'm with somebody.'

The girl's eyes were immediately on Leah. 'Introduce us then,' she said brightly.

'Leah, Ruth,' he said waving a hand between them. 'And this is Carl.'

'We went to the same school,' said Ruth. 'I used to look after him when he was little, and I was his agony aunt until he started doing things he couldn't tell me about.' She chuckled at her own joke, her eyes still on Leah, then crouched down beside the pushchair and tickled a finger round Jo-jo's face. She was rewarded with a succession of dribbly smiles. 'Isn't she sweet.'

'He,' corrected Leah. 'His name's Jonah.' She sounded perfectly friendly but Patrick could see she felt intimidated by the way Ruth was scrutinising her; she seemed almost to shrink against Ruth's large bulk.

'I might come round tomorrow,' he said, turning as though he meant to walk on.

'Hang on,' said Ruth. 'We're going your way.'

They walked along together. Ruth began asking questions about Jo-jo, his age, if he had teeth, all sorts of things which, Patrick thought, weren't really the questions she wanted to ask. But she fired away, hardly giving Leah time to answer. She dominated the conversation even when it turned to other things like Patrick's room and their friends back home. But in an odd way Patrick enjoyed having her and Carl there. Their presence seemed to have subtly altered the balance of things, brought back his usual strut of confidence. Leah, on the other hand, had become subdued. It made him feel protective towards her, and he put his arm round her again. Seeing Ruth's eyes on them, he slipped his fingers under her hair and gently squeezed her neck. Leah glanced sideways at him with a little warning frown, but he just smiled, then took her hand and held on to the pushchair with it enclosed in his own.

'Are you still looking for a car?'

Patrick turned his head towards Carl. 'Yeah, I am. Why?'

'I've got one that might interest you.'

They had come to a narrower section of the pavement; the crowds were thicker and Carl walked ahead. Patrick let go of Leah's hand and went to catch him up. Engrossed in talk of the car, he was only vaguely aware of Ruth's voice, her monologue of their school days and

Leah's barely audible replies. Then, alerted by a short silence, he heard Ruth ask, 'Is he Patrick's baby?'

He looked over his shoulder just in time to see Leah shake her head, and Ruth compose her face to hide her curiosity. Carl carried on telling him about the car, but Patrick cut him short and slipped back to Leah. The day was turning out very differently from what he had expected. He put his arm round her again. A little breeze blew wisps of hair round her face and she kept hooking them behind her ears, wetting her finger to make them stay in place. Patrick remembered her doing the same thing on those walks in the pine forest, how it had reminded him of a cat washing behind its ears and how he had watched her then, burning with thoughts of what he wanted to do to her. By some miracle it had all come true; now it was going to be over.

'Look, there's Corpus Christi,' Ruth was saying. 'That's where Patrick's going.'

'If I get my grades,' said Patrick.

'Of course you will.' She leant slightly towards Leah. 'His father taught English—Patrick had a head start on all of us. He had William Blake instead of nursery rhymes,' she laughed, 'and Kubla Khan for a bedtime story. We all knew he'd come here. He's sickeningly brilliant.'

Patrick gave a dismissive grin. 'Shut up, Ruth,' he said, 'you'll bore Leah to death.'

Leah just smiled quietly between them.

They cut through Trinity Lane and crossed the river. Once Patrick leant his head to Leah's and whispered, 'I'll get rid of them in a minute. We'll go and sit down somewhere.'

'Don't worry,' she whispered back, 'I don't mind them,' and a bit louder, 'There's plenty of time.'

The breeze had dropped; groups of people were dotted everywhere across the expanse of mown grass the other side of the river. Some were sitting talking or having picnics, others were stretched out sunbathing. The odd one had an open book propped over their face as a shield against the sun.

Ruth flopped down on the grass and patted a space beside her for Leah. 'Can I hold the baby?' she said.

'No, don't let her,' said Carl. 'She'll be getting ideas.'

'No I won't.' said Ruth. 'I don't intend to have any children until I'm at least thirty.'

Leah handed Jo-jo to her. He stared into Ruth's face, his lips turning down, the bottom one beginning to tremble.

'He's going to cry,' said Carl.

'No he's not.' Ruth bounced him up and down and whistled in his face. Jo-jo's eyes grew big, then he startled to gurgle and wave his arms about.

A couple passed by them and spoke to Carl.

'God, this is embarrassing,' he said. 'They probably thought he was ours.'

'How can a baby be embarrassing?' said Ruth. She had Jo-jo in her lap now and was swooping a hand up and down like a dive bomber to tickle him.

'You'll scare him,' said Carl, pulling up a dandelion to tickle Jo-jo's nose. 'This is how you're supposed to do it.'

'That's unhygienic,' said Ruth. 'A dog could have pissed on that.'

Patrick looked at Leah with raised brows, and she smiled at him as though to say she didn't mind what they were doing with Jo-jo. They were all sitting on the grass now, Patrick stretched out full length, his head level with Leah's hip.

'How long can you stay?' he asked quietly.

'An hour or two.'

He shifted over a bit so that his cheek was against her. 'Or three?' he said.

She shook her head, plucked up some blades of grass and playfully sprinkled them over his face. He screwed up his eyes and blew them away with his bottom lip, but she did it again. This time he caught her wrist. As soon as his fingers closed over her warm skin, the urge to put his arms round her was there again. He hesitated, wondering what she would do if he just slipped one arm across her knees, but she turned to answer something that Ruth had said, and he contented himself with stroking a thumb over her palm. She eased her hand away and carried on talking to Ruth.

Patrick closed his eyes and listened to them for a while. Ruth had just discovered, by her roundabout questioning, that Leah had another son, and this opened up a whole new realm of investigation. She quizzed Leah using subtle little traps. Patrick only heard half of it because someone sitting near them had turned on a radio, but he soon realised that Leah stubbornly refused to answer anything she didn't want to. And once or twice she had Ruth almost speechless with her bizarre remarks. He heard Ruth say, 'Really?' and Leah laugh and tell how she had spent a whole day and night hidden in the cupboard under the stairs because she'd eaten a box of chocolates that had been given to her sister Justina by a boy friend. 'I was terrified. She was always threatening to throw me down an old well we had in the back garden—I thought she might really do it this time.'

'Really? How horrible,' said Ruth, sounding more fascinated than horrified.

Patrick closed his eyes, letting their voices drift over him and mingle with the music from the radio. He still had his face against Leah's hip, and he could feel every movement she made, each little vibration of her body recorded against his skin. He snuggled closer to her.

'Is he asleep?' he heard Carl say, then he felt Leah's hand cup his chin.

'I think he's pretending,' she said.

'What?' said Patrick, sitting up, not sure himself whether he had dozed off.

'Jo-jo's getting restless. I'll have to go back to the car to feed him soon,' Leah said quietly. She had Jo-jo on her own lap now.

Patrick heaved himself to his feet, then it seemed natural to take the baby from her while she got up. He saw Ruth look, knew her curiosity was far from satisfied, and he gave a defiant little grin. 'We've got to be off now,' he said.

As he and Leah walked away, he felt in high spirits though he wasn't exactly sure why. He just felt good.

'I'm sorry we got lumbered with those two,' he said.

'It doesn't matter. I'm just sorry that we haven't been able to talk about Cody.' She glanced up at him. 'Don't your friends know about him?'

'I've only told one of them. It's not a thing I talk about, except to you. There're lots of things I've talked about with you that I wouldn't with anybody else.'

She looked at him again but said nothing, and then they were back in crowded King's Parade and a couple of German tourists asked Patrick to take a photograph of them. They positioned themselves on the low wall that separated the pavement from the sweep of lawn in front of King's College, shifting first to the left, then to the right, asking him to take another and another so that they had a different background in each. Patrick pulled a face at Leah over his shoulder and she laughed. The Germans promptly invited her to sit between them but she shook her head, and laughed again because Patrick had pressed something wrong on their complicated camera, and an extension had shot out of the side. The woman looked horrified and snatched it back, but the man patted Patrick's shoulder and kept saying, 'Vimmen alvays panic, alvays panic, vimmen all ze same, panic, panic.'

Patrick apologised in German but was hard put not to burst out laughing himself.

It set the mood for the final lap back to the car, or rather Leah's mood. She chattered on about things they passed, coming out with her odd little phrases, what her father had said, what Tanya had said, what Kim or Jo-jo had done. She also mentioned Cody a few times. But the things she said were vague and trivial, and Patrick scarcely listened anyway; all he could think of was how he could delay her. As they approached the house, he said to her, 'It's far too hot to sit in the car.' He took in a little breath. 'Come up to my room, just while you feed him.'

She shrugged and tapped her fingers on the handle of the pushchair. 'Patrick, it's been a lovely day. I don't want to—'

'I won't jump on you the minute I get you up there. Don't panic,' he went on in a German accent, sensing her indecision and desperate not to let her go. 'You vimmen, you alvays panic.'

She smiled and looked away. 'It's not that,' she said with a little shrug. 'I feel awkward feeding Jo-jo in front of you.'

They had stopped while they talked, and he stuck his thumbs in his pockets and walked on. He knew it was stupid to be hurt by her words, but they had shattered an illusion that had been building up over the last couple of hours. Walking through the town with her, sitting down by the river with Ruth and Carl, they'd been almost like a couple. Ruth had certainly thought this was the case, he was sure of that. And now Leah had made him feel like a randy schoolboy.

'Are you hungry?' he said coldly.

'I am a bit.'

'Right. I'll go and get us a couple of pizzas.' He tossed her his keys. 'You go up by yourself. You can leave the pushchair in the hall.'

'Patrick, I have to go home soon.' He walked off while she was still talking. 'I'll eat with you, then I have to go,' she called after him.

He swung round and took a step back towards her. 'You can't wait to get away from me, can you?'

'That's not true,' she said gently, but he ignored her.

'Why do you do this to me?' he said. 'Why have you been so...so nice to me for the last couple of hours, and now you just...you just switch off.'

'I haven't switched off, as you call it. You're being unreasonable.' Jo-jo began to cry and she lifted him out of his pushchair. 'Go and get the pizza, we'll talk when you come back.'

He felt a sneer twisting his mouth. Go and get the pizza like a good boy, he wanted to say, but he could see that she was near to tears. He stood there, his arms hanging by his sides, not wanting to go in case she didn't wait for him. 'You won't go before I get back, will you?' he said at last.

'No, of course not.' Jo-jo was crying quite loudly now. 'Do you want some money?' she said, holding the baby's cheek against hers.

Patrick shook his head and turned on his heel,

back the way they'd come.

Buying the pizza, he was rude to the assistant who tried to hurry him because a queue was forming while he decided what to have. He had no idea what Leah liked, and the thought of taking back something she hated made him feel ridiculously agitated.

When he got back she'd cleared a space on the table ready for them to eat. Jo-jo lay on the bed.

'He's asleep,' Leah said, in her usual happy tone. 'Your friend Ruth tired him out.'

'She'd tire anyone out.' Patrick lowered his voice but made it obvious that he wanted to forget the argument too.

'No need to whisper.' She went and switched on his radio, turning down the volume from the full blast he usually had it. 'There. We won't disturb him at all now.'

Patrick had bought wine as well, and she came to look at the bottle. 'I thought you were a poor student.'

'I get an allowance from a trust fund my grandfather set up. It was pay day yesterday.'

'You're very lucky,' she smiled. 'Let's drink a toast to you and these exams then. Now, have you got plates, or are we eating it out of the box?'

He looked up from where he was raking through a tray of old cutlery that Ginny had given him. 'I have got some plates but they need washing up.'

'Why are boys always so pathetic about washing up?'

'Don't call me a boy.'

The smile left her face. 'It's just a word. Don't be so sensitive.'

'I can't find the bloody corkscrew,' he said, still clattering around with the cutlery.

'It doesn't matter. I can't drink much anyway.'

'But I bought it for you. I don't normally drink wine—I got it for you.'

'Calm down, Patrick. It was sweet of you, but—'

'Ah, got it!' He held up an old-fashioned corkscrew, then jammed the bottle between his knees to open it. Leah went and rinsed two plates at the washbasin.

As they began to eat, a ballad came crackling over the radio. Patrick reached over to tune it in properly. 'Last night, you made another promise,' came the voice. Leah hummed along with it. 'This is a beautiful song,' she said, carefully picking slivers of mushroom from the top of the pizza and piling them on the side of her plate. 'Bit before your time though.'

'I've heard it. Don't you like mushrooms?'

'I used to, but I picked some in the woods once and when I put them in the frying pan I noticed all these little insects crawling out of them.'

Patrick looked at her in disbelief. 'Didn't you wash them?'

She stuck out her bottom lip. 'I don't think you're supposed to wash mushrooms, are you?'

'They probably weren't mushrooms,' he laughed. 'They were probably toadstools.'

128

'Or magic mushrooms,' she laughed back. 'Have you ever tried them?'

'No,' he shook his head. 'I'm not into drugs. I've tried cannabis at parties once or twice, but that's all.'

'I think Kim's tried more than that.' Her face grew serious, then she cocked her head to one side. 'I wish he could be like you, studying and everything.'

'You make me sound really boring.'

'You're far from that, Patrick.' Her eyes met his for a second. 'But you still play your games of love with me,' the singer finished. He thought of the day before yesterday, glanced at his watch and tried to imagine what they had been doing at this exact moment. 'Don't look so solemn.' She rolled up the last of the pizza and put it in her mouth.

'I feel solemn.'

'Well, don't,' she said firmly. 'I want to see a smile on your face when I leave this time.'

'Why?' He chewed on his thumb, biting into his flesh. 'So you can go home with a clear conscience?' He stared hard at her but she stared unflinchingly back. Don't spoil it, he told himself, stop now, but he couldn't help adding, 'None of it meant anything to you, did it? I was just an afternoon's entertainment, wasn't I? Wasn't I?' He crunched his thumb between his back teeth.

'Patrick, don't.' She reached out and pulled his hand away. 'Don't do this all the time. I can't bear it.'

'Nor can I,' he said miserably. 'I don't want you to go.'

'You know I have to, we've been through all this before. I can't go on seeing you.'

'Why?' he breathed into her face. 'It could just be like today. I wouldn't...' He clicked his tongue, impatient with himself and the need to explain all that was in the tug of his feelings for her.

'You would,' she said softly. 'That's exactly why I have to go—and why I can't come back.' She held his hand sandwiched between hers, playing with his fingers. 'I'll find you another photo of Cody. I'll send it to you.'

'I wish I'd never started looking for him.'

To his surprise, she smiled and said, 'So you wish you'd never met me, do you?'

'Yeah, I do,' he said stubbornly.

Her face clouded over; there was a flicker of disappointment in her eyes. 'Don't say that.'

He wanted to take it back, say he didn't mean it, but he was caught in a dither of wanting to hurt her and make her feel as unhappy as he felt She let go of him and stood up. 'Are you coming down to the car with me?' she said, going to pick up the baby.

'If you want me to.'

'It's up to you.'

On the way down to the car park she said, 'When is it you get your exam results? I'll phone you. I'd like to know how you get on.'

'Next week. I'll be back at home.'

'Please don't be unhappy, Patrick,' she said, just before she got into the car.

'I won't,' he muttered, looking towards the entrance where another car was pulling in. 'See you then.'

The door of Leah's car was still open. She beckoned him down to her, and he bent his head, unable to resist. 'I will think about you,' she said, hooking a hand over his shoulder. 'Truly I will,' and she pulled him a little closer and kissed him on the lips. Without a word, he straightened up and walked away.

He wandered aimlessly round the town for a while, feeling lonely and miserable, wishing he was back with Mansour and his old school friends. When he bumped into Ruth and Carl coming out of a pub, it was almost a relief to see someone he knew, and he tagged along with them despite the fact that it was sure to mean an interrogation.

'Has she gone?' said Ruth almost immediately, linking an arm through his, the other through Carl's.

Patrick nodded.

'What, home?' she persisted.

'No, to the moon,' he said, screwing up his eyes. He had the beginnings of a headache from having drunk most of the wine he'd bought for Leah.

'I meant home, as in home to a husband.'

'You've got it in one, Ruth.'

'I thought you were looking a bit forlorn. What do you want to get involved with a married woman for?' A waft of the Guinness she always drank blew across his face. 'Apart from the fact that she's very pretty, I wouldn't

131

have thought she was your type at all.'

'You don't know anything about her.'

'I know she's a lot older than you.'

'I'm very mature for my age,' he said with a long weary yawn.

'I thought she was nice,' said Carl.

'I didn't say she wasn't *nice,*' said Ruth. 'I just said she was too old for him. And she's got funny eyes. And she says odd things.'

Patrick put his hands over his ears. 'Don't keep on, Ruth, you're doing my head in.'

'All right, I won't say another word about her.' She sounded a bit huffy, but in the next breath she'd invited him to go home with them and then on to a party that evening.

The party was in the house next to theirs, and Ruth seemed to know everyone. She also seemed intent on introducing Patrick to every girl who wasn't obviously with someone. Downing a can of lager between each introduction, the girls' faces soon became blurred, and he ended up dancing, or rather wrapped in the arms of a tall Swedish girl. At one point he straightened up, put his hands on her shoulders to steady himself and kissed her. She responded with great enthusiasm, and he thought dully that perhaps he'd ask if she wanted to go home with him. The thing that attracted him most was the skimpy two-piece outfit of black Lycra she wore, and the band of naked torso it left exposed. He tried to encircle her waist with two hands, hooking his thumbs under the top of her skirt.

'Your hands are too small,' she laughed,

132

pushing them down to her hips. 'But you know what they say about tall men with small hands, don't you?'

He didn't, but guessed it was something crude, and suddenly she had lost her appeal for him. He pretended he had to go for a pee and went out to the kitchen for more lager.

A group was gathered there, deep in discussion. He heard somebody mention T.S. Eliot and the film they had just seen about him, and someone else quoted a line from 'Portrait Of A Lady'. It was wrong and he longed to get involved. But he didn't know any of them; they would think him an intruder, an upstart who thought he knew it all. He was at the stage where thoughts don't always convert smoothly into words, but just sober enough to realise it and know he ought to keep quiet.

Two girls sat on the kitchen table sharing a joint. He watched them pass it backwards and forwards between them. They looked alike, with the same hairstyles and clothes, and it made him think of the twins and home, and of his friends again. He picked up a can of lager from a stack on the draining board and went and sat on the stairs to drink it, debating whether to stay or not. In the few minutes it took him to finish it, he'd decided that he'd not only stay, but he'd get hold of the Swedish girl and take her back to his room for the night. He could count on one hand the times he'd spent a whole night with a girl, and it had never been in his own bed.

But when he went back through she was dancing with someone else. She smiled at him over her partner's shoulder and made a little gesture which he didn't understand. He shrugged, and squeezed through the crowd over to where Ruth and Carl were sitting on a window seat, a polystyrene tray of food between them. Ruth gathered it up and patted the space for him to sit, but he had the feeling that he might not be able to judge it quite right and he slithered to the floor beside her legs.

'You look pissed,' she said, patting his head.

'It's drinking on an empty stomach,' he said, looking towards the food.

She began feeding him pieces of spicy-tasting chicken, dropping it into his mouth like a mother bird feeding young. He sat with his head against her legs, opening his mouth every time her hand descended in front of his face, watching the Swedish girl watching him.

'She fancies you,' said Carl. 'She asked us where you lived.'

Before he could think of an answer, Ruth had stuffed the end of a folded bap in his mouth. 'He's not interested,' she said. 'He's dreaming of Leah.'

'Yeah, I am,' said Patrick with his mouth full. Just the mention of her name and his head was suddenly full of her. He stopped looking at the Swedish girl and closed his eyes, imagining that when he opened them, it would be Leah he saw—and Leah he would be taking home with him.

'It's best to give up women for the first six months you're here,' said Carl. 'They're too much of a distraction.'

'Like you did,' snorted Ruth.

'Sex inspires you to work better,' said Patrick, feeling sure he'd made some deeply profound remark.

'Don't talk rubbish,' said Ruth.

He twisted round, an elbow on her knees. 'What about the romantics?' he said.

'Oh, here we go. What about Coleridge?' she mimicked.

Her mocking tone sent him straight back to his third year at school when his grandfather had used an essay he'd written on Coleridge to demonstrate something to the sixth form. Someone had discovered it was his, and Ruth told him they were saying he hadn't really written it, and that he always had help with his homework and exams. It led to the first fight he'd ever had and the beginning of establishing himself in a lot of ways. But he had never forgotten the pain of being mocked and called a cheat. And now, when Ruth leant over and tugged at the back of his hair and said, 'What about the Brontës then?' he felt a spark of aggression towards her.

'They probably spent half their time wanking,' he said. 'Like all women.'

She jabbed her knee hard against him. 'Don't take your sexual frustrations out on me.'

Carl laughed. 'Go and dance with Nina, we won't tell Leah.'

'It wouldn't make any difference if you did,' said Patrick.

'Oh?' said Ruth. 'So it's not the big romance it looked like?'

135

'You must have been seeing things.'

'I know you, Patrick, I know when you're smitten.'

'Smitten, eh?' he laughed.

She banged her knee against him again. 'You won't be laughing when her husband comes and beats you up.'

'No chance. He's old as the hills. Anyway, it's over.' The food had sobered him slightly and he was slipping into a morose, self-pitying mood. 'She doesn't want to know me. I spent a whole afternoon fucking her, and she doesn't want to know me.'

Ruth slapped him round the head. 'I don't blame her.'

Patrick yelped and dodged away from her, then got unsteadily to his feet and looked across the room. The Swedish girl was sitting on the arm of a chair talking to someone, her long legs provocatively crossed, her skirt hitched up to the top of her thighs. 'What did you say her name was?' he squinted at Carl.

'Nina. Go on, you drunken pest,' laughed Carl. 'I think you're getting on Ruth's nerves.'

'I need a drink,' muttered Patrick. He made his way back to the kitchen but there were no cans of anything left so he filled a tumbler from a bottle of red wine he found on the table. The girls with the joint were still there, and one of them turned to see what he was doing just as he began to gulp it down.

'Is that your party piece?' she giggled.

'This is just the preliminaries,' he said, stumbling over the word and then perching

136

on the table next to her. He watched while she rolled a new joint, and wondered whether he should sit here and talk to her and her friend for the rest of the evening; they seemed interesting, slipping from one subject to the next in a fast flow of impressive words. She offered him the joint and he took it, inhaled, coughed a bit, inhaled again and washed the next cough down with a swig of the red wine.

'Black Moroccan,' she said.

He nodded as though he knew.

'Do you usually mix it with wine?' she said.

'Sometimes.'

'What I really like...' His head swam a little and he missed her next words but thought they must be funny because the other girl was giggling as though she'd never stop. 'And what about you?' she said.

It was on the tip of his tongue to say mushrooms, but he had the feeling he might start talking about Leah, and he didn't want to because he was beginning to be nagged by guilt, sure he had betrayed her in some way. He took a final swig of the wine, and went back to find Nina.

The next morning, opening his eyes very cautiously because there was a hammering in his head like a manic woodpecker, he wondered for a moment whether Nina would be there beside him. He moved his arm sideways and found he was alone and still dressed. It was difficult to move because the bottom sheet was somehow twisted round his legs. He raised his head and saw that it wasn't a sheet but a long coat, and it was the belt that was trapping his legs. And he wasn't back in his room, but on Ruth and Carl's sofa. He stared at his two bare feet sticking out from the bottom of the coat, and bits of the previous evening came back to him: Carl trying to get him into someone's car, then giving up and threatening to leave him on the pavement, and then Ruth helping to lift him upright.

A long chink of too bright sunshine came from a gap between the curtains, and he pulled the coat over his head. In the movement, he caught a whiff of perfume from his shirt sleeve, and more images of last night came drifting back. He remembered kissing Nina, cuddling and kissing her and then rolling about on the back lawn with her. The thought of it and the remembrance of fierce and unhappy sexual arousal gave him a slight erection now. But he could also remember that it had not come to anything, and that he must have done something to offend her because she'd leapt up and sworn at him, and he'd stormed off, ending up crashed out on the hall floor.

He felt no happier this morning, but the blur of his hangover was strangely soothing; even the hammering in his head was not particularly painful. Perhaps it was the aftereffects of that joint he'd smoked. He vaguely remembered going back for more sometime between falling over in the hall and ending up on the pavement. He closed his eyes and his brain was swamped with floating shapes, chunks of prose and poetry he'd crammed into it for his exams. And dancing along the top of the letters was a tiny Puck-like figure, jigging up and down in time to the hammering. A limber elf, he thought, smiling to himself as he remembered Ruth teasing him about Coleridge, and his remark about the Brontës. The figure became clearer, its dancing winding down to a slow rhythmic motion. Kim, it's Kim, he thought with another drowsy smile. He glided down into sleep again. And this time it was filled with beautiful erotic dreams where Leah lay on her back with her mouth open while he trickled a bottle of Kim's love potion down her throat.

## Chapter 8

A week later, Patrick was speeding towards his grandmother's at the wheel of his first car. He'd gone back home to London after the party. It had been such a packed and exciting seven days, what with the car and his exam results, that it had helped ease the hurt of another rebuff from Leah. She'd phoned to ask about his results and, on the spur of the moment, he'd asked her to the celebration party he and Mansour were holding. Her refusal had been backed by a string of reasons why she couldn't possibly come, and he'd made up his mind there and then to forget about her. But there was no reason why he shouldn't stay friendly with Kim. In fact Kim

139

was the very person who might help him with an idea he had for the celebration party. It had come to him along with the dreams of his hangover; one minute he'd been tipping the love potion down Leah's throat, the next he'd been spiking everyone's drinks with a foaming black liquid that Ruth had brewed up for him. He'd woken to find Ruth dripping Guinness onto his face. For the next half-hour she'd lectured him on the dangers of drugs and married women, and he'd sat there in a stupefied daze until Carl had laughingly rescued him and taken him off to see the car he had for sale.

But when Patrick finally emerged from his hangover, the idea was still there. And this, he told himself, was the sole reason he was going to see Kim again. He put his foot down, watching the needle flicker towards the eighty mark and trying to remember something those girls with the joint had told him.

His grandmother came out to meet him. She hadn't yet seen the car but he'd painted a glowing picture of it the evening he'd phoned to tell her his results. Old but very reliable and well looked after, had been his description. He had made it fit her idea of what sort of car he should have, leaving out Carl's boast of the speeds it could reach on the flat, and Larry's remark that the insurance would cost him a bomb. Whether it had been this carefully doctored description, or his exam results, he wasn't sure, but the cheque had arrived two days later. Ginny had been surprised, even a little jealous, he'd thought. 'You've got everything now,' she'd remarked with a hint of sarcasm. 'She's just proud of me,' he'd replied. 'I'm proud of you too, Patrick,' Ginny had said. 'But I don't think my opinion counts for much these days.' He'd walked off without answering.

'Well, I like the colour,' said his grandmother. 'We had a blue Cortina years ago when Ginny was little. It was your grandfather's favourite car. Pale blue for Cambridge,' she smiled up at him. 'He would have been so proud of you.' She reached up to give him a peck on the cheek. He couldn't remember the last time she'd kissed him; even when he was small they'd been reserved for goodbyes only. He turned abruptly away, reaching into the back of the car to get the flowers he'd bought her. It bothered him that he felt so devoid of affection for her. Yesterday he had seen Mansour shed tears because his family had left to visit relatives in Pakistan. Patrick wondered if he would ever feel the same way about his own family.

He handed her the flowers. 'I appreciate you buying me the car,' he said, carefully avoiding her eyes.

'Did you get the insurance sorted out?' she said, peering at the tax disc, back to her practical self.

'Yes, Larry lent me the money.'

He followed her inside, had tea with her, smiled and chatted and forced himself to be patient and answer all her questions.

'Well, here's to your future,' she said, raising her glass of the ginger wine she always produced on special occasions. 'I expect you've been

141

celebrating with your friends, haven't you?'

'Not yet. We're having a party at Mansour's house next week.'

'Oh yes, Ginny told me.' She fell silent, opened her mouth as though she was about to say something and closed it again. 'How are you managing with the allowance?' she asked after a few seconds. 'I expect most of it goes on your rent, doesn't it?' He glanced up, wondering if she was about to offer him some more money, but she said, 'You could always move in here for the rest of the holidays.'

'I'm managing OK—I like it there.'

'Only...' She paused again. 'Ginny's been a bit worried about you.'

'I don't know why,' he shrugged.

'She... Well, as long as you're managing. You've got so much ahead of you now. If you do need anything, come to me, won't you?'

'Yeah. Thanks.' He picked up another buttered scone, trying not to let her see how eager he was to be off.

It was nearly five when he got to the shop. Kim was getting ready to close, bundling up the garments that hung in the doorway. His wild curls were loose and he wore a pale pink shirt of some softly feminine material. From the back, he could have been Leah. Patrick crept up and gave his hair a tug. Kim spun round.

'Patrick!' He slapped a hand against his chest. 'I thought you were Tanya checking up to see what time I closed.'

142

'Guilty conscience,' laughed Patrick. 'Isn't she here then?'

'No, she went home early. We've got guests and she's doing the cooking. Come on in.'

The shop looked different from last time: there was a new counter, and background music drifted down from two speakers.

'Mozart, eh,' Patrick said. 'Coming up in the world, aren't we?'

'Is it?' said Kim. 'I wouldn't know. It's Tanya's idea. She's trying to change the image of the place.' He dumped the pile of clothes and went to shut the door and turn the open sign round.

Patrick stood listening to the music, and for a moment he was caught up in memories of a remote and serious man shut in his study for hours on end and not to be disturbed on any account. How different things might have been if he'd known that the man was his grandfather, not his father.

'What have you been doing with yourself then?' said Kim, coming to lean on the counter. 'You keep saying you'll call in and come out for a drink with us, but you never do.'

'I've been busy. I—'

'Oh, by the way,' Kim butted in. 'Shame about Cody, wasn't it? Still you never actually knew him, so...' he broke off with a shrug. 'My mum was really upset about it. She said she was dreading phoning you. She hates telling anyone bad news.'

Patrick was suddenly cautious. It sounded as though Leah still hadn't mentioned they'd met.

And perhaps there was good reason now. He looked round the shop, gaining time to think. There was a book open and laid face down on the counter. He picked it up. "The House of Dr Dee,'" he read. 'Are you planning to grow your own incubus out in that little room of yours?'

'Do you know it?' Kim swivelled round, his eyes registering pleasure. 'It's brilliant, isn't it? Imagine what you could do with it.' Patrick smiled with patient amusement. It was easier to talk to Kim without Tanya there. 'Did you do chemistry at school?' Kim asked.

'Not in the sixth form.'

Kim flung an arm round his shoulders. 'I'd forgotten. How did you get on? Are you going to Cambridge?'

'Yep,' said Patrick, trying to remember if it was him who'd told Kim about it. Or had Leah been talking about him? Kim smelt of her, or rather, like her, the same warm, soapy smell. 'I got three straight As.'

'Wow. That definitely needs drinking to.'

'That's why I came really. Do you want to come out for a drink now?'

Kim made a fist of annoyance. 'Shit, I can't. We've got these guests, see—my mother's expecting me home. Tanya'll be here to pick me up at half five.'

Patrick glanced at his watch. What he wanted to ask Kim would have been so much easier over a few drinks in the smoky anonymous atmosphere of a pub. Kim's arm was round him again. 'Did you come all the way specially?'

'And to ask you a favour.' He hesitated,

144

worried that Tanya might turn up. 'I'll run you home,' he said suddenly. 'I've got a car now.'

'What have you got? Let's have a look.'

'Hadn't you better phone Tanya first?'

'Good thinking.' Kim raced out to the back. 'What was the favour?' he called as he dialled the number.

Patrick waited until he came back in. 'Have you got anything to add extra stimulus to a little celebration party?'

Kim eyed him coolly, almost suspiciously. 'Dope, you mean?'

'Well...' Patrick shrugged. 'Whatever you've got.'

'What do you take me for?'

Patrick was thrown; Kim's mood seemed to have changed in a flash. He waved a hand in the direction of the back room. 'I thought you might have something—you've got so much gear out there.'

'I experiment, I don't deal in drugs.' Kim stared at him, totally serious. Then suddenly he grinned and caught Patrick by the shoulders. 'But as it's you...' He patted Patrick's cheeks. 'Come with me.'

Patrick followed him through to the little back room. 'Nothing too strong,' he said as Kim leaned round to close the door behind them. 'It's just for a laugh.'

'You'll have more than a laugh with this. I've perfected it now.'

'Oh, no, Kim. Not the dreaded love potion.'

'I'll mix in something to give it an extra kick.' Kim took a little notebook from a drawer. 'I

145

promise you this'll give you the best time you've ever had.'

'Is this the same stuff you gave to your mates at school?'

'No, I've altered the formula. Anyway, mind-altering drugs are a lot more powerful than aphrodisiacs; I'll have to adjust the balance. It's only the timing I'm not certain about.'

'The timing?' Patrick echoed.

'Yeah, how quickly it works and how long it lasts.'

'Is this stuff safe?'

'Course it is. And it's a better high than all that crap they smoke, and cheaper. In fact I'll let you have it for nothing, on one condition. You come back and tell me how you got on.'

'Come back?' Patrick echoed Kim's words again. 'Yeah, I'll do that.'

Kim was absorbed in the notebook. When he looked up, his expression was dreamy, almost blank, Leah's exactly. He blinked once, then smiled Leah's smile. 'We'll go for that drink when you come again. If I'm not here, I'll be at home. Come and pick me up.'

Patrick nodded and licked his lips, reminding himself of his intention to forget all about Leah.

'Six drops,' said Kim, suddenly more lively. 'Depending on the results you want and how quickly you want it to take effect. The more you take, the quicker it works. The best idea is six drops, take advantage of the short-term high, then sleep on it for the long-term effect to start working.'

146

Patrick stared at him. 'You're fucking nuts,' he smiled, peering over Kim's shoulder at the notebook.

Kim promptly spread his hand over the page. 'I've let you into enough of my secrets for one day. You go and start counting the till money, and I'll bottle this up for you. You wait,' he called as Patrick walked off. 'The word ecstasy will have a whole new meaning once you've tried this.'

As they pulled up outside Kim's house, a small bottle of the love potion wrapped in tissue paper and stowed away in the glove compartment, Patrick said, in what he thought was a nonchalant voice, 'Say hello to your mother for me, won't you?'

'Come in and say hello yourself,' Kim replied as though it had just occurred to him. 'She'd like to meet you. Tanya told her you looked just like Cody.'

Patrick wrenched up the handbrake with twenty times the force it needed. So Tanya didn't know they'd met either. God! Leah had certainly left him in the dark about who knew what. 'You've got guests, I can't just barge in.'

'Yes you can. Oh, come on, we can have that drink. I get so bored when they all start prattling on.'

The engine was still ticking over and Kim reached across and switched it off.

'Kim!' Patrick protested, but Kim was already out of the car. He came round to the driver's

147

side and pulled open the door.

'Just come in for half an hour. They won't mind.'

Patrick could think of no excuse not to, and half of him was already stirring with excitement at the prospect of seeing Leah again. The other half, however, was quaking with nerves as he followed Kim round to the back of the house.

'Just one thing,' said Kim, as he opened the gate with the 'Beware of the Dog' sign. 'Don't mention the love potion. They get a bit paranoid about my experiments. Oh, and another thing.' He came to a halt now. 'Better not mention about Cody being your father, unless my mother does. I don't know if she's told Carew about it. We don't tell him everything,' he finished in a whisper.

'I'd better not speak at all,' said Patrick, making a joke of it, though all these last-minute instructions were making him wish he could back out. But Kim was already through the gate and announcing that he'd brought a friend home with him.

The back garden was all lawn except for the top where a wide flagstoned terrace ran along the whole length of the house. It was dotted with overgrown pots and tubs of flowers, and bordered by a low ornamental wall. In the centre of the terrace was a large table where a forest of bottles and glasses winked and glinted in the late afternoon sun. And round the table sat four people. One of them was Leah. Lingering behind Kim as they came on to the terrace, he looked at everyone but her.

'This is Patrick, everybody.' Kim pointed a forefinger at him. Then in quick succession he jabbed it at each of the people seated at the table. 'Maurice, Simone, my mother and Carew,' he said.

'Kim, Kim,' said Carew with a frown, getting up and extending a hand towards Patrick. 'How are you, Patrick? I'm Kim's stepfather. This is my wife Leah,' he went on. 'And this is Simone, and Maurice, very dear friends of mine.' Simone and Maurice both shook hands with him. Leah did not. She raised her eyes and said a barely audible, 'Hello, Patrick,' and he wished he had not done this to her. He sank down on the chair that Carew pulled out for him, determined to go as soon as it was politely possible.

'Now what would you like to drink, Patrick?' said Carew. 'We've been having a little aperitif.'

'For the last two hours,' laughed Simone.

'I'm driving, actually,' said Patrick.

'A shandy then?'

'No, get him something stronger than that,' said Kim. 'He's celebrating. He's just got through to Cambridge.'

'How wonderful. Congratulations,' said Carew as though he really meant it. There was murmured approval from Simone and Maurice. Kim winked at him and looked pleased as though he had achieved something special himself.

'A shandy will be fine, thanks,' said Patrick.

'Stay to dinner then,' said Kim. 'You can have something stronger if you're eating.'

Patrick's feeble, embarrassed protests were immediately brushed aside by Carew; never had he met anyone so unconditionally welcoming. He was nothing like Patrick had imagined—and he'd pictured this man many times recently. Carew was big, broad and tall, with a shock of near-white hair and strong, almost rugged features. But his voice was soft and cultured, and there was something inherently gentle in his movements and his expression.

'I'll go and get our drinks and tell Tanya you're stopping,' said Kim.

Leah got to her feet as well. 'I'd better get Jo-jo. I expect Tanya's getting fed up with him by now.'

They disappeared into the house together. As soon as they were out of earshot, Carew said, 'Well, I'm glad to see that Kim has at least one sensible friend.' He turned to Patrick as he spoke, smiling as though he meant it jokingly. Patrick wasn't sure if he was expected to answer; it was just the sort of patronising remark his grandmother would have made.

Simone saved him. 'I hear he's been suspended from school,' she said.

'Yes,' said Carew, relighting the stub of a cigar that he had been rolling between his fingers. 'For passing round some kind of drug or alcohol or something. I'm hoping it's not too serious, but I never can get to the bottom of what he does, and of course Leah defends him all the time.' His voice had dropped; the conversation was suddenly between the two of them, and Maurice had begun to question Patrick about his degree. Patrick did his best to answer politely, but his attention was on the lowered voices the other side of him.

'That's natural,' he heard Simone say. 'But I suppose it makes it difficult for you.'

'Yes, it does. As you know, I do my best for Kim. I try to avoid open confrontation, but it's not always easy.'

'Couldn't you take him to Florida with you next week?'

'No, I think he's better off here with Leah. And anyway, I don't like leaving her with just Tanya.'

'She's not coming with you then?' Simone's voice had risen. Patrick pricked up his ears.

'She won't come, not with the baby. Anyway...' Carew leant back in his chair and puffed a cloud of pungent smoke into the air. He waved it away from Simone and glanced at her with a little smile.

Patrick turned quickly back to Maurice.

'...that was in Gonville and Caius, and of course everything was different in the fifties,' Maurice was saying. 'Did you say you were in Trinity?'

'Umm...' Patrick's mind had gone completely blank.

'And perhaps she needs a little break from me,' he heard Carew say.

'Umm, no, no, Corpus Christi,' said Patrick.

'Ah, Kit Marlowe's college,' beamed Maurice. 'I expect you've studied his work, haven't you? Faustus is usually in there somewhere.'

'Yeah,' said Patrick. Why don't you shut up, he thought, straining his ears because Simone's

151

voice had dropped again and she had her head bent close to Carew.

'Some women take longer to get over...'

'Oh no, it's not that. She was fine, even talking about having another...'

'And if she's worried about Kim...'

Patrick could only hear snatches of their conversation now. Maurice had started on about student loans, losing Patrick completely. He was about to admit that he hadn't heard, when Kim came back with a tray of drinks. Leah was close behind with Jo-jo tucked on her hip and a little snowy blanket trailing from the other hand.

'Carew has been telling me about his lecture tour,' said Simone. 'It's a shame you aren't going.'

'It's too far for Jo-jo,' said Leah, unsmiling and not even bothering to look at Simone as she spoke.

Carew reached out to Jo-jo. 'Have you been helping Tanya do the cooking?' he said, shaking the baby's little fist up and down. Jo-jo cooed with delight.

Leah wrapped the blanket round him and took him over to Kim. 'Here, look after your little brother for a minute while I go and help bring the food out.'

Kim pulled a face but took him, and Carew held his cigar towards Simone. 'I'm not allowed to have him if I'm smoking,' he said.

'I should think not,' said Simone.

Across the table, Kim was tossing Jo-jo up in the air and singing loudly, 'Noah in the ark and Jonah in the whale!'

'Kim, don't do that to him,' said Carew.

'Why?'

'He's going to bed soon, You'll get him over-excited.'

'He'll start bawling if I don't,' said Kim defiantly. He was about to toss Jo-jo up again, when Tanya appeared.

'You'll start bawling if I give you the smack you deserve,' she said, flicking Kim with the handful of serviettes she was carrying.

Kim laughed and ducked his head. Tanya stood beside him and looked across at Patrick. 'How lovely to see you again,' she said. She blew him a kiss, her eyes fixed on him in a way that said, I know all your little secrets. He told himself not to be so stupid, and smiled back at her as confidently as he could.

'Ah, food,' said Carew, as Leah came out carrying a tray laden with plates and serving dishes. He stood up to help her, and everyone began rearranging chairs, shifting glasses and bottles and passing round cutlery.

In the general hubbub that followed, Patrick was able to look at Leah for a few magical seconds. He thought of that day by the river when he'd said she was perfect. She certainly looked perfect tonight. She wore a white silk dress, the bodice crossed over to form a halter neck, leaving her back and shoulders bare. It was trimmed with gold braid, and she had gold combs holding her swept-back hair in place, and a cluster of thin gold bangles on each arm. And something he'd never seen before—her lips and nails were painted bright red.

153

When she'd finished unloading the tray she went and took Jo-jo from Kim and brought him round the table for Carew to kiss goodnight. Patrick thought of last week; not the day she had come to tell him his father was dead, but the day they had sat by the river with Ruth and Carl. He looked away, smarting with sudden unhappiness, and debating whether to just get up and walk out.

Simone had put something on his plate. He looked up and smiled his thanks, an eye on Leah disappearing into the house.

'Do help yourself, Patrick,' Carew said. 'We don't stand on ceremony here.'

Simone dished something else out for him; Maurice was telling him about their own three sons, to which Patrick murmured polite responses. Then Leah was back, slipping into her seat beside Carew and giving a brief little nod at something he asked her. Patrick saw Carew gaze at her. She seemed not to notice, but sat there still and silent while everyone else was talking and helping themselves to food. Carew looked at her again, then reached out and took her hand, drawing it towards him as though he was going to kiss it. But she pulled away and picked up her glass, holding it between her palms, her eyes fixed on its contents.

She doesn't love him; Patrick was suddenly convinced of this. A tight ball of excitement formed in his chest.

'Now tell me, Patrick,' Simone was saying. 'Whose friend are you, Kim's or Tanya's?'

'Well...' Why did older people always ask

such stupid questions? 'I met them at the same time.'

'We share him,' said Kim.

'Yes, we just have to decide who has what bit of him,' added Tanya suggestively.

Kim smiled innocently round the table, then spluttered with laughter.

'You'll have to excuse them,' said Carew. 'Kim, alcohol and Tanya are not a good mix.'

'Young people seem to drink so much more these days,' said Maurice, with a good-humoured smile as though he was trying to keep the peace.

'It's *what* they drink,' said Carew. 'What is it you've got there, Kim?'

'Only vodka,' said Kim, defensively.

'In a lemonade glass?' smiled Simone.

'Saves me having to keep getting up.'

'Kim!' said Leah sharply.

Patrick saw Kim stare back at his mother for a moment, then look away with a sulky frown. Why don't you all get pissed, he thought, imagining a scene where the rest of them slid to the floor in a drunken stupor and he was left alone with Leah.

The conversation began to flow again. Kim seemed a bit subdued, but when Leah went to fetch the dessert, he followed her out, and they came back laughing together as though he had been forgiven.

As Leah started to ladle fresh fruit salad into bowls, a little whimpering cry came from an open window above them.

'I'll go, dear,' said Carew.

'No, you finish this,' she said, handing him the spoon.

'He's at the age when he only wants his mother,' Carew said, getting to his feet, syrup dripping from the spoon on to the table. 'Now then, who's for Tanya's special fruit salad?' He proceeded to fill the bowls, looking too big and clumsy. With a little click of her tongue, Tanya got up to take over.

'You're still chief cook and bottle washer then?' said Simone.

'It's a case of having to be,' said Tanya mildly.

Kim leant rudely across in front of Maurice to speak to Patrick. 'We'll go and have a game of snooker when we've finished this,' he said.

Patrick nodded; Kim might just as well have said, we'll go surfing on Bondi Beach. 'Where's the loo?' he asked.

'By the hall stairs,' said Kim.

Of course, they would have a bloody downstairs cloakroom.

'No, the bulb's gone in there,' said Carew. 'You'll have to go upstairs, if you don't mind. Top of the stairs, turn right. Ask Leah if you get lost.'

I'm definitely going to get lost, Patrick wanted to sing out, elated by this piece of luck. He got to his feet, carefully squeezing between his chair and Simone's. She caught his arm. 'They have fascinating little plaques on all the doors upstairs,' she said. 'Do have a look while you're up there.'

'Particularly the one with Leda being shagged

by the swan,' said Kim.

Patrick stopped in his tracks, thinking for a moment that Kim had said 'Leah'. Then he remembered what the woman in the pub had told him about Carew teaching Greek.

'Kim, you're being insufferable this evening,' said Carew.

'Isn't he just,' said Simone.

'I believe the correct term for the copulation of birds is treading,' said Maurice, eyeing Kim with friendly triumph.

'Well, she wasn't a bird,' retorted Kim.

'Actually, in some versions of the story, she turned herself into a wild goose,' said Carew, with a wink at Maurice.

'I'll know what to look for anyway,' said Patrick. The few seconds' delay was enough to let him worry a little about what he was doing, but he could hardly say he'd changed his mind, and once in the house he quickened his pace. As he reached the landing, Leah was backing slowly out of the door opposite and almost jumped out of her skin when she turned and saw him. She put a finger to her lips.

'I came up for the loo,' said Patrick in a whisper. She pointed to her left and came towards the stairs but he barred her way. 'I didn't really. I came up to see you.'

'Please, Patrick, not in my house.'

'I only want to talk to you on your own for a minute.'

'You shouldn't have come here. If you cared anything about me you wouldn't have put me through this.'

He swallowed. 'Kim asked me. What was I supposed to say? I can't come because it upsets your mother to see me.'

'It doesn't upset me, don't twist things round to defend yourself.'

'I'm not trying to defend myself,' he protested, turning away to stare along the landing. It was in semi-darkness, a huge fern blocking the light from the only window. He imagined drawing her into a shadowy comer, kissing her and saying, don't be angry with me for coming, I know you don't really love him. 'I wanted to come,' he said. 'I wanted to see you again.'

'Oh, Patrick,' she said with a little scolding frown.

'If you won't come to my party,' he said, detecting that she wasn't really very annoyed with him, 'would you meet me somewhere else, just once more?' Her expression softened, her eyes met his for a second, and it was as if a little crack had opened up. He looked along the landing again—both ways this time—then caught a quick glance over his shoulder to check the hall below. 'I wish you would come to my party,' he said.

'I've told you, I can't.'

He thought back to the phone call last week and how he'd argued with her until she'd put the phone down.

'But you can now. Your husband's going away. You can come to London—he won't know.'

'Shh, keep your voice down. Now listen, Patrick, even if Carew goes a million miles

158

away, I'm still married to him.'

'I'm only asking you to come to a party,' he said stubbornly. 'That's all.' But that wasn't all; and she knows it, he thought, watching her shake her head. All this was pointless; he should have stuck to his intention to forget her; she wasn't going to change her mind. He must have been mad to think she was, mad to come here, and even madder to get mixed up with that crazy idiot Kim. 'You're right, I shouldn't have come,' he said. 'I'm sorry. I shan't pester you any more.'

'I forgive you.' Her voice sounded different; he wasn't quite sure how, but before he had time to think about it, she reached up and touched his cheek. 'Don't be sad. I don't want you to be sad.' Her fingers lingered against his skin.

'I'm not,' he said woodenly, turning his face away from her. 'Can I get out the front way? There's no point in me hanging about here.'

'No, wait a minute.' She folded her arms across her chest. 'Don't go yet. Kim will be disappointed.' Then almost immediately, she looked up at him and said, 'All right, I'll come to your party. But only for an hour or two.'

Before he could say a word, she was shushing him again. 'Was that Jo-jo?' She listened, head tilted. 'I'd better check. He's in a new big cot and it's a bit strange for him. You go down.'

But Patrick didn't want to go back down, he wanted reassurance that she meant what she'd said; her change of mind had been so abrupt, he could hardly believe it. He watched her tiptoe across the bedroom. Through the open

159

door he could see a double bed. There were clothes carelessly strewn across it, all Leah's by the look of them, but on one of the pillows, neatly folded, were a towelling robe and a pair of maroon pyjamas. He went to stand in the doorway, keeping one eye on the stairs. The room was all Leah and the baby: talcs and lotions, odd pieces of jewellery, underwear and soft toys. Nothing of Carew except the awful pyjamas. Everything was bathed in pale yellowish light from a bedside lamp, and he could see himself dimly outlined in a dressing table mirror, framed in the doorway like a voyeur lurking in the shadows. Over by the far wall, Leah completed the picture, standing perfectly still beside the cot, her back to him. He glanced towards the stairs again, then crept across to her, taking careful light steps, absurdly fearful that he might leave a trail of footprints in the deep pile of the carpet.

'Look at him,' she whispered without turning. 'Doesn't he look beautiful?'

Patrick peered over her shoulder into Jo-jo's cot. The baby lay with an arm curled above his head and one chubby leg kicked free of his sleeping suit. His eyelids flickered open a fraction, then slowly fell closed again, his shiny dark lashes settling against his cheeks as though he was just too tired to stay awake any longer. But as far as Patrick was concerned it could have been a plastic toy lying there; he had eyes only for Leah: the smooth bare skin of her back and shoulders, and the swell of her breasts beneath the white silk. The warmth of her drifted up

160

into his face. An inch or two and he could put out his tongue and lick her neck. It was like that time in the car park when he'd longed to touch her and couldn't. But worse now because of the insinuations of this room: the bed just a few feet away and all the other soft and intimate things that she would rub or spray on her body, or slip in or out of late at night and early in the morning. He looked at her red-tipped fingers balanced lightly on the edge of the cot, then back to her profile and the curve of her ear exposed by the upswept hair. But he mustn't touch her or she might change her mind and say she wouldn't come to his party after all.

'Leah,' he began, his voice choking with all he wanted to say. Her finger shot to her lips, then to his. 'You do mean it, you will come?' he whispered, taking hold of her wrist. She pulled him away from the cot, wriggling her hand free as she went.

'Just for a little while,' she said. 'And on one condition.' A little breeze came to interrupt her. It sent the curtains fluttering inwards from the open window and brought the hum of conversation from below. She went and closed the window, then beckoned him to follow her out to the landing. 'I'll come if you make an excuse and go home now,' she said.

'All right.' He wanted to hug her, kiss her, swing her round and say I'll do anything you say, anything, but she gave him a little push.

'Now go to the bathroom or they'll wonder what's going on.'

When he finally went back downstairs, they

161

had lit a string of lanterns across the terrace. The sun had only just set, but the terrace was already shrouded with the feel of dusk. There was a faint chill in the air and moths were beginning to gather around the lights, fluttering blind and bewildered against the glass. Carew was busy topping up drinks, and someone had brought out cheese and biscuits. Patrick saw that his half-eaten bowl of fruit salad was still there, abandoned amongst all the other leftover food. He cleared his throat ready to announce that he had to go, when Carew looked up and saw him.

'Patrick!' he said. 'I hear my wife waylaid you in her bedroom. We were just about to send out a search party.'

'Don't embarrass him,' said Simone. She smiled up at him. 'Don't worry, Patrick, we all get dragged to see little Jonah asleep sooner or later.'

It was said perfectly kindly—he saw Leah smile as well—but Kim piped up, 'My little brother is a real star, did you know that, Patrick?' His tone was petulant, verging on irritable, and he leant forward and began to hack off great uneven slices from a truckle of cheese. Leah had changed seats to sit next to him, and she reached out and stroked his hair but didn't say anything. Carew gave them a quick sideways glance then asked Patrick if he'd like another drink.

'Actually, I have to be off,' said Patrick. 'I've got to drive back to my grandmother's.'

Kim straightened up. 'You don't have to go yet. It's early.'

'I don't want to leave it too late and disturb her.' Patrick noticed Tanya watching him with an amused smile. 'She goes to bed quite early,' he finished.

'Give her a buzz—you can stay here,' said Kim.

'No, I can't, I—'

'Course you can,' said Kim loudly.

'He has his arrangements, don't interfere,' said Carew. 'And could you please stop hacking that cheese about.'

Kim glared at Carew and slumped back in his chair, his head leaning against Leah's shoulder. 'You've had too much to drink,' she said, putting an arm round him. 'Why don't you go to bed?' Kim closed his eyes and snuggled up against her.

Patrick began to say his goodbyes, suddenly wishing Leah had not imposed this condition on him. There was something beguiling about the atmosphere on the terrace; an exciting undercurrent of things he didn't want to miss. Carew stood up and shook hands with him.

'Nice to have met you, Patrick. I hope we'll see you again, but if not, all the best for the future.'

The others remained seated; Tanya waggled her fingers in the air and Simone swivelled round to smile and wish him good luck. There was no way he could single Leah out to say goodbye, but he chanced a look across at her. See you next week, he wanted to shout, and found himself saying it instead to Kim. Kim leapt up and came round to him. His eyes

163

were bright with alcohol, his long hair stuck to his face where he'd been leaning against Leah. He put both arms round Patrick and whispered, 'Don't forget, come back and let me know how you get on.'

Patrick froze; he had completely forgotten about his promise to Kim and the bottle of god knows what, tucked away in his car. 'Yeah, course I will,' he muttered.

'Six drops,' whispered Kim, almost cheek to cheek with him.

Over Kim's shoulder, Patrick could see the circle of watching faces. He gave what he thought was a tolerant, amused smile and patted Kim lightly on the back, acutely aware that Kim could start blabbing on about anything in this state.

'It can't fail. You'll be back for more,' whispered Kim far too loudly. He gave Patrick a great hug and kissed him noisily on the cheek.

'Stop acting like an arsehole, Kim,' said Tanya. There was an awkward silence, then Leah got up and gently levered Kim away.

'Goodbye, Patrick,' she said. He took a couple of steps backward, raised a hand to everyone, and made his escape.

Once in the car, he collapsed with laughter and disbelief at the whole evening, and a wild sense of happiness that Leah had agreed to see him again. When he turned the ignition key he got only a wheeze of sound from the engine. He sat there a moment, the key between his fingers, entranced by a vision of staying here the night, sleeping in one of

164

those low-ceilinged rooms—sleeping and waking under the same roof as Leah. Then he turned the key again and the engine burst into loud pulsating life.

## Chapter 9

Telling Mansour about Leah was a relief, a safety valve for the pent-up emotions that had led to yet another row with Ginny. Patrick didn't spill out his feelings in the crude way he had that drunken night with Carl and Ruth, but told Mansour how she'd helped him, how kind she'd been, and how the more he saw of her, the more he liked her.

'I suppose I fancied her right from the start,' he said, admitting a little more with each sentence. 'And now...' He shrugged and smiled at Mansour's expectant face. 'I can't think about much else.'

'And because she's married to an old man, you think you're going to supply her with what she's not getting off him.'

'Don't take the piss, Mans. It's not like that.'

'What is it like then?'

They were sitting in what Mansour's mother called the children's room, a large conservatory leading directly off their equally large dining room. It was furnished with a series of low divans heaped with bolster size embroidered cushions. Normally the room was alive with Mansour's sisters' noisy chatter as they played games or did each other's hair, or just lounged on the divans swapping gossip. But they had all gone to Pakistan with their parents for the holidays.

'It's like...' Patrick stretched full length, manoeuvring one of the cushions under his head. It was good to relax with just Mansour; they hadn't been together like this for ages. Patrick stared up at the sloping glass roof where the fallen petals of a climbing plant lay like a drift of purple snow. 'I can't explain exactly how I feel, but it's not just sex.'

'Sex has come into it then?' Mansour kicked him lightly on the leg to make him answer but Patrick would only nod. 'I thought you were looking a bit haggard, you secretive bastard.'

'It's not like you think, Mans. I like her so much I feel bad talking about her but in another way I want to.' He turned on his side to look at Mansour. 'Does that sound crazy?'

'No, it sounds like the arrow through the heart.' Mansour pulled a serious face and stabbed himself in the chest with a forefinger. 'But you've suffered from that before and recovered.'

Patrick smiled. 'Leah's different from anyone I've ever met.'

'And I suppose she's also the most attractive girl, or rather woman, you've ever met.'

'Yes, she is. She's really beautiful.'

'Long blonde hair and...' Mansour shaped an hourglass figure with his hands.

'Wait and see. She's coming tonight.'

'What, here? To our party?'

'Here to our party,' repeated Patrick.

'With her husband's permission, I suppose.'

'He's working away. They've got a house in Camden. She'll come from there.'

Mansour stood up, stretching and grinning down at him. 'I hope you know what you're doing.'

They spent the next hour shifting furniture around ready for the party. Patrick avoided talking about Leah any more. He knew he'd given Mansour the impression that he was having an affair with her, and he told himself this wasn't totally false. She wouldn't be coming tonight if she didn't care about him and want to continue seeing him. Over and over he'd thought of that moment she'd pulled her hand away from Carew's. Once upon a time he would have shared everything with Mansour, but now he held back; things had changed and he felt older, different. His life was suddenly split in two, and one half contained things which he didn't want to tell anyone about.

Ginny was ironing when he got home, and she looked up with a smile and asked him if he needed anything ready to wear for the evening. He knew it was an attempt to make up for the row they'd had this morning, but the gesture made him bristle with hostility for some reason.

'No thanks,' he muttered, and went to make himself a sandwich.

167

'I bought you some booze for tonight,' she said, pointing to the corner of the kitchen where packs of lager were stacked on the worktop. 'Larry said he thought Hoffmeister would be all right.'

Patrick glanced over his shoulder at her. Only a few hours ago at breakfast she had caused a scene when she discovered that Larry had said he needn't pay back the money he'd borrowed for his car insurance.

'Mum's paid for his car, he can't have it all ways,' she'd protested. 'He's got the allowance from Dad's money, let him pay it back out of that.'

'He'll need that,' Larry had said. 'His grant won't go far.'

'Then he'll have to get a holiday job like everyone else.'

Patrick had sprung up from the table. 'I might get a permanent job,' he'd said. 'Then you can have every penny back.'

Now, he looked at the cans and thought of the money Mansour's parents had left for them to get stuff for the party. It was on the tip of his tongue to say, 'I suppose you'll want the money for those,' when the phone rang.

Ginny went to answer it. When she came back into the kitchen, the smile and the tone of reconciliation had vanished. 'It's her,' she said, indicating with her thumb. 'That woman from Norfolk.'

Patrick dropped the sandwich and dashed out to the hall. Emma and Heidi had just come in from the garden and went to follow him but Ginny dragged them back and shut the kitchen door.

'Leah?' he said, mouth close to the receiver.

'I'm a bit nervous about tonight.'

He gave a sigh of relief and leant back against the wall. 'I thought you'd changed your mind about coming.'

'I wouldn't do that, I wouldn't let you down.' There was a little pause. 'But I want you to meet me at the door.'

'Shall I come and pick you up?'

'No, you can't do that, Tanya's here with me. I've ordered a taxi for nine. I've told her I'm going to a friend's birthday party.' She gave a little laugh. 'She knows I don't have any friends in London so I've had to invent one.'

He smiled at her through the receiver. 'Does she believe you?'

'You never know with Tanya. But it'll be all right. Carew gave me some money to come up here shopping, and I let her spend most of it. Babysitting fee.' She laughed again. 'She's upstairs now trying on the things she bought. That's the other thing I called for. What shall I wear?'

'Anything you like. Wear what you had on the other night.'

'I don't want to look out of place.'

He thought of the girls he knew. Some wore minis and Docs, other swathed themselves in black from head to toe. Or there were the girls like Nina who wore as little as possible and painted their faces like dolls. Leah wasn't like any of them.

169

'It doesn't matter what you wear. As long as you come.' He lowered his voice, thinking he heard movement by the door. 'I just want to see you.'

'Patrick,' she warned. 'I'm coming as your friend, that's all.'

The door opened a fraction and one of the twins' heads appeared, then they both came wriggling through the gap, checking to see that Ginny wasn't watching.

'I've got company' said Patrick. 'I've been joined by two horrible little monsters.'

The twins giggled, and in a sudden rush of happiness, he let them say hello to Leah. They took it in turns to speak to her, their heads pressed over the receiver. Leah asked them silly questions like, was Patrick mean to them? Did he make them run around fetching things for him, and did he sneak into their room to pinch their teddy bears to take to bed with him? It made the twins laugh, and it reminded Patrick of times when he had interrogated the friends of girls he liked, to discover things about them.

'She wants you again,' said Heidi, thrusting the receiver at him.

'That's what I was hoping,' muttered Patrick.

'What was that?' said Leah.

'Nothing.' He settled back against the wall, ready to spin out this conversation, happy to talk nonsense for the rest of the afternoon. But Leah said she had to go because Jo-jo was crying.

'She's a nice lady,' said one of the twins as he replaced the receiver.

Patrick laughed and hoisted her up onto his

shoulders, ducking down as he went back into the kitchen.

'My turn,' said the other twin, raising her arms.

Ginny was still ironing. There was rarely a minute when she wasn't doing something around the house, and in term time she worked in the office at the twins' school. As they came through the door, she glanced up and it crossed his mind that she was only a couple of years older than Leah but looked more because she was so often frowning.

He lowered Heidi to the floor. Or was it Emma? He pretended not to know, and as they laughed and pretended to be each other, he went over to Ginny. 'Umm, thanks for the...' he began but she started to speak at the same time, her voice raised above his.

'I suppose that was more news about your father,' she said without looking up from her ironing. Patrick watched the iron go whizzing back and forth across the same garment. It caught on a button and split it but she didn't stop. 'It's the only thing that puts a smile on your face these days—your little secret search.'

Her words wouldn't have hurt so much if they had come this morning, thrown into the heat of their row. But now, sandwiched between his conversation with Leah and his intention of thanking her for the lager, they sounded full of spite.

'If you really want to know,' he said, surprised to find himself suddenly very upset, 'my father's dead.'

171

The kitchen became very quiet; Ginny bent over the ironing board as though she was inspecting something. Her hair slid round her face and he couldn't see her expression.

'Mummy?' said one of the twins in a testing voice.

Ginny straightened up and reached for the pile of ironed clothes. 'Take these upstairs and put them in the airing cupboard,' she said, giving half to each twin. 'Hurry up,' she added sharply, hooking her hair behind her ears with two fingers. 'How long have you known?' she asked as soon as they'd gone.

'A couple of weeks.'

'I see.'

Patrick stood there shaking slightly with emotion. 'I was in Cambridge.'

'Oh, I know when it was. I've got all her phone calls logged in here.' She tapped her head. 'You might think I'm stupid, you might think none of this...' She stopped, visibly fighting back tears.

'I would have told you,' he muttered. 'But you didn't want to talk about him.' She snatched up a pillowcase and began ironing again, and he saw the tears splash down, staining the cotton for a second before they vanished under the iron's heat. 'It was two years ago, a car accident,' he said miserably. This was spoiling everything. Talking to Leah he'd felt on top of the world, now Ginny had wrecked everything. 'It's not worth crying over now,' he said, battling with his own angry tears. 'It's a bit late for that.'

She banged down the iron. 'You don't understand anything, anything,' she cried, shaking her head until her hair whipped round her face.

'No, because you won't tell me,' he shouted. He waited, arms hanging at his sides, giving her the chance to say more but uncertain if that's what he wanted right now. 'I'm going for a shower,' he said after a few seconds. Ginny said nothing, and he stormed off up to the bathroom, ignoring the twins as he passed them on the stairs. They came knocking on the door, but he turned up the water to drown out their tapping, and stayed there long after it had turned icy cold.

When he finally went back downstairs, Larry was home and had loaded the cans into his car for him. Patrick drove off without a word to anyone.

Mansour's house was almost shaking with the volume of music pouring from the ground floor.

'Won't we have to keep the noise down?' said Patrick as he struggled into the hall loaded with the packs of lager.

'Don't worry,' said Mansour. 'I've personally visited all our neighbours and apologised in advance and promised it will stop around midnight.'

'Midnight? Bit early, isn't it?'

'We'll worry about that when it arrives.'

'You're in a reckless mood tonight,' said Patrick jokingly, wishing he could feel more reckless himself.

He dumped the lager and joined a group who

were making tequila slammers. A girl came up and hooked her arm round his neck.

'Patrick, you look miserable,' she said. 'What's up?'

'I'm a few drinks behind you lot, that's all.'

'Well, that's easily solved,' she said, handing him a glass.

Mansour came to stand behind him. 'Is it the beautiful Leah?' he whispered. 'Isn't she coming after all?'

'Of course she is.' He downed the drink in quick gulps, and felt slightly better. The others had been here longer, and he was conscious that he had a lot of catching up to do to get in the party spirit. He had left home soon after six but not come straight here. Instead he had driven across London to Leah's house, a slow and tedious journey in the rush hour traffic. And he wasn't quite sure why he did it; all he could do was park within view of the house, there was no way he could knock on the door. He'd sat there for over half an hour occasionally gazing towards an upper window where a light shone through the closed curtains. The baby must be in bed, he'd thought, and perhaps Leah was getting ready in the same room. He'd found himself dreaming about her, just as he used to do during the nights after he'd been walking with her in the pine forests. Kim's so-called love potion was still in the glove compartment. He'd taken it out, uncorked the little bottle and sniffed at it. It smelt strongly of alcohol and there didn't look much in the bottle. He

174

shook a drop on to his finger and stuck it in his mouth. But all he could taste was the salt from a packet of crisps he'd just eaten. Still it didn't matter now, not now that Leah was coming. He wouldn't need any artificial stimulants to enjoy himself tonight. He pushed the cork back in, thinking maybe he'd spike some of his friends' drinks with it as he'd planned, just to see what happened.

By nine o'clock he had forgotten all about it. The party was coming to life as more people arrived. It was mostly his own age group but some of his friends had brought along older members of their family, and some of the girls in his year had older boy friends. He was glad about this as he'd told Leah there would be all ages here. At quarter past nine he went out to wait for her.

Two fifth-years who belonged to the local kick boxing club had been assigned to guard the front door against gatecrashers. Patrick sat on the front steps with them, a can of Red Rock between his feet.

The minutes ticked by. He kept looking at his watch, taking a gulp of the cider and looking at his watch again. One of the fifth-years was balancing on the iron balustrade alongside the steps. 'Cab approaching,' he said. Patrick jumped up, cursing as he kicked over the Red Rock.

'I hear she's married, this girl friend of yours,' said the other boy, a trace of admiration in his voice.

'So what?' said Patrick, tipping the can upright

175

with his foot, then kicking it into the air and catching it.

The boy shrugged. 'So nothing.'

The cab pulled to a halt. Patrick tossed the can into a hydrangea bush, gave the boy a confident wink, and strode across the pavement to meet it.

Leah looked even better than she had the evening at her house; and tonight it was all for him.

'It's ages since I've been out like this.' She stood there straightening her dress. It was bright yellow and clung to every inch of her, the off-the-shoulder neckline exposing not only her shoulders but the generous curve of her breasts, their fullness accentuated by the line where her lightly tanned skin ended. 'This is Tanya's,' she said. 'She bought it today with my money. The sandals are hers too.' She laughed. 'They're too big and the dress is too small.' Her hair was swept back the same as she'd worn it the night he went to her house and she was wearing bright red lipstick again.

As they went up the steps, she said, 'What would have been the best idea—I only thought of it today—was if you'd asked Kim to come to your party. I could have come with him.' She stopped and smiled up at him. 'It would have looked better.'

Patrick wasn't quite sure what she meant, but the mixture of drinks he'd downed over the last hour or so was already affecting his ability to think clearly, and he interpreted her words to mean what he wanted them to mean. 'I like

176

Kim,' he said to please her. 'But I only want you here tonight.'

She shook her head at him, then slipped her hand in his. 'Come on, Prince Charming,' she smiled. 'I have to go long before midnight.'

## Chapter 10

'Are these all your school friends?' Leah asked as Patrick steered her through the crush of bodies and out to the conservatory.

'Some are.'

'It isn't quite what I expected.' She ducked out of the way as someone threw out a hand to emphasise a point they were making.

'Well, you're here now,' he said, enclosing her in a protective arm.

She laughed and held on to him. 'So I might as well enjoy myself, is that it?'

'Yeah, that's it,' he said in a sudden whirl of happiness.

He found a quiet corner in the conservatory and left her there while he went off to get drinks. When he came back, Mansour and another boy from their year were talking to her.

'I've been hearing all about your trip to the Lake District last summer,' said Leah.

'Oh yeah.' Patrick handed her the drink and gave Mansour a warning look over her head. The week-long camping trip to the Lakes, supposedly part of their A-level studies, had

177

been spent chasing after a party of Japanese girls, two of whom he and Mansour had smuggled back to their tent on the last night. It seemed pathetically infantile now.

Leah sniffed at the drink. 'What is it?'

'Malibu and pineapple.'

'Plenty of pineapple, I hope,' she said, smiling up at him.

'Not if I know Patrick,' said the other boy, who had sat himself down next to her and spread out an album of school photographs across their laps. 'Look, this one's just before we left,' he said, reaching across her to point it out. Patrick could see the upside-down picture of them all standing in front of the coach.

'It must have been a lovely holiday,' said Leah in that special interested voice that Patrick knew so well. 'Did you stay in the tent all week?'

'Yes. Luckily it didn't rain.'

'I think I'd like camping. I love sleeping outside.'

'You look as though you've been out in the sun a lot,' said the boy, smiling round at her. 'Or do you have your hair highlighted?'

Leah looked at him as though she wasn't sure if she'd heard right. 'No, it's the sun,' she said finally with a little laugh. She glanced up at Patrick, then asked the boy, 'What about yours?'

'Oh, I have mine done,' he said, slightly self-conscious and not realising she'd asked the question jokingly. 'My friend's a hairdresser so I get it done cheap.'

'Yeah, we can see that,' said Patrick.

178

The boy looked up at Patrick now, his mouth turned down in an odd little expression of hurt. Leah frowned and looked from one to the other of them, then flicked over a page of the album. 'Is this your school play?'

'Yes.' The boy perked up. *Death of a Salesman*. I wasn't in it, but Patrick was. He played Happy. Look, there's some more over the page.'

'Did you take all these?' asked Leah. 'They're very good.'

'Yes, it's my hobby.' He smiled at her and laid his hands prayer-like on the page. 'Well, one of them.'

Patrick leant down and slammed the album shut, trapping the boy's hands inside. He heard Mansour say 'Leave him, Patrick', and saw Leah look bewildered. With a little twist of the album he let the boy go, but couldn't stop himself from saying, 'There's a couple of pretty little fifth-years out the front—can you go and bore them instead?' The boy looked stricken; he gathered up the album and marched off without a word.

'That was unkind,' said Leah with a hesitant smile.

'You're getting to be a bully, Patrick,' said Mansour. He smiled at Leah, gave Patrick a little punch on the arm, and walked off as well.

'And you're getting to be a gossipy old woman like him,' Patrick called after him.

A couple of heads turned but there was too much noise for anybody to take much

179

notice. Patrick sank down on the divan, legs stretched out and hands stuck in his pockets. Leah sipped her drink, looking at him now and again but not speaking. He shifted his position, resting his arms on his knees and staring down at the floor, wondering why the hell he'd behaved like that, what he'd been trying to prove. He felt Leah touch his arm. 'I don't think I should have come,' she said gently. 'I don't want to make you fall out with your friends.'

He turned his head towards her. 'It's not your fault, it's me.' He laced his fingers together, turning them over to inspect them. It was just like at home earlier: one minute he'd felt on top of the world, now it was all going wrong. And he'd so wanted to impress her, let her see what he was like amongst his friends. She nudged him and pulled his hands apart, taking hold of one.

'I shall go home if you don't start enjoying yourself. I didn't come all this way—and tell lies—so you could make me miserable.'

He tightened his fingers round hers, noticing, as he had before, how different her hands were from all the others he'd held: small and hot and rough, the nails slightly bitten. Tonight she wore other rings as well as her wedding band, and he rubbed a thumb across the stones. The largest looked like a diamond, the way it winked and sparkled in its brilliant gold setting. The other was no more than a chip of green held in a complicated design of two clasped hands. He wondered if either of them was an engagement ring, and who had bought them. 'I shan't let you go home,' he said, clamping his hand round her wrist.

'Do you think that'll stop me?' Quick as lightning she darted out to pinch the inside of his thigh. He let go of her with a little laughing yelp, and she was immediately digging her fingers into his side, tickling and pinching him, until he curled away from her. 'That's better,' she said. 'You can be far too serious—too moody,' she added with a final prod.

He moved back closer to her. He wanted to tell her about the row with Ginny, explain that it was on his mind. But it didn't seem the right time or place to bring it up. 'I drove over to your house earlier,' he found himself saying. 'I sat in the car for ages.'

'Oh, Patrick.' She took his hand again, wrapped his fingers round her own. 'What am I going to do with you?'

They were suddenly drenched in a spray of water. 'Sorry, guys,' somebody shouted, and another spray hit the roof of the conservatory and went dripping over a couple embracing on one of the divans. 'He's got that fucking water pistol again,' somebody else shouted, and there was a stampede out to the back garden where the laughter and shrieks carried on in the darkness.

Leah brushed drops of water from her shoulder, then took a tissue from her bag and wiped Patrick's face. It felt lovely having her dab away at him as if he was a little child, and he closed his eyes. 'Keep them closed,' she

181

said, putting a hand to his face. 'I've got a present for you.'

'A present?' He immediately opened his eyes and saw her take a parcel from her bag.

'Yes. Something I promised you.'

At first he thought it was a book. But when he pulled away the wrapping paper he found a pair of matching silver picture frames joined together with narrow blue ribbon; one held a photograph of his father. It was a close-up, just head and shoulders, and not as formal as the wedding photo. Cody's black hair was tousled, his lips parted as though he was about to laugh at something. Patrick was swamped with emotion; the face was so alive, so happy.

'Blue ribbon for blue eyes,' smiled Leah. Then she added softly, 'It's a lovely photo, isn't it? It was taken on the terrace where you sat the other night. I've written the date on the back.'

Patrick slid the photo out to look. The date was written neatly in red. Underneath, in another hand, was written 'Gabriel at Kim's birthday party'.

'Justina always called him Gabriel,' said Leah. 'Scribble that out if you like.'

Patrick replaced the photo and fingered the filigree pattern of the frame. 'Thank you.'

'The empty one is for a picture of you.'

'Thank you,' he said again. 'It's the best present anyone's ever given me.'

'As long as it's made you happy.'

Someone turned the lights out in the adjoining room, and then the lights in the conservatory went off for a moment. A girl shouted, 'I hope you're going to clean this place up for Mansour, you just knocked my bloody drink over.'

'You make me happy.' Patrick's words were lost in the answering shouts and he leant close to her and said louder, 'Being with you makes me happy.' His face was inches from hers. 'You know that, don't you?' He saw her nod, and began kissing her. A group of people moved in front of them, laughing and stumbling against the divan. Behind them, oblivious of it all, Patrick went on kissing her, swept away on a high of alcohol and desire and all those times he had wanted to touch her and couldn't. The thrill of feeling her respond banished any last vestige of restraint, and he pushed his tongue deep into her mouth. She was immediately twisting away, hands against his chest.

'I knew this would happen,' she said, resting her forehead against his chin, her arms looped over his shoulders.

'But you still came.'

'You bullied me into it.'

Someone had dimmed the lights again, leaving only one bulb burning at the far end. There was more laughter and a girl shrieking obscenities from the garden.

'Where's my drink?' said Leah.

He fumbled on the floor for it, dazed and light-headed with arousal, and found his own as well, hardly touched. Leah drained her glass with a little flourish and handed it to him. 'Just lemonade or something this time,' she said. He got to his feet, but Mansour was there taking the glass from his hand, and they were surrounded and dragged up into a line forming across the conservatory. A girl clamped her hands on his waist from behind. 'Patrick, you're sweating like a pig,' she said, rubbing her palms up and down his sides. 'Whatever have you been doing?' He laughed and wrapped his arms tight round Leah in front of him.

The conga line wound up the hall, heading for the open front door, squashing up like a concertina as the leaders slowed to negotiate the steps. Everybody was singing loudly; it was like a football match with two opposing sides, one belting out the latest Take That hit, then being shouted down with an old Gary Glitter number accompanied by stamping feet and bursts from a referee's whistle. And from somewhere way back, a high-pitched solo of an irreverent 'God Save the Queen'.

Out in the street, the line began to break up with just a few continuing on up the pavement. Patrick held on tight to Leah for a moment, lifting her off the ground before letting her go. She swivelled round to face him, taking his wrist to look at his watch.

'Another hour,' she said.

He shook his head, his heart sinking a little. 'You can stay longer than that.'

'Patrick, don't start,' she warned, but she was smiling, and leant close against him as what remained of the conga line squeezed back past them, and he had the feeling that it wouldn't take much to make her stay. She just needed a little persuasion. He looked across the road to

184

where his car was wedged between two others. On the dashboard lay the empty packet from the crisps he'd eaten earlier, shining bright blue in the light from a street lamp.

Leah drilled a finger under his chin. 'You're getting that serious look again, you'd better have another drink,' she joked.

He stared down into her face, then suddenly clasped her hands as though he was glueing them together so she wouldn't move. 'Wait here, I won't be a minute,' he said. He ran across the road to his car. Fumbling with his keys, and having to try all four, even the one to his room at Cambridge, made him realise that another drink was the last thing he needed. It was Leah who needed that—or something. He glanced over his shoulder to where she stood against the iron railings, half hidden by a crowd of people on the steps, then pulled the door open. Kim had said it was perfectly safe. What else he'd said Patrick couldn't remember. All he could think of was that he wanted Leah to forget about the time. He glanced round again, suddenly excited about what he was going to do.

'I forgot to lock it,' he said, coming back across the road, a hand in his pocket where the little bottle lay snug against his hip.

'You won't drive home tonight, will you?' she said.

'No, I'll walk—or stay here.'

The house was in semi-darkness now, and in the hall they passed two boys embracing, one of them the boy who had shown Leah the photos.

Patrick made a little thumbs-up gesture at him but the boy turned pettishly away.

'Is he gay?' whispered Leah.

'No, we all snog each other for the fun of it. Course he is,' he said, throwing an arm round her, oddly pleased by her naivety.

A cheer came from the kitchen; loud singing began, for he's a jolly good—and was drowned in a fresh burst of music from the stereo. Mansour appeared in the doorway holding up a magnum of champagne. 'Felix brought it round. You've just missed him. Our headmaster,' he explained politely to Leah. They followed Mansour into the kitchen where noisy toasts were being made. He shut the door behind them. 'Only the chosen few,' he said.

'Can't we mix something with this?' said a girl, as Mansour filled her glass. 'Give it a bit more kick.'

'No, you don't mix anything with champagne,' said Mansour.

'Don't be such a purist, Mansour. It's overrated, overpriced and boring.'

Patrick fingered the little bottle in his pocket. No, he thought, you can't have this, I've changed my mind. This is for me and Leah.

'How about a splash of Southern Comfort?' someone suggested.

'Good idea.'

There was more laughter as glasses were topped up with generous measures of Southern Comfort. Leah refused it, earning a few glances, but nobody said anything.

The group gathered together, perched on

the worktops and high stools at the breakfast bar. They swapped news, told jokes, gossiped about who was going out with whom. One of the girls was trying to fix a date when they would all meet up again, and she kept crying and kissing everyone. Patrick was drawn into the conversation, asked about his room at Cambridge and his car. He answered questions but asked few, conscious of the minutes ticking by. Leah looked slightly bored; she had hardly spoken a word since they came into the kitchen.

'Do you want any more?' he said quietly, tapping a finger against her glass.

'No thanks.' She flashed him a brief smile and turned to Mansour. 'Do you mind if I make myself a coffee?'

'No, of course not. I'll do it for you,' Mansour replied quickly, ever polite and, apart from Leah, the only one still sober. 'Anybody else want coffee?'

There was an uninterested shaking of heads, barely a break in the conversation. Patrick had detected a hint of hostility towards Leah. It was no more than the odd look, a sideways glance from a couple of the girls summing her up. It didn't bother him, he felt detached from them tonight, and the tricks and secrets of the coded language they used seemed tedious rather than clever.

He hopped down from the worktop. 'I'll do it, Mans,' he said. 'I fancy one myself.' He turned to Leah, encircling her where she sat. 'Black or white?'

'White—with three spoons of sugar. But you

ought to have black.' She put her hands on his shoulders and jumped down too. 'I'll come and help you.'

'We'll take this outside.' The idea came to him as he struggled to tear open a carton of milk. Something about the picture on it of cows grazing in the sun reminded him of the swing bed on Mansour's back lawn—only there would be no sunshine out there now. He looked out of the window. It was almost pitch dark. The cardboard gave way and he slopped milk carelessly into both mugs as if he was watering a row of plants.

'Careful.' Leah grabbed his wrist but the carton tipped over and sent milk pumping across the draining board. It cascaded like a waterfall into the sink.

'What are you doing over there?' called Mansour.

'Nothing.' Patrick stood the carton upright and Leah giggled helplessly as it tipped over again. She wanted to carry the mugs but he wouldn't let her, and she laughed all the way down the lawn as the very milky coffee splashed down his trousers and on to the dew-soaked grass.

'You wouldn't make a very good waiter,' she said, plumping down on the swing bed and kicking her feet against the ground so that it swung backwards and forwards.

Beside the swing bed was a small wrought-iron table. Patrick put the mugs on it and waited, listening to the creak of springs. Leah started to sing quietly in time to her rocking.

'Tonight, I'll dream again of Limerick, and count the days until I'm free.'

Patrick eased the little bottle from his pocket and tipped a few drops into Leah's coffee. When he went to pour the remainder into his own, he found the bottle was empty. He kept shaking it over the cup but nothing came out. Leah craned round the awning to peer at him, in the darkness. He quickly folded his arms, the bottle enclosed in his palm, wondering what the hell he'd done and which mug he should give her.

'This is lovely,' said Leah, kicking the swing bed into action again. 'I wish I had one of these at home.'

'Why don't you ask your husband to buy you one?' Patrick said. 'I expect he gets you everything you want.'

'No, he doesn't get me everything I want,' she answered sharply. She planted her feet on the ground. 'Pass my coffee and stop being silly. I have to go in a minute.'

He picked up both mugs and went to sit with her. They sipped at the coffee in silence, then Leah said, 'This is awful. It's stone cold and I don't think you put any sugar in it.'

'I did. You saw me.' He paused only a second before blurting out, 'Here, I'll sling it away if it's that bad.'

'No you won't,' she laughed, swivelling away from him as he went to take it from her. 'I don't want you having another one of your moods.' She put the mug to her lips again and he watched helplessly as she drained it down to the last drop.

He finished his own, its milkiness making him feel slightly sick on top of all the alcohol. Leah curled her feet under her and rested her head against his shoulder. 'It's nice out here, I could fall asleep,' she yawned. She'd hardly got the words out when there was the sound of someone coming down the lawn. They stopped a few feet away and began to urinate into the bushes. Patrick felt like murdering them, but Leah giggled and whispered, 'That's what I want to do. Come on, you can ring for a taxi while I go to the loo.'

He put their mugs on the table and followed her back indoors. The group in the kitchen were still deep in conversation; the whole atmosphere of the party seemed slower. The music was just as loud but it was a melodious ballad, and more people were entwined in corners than racing around the house. Patrick watched Leah try the handle of the downstairs cloakroom, not sure whether he was relieved or disappointed that she still seemed perfectly normal. A muffled 'Go away' came from the other side of the door and she stuck an impatient hand on her hip and went marching over to the stairs. Earlier that day, he and Mansour had tied a rope across the bottom of the stairs to keep people out of the bedrooms. It looked like a stately home with the little cardboard notice that said, 'PRIVATE BEYOND THIS POINT'. Leah tugged at it, though it would have been easy enough to crawl under.

'Undo this, Patrick,' she said. 'I'm desperate.'
He went to unhook it for her but she sank

down on the bottom stair. 'Goodness, I feel so dizzy,' she said, resting her head on her knees. 'It must be the champagne, or that Malibu stuff you gave me.'

Patrick crouched beside her, a little roar beginning in his ears. She twisted her head round to look at him. Two bright red dots had appeared on her cheekbones and she was breathing heavily through parted lips. 'I must go to the loo,' she said, clutching at him to heave herself up.

Halfway up the stairs she stumbled badly and would have fallen if Patrick had not been holding her round the waist. She slumped against him and kicked off her high-heeled sandals. He picked them up and she laughed, 'Don't let me go home without them or I will be in trouble.' At the top she slapped both hands against her chest. 'Where's my bag? Can you go and look for it?' Patrick ran back down the stairs to find it.

It was on the bottom stair, open because of the picture frames sticking out of the top, and too tempting not to look inside. He wasn't normally inquisitive; never before had the contents of a woman's handbag held any interest for him. But Leah was different, she invited curiosity in a hundred different ways. He wriggled his fingers through the contents. There was a lipstick, a small purse, a tissue, a number of till receipts from Harrods and Selfridges, and two small round pads of cotton wool. He quickly held one of the till receipts towards the light. It was for ninety-six pounds. Ninety-six pounds for a dress or shoes or whatever it was that she and Tanya had bought. He stuffed it back, wishing he hadn't looked. It seemed to represent Carew and all the reasons why she must soon go home.

She was in the bathroom when he went back up. He listened to the sound of running water. It went on and on. 'Leah,' he called, tapping on the door. 'Leah, are you all right?' The water stopped and the door swung open. 'I thought you might have fainted or something.'

'No, I'm fine,' she said, as though she had never been anything else. She was standing in front of the washbasin, peering at herself in the mirror above. 'What a mess I look. Have you got my bag?' He handed it to her with her sandals. She dropped the sandals in the basin, propped the bag on top of them and fished out her lipstick. With random little dabs she smudged it across both lips, then tidied it with her fingertip, glancing round as she did so. 'Don't stare, it's rude,' she smiled. Then in a sudden quick movement she reached out and dashed a stripe of lipstick across his cheek. It was typical of her, but when she did it again, painting his other cheek, the action was more provocative than playful. He came up behind her and looked over her shoulder at his red-streaked face. She put away the lipstick and began to search through her bag.

'What are you looking for?'

'A comb.'

He smoothed down the back of her hair, then mussed it up again. She didn't move, just stared at him in the mirror, and he wrapped his arms round her from behind. 'Don't go,' he said. 'I don't believe you really want to.' Voices echoed up from the hall below: someone was leaving. Patrick stretched out his foot and kicked the bathroom door shut. 'Stay here with me, Leah,' he murmured, tightening his arms round her. He felt her breasts heave in a long sigh. How very badly he wanted to close his hands over them, press his fingers into their softness. He moved back a fraction and ran his fingers across her bare shoulders, imagining how it would be to slip her dress down and watch in the mirror as he handled her naked breasts. Shouts of laughter came from downstairs. Patrick tensed with irritation; it would only take the smallest interference to spoil this. He lowered his eyes and found Cody smiling at him from the top of Leah's bag. It felt like another intrusion and made him think of Ginny crying over her ironing. He reached out to push the photo out of sight but his hand caught the tap and water began to flow into the basin. 'Oh, shit,' he muttered.

Leah giggled and rescued her things. 'I don't think you know what you're doing this evening.'

'I know what I want to do,' he said in a fluster of laughter and frustration.

She swivelled round; the heel of the sandal she was holding caught against his chest. 'And I know what you want to do.' The invitation in her voice was unmistakable but he stood there like a fool, staring down at her red-smudged mouth and tangled hair. She smiled and butted her forehead against him, and he came to life, grabbing hold of her and kissing randomly and wildly across her neck and shoulders. They stumbled against the washbasin and she ducked away, whispering, 'Not here.' He remembered her saying the same thing, sitting on the table in his room at Cambridge. But this was a different Leah, different even from that afternoon. She led the way out on to the landing. Opposite, a bedroom door stood ajar. Patrick thought of other parties and other bedroom doors, of checking to see that rooms weren't already occupied. And always there had been the thrill of anticipation and the mounting excitement. But never had it felt like this.

'Is it all right in here?' she said, going to stand in the doorway. 'What a beautiful room.'

He followed her in and closed the door. It probably belonged to one of Mansour's sisters, or perhaps two of them shared it. The bed was a double, covered with quilted ivory satin and heaped with numerous fluffy toys, their glass eyes glinting wickedly in the light from a street lamp. There were more of them scattered around the room, perched on white wicker chairs and lined up on the dressing table amongst rows of perfumes and bath oils and heaps of bright gold jewellery.

Leah turned in a slow circle as though she was entranced by it all. Then she sat down on the end of the bed. There was just enough light from the street lamp to see that her face had grown serious; or was it worried? Patrick went and stood in front of her, almost too

194

scared to touch her in case she was having second thoughts and this would all fall apart like some crazy fragile dream. Very carefully, he put his hands on her shoulders, waited a moment, then took hold of the top of her dress. It was stretchy and easy to roll down, but he did it little by little until it reached her elbows. She did the rest, pulling out her arms. She had on a strapless bra; it was made of stiffened cream lace and so heavily boned that it didn't slip down with her dress. He knelt down and was about to reach round to unhook it when she caught hold of his arms.

'Leah, please,' he began, desperate to do this just as he'd imagined. But she took his hand and pressed it between her breasts.

'The front,' she whispered. He felt the bump of hook and eye under his fingers, and understood. He was already shaking, but undoing the tight hooks, his knuckles pressing into her soft flesh and her open-mouthed breathing noisy and stimulating, he could hardly control himself.

As the stiff band of lace fell away, he raised his head to look at her, wanting to know it was all right to touch her. Her eyes were closed and he could see little drops of moisture forming beneath her lashes. For one awful moment he thought they were tears, then he saw that her whole face was wet, her neck and shoulders were wet and her beautiful breasts were wet. She opened her eyes for just a second, then flung herself backwards to lie amongst the heap of fluffy toys. He stood up and stared down at her, mad with love for her.

All he could think of was that he mustn't rush this. It was his last chance to impress her, and make her want him again after this night was over. He began to take off his own clothes. She looked up once, smiled at him, then wriggled the dress down over her hips and threw it at him. He caught it, flung it aside and dived on the bed.

Her legs were bare; all she had on now were her pants, the same plain white schoolgirl style that he'd seen her in before. They were tight over the swell of her stomach and not big enough to conceal the thick dark hair in her groin. He leant over and kissed her just above her navel. She lay very still and he kissed her again, lower, and then lower until his mouth was pressing against smooth dry cotton. He felt her pelvis arch up towards him, and as soon as he hooked his fingers over the waistband of her pants, she rose higher to make it easy for him to take them off. It was so difficult then to hold back. She had opened her legs and drawn up her knees; the position of childbirth. The whole idea of it usually revolted him but it had just the opposite effect as he looked at Leah's thighs.

With a little moan, he buried his face between them, sucking at her and pushing his tongue into her. She began to writhe about, sliding on the padded satin, but he kept his mouth tight against her, wanting to experience the feel of her orgasm. And taste it, he thought, delirious with excitement and aware that he was only seconds from ejaculation. But at the last moment, she jerked away from him and rolled onto her side, curling up with her hands between her legs as though she was in pain. It startled him; worried and calmed him. He leant over her, only to find her smiling at him.

'It was too nice,' she murmured. 'I've never felt anything like it. I thought I would faint if I didn't get away from you.'

He gave a little laugh of relief. 'Really? Was it really?' he said. In answer she reached out and picked up two of the fluffy animals and tickled them against his stomach.

'Don't,' he laughed, kneeling up away from her. 'Stop it.'

She did it again. 'You like it,' she said. 'I can see you like it.' She dropped them and knelt up with him. He kissed her very lightly and ran his fingers over her breasts. 'Are you glad you stayed?' he whispered, feeling himself grow unbearably hard again.

'Don't talk about that,' she said, and hit him quite spitefully with one of the toys. But before he could say or do anything she had dropped down in front of him and taken him into her mouth. Shock waves of pleasure hit him. He clutched at her, twisting one hand in her hair and gripping her shoulder so tightly with the other that he was pinching her sweat-soaked skin. But she didn't complain, not even when he caught hold of her head and held it in a vice-like grip while he sent great spurts of semen to the back of her throat.

He crouched there, stunned and half ashamed, unable to look at her. In all his dreams of her, he had never imagined this; had never even done this before. He felt her cheek press against his stomach for a moment, then she had slipped away, over to the basin in the corner of the room. When she came back, she folded her arms round him and rolled him down beside her, pulling the satin coverlet over them.

'Don't go, will you?' he said. 'Stay here with me all night.'

'Shh,' she murmured, pressing his face into her neck and curling herself round him.

The next thing he knew, someone was tapping on the door. He sat up, disorientated, looking round the room in the beam of the street light.

'Patrick, is that you?' came in a loud whisper.

Leah raised her head. He put a finger to his lips, pulled the coverlet over her and went to the door. The party was still going strong by the sounds of it.

'I thought it must be you.' Mansour peered in at him. 'I've brought you some refreshment.' He held up a champagne bottle, tilting it to show what remained. 'I thought you might need it.'

'Yeah,' Patrick smiled. 'Thanks. Sorry about earlier.'

'I just hope you know what you're doing. I don't want her husband coming here and beating you to a pulp in my sister's bedroom.'

'No chance, he's in the States.'

'Seriously, you could be getting yourself into all sorts of trouble.'

'Let me worry about that. What's the time?'

'Nearly one. I'll have to start kicking them

out in another hour or so. But I don't expect I'll get rid of you, will I?'

'No way.' He gave a confident grin and closed the door, swigging from the bottle as he went back to the bed.

Leah propped herself on her elbows, shaking her head as he offered her the bottle.

'What did he say the time was?' she asked.

'Eleven o'clock.'

'Liar.' She sat up and stretched, reaching high above her head, naked and smiling. He stood the bottle on the bedside table, carefully blocking her view of his watch which he'd put there earlier.

Later, he caught sight of its luminous dial and saw that it was now past two. But it hardly registered, he was gripped in the consuming pleasure of orgasm once more, Leah face down beneath him. It wasn't a need for variety, or even her admission that she'd never done it like this with Carew; it wasn't even Patrick's idea. She'd rolled over herself, and Patrick hadn't hesitated for a second. He was clumsy with eagerness and made her cry out, but it only heightened his excitement, and he burrowed his hands under her body to squeeze her breasts.

They both lay silent and still for a long while, then he hoisted himself up and kissed her shoulder. When she didn't move, he did it again. She wriggled, and he started kissing her along her spine, going all the way down until he came to the swell of her buttocks. He kissed her there; she laughed and he tickled her until she twisted away, jackknifing her legs and snatching at his wrists.

'Stop it!' She rolled onto her back and he leant over her, a hand each side of her head. 'You hurt me,' she said, her tone lightly scolding.

'I'm sorry, I didn't mean to.'

'Yes you did.' There was a funny little smile on her face. He stared down at her, unable to decipher it, and wanting only to please her.

'I got carried away...' He hesitated. 'Because I love you so much.' He dropped his face into her neck. 'I really love you, Leah.'

The noise of a car revving up came from the street below. He curled his arms round her head, hoping she wouldn't hear and be reminded of the time. There was more noise: banging doors and laughter and someone shouting, 'Be quiet, you noisy fucker.' The laughter stopped for a moment, then broke out again in a loud burst. The car pulled away, racing off with a screech of tyres.

Leah sighed and freed herself to sit up. She raked her hair back from her face and held both palms to her cheeks. Patrick sat up beside her. 'What's the matter?' he said softly, thinking, here it comes, she's going now.

'I feel peculiar again.'

'How do you mean?' He tried to hold her but she pulled away.

'Just peculiar,' she said impatiently. She kicked out her foot, sending a pink cat flying across the room. It landed on the dressing table, knocking over a couple of bottles. She put a hand to her mouth, gave a short laugh and slumped back on the pillows. Within seconds she was sound asleep.

Patrick reached round for the remains of the champagne. He really wanted water but didn't want to disturb her by getting up from the bed; while she was asleep she couldn't go—it seemed as simple as that. As he settled down, an arm round her, a hand resting on her breast, he had a vague sense of guilt that he was tricking her in some way by letting her sleep. But it merely danced on the outer edges of his consciousness, and soon he was asleep himself.

## Chapter 11

When he woke, Leah had gone. The house was silent, the room stuffy with the lingering odours of alcohol and sex, and dark because she had pulled the curtains. He rolled over to look at his watch. It was just after five. Maybe she had gone to the bathroom. But when he raised his head and saw that her clothes had gone too, he wasn't surprised, and something told him that she'd left some time ago.

He got up and wandered round the room, half-heartedly looking for something, though he didn't know what. Anything would have done. But there was no trace of her, not even a waft of scent. He remembered her telling him once that she never wore it because it made Jo-jo sneeze. All that remained were the picture

201

frames which she'd propped on the bedside table. Cody was watching him again, just as he had last night in the bathroom in those crazy few minutes when Leah had changed her mind about staying. Patrick stared back at the smiling face. How could she go without even saying goodbye? Perhaps she had tried to wake him and couldn't; God knows how much he'd had to drink. He blew out a long breath. What now? he thought. What do I do now?

Downstairs, Mansour and two girls were tidying up. Patrick went out to the kitchen and drank two glasses of water straight off, then beckoned Mansour aside. 'Did Leah get her cab all right?' he asked lightly.

'Yes, I called it for her. She said you were completely zonked out.'

Patrick nodded and smiled in agreement. 'Do you need any more help to clear up?'

'No, we've nearly finished.'

'I'll get off home then.' He hesitated, then swung off upstairs again. 'I'll just go and straighten the bedroom,' he called over his shoulder.

Mansour had a phone extension in his room; Patrick crept in and called Leah's number. It rang for ages, and he kept thinking just one more ring and I'll put it down. Then Tanya answered and he could tell that she'd snatched up the receiver in a temper. 'Hello? Who's that?' she said.

He couldn't risk speaking, and waited, dumbly imagining that Leah would soon come and take the receiver from her.

'Who is it?' Her voice was a bellow this time but still he didn't answer. 'Do you realise what time it is, you fucking pervert?' she shouted and banged down the receiver.

Larry was already up, sitting at the kitchen table with his paper and a cup of tea.

'Good time, mate?' he said without looking up.

'Yeah,' Patrick grunted and brushed past him. In his room, he stood the picture frames on his chest of drawers, and then, for the second time within a few hours, he pulled off his clothes and fell into bed.

Ginny was picking them up when he woke. He watched her hang them over the back of a chair but quickly closed his eyes when she turned round. She went to open the window, and he curled under the duvet, battling the dual discomforts of a starry headache and an erection.

'Patrick! Cup of tea,' she said loudly.

He emerged, shading his eyes from the light as though he had just woken, and found the tea on the chair beside his bed.

'Thanks,' he muttered, following on with a genuine yawn.

'Did you have a good time?' she smiled. 'You look as though you did.'

'Yeah, thanks,' he nodded, bleary and sniffing.

'I don't think you should have driven home, but never mind, I know you're usually careful.' She came to sit on the bed. 'It's nearly

203

lunchtime, you know.' He looked up, aware of a certain tension in her voice and saw that she was holding the frames that Leah had given him. Her eyes followed his into her lap. 'It's a very good likeness.' She stopped, licked her lips and cleared her throat. 'It'll be you in a few years' time,' she went on, smiling again.

Patrick reached for his cup, wishing to God he'd put the frames away.

'I'm sorry he's dead, Patrick, really I am.' After a few seconds, she asked gently, 'Who gave you this? Not his wife, I don't suppose.'

'No. Her sister.'

'The one who's been phoning you?'

'Yeah.'

'I know how you contacted her. I wasn't prying. You left the cutting in the pocket of your shirt. I nearly put it in the washing machine.'

'It doesn't matter.' He sipped at the tea, eyes fixed on the tiny bubbles that gathered and shifted round the edge of the cup.

More seconds tripped away. Ginny held the frames in her lap, staring down at them as though she was reading a book. 'You've met them then,' she said, so quietly he could only just hear her. 'His wife and her sister, I mean.'

'His wife lives in Spain. They were divorced years ago. It's her sister who found out everything for me.'

'And she's still in Norfolk, at that house?'

He nodded. This was going to get complicated. The last thing he wanted was to discuss Leah with her.

Ginny cleared her throat again. 'I went there once.'

He stopped drinking, saw her hands twist together over Cody's face, and had the feeling that this was what she had been working up to say from the beginning.

One of the twins called up the stairs, could they put the television on? Ginny jumped up and went to the door, called down, 'Yes, just for half an hour,' and came straight back.

'It was about a year after you were born. I thought if I could get some recognition from him, perhaps some sort of financial support...' She glanced down at the photo, then up at Patrick. 'You see I did try.'

Patrick fidgeted, uncomfortable; this was no longer what he wanted.

'His wife said she didn't know where he was. I didn't tell her why I wanted him, but I think she guessed because she was hostile right away.' Ginny was speaking quickly now as though she had to get it all out. 'There was a girl there, standing behind her in the hall. I wasn't invited in. She...Justina, I mean... She caught hold of the girl by her wrist and dragged her in front of me. I remember thinking they must be sisters. She shouted at the girl, "Look, here's another one after him." I was scared because she was so angry. She kept shaking the girl. I thought she might start on me. Then all of a sudden, the girl bit her on the hand.' Ginny gave a little watery smile. 'Justina slapped her really hard round the face. I couldn't believe it, fighting like that in front of me. After that I knew I wasn't going to get anywhere, so I went home. I never told Mum where I'd been. I never told anyone.' She began to cry; just silent tears at first, then little shaky sobs. She pulled a handkerchief from her sleeve and blew her nose. 'We were living near Aunt Cath then. I was staying with her when I found that picture in the local paper. It was just before you were born.' She was struggling to control the tears but they overwhelmed her and she covered her face with the handkerchief. 'I had no one to talk to.'

The door suddenly burst open. Ginny quickly dried her eyes and closed up the picture frames.

'I thought you were watching TV?' said Patrick, to save Ginny having to speak.

The twins edged their way in, one after the other. 'It's gone wrong,' said one of them. Every now and then, the sound faded and the set needed fiddly adjustment with a screwdriver.

Apart from Larry, Patrick was the only one who could fix it properly.

'So you've come to drag me out of bed, have you?'

They laughed and came bounding over to climb in with him.

'Yes, we have.' One of them began pulling at him, standing behind him on the pillow, arms round his neck. Her little warm hands on his skin and the soapy smell of her hair felt shamefully stimulating and he twisted away from her.

'Get off there with your shoes on,' said Ginny sharply.

They obeyed at once, clambering down to sit

side by side opposite her. 'What did you do at your party?' said one of them.

'Drank lots of lemonade.'

They giggled, wise to his teasing even if they didn't always understand. 'We're having Coke at our party.'

'We thought it might be nice to go out for Sunday lunch on their birthday,' said Ginny. She composed herself, giving her nose another blow and smiling through wet lashes. 'Larry suggested it. We can celebrate your results as well.'

Patrick nodded, looking at his watch. 'I'd better get up.'

'Are you staying here tonight?' There was unfamiliar eagerness in her voice. 'I expect you could do with a quiet evening in.'

He had planned to go back to Cambridge, but was suddenly unable to disappoint her. 'Yeah, I might,' he said, his tone noncommittal.

'Goodee!' shouted the twins.

'Now let me get up.' He poked the nearest of them in the ribs. 'Or it'll be time to go to bed again.'

Ginny stood up and held out her hands to them. 'Come on, let Patrick get dressed now.'

In a flash of mischievousness, one of the twins darted across the room and snatched his trousers off the chair. Patrick saw the little bottle fall onto the carpet and roll under the chest of drawers. She flung the trousers on the bed with a laughing 'Hurry up!' and then Ginny was herding them out of the room.

Ginny cooked him a late breakfast, and called up the stairs to say it was on the table and she was popping out to the shops. As soon as she'd gone he tried to phone Leah again. This time the answering machine was switched on. He made a cup of tea, then tried again, but it was still the machine. Folding two rashers of bacon between a slice of toast, he went out to his car and drove to her house. He knew they'd probably gone back to Norfolk, but he wanted to make sure.

The parking space was empty and the gate to the back garden padlocked. He vaulted over it and went to look through the kitchen window. It was tidy and deserted. A man came out from the house next door and asked if he could help.

'Oh, I was, er, looking for Mrs Carew.'

'I'll pass on a message if you like,' said the man, eyeing him suspiciously.

'You don't know her number, do you?' Patrick blurted out. 'In Norfolk, I mean.'

'Ah, well, I can't really say. If you leave a message I'll make sure—'

'Don't worry,' said Patrick. He hesitated, knowing he had to jump back over the gate, and how bad it must look. The man would be sure to mention it. 'It's her son I'm after actually. Kim. I'll see him sometime. Don't worry.'

By the time he got back home, it was mid-afternoon. Ginny and the twins were busy making cakes. The kitchen echoed with their happy chatter and the whole house smelt of baking. Patrick stopped only long enough to

208

gather up the few things he'd brought with him from Cambridge.

Ginny was at the bottom of the stairs as he came down. 'I thought you were staying.'

'I've changed my mind.' The words came out brusquely, a defence against any delay.

'Are you going to that big school now?' said one of the twins, running after him as he made for the front door.

'Soon,' he said, bending briefly to kiss her, then doing the same to the other one.

'University,' corrected Ginny. She caught the strap of his holdall. 'You're not in any kind of trouble, are you?' she said.

'Of course not.' He eased away from her but she kept hold of the strap for a moment.

'It must be me then,' she said with a catch in her voice.

'It's not you, it's not anything,' he said. 'I just have to get back. I've got a lot to do.'

## Chapter 12

Leah's car was the only one there, parked on the square of gravel at the side of the house. It was more than he'd hoped for to find her alone. But as he went to go through the back gate, Zula came bounding up, barking furiously, and almost at once he heard Kim's voice bellowing at her. The dog stopped in her tracks. Patrick clicked his tongue at her and called her name.

Her tail lowered and began to wag, then she was barking again, her head thrown up, howling like a wolf, and he was almost glad to see Kim appear.

'Hey, Patrick, it's you.' Kim had nothing on but a pair of shorts. He aimed a barefooted kick at the dog's rump. 'Go and lie down, you pain.' The dog slunk away, dropping down on its belly a few feet from them. 'I was wondering about you,' Kim said. 'Come and tell me all about it.'

Patrick followed him round to the back of the house. There was a blanket spread out below the terrace. It was covered with an assortment of cans, plates, books and sweet wrappers. A radio lay on its side crackling away, slightly off channel. Kim flopped down on the blanket, sweeping aside some of the debris to make room for him. 'What happened then?' He lay back, shading his eyes from the rays of sunshine that came slanting across the lawn. 'Have you had a whole week of unbridled passion?'

Patrick couldn't help smiling. 'You're joking,' he said, trying to keep his tone as light-hearted as possible.

'Tell me then. Did you try the stuff I gave you?' Kim eyed him from beneath the angle of his hand. He wasn't the easiest of people to lie to. Beneath the ready smile and the friendly gestures, there was something disconcerting about him. Patrick felt it more strongly than ever today but knew it was because of last night and this act he had to put on. He gave a dismissive shrug, avoiding those watchful eyes of Kim's. 'I got pissed and forgot about it.' He picked up the radio and fiddled with the knob. The garden was suddenly filled with reggae music. 'I just came out here for the drive—see how you were doing.' He turned up the volume and made himself look Kim in the face. 'You don't mind, do you?'

'No, I'm glad to see you. It gets boring here on my own.'

'On your own?' Patrick glanced casually towards the house. 'Is your father still away?'

'Carew you mean? Yeah, he's gone for two weeks.'

'And Tanya's at the shop, I suppose?'

'Yeah.' Kim rolled onto his stomach, his head turned sideways on his arms. 'She's not very happy with me. She and my mother stayed in London last night, and I was supposed to open up the shop this morning, but I overslept.'

Patrick paced himself, flicking over the pages of one of the books. 'Is your mother with her?' The words seemed to come out unnaturally loud. Kim raised his head, his thick brows knitted together.

'Do what?'

'I just wondered if your mother was with Tanya.'

'No, she never works in the shop. She's in bed.' Kim squinted towards the house. 'She's not well. She was ill on the way home this morning.'

Patrick turned a few more pages, the words forming one long blurred line. Yeah, and it's your fucking fault, he wanted to say. But of

211

course he couldn't—and anyway, it wasn't.

'She went out to a party,' Kim went on. 'But it's not a hangover, she doesn't drink much.' He sat up, arms round his knees, chin resting on them. 'I hope she's not pregnant again.'

'That's not very likely, is it?' Patrick wanted to gulp the words back, but Kim was already grinning with amusement.

'Carew may look over the hill, but he can still raise a hard-on now and again, I assure you.'

Patrick let out a little snort somewhere between disapproval and laughter. 'Don't you want another brother, or a sister?' he said, staring intently at the book and feeling as though he had waded into quicksand.

'Nah, not particularly,' said Kim, resting his head back on his arms.

The dog had moved nearer to them. It sat watching, its ears flicking backwards and forwards as though it was listening to their conversation. Kim reached round for an empty can and tossed it at the dog's head. The dog manoeuvred it between its paws and began licking at the trickle of brown liquid that ran from the lid.

'Does he go away a lot?'

'Carew?' said Kim, as though Patrick had started on a completely different topic. 'Yeah, a fair bit. Usually it's only to London, and my mother goes with him.'

'Is that where they met?' Patrick asked.

'Sort of.' Kim threw another can at the dog. 'We were hitching there and he picked us up.' He looked round as if to say, how about that then?

'Yeah?' said Patrick. 'Why were you hitching to London?' he added, unable to resist questioning Kim, driven by a compelling fascination to hear more about Carew.

'It was after that cow Justina locked us out. She shut us out all night. We had to sleep in a little tent I had pitched on the lawn.'

'Why did she lock you out?'

'Oh, she was just having one of her tantrums. Tanya let us in the next morning, but my mother went straight and packed a case and we were off. Just like that.' He clicked his fingers in the air. 'We got picked up by a couple of lorries.' Kim grinned across at him. 'My mother didn't give a shit in those days. Then Carew pulled up. He said he was going to London. When my mother got in the car I thought perhaps we were going to stay with my father, or even go and look for Cody.' Kim fell silent as though that was the end of the story. But Patrick was more eager than ever to hear more.

'What happened then?' he urged.

'He kept looking at my mother.' Kim swivelled round to face him. 'I mean, you don't really like any guys staring at your mother, do you? But an old bloke like him...' He began tugging up little chunks of grass. 'I was only about ten, but I wasn't stupid. When we got to London and he asked her where she wanted to go, she started crying.' Kim stopped again and made a little whistling sound through his teeth. 'I can't say anything bad about him. He was really good to us. But my mother didn't like it in London. She missed Tanya and the dogs.'

'So you didn't go to your father's, or see Cody?'

'Nah.'

'Didn't you want her to marry Carew?'

'Oh, I didn't mind.' Kim looked at him again. 'I'm not jealous or anything, don't think that. I knew she'd get married again—she's so beautiful. Still you know that, don't you?' He grinned. 'I saw you looking at her last week when you were here. Go on, admit it.'

Patrick felt himself smile stupidly while a little splutter of astonishment escaped his lips. 'Are you hoping I'll say yes, so you can punch me in the mouth?'

Kim gave one of his high croaky laughs. 'You take everything so seriously. I think you've been at school too long.' He leant over and swiftly hooked an arm round Patrick's neck, catching him in a half-nelson and pulling him back on the ground. There was the smell of sweat and the feel of Kim's coarse hair flicking in his face, and out of the corner of his eye Patrick saw the dog bounce up. It started to yelp and growl, and he wrenched away.

'Leave off, Kim,' he said. 'I don't want that fucking hound tearing my throat out.'

Kim lay back, giggling like a girl. 'She's all right.' He reached out a hand to twist the dog's muzzle. 'You're a pussycat, aren't you, Zula?' The dog suddenly shot round, ears pricked. There was a scrunch of gravel, and she started

214

to whine and wag her tail furiously.

'Good, that's Tanya. We can get some grub now,' Kim said, leaping to his feet. He stood astride the dog, trapping it between his legs and flexing his biceps in a bizarre little show of power. It tried to pull away, twisting its head to snap at him. 'Stop that, you vicious bitch,' he said, slapping it round the ears before releasing it. The dog shot off and Kim turned back to Patrick. 'Come on, let's go and tell Tanya to cook plenty.'

'Won't she mind?' Patrick hung back. 'I don't want to keep barging in.' There was nothing he wanted more than to follow Kim, but he'd lived for years in a house where inviting anyone for a meal without asking first was unheard of.

'Don't be stupid, she'll be pleased to see you. She reckons you're the sexiest schoolboy she's ever come across,' he added with a burst of his childish laughter.

But Tanya barely acknowledged him. They had come in by a side door directly into the kitchen. The dog had followed them, and Tanya immediately screeched at it to get out, then started gathering things from different cupboards, banging about as she went. Kim seemed totally unconcerned and went over to rake amongst some clothes piled on top of an ironing board.

'Dressing for dinner,' he joked, pulling out a V-necked jumper and dragging it on. He eased out his imprisoned hair and jerked his head towards Tanya. 'She doesn't like naked bodies at the table.' Tanya ignored him, and

Patrick wasn't sure whether to smile or ignore him too.

The kitchen was a huge L-shaped room and very hot despite all the windows being open. There was clutter everywhere and it all seemed to be in the wrong places, like the tins of dog food lined up on a plant stand and the newspapers soaking up water on the draining board. Tanya was cooking on a maroon-coloured Aga set back in the alcove of an old chimney breast in the far wall. At her elbow was a clotheshorse hung with baby clothes, the ones along the bottom rail wet and dripping puddles on to the quarry-tiled floor. Patrick couldn't help comparing it with his own home where a single wet footprint was enough to make Ginny complain; his grandmother would have had a seizure in here.

Kim fetched a jug of orange juice from the fridge and poured generous glasses for them all. He took Tanya's over to her and stood there, his chin resting on her shoulder to see what she was cooking.

'You could have started this instead of dossing around all day,' she said, elbowing him hard in the ribs.

He yelped. 'I haven't been dossing, I've been looking after my mother.' He came to sit at the table where Patrick was already perched on a wooden chair doing his best to look relaxed.

From where he was sitting he could see out into the hall. There was a path of pale sunshine spilling in from the terrace, dappled now and again with the flickering movement of

216

leaves round the door. Kim had fallen silent, concentrating on digging a splinter from the side of his hand. There was only the sound of Tanya frying onions round the corner, and Zula's panting from the doorway.

Kim stretched. 'That smells lovely. When will it be ready?'

'Not for hours,' replied Tanya. 'Could even be days.'

Kim clicked his tongue and pulled a face. Patrick gave a little smile to show he was listening—but he wasn't, not properly, because he'd heard movement above them. It was only the faintest creak, but enough to compel him to keep an eye on the hall and the stairs, the bottom six of which he could see without moving his head.

When her feet appeared, then her legs, bare and shiny brown in the beam of sunlight, he quickly picked up his glass for something to do. Two seconds later she stood framed in the doorway. She saw him at once, her flickering look of surprise changing almost immediately to pleasure. The last mouthful of orange juice bubbled in his throat, and he rubbed a hand across his mouth, fearful that it would spray out in a great gush across the table.

Kim turned to look over his shoulder. 'Mum! I didn't hear you come down.'

She was wearing a crimson silk kimono flowing loose and open over a short white nightdress. Her face was pale but her eyes feverishly bright. She pulled the kimono round her, fastening it with a narrow belt. 'You didn't

217

tell me you had company,' she said, coming to stand behind Kim's chair.

'It's only Patrick.' Kim strained backwards to look up at her. 'And he's nearly one of the family.'

Patrick knew he must say something but he was terrified the words would come out garbled or that a great clownish grin would spread across his face. She saved him by speaking first. 'Hello, Patrick. Excuse me, won't you,' she smiled, pulling at the kimono again, 'but I've only just got up.'

'Er, yes, Kim said you weren't feeling too good. Are you feeling better now?'

'A lot better, thank you.' Her eyes lingered on him for a moment, then she went over to Tanya. 'Can you do Jo-jo another bottle for me? I daren't feed him. I tried earlier and he was sick straightaway.' She laced her hands across her stomach and frowned. 'I feel as though my whole body's been poisoned.'

Tanya fished a baby's feeding bottle from the sink. 'About time he was weaned anyway, or he'll end up like Kim, breastfed at ten years old.'

Kim's mouth flew open and he turned angrily towards her, but Leah fluttered a hand at him as if to say, ignore her, and he contented himself with a scowl and a muttered, 'Crude bitch.'

Tanya smiled to herself, swilled the bottle round under the tap and went back to her cooking. 'Hope you like spaghetti Bolognese, Patrick,' she said, looking over her shoulder, friendly as could be.

'Yes, I do, thanks.'

Leah came over to them and poured herself some orange juice. Kim got up to give her his chair which was the only one lined with cushions.

'I went out last night,' she began slowly and deliberately, looking at Patrick across the table. 'I really enjoyed myself, but I don't think it's done me a lot of good.'

Kim was hanging over her. 'What did you have to eat?' he asked, gently smoothing back the hair from her forehead.

'Nothing much.' She yawned, stretching up with both hands to pat his cheeks.

'Perhaps it's a bug then,' Kim went on, combing his fingers through the tangled length of her hair.

'Stop doing that,' grumbled Tanya, coming to drop a collection of cutlery on the table.

'What's wrong now?' said Kim.

'Getting hair all over the table.'

'I'm not.'

'You wouldn't do it if Carew was here,' Tanya said with a little smirk.

'Do what?' said Kim, getting agitated.

'Try to be Mummy's little baby boy.'

'You do talk a load of old bollocks,' said Kim angrily, but there was something in his tone that hinted he wasn't so very far from tears.

Leah caught hold of his hand. 'Will you do something for me?' she asked. 'Will you go and get Jo-jo? Please,' she added as he lingered there, glaring at Tanya.

He stomped off, but stopped in the hall to

call back at Tanya, 'You know what you need, don't you?'

Tanya laughed and kicked the door shut behind him.

'Do you have to torment him?' said Leah. 'It only gets him in a temper, then he gets in trouble.'

'You've got no control over him, that's his trouble,' said Tanya. 'Can't we swap him for Patrick?' She gave a little trill of laughter and went off to her cooking again.

Leah waited until Tanya was at the Aga with her back to them, then whispered across the table, 'What are you doing here?'

'I had to come,' he whispered back. 'I had to see you.'

Keeping an eye on Tanya, she reached across and touched her fingers to his face. He immediately pressed his lips into her palm. But Tanya was already turning round. 'Leah, are you having any of this?'

Leah pulled away just in time. 'No thanks. There's only one thing I want right now.' She paused; her eyes flicked towards Patrick for one brief second. 'And that's some more sleep.'

Kim came back with Jo-jo bundled up in a towel and screaming his head off.

'He's soaked,' he said, placing him unceremoniously on Leah's lap.

She unwrapped him and cuddled him against her, a hand splayed round his little dark head and her cheek against his. 'Poor baby,' she murmured to him. He stopped crying and she held him in front of her and blew little kisses at him. His tear-stained face crinkled into gurgling smiles and she bounced him in the air, disturbing the kimono and revealing the glistening dark channel between her breasts.

Patrick dragged his eyes away from her. He examined his knuckles, then raised his head to look at a lacy pattern of cobwebs on the ceiling, as if they were the most interesting things he'd ever seen. He was about to steal another look at Leah when Tanya came up and handed her the bottle of milk. Leah tested a few drops on the back of her hand. 'It's too hot,' she said ungratefully, then disappeared upstairs with the baby.

After they'd eaten, Kim asked him if he wanted to play snooker.

'What, here?' Patrick vaguely remembered him mentioning snooker that other evening when persuading Leah to come to his party had been the only thing on his mind.

'Yeah, we've got a games room.' Kim was up, leaving the debris of his meal: pieces of French bread scattered round his plate, his knife and fork left on the table and an apple core fallen on the floor. Force of habit made Patrick gather up his own things and take them to the sink.

'I think we really will swap you for Kim,' said Tanya, with one of her sly smiles.

Patrick answered with a brief grin, and glanced at his watch.

'Stop worrying about the time,' said Kim. 'You're always looking at your watch.'

'It's habit,' said Patrick, wondering himself why he did it.

The games room was in an extension built on the side of the house and was dominated by a full-sized snooker table. There was also a dartboard, a huge television on a swivel base, and a music centre, and the room was showily furnished with a white leather sofa and chrome and glass coffee table. It looked smart and modern compared to what Patrick had seen of the rest of the house.

Kim went to pull down the window blinds, then switched on a shaded light hanging directly over the snooker table. The room was transformed; it reminded Patrick of the smoky, dimly lit snooker clubs where gangsters meet in films. He settled himself on the sofa, rubbing a hand along the squeaky smooth arm. 'It's smart in here,' he said. 'You lucky devil.'

Kim looked pleased. 'Yeah, and it's all mine—nobody else uses it now. My grandfather had it built. He used to practise in here.' He went over to a corner and came back with a very plain wooden guitar. 'This was one of his. Spanish guitar. He wasn't exactly Eric Clapton.' He rested a foot on the sofa beside Patrick, the guitar balanced on his leg, and began to pluck at the strings with one finger.

'Can you play it?' said Patrick.

'A bit. He tried to teach me but he didn't have a lot of patience. And my fingers were too small. I was only a kid then. I can remember when I was really small sitting on his lap while he was playing. Or it might have been Cody.' His brows drew briefly together. 'I forget now.'

'Did he practise in here as well then?'

'Yeah, I think so. It was him who had the snooker table put in, I know that.' He ran a thumb right across the strings and glanced up at Patrick. 'I'm not supposed to talk about him—I promised my mother. She said I'd remember all the wrong things. She said it was bad enough for you as it was.' He sat down on the sofa, the guitar on his lap. 'I don't know what she meant really. I don't remember anything bad, he was always nice to me—when he was here, that was.'

'I just wish I'd had the chance to meet him, that's all.' Patrick took the guitar from Kim and tried a few testing chords.

'Yeah,' said Kim with a sympathetic smile. 'Specially as you might have been his only child. It's tough he died without knowing about you.'

'Don't you need a plectrum for this?' said Patrick, swallowing down the lump that had risen stubbornly in his throat.

'Nah,' said Kim, standing up and taking the guitar back. He went over and put on a cassette. The music came through only one of the speakers at first, and the room echoed with the sharp vibrant clack of castanets and the thud of stamping feet. Kim drummed away on the body of the guitar, his expression rapt as though he was completely absorbed. Suddenly there was a hoarse shout from the other speaker and then the whole thing burst into life with a rush of guitars and the plaintive notes of raw flamenco. Once the music was under way, Kim joined in, both playing and singing. The sound was helped by his naturally husky voice, but the demands of the music were too much for him, and after a while he gave up.

'You have to be born to it to do it properly,' he said. 'And it can get boring when they drone on and on.'

But Patrick thought the music infinitely sad and beautiful. He sat there watching Kim's small square fingers move idly over the strings. 'Does *your* father play?' he asked when Kim stopped.

Kim shrugged. 'S'pose so. He was in the group with Cody.'

'Do you see much of him?'

'Nah.' Kim banged the heel of his hand against the guitar in time to the last crescendo of music.

'Do you wish you did?'

'Nah.' Patrick had the feeling that Kim wanted to end this conversation. Then, out of the blue, he said, 'Fathers are no big deal, take it from me. I can't say I'd be devastated if I never saw mine again.'

'Does your mother see him at all?'

Kim shook his head. 'No, they were divorced years ago.'

'How long were they married?'

'I dunno.' After a little pause, Kim added, 'They made her marry him 'cause she was expecting me.'

'They?' asked Patrick cautiously, sensing a certain aggression in Kim's tone.

'Her father, Justina, Cody—I dunno.' Kim rubbed the back of his hand to and fro across his forehead. 'It was such a fucking mess in this house until Carew came.'

'In what way?' Patrick ventured.

'In every fucking way.'

Patrick stared at him, wanting to delve further but wary of upsetting him. 'So you're nearly as fatherless as I am?' he said at last.

Kim didn't answer but gave the guitar a great thump and burst into a mad little frenzy of playing and singing. When he finally stopped, he began to laugh as though it had all been one big joke. 'It's a miracle I grew up to be so normal,' he grinned.

'Normal!' Patrick said, shaking his head and laughing too.

They played snooker to the sounds of flamenco. The games were short because Kim was a far superior player and wouldn't give an inch. He was a bad winner, cocky and bragging as soon as he was in the lead and making a meal of his final pots when Patrick hardly got to the table. But Patrick still enjoyed himself, and not just because of the thrill of being here in this house; he was becoming oddly fascinated with Kim.

They were nearing the end of their third game when Leah put her head round the door.

'Would you like a drink?' she asked, smiling at Patrick.

Kim swung round from the table. 'A couple of lagers would go down well, Mum,' he said.

'I meant coffee, actually.' She came into the

225

room. Her hair was wet and combed flat against her head as though she'd just come from the shower, and she'd changed into jeans and a white tank top.

'Lager helps me sleep,' said Kim, positioning himself to pot the final black.

'Then you should sleep for the rest of the week, judging by the cans out on the lawn.' She smiled indulgently at him, then looked at Patrick. 'What would you like, Patrick?'

He glanced at Kim leaning over the table. 'You,' he mouthed at her, then said out loud. 'Nothing thanks, I'm driving.'

Kim hit the ball, shouted, 'Yes!' and swung round again. 'Stay here the night. You haven't got to get back for anything, have you?'

'Well, not really, but...' He looked helplessly at Leah.

'Yes, why don't you? We've got plenty of room.' She rested a hand on his back. 'It's so nice for Kim to have company. He gets bored when he's confined to quarters.' She moved her hand to his waist. 'And I'll feel safer with two men in the house.'

Patrick's heart began to pound; he felt ecstatic. 'OK, I will.' He gave a great happy smile, smothering it with a yawn to stop it going on and on.

'Tired?' she said, giving his back a little pat before removing her hand.

'No, not really.' He smiled again, taking in a gulp of her soapy fragrance. 'You're looking much better,' he said.

'Did I look awful before then?'

He hesitated, not sure how to answer in front of Kim. But it was Kim who spoke. 'Stop fishing for compliments, Mother,' he said, scooping the balls back into the triangle ready for the next game. 'And go and get our drinks.'

'See what I have to put up with?' smiled Leah.

Kim clapped his hands at her. 'Don't try and get Patrick on your side. I'm getting him out of his goody-goody ways.'

She gave a little affectionate growl and tugged the back of Kim's hair. Patrick watched, wishing he had this sort of relationship with his mother.

They played until after midnight, drinking and talking between games, and were amiably drunk when they finally went to bed. Patrick hadn't wanted to drink so much; he felt certain he would be spending the night with Leah. He wasn't sure how it would happen, but he was confident it would. She came to say goodnight to them about eleven, kissing Kim, then coming over and raising her face as though she expected to do the same to him. Taken by surprise, he bent and brushed his lips clumsily against her cheek. Kim seemed unconcerned, and Patrick reminded himself how freely and openly this family bestowed their affections.

He spent the next hour fighting the growing haze of intoxication, aware of having to guard his tongue as, relaxed with alcohol, they laughed and joked and swapped confidences. How easy it would be to let slip the biggest secret of all.

Kim showed him up to his room. It was on its own at the end of the landing on the opposite side of the stairs to Leah's. The bed was not made up, and Kim gigglingly helped him stuff pillows in pillowcases and the duvet in its cover. Patrick felt an odd sense of disappointment, expecting Leah to have done this, carefully preparing it all for him. But after Kim had gone, thumping noisily along the landing, Patrick had the notion that perhaps it was a hint that she wasn't expecting him to sleep in this bed at all. He lay there in the darkness, wondering what to do and whether she might be waiting for him. Never had he stayed anywhere so quiet and dark. He wanted to go to the bathroom but was almost frightened to move, worried that any noise he made would echo through the house. But in the end he had to. Out on the landing he heard the sound of a radio coming from Kim's room. It was turned down low, but enough to cover the sound of his footsteps.

He splashed cold water over his face to sober himself up. If only he had the courage to go to Leah. Back in bed he tortured himself with the thought that he was going to miss this chance of sleeping with her. He began to count, promising himself that when he reached one hundred he would get out of bed and go to her. But long before he reached even fifty, his thoughts had merged into dreams. He found himself climbing into bed beside her, only to discover that Carew was there.

He woke with a start, trying to focus his eyes in the inky darkness. She was sitting on the edge of the bed.

'I didn't know whether to wake you,' she

228

whispered with a soft little laugh. She was wearing only the scarlet kimono, and slipped it off as she spoke. 'Did you want me to?'

'Yes, yes...oh, Leah,' he murmured, pulling her under the duvet with him.

'You knew I'd come, didn't you?' she said, wriggling up against him.

'Yes, yes,' he whispered, running his hands down over her buttocks and pulling her so close that it felt almost as good as if he'd already penetrated her. She twisted her arm free and held up a fist to let him feel the ring of rubber in her palm. But when he went to take it, she whispered, 'I'll do it.' She slid her hands down between his legs, caressing him as she went, then trailed her fingers slowly up again. 'You must have been dreaming about it,' she giggled against his shoulder.

'No, I'm like a fast car,' he said, licking at the lobe of her ear. 'Nought to sixty in five seconds.'

'I love it when you're like this,' she murmured, hooking an arm round his neck and a leg round his back.

'Do you?' he breathed, pushing his hands up under her breasts. 'I'll always be like this with you.' He carefully eased his thumbs across her nipples. They felt large and soft and slightly damp. He bent his head and put his lips to one, waiting a moment to see if she stopped him. 'And what about you?' he whispered against her skin. 'What's your rate of acceleration like?'

She giggled again, tilting her pelvis towards him and rubbing her heel up and down between

229

his buttocks. 'Put your foot down and find out.'

His own soft laughter was smothered against her neck, and lost in a sigh of pleasure as he felt her nipple stiffen between his fingers.

She left before dawn, not creeping away while he slept as she had at Mansour's, but extricating herself from his arms as he started to kiss her on waking.

'You always go away from me,' he said, flinging over on to his back and kicking the duvet from his legs.

'I have to. The baby wakes early.'

But soon after she'd left, Patrick heard the phone ring. It was picked up at once, and he knew instinctively that it was Carew, and that was why she'd gone. He rolled on to his side and punched a fist into the pillow, screwing his knuckles into its softness as he imagined her chatting away, perhaps even saying she missed him. But what did it matter? He relaxed, knowing it didn't matter at all; it would only be pretence. She didn't love Carew, he was quite sure of that. He turned over again and curled back to sleep.

## Chapter 13

Patrick lingered over washing and dressing, putting off the moment when he would have to go down and face them all. This was very different from yesterday morning, stumbling

230

downstairs hungover and surrounded by friends who knew what he'd been doing. The act he would have to put on with Leah was going to be bad enough; facing Kim was something he didn't relish at all.

But when he finally went downstairs Kim wasn't there. Tanya and Leah were sitting at the kitchen table, both engrossed in newspapers while pop music blared from a radio perched on the bread bin. Leah looked up and smiled but it was Tanya who spoke first.

'There's some bacon and some tomatoes for you in the Aga,' she said, pointing a thumb over her shoulder. 'Fry yourself an egg to go with them.'

'Right. Er, thanks.' He went over to the Aga. The twin lids were up and a frying pan was half over one of the rings. He moved it to the centre of the ring but it didn't feel very hot, nothing like the hotplates on the electric cooker at home. He looked down for some kind of dial but there wasn't one, and he wondered if you had to close one of the lids. 'I'm not sure how you do this,' he said, holding a tentative hand over the ring to test its heat.

Leah put down her paper and came over to him. Without a word she moved the pan to the other ring, then broke an egg into it, smiled up at him, and broke another.

'I expect you're hungry, aren't you?' she said.

He nodded, feeling an instant longing to touch her. She had on the white nightdress and red kimono again, and looked as if she had

231

just crawled from bed, her hair falling round her face and shoulders in a mass of knotted curls, and her cheeks flushed and puffy. Her lips also looked vaguely swollen, and redder than usual. My doing, he thought. She's stamped with everything I did to her, her whole body probably looks the same. She reached across for the egg slice, purposely leaning against him.

There was the scrape of a chair and a rustle of newspaper as Tanya stood up. 'I can't wait any longer for Kim,' she said. 'I don't want to be late opening up again. You'll have to bring him in, Leah. Or perhaps you could drop him off on your way home, Patrick.'

'Yeah, sure.' His heart sank. He knew there was no reason for him to stay here any longer, but Tanya putting it into words made him feel he was already being wrenched away.

Leah carried on with the eggs, she didn't even look round. But as soon as Tanya had gone, Patrick put his hands on her shoulders, swivelling her round to face him. 'Will you come back with me?'

'What do you mean? I can't come in the car with Kim.'

'No, I mean in your own car. Come back to Cambridge with me, stay a few days.'

'I can't. What could I tell them?'

'Make up something. Please, Leah, just for a few days.'

She tapped the egg slice playfully against his cheek. 'I should think you've had enough of me to last you a week. A month,' she added, tracing a circle on his face where she'd streaked it with fat.

He snatched her hand away, rough and impatient. 'It's not just sleeping with you, you know it's not just that. I want to be with you—while we've got the chance.'

'Here,' she said reaching for a tea towel, 'wipe your face.'

He gave it a brief rub. 'Is it clean?'

'Let me see.' He bent his head and she kissed his cheek. 'We have to be careful, Patrick.'

'I know, I know.' He put a hand to his face again. 'I need a shave. I've got my things in the car.'

'No, leave it, you look older.'

'Do you wish I was?'

'I don't care about your age.' She put a sudden finger to her lips. 'Shh, Kim's coming.'

Patrick let out an impatient breath. This precious time with Carew away seemed to be constantly stolen by other people.

In a flash she had tipped the eggs on to a plate with the bacon and tomatoes, and Patrick was sitting at the table by the time Kim came sauntering into the kitchen.

'Is there any left for me?' he said, sidling up behind Patrick and quickly swiping a rasher of bacon from his plate.

'I'm just doing yours,' said Leah. 'Leave Patrick alone and stop behaving like a hooligan.'

'It's all right, I'm used to him now,' said Patrick, swinging round to grab Kim's wrist and twisting it until he dropped the bacon.

'Ouch.' Kim laughed and jerked away. 'See,

233

he's not as angelic as you think,' he said, rubbing his wrist.

'He's angelic compared to you.'

Kim sat down opposite him. 'Blue-eyed boy, eh?' he said good-naturedly, tapping his palms on the table in time to the music. 'Do you want to borrow a comb and stuff?'

'It's OK, thanks, I've got my things in the car. I came here straight from London.'

Kim looked surprised. 'You didn't say you'd been to London.'

'I went home—to a party. I told you.' Patrick filled his mouth with food and began to chew. 'To celebrate our A-level passes,' he mumbled.

'Ah, that's why you look so debauched. Too much...' Kim raised his hand as if he was lifting a glass to his mouth. 'Doesn't he look debauched, Mum?' He repeated the word, as pleased with himself as if he'd just invented it.

Leah put a plate of breakfast in front of him. 'No, he doesn't, not in the slightest. Now get a move on or you'll be in Tanya's bad books again. Patrick's going to give you a lift in.'

As soon as Kim had finished eating, he was up from the table and asking Patrick if he was ready to go. Leah had gone upstairs to fetch Jo-jo.

'I'd better say goodbye to your mother.' Patrick got reluctantly to his feet. 'We'll shout up on our way out,' said Kim. 'She could be ages fiddling around with the baby.'

Leah came to the top of the stairs, Jo-jo in her arms.

'Thanks for the breakfast, and everything,' Patrick called up to her.

'Come on.' Kim gave him a little shove. 'You don't have to try for extra Brownie points with my mother, she already likes you.'

It suddenly felt as though Kim was responsible for him having to leave, and Patrick marched off out to the car with resentment burning in his chest. He knew it was ridiculous, Kim was the one who'd invited him to stay, and the only one who could invite him back again. In the meantime there was nothing he could do but go back to Cambridge and wait for Leah to phone.

But on the drive to the shop, Kim said, 'Do you have to go back to Cambridge this morning? Why don't you come to the shop with me? We could have a laugh.'

'I ought to get back. I've got reading and stuff to do.'

'You can have one day off surely,' said Kim. 'It's the holidays.'

'I know but...' Patrick hesitated. A short while ago the thought of getting back to Cambridge had been the last thing on his mind. But now, he wasn't sure; he did have things to do, and there could well be messages and post for him. But Kim's offer was tempting. He weighed it against the chance that Leah might phone him today. And Ginny was sure to phone after the hasty way he'd left. He ought to get back.

'You could help me with my catalogue.'

'What?' Patrick glanced across at him. 'What catalogue? What are you talking about?'

'A mail order catalogue. That's how I'm going to sell my love potion. I'm going to make a fortune, you wait and see.' He rubbed his palms together, dashing them hard against each other and making the signet rings he wore on both hands click like castanets. 'I've got other things to sell as well.'

Patrick looked towards him once more. 'I'm beginning to wonder about you,' he said.

'Wonder all you like, but I'm telling you, there's money in it. You can have a cut if you help me.'

'Help you do what?'

'The catalogue. How many times do I have to tell you something? I need someone who's good with words to write the advertising blurb. And you've got transport. I need that for something else I'm planning.' He clicked the rings again in a little burst of enthusiasm. 'Go on, stay on a few days and help me. We'll go fifty-fifty,' he added, dangling a final carrot.

It could have been ten per cent, one per cent, nothing.

'Stay on at your house, you mean?' said Patrick.

'Whoa, back!' shouted Kim. 'You've passed the fucking turning.'

'It's all this high finance,' said Patrick, craning round to look over his shoulder and then screeching back in reverse.

'Will you then?'

Kim, I love you. 'You'll have to phone your mother and ask her,' he said, smiling to himself at how, not long ago, he'd been blaming Kim for having to leave.

'She won't mind. I've told you, she really

likes you. Carew was quite impressed by you as well. They don't always like my friends. Not that I've got many round here. They're all—fucking hell!' Kim yelled, bracing himself against the dashboard as Patrick shot forward and swerved round the corner.

'You should put your seatbelt on,' said Patrick. Especially now you're so precious to me, he thought, smiling again.

Tanya was not so excited about the idea of them being in the shop together. 'I hope this doesn't mean you're going to spend all the time fart-arsing about with those bloody drugs,' she said when Kim told her Patrick was staying. Kim looked genuinely indignant and denied it, but she was still sceptical. 'You two are getting a bit too thick,' she said.

But later on, when Patrick had served a few people, taking to it like a duck to water, she relented and went off to do some shopping, leaving them in charge.

As soon as she'd gone, Patrick insisted that Kim phone home. He lingered at Kim's elbow, and halfway through the call he pulled the receiver from him. 'It was Kim's idea, I hope you don't mind,' he said.

'I don't mind at all,' said Leah, her voice completely neutral.

But Patrick wanted more than this from her. 'I don't want to be a nuisance,' he said.

'Patrick, I can't imagine any way in which you could be a nuisance,' came back down the line.

'Oh, I can.' He felt reckless. 'You just don't know me very well.'

'I think I do,' came back, almost whispered.

'Come on,' said Kim, 'hurry up. I want to get on before Tanya comes back.'

'I'll see you later,' Patrick managed before Kim took the receiver from him.

They spent the next half-hour making a list of all the potions that Kim had already bottled. Patrick was amazed by what he saw. Kim seemed to have been working on this for months, maybe years. He had all sorts of herbal remedies made up and neatly stacked away in labelled bottles. Some looked a bit amateurish with handwritten instructions and second-hand corks but Kim brushed this aside and said they could easily redo them. When it came to the love potion, Kim was even more enthusiastic. He hauled up a giant demijohn from under the worktop and carefully pulled out the stopper.

'I've made this since last week,' he said, taking a long glass rod and giving the liquid a thorough stir. 'Pity you didn't try what I gave you, I can't be certain that I've got it right until it's tested.'

Patrick said nothing but Kim's intent expression and the sound of the rod clanking on the sides of the demijohn made him vaguely uneasy. Although common sense told him that Kim's claims for the love potion were nonsense, he did wonder about the power of the aphrodisiac content. Not so long ago he'd read a newspaper report about a man who'd given a young girl what he claimed was a cold cure when really it was a sexual stimulant. The name of it came back to him now.

'Do you put amyl nitrate in that?' he asked.

Kim frowned and drew in his breath through pursed lips, as if Patrick had said something quite scandalous. 'Whatever gave you that idea?' he said, whisking the liquid into a froth.

'Is it that cantharides stuff then?' said Patrick, watching the trails of honey-coloured bubbles slip down the bulging sides of the glass.

'Tumera aphrodisiaca,' said Kim with a mysterious little grin. 'Damiana to you. And I use lemon verbena.'

'Is that what makes it golden?' Patrick was becoming intrigued by the little sunbursts of colour.

Kim gave a vague shake of his head. 'It'll change to blue when I put the time crystals in. They're white but...' He withdrew the rod, placed it carefully on the worktop, and rubbed his hands together, clicking the rings. 'It's the way the ingredients react with one another. They echo the chemistry between human beings.'

'Is there any madness in your family?' said Patrick.

The smile left Kim's face. 'Don't take the piss.'

'I only asked.'

'One minute you act interested, the next you start fucking about.' Kim rammed the stopper back in the demijohn and accidentally knocked the glass rod onto the floor. 'Oh shit! That's your fault,' he shouted as it shattered into a thousand pieces.

'Calm down,' said Patrick, raising his palms. 'I am interested. Honest. Now tell me how

239

you're going to make this vast fortune.'

'Are you serious? Do you really want to help me?'

'If there's money in it, yes.'

Kim leant against the worktop chewing on a knuckle, then was suddenly all smiles again. He kicked the splinters of glass out of the way and crawled under the worktop, emerging seconds later with a new-looking cardboard box. 'Check Tanya hasn't come back,' he said.

Patrick went and stuck his head round the door. 'All clear. What the hell have you got there, Kim?'

'Come and see.'

Patrick gingerly flicked open the flaps of the lid and peered in. It was filled with tiny dark brown bottles, their lids fitted with rubber drop dispensers. Six had white labels and six had blue; all were printed with a new moon emblem and a row of tiny flowers round the edge. Patrick lifted one out. '"Moon Rocket",' he read. '"Sexual energy on the wane? Take three drops of Moon Rocket and see *your* moon wax beyond your dreams."' He burst out laughing and picked up a bottle with a white label. '"Moon Flower."' He swivelled the bottle round to read the other side of the label. '"Ladies, do you..."' he began. 'Where the hell did you get these, Kim?'

'I sent off for them. They were a bit pricey so I couldn't get the full range.'

'How much?'

'Tenner a bottle.'

Patrick's mouth fell open.

'I'm going to resell them at twelve quid. Or maybe fifteen.'

'Can you do that? Isn't it illegal?'

'There you go again, worrying about rules and regulations. Of course it's not illegal. Anyway, I'm going to change the labels and sell them with my own stuff.'

'Do you know what's in them?'

'Some of it.'

'And is it the same as you put in your love potion?'

'Not exactly,' said Kim evasively.

'But it's the same sort of thing,' persisted Patrick.

'I use my own ingredients. These,' he indicated the box of little bottles, 'are made mostly from herbs imported from China.'

'But wherever the stuff comes from, it's only herbs or drugs. Whatever you mix up, it can't make someone fall in love. That's a load of crap.'

'Why is it? Some drugs can alter the way your mind works. Take cannabis, for instance. And Ecstasy and speed. They can make you feel good, they can make you feel bad. Why shouldn't there be drugs and herbs that can make you fall in love—with a little experimenting, of course.'

'OK, say there was,' said Patrick. 'How could you guarantee that you'd fancy one person and not another?'

'That's done with the time crystals.'

'What are they made of then?'

'A secret ingredient,' said Kim, perfectly straight-faced.

'It's your brain that's made of secret ingredients.'

'You believe what you like, I know what I know.'

Patrick held one of the tiny bottles up between forefinger and thumb. 'And do you know who's going to part with twelve quid for this?'

'Hundreds of people. Thousands.'

'Who said?'

'They told me—the woman at New Moon Dream Products told me. We'll drive up there tomorrow, it's only about eighty miles.'

Patrick stared at him, a smile of disbelief spreading across his face.

'You won't laugh when you see the set-up. There's definitely potential in this.'

'It's the present I'm worrying about,' said Patrick. 'Who's paying for the petrol, for a start?'

'Your tank's half full,' said Kim. 'We'll put it against the free meals you'll be getting for the next few days.'

'OK, it's a deal,' said Patrick, unable to resist adding, 'a very good one.'

Kim's eyes settled on him for a moment, his expression blank, then he smiled and said, 'By the way, don't tell anyone about this, especially not my mother.'

By the time Tanya returned, they were back out in the shop and convincingly busy tidying shelves. The rest of the day passed quickly.

Customers came and went. Some bought things, others just browsed; many of the younger ones stopped to chat. Kim seemed very popular and flirted with them all, girls and boys alike. Patrick was soon doing the same, only he stuck to the girls. At closing time, as they brought in the garments from the doorway, he was surprised how much he'd enjoyed himself.

They ate out on the terrace and lit the lanterns. Leah had put on the white dress with the gold braid, and apart from the food—one course of beefburgers and chips—it reminded Patrick of the first time he'd come to the house. But tonight she was sitting next to him. He thought again of how she had pulled away from Carew, and in a secret move beneath the folds of the tablecloth, he felt for her hand himself. She responded by twining her fingers round his.

Tanya was making sarcastic remarks about the meal. 'You must have spent hours cooking this,' she said, lifting a whole beefburger on her fork.

'Don't eat it if you don't like it,' said Leah, smiling sweetly across the table at her while she squeezed Patrick's hand.

'I'll have yours,' said Kim, angling for the beefburger with his fork.

'Here.' Tanya tossed it on to his plate. 'I hate the bloody things.'

Patrick imagined someone behaving like this in his house. It was the first time he'd thought of home all day. He glanced at Leah and she

243

eased her hand away and carried on eating. 'Do you like the beefburgers, Patrick?' she asked, her voice slightly anxious.

'Yes, they're lovely,' he said.

Tanya laughed, and to his great humiliation Patrick felt himself blushing. He gave an exaggerated yawn, a hand to his face.

'You'd better not keep Patrick up so late tonight,' said Leah, looking first at him then across at Kim.

'He's got no stamina. A day's work and he's finished,' said Kim, but he began yawning too.

'You don't call what you two did work, do you?' said Tanya, leaning over to tip the rest of her meal onto Kim's plate.

Under cover of their banter, Patrick felt for Leah's hand again. After a few minutes, she said that she'd go and make Tanya a sandwich. But when she went to stand up, Patrick kept hold of her, and she sat there with her hand trapped in his. 'Do you want to come and help me, Patrick?' she smiled at him. 'You can make some coffee.'

'Yeah, all right,' he said, releasing her. It felt like an exciting game doing these secret things in front of Kim and Tanya, and as soon as they were in the kitchen, he shut the door and pushed her against it.

'So you're staying here for a few days, are you?' she said teasingly, hands spread on his chest to hold him off.

'I'm going to stay here for ever,' he said very softly, his lips already closing over hers.

# Chapter 14

Once more the phone rang in the early hours just after Leah had left him. He'd asked her if it was Carew, slipping the question in as they lay there talking after making love. They'd talked late into the night, heads close together on the pillow, whispering and laughing in the darkness. But when Patrick had mentioned Carew, she'd said only a simple yes, then put her hand over his mouth, something she did whenever he asked her things she didn't want to answer. He fell asleep soon after she'd gone, the words of a little song she'd been singing quietly to him echoing in his mind.

The tune was still with him the next morning. He whistled it as he ambled downstairs, confident and happy. In the hall, the smell of frying bacon came to meet him, and the sound of raised voices.

'It's the busiest day, you know very well it is,' Tanya was saying. She looked up as Patrick came through the door. 'Is this your idea to go swarming off for the day?'

Before he had a chance to answer, Kim said, 'Don't start on him, it's all down to me.'

'You couldn't go if it wasn't for his car,' snapped Tanya.

'Exactly,' said Kim with one of his annoyingly

innocent little smiles. 'I'm making the most of him while he's here.'

By the looks of it, they had already eaten. Kim was smartly dressed and his hair was slicked back and held with a rubber band.

'Your breakfast's on the Aga,' said Tanya with a wave of her hand in that direction.

Patrick went to get it and found Leah there, Jo-jo on her hip while she searched through the baby clothes on the clotheshorse.

'Hello, Patrick,' she said, smiling round at him. 'Sleep well?'

'Very,' he said, smiling back at her.

She straightened up, a tiny blue T-shirt in her hand. 'Stop moaning,' she called across to Tanya. 'I'll come and help you for a while.'

'That's it, let him get his own way again. And what about Jo-jo?'

'I'll bring him with me of course.'

'That's the last thing I need, a screaming baby in my shop.'

'Please yourself,' said Leah, taking a couple more things off the clotheshorse. 'I'm going back to bed if you don't want me to come with you.'

'Of course I want you to,' said Tanya crossly.

Leah went to sit at the table and began dressing the baby. 'And it's not your shop, it's Carew's,' she said, looking up as she pulled off Jo-jo's sleeping suit.

'Does the shop really belong to Carew?' Patrick asked Kim, after Leah and Tanya had gone. 'I thought you said it was Tanya's.'

'She rents it off him.'

'But I thought it used to belong to your great-great-grandfather or somebody,' said Patrick.

'It did.' Kim sniffed and looked away.

Patrick could see that he didn't want to talk about it. 'Well, how come it belongs to Carew then?' he persisted, sure that if it was the other way round and Kim wanted to know something, he'd wheedle on until he found out.

'It was left to Tanya, she got into debt, Carew bought it when he married my mother. Satisfied?'

'He must be loaded,' said Patrick lightly, determined not to let Kim's tone annoy him.

Kim's head jerked round. 'She didn't marry him for his money, if that's what you're trying to make out.'

'I never said she did.' They both fell silent. Patrick finished the piece of toast he was eating, and stood up. 'We'd better clear this lot up before we go, hadn't we?'

'Nah, leave it, Tanya'll do it when she comes home,' said Kim, back to his smiling self. 'Come on, we'd better get you smartened up.'

'What?'

'We want to be taken seriously. We're businessmen, don't forget.'

'I haven't got anything else with me.' Patrick glanced down at his jeans and crumpled shirt, then back at Kim. 'What are you plotting now? Your clothes won't fit me.'

'Follow me,' said Kim, looking suspiciously pleased with himself. But when Kim led him upstairs and into Leah's bedroom, Patrick hung back and shook his head. 'I'm not wearing any of Carew's gear.' He didn't even want to be in their bedroom with Kim.

'Don't be stupid, it's far too big.' Kim went over to a walk-in cupboard built in an alcove. 'You can wear your father's.'

Patrick watched in stunned silence as Kim squeezed between two packed rails of clothes. 'Didn't he take all his things with him?' he said quietly as Kim emerged with a couple of suits protected in plastic bags.

'Obviously not. I know they're his because my mother told me. Justina was going to burn them apparently.' He held one up. It looked very expensive and surprisingly undated with the longish single-breasted jacket.

'I'm not wearing it,' said Patrick suddenly. 'Put it back.'

'Why not? You'll look the part in this.'

'Put it back, Kim.'

'Don't be—'

'He's dead and I'm not wearing it.'

'Why not? I would if it was my father.'

'Yeah, because you're fucking weird, everything you do is weird, especially your fucking potions.'

Kim threw the suits on the bed. 'And you're fucking boring.'

'If that's what you think, find your own...' Patrick broke off, stuck his hands in his pockets and turned away, staring down at the carpet. The last thing he wanted was to fall out with Kim and throw away precious days at this house over a few hasty words.

After a minute or two, Kim said, 'I didn't know you'd feel like that about it.' His tone had changed again, it was conciliatory, apologetic almost.

'Well, it's not your father, is it?' said Patrick grudgingly.

'OK, I'm sorry.'

Patrick allowed himself a look at the suits. He'd never owned anything as smart or expensive, though he was quite interested in clothes. Kim had taken one out of its cover, and he picked it up. 'Did you ever see him in this?' he asked.

Kim sat on the edge of the bed, hands held loosely between his knees, his head slightly bent. 'I don't remember. We're still going, aren't we?' he said, looking up.

'Yeah, OK.' For the first time since they'd met, Patrick felt he was the one in control. He walked over to Leah's full-length mirror and slipped on the jacket. He buttoned and unbuttoned it, slid his hands in and out of the pockets, taking his time—and telling himself that he was doing this to stay friends with Kim.

'You look like the guy in the Armani advert,' said Kim. 'All you need now is a black polo neck.'

'And a Rolex and Ray-bans.'

Kim laughed, breaking off almost at once to sit in silence again. Patrick picked up a comb from Leah's dressing table and ran it through his hair. Then he picked up a spray can and angled it at his head, giving the button a few short bursts.

'That's deodorant,' giggled Kim.

Patrick nearly dropped it. 'Fucking hell, why didn't you tell me?' He turned to Kim. 'Give us the trousers then.'

New Moon Dream Products was run by two women working from a converted Nissen hut. Patrick was nervous at first, imagining that the women eyed them suspiciously. But Kim wasn't in the least daunted; they'd hardly got inside the building when he launched into his planned spiel about having just opened a shop selling herbal remedies.

'The premises belong to my sister,' he said confidently. 'She's a pharmacist but, er, Patrick and I,' he paused to indicate Patrick standing dumbly admiring beside him, 'we're taking over a section to set up on our own.'

'Does she approve of this sort of stuff?' said one of the women. She was the friendliest and had introduced herself as Kelly. The other one listened but said little.

'She just hopes it's going to be a money-spinner for us,' said Kim.

'It will be if you get the right customers,' said the woman.

'Who are they?' asked Patrick, feeling he ought to say something, though his question earned him a black look from Kim.

'Well,' said the woman, with a this-is-between-you-and-me look. 'A lot of it's bought by old guys chasing after young girls and finding they can't get it up. Pathetic really, but there you go. It started in the States, a lot of it over on the

West Coast. You know what it's like, the thing they have about eternal youth. They think they can buy it.'

'But there's a lot of research to show it works,' said Kim, sounding so knowledgeable and serious that Patrick had to look away.

'Yes, there is,' said the other woman. 'I'm a trained herbalist. I've studied which herbs work on different parts of the body. The Chinese have used them for centuries. It may be big business now, but all the claims have a sound basis in ancient practice.'

'And we've got our reports,' said Kelly with a smile. She took them through to a little office and showed them a file detailing what appeared to be bona fide tests of the products on members of the public. 'As you can see, they're not just to help cure impotency, plenty of young people use them for extra stimulation.'

'Could we have some copies of these?' said Kim. 'For advertising.'

'I don't see why not.' Kelly looked at her colleague.

Patrick flicked through the file, hardly able to keep a straight face at what he read. Kim, meanwhile, had started to discuss supplies.

'We couldn't give you much of a discount unless you buy in bulk,' Patrick heard the less friendly woman say. 'And we'd want cash up front.'

'No problem,' Patrick chipped in. She was beginning to annoy him. 'We'll sort out what we want and get back to you. All we want now are a few samples for our catalogue.'

251

Kim looked at him with a flicker of a smile, and Kelly pursed her lips and said, 'That should be OK. Once you get going you can open an account with us.'

Patrick smiled at her, growing more confident. 'Have you tried any of them yourself?' he asked.

'Of course,' she said, straight-faced. 'Have you?'

'Like all herbal remedies, they should be used with care,' butted in the other woman.

'I'll remember that,' said Patrick.

'My partner likes to experiment,' said Kim, giving Patrick's arm a tap with his knuckles. 'He thinks word-of-mouth recommendation is the best way to promote sales.'

'I'm sure he's right,' said Kelly. She looked in her late twenties and reminded Patrick of a lady doctor, the way she stood there with her hands in the pockets of her unbuttoned white overall.

'We'd need references for an account,' the other woman was saying.

'Yes, of course,' said Patrick, a little high on the whole charade. This was even more fun than the shop. 'We do have other suppliers,' he added for good measure.

Back in the car, Kim burst into whoops of triumph.

'Christ, I never guessed it would be that easy,' he said. 'I thought there might be some sort of restriction on their sales. It was definitely that suit.' He turned laughing to Patrick. 'You could persuade a woman to part with anything in that.'

A tinge of unease stirred in Patrick; it wasn't guilt or regret that he'd worn the suit, it was more a feeling that he was doing something irreversible, like things said that could never be unsaid. He aimed a breezy punch at Kim and rammed down the accelerator so that they sped off with a screech of tyres, like two robbers leaving the scene of a crime. Most of the way home he broke the speed limit, overtaking with barely enough time to tuck back in before a bend or an approaching car, taking chances he wouldn't normally take.

A couple of miles before home, they pulled up in a layby and Patrick changed into a tracksuit he had in the car, in case Leah was back before them.

Despite instructions to Patrick not to tell anybody where they'd been, Kim was soon throwing out hints himself, saying that they were going to set up in business together but couldn't reveal what it was yet.

'You're going back to school,' said Leah firmly. She was busy changing Jo-jo and didn't even bother to look round. 'Even if it means starting at a different one.'

'OK, OK,' said Kim impatiently. 'I know that. We're going to do it in the evenings and weekends.'

Leah looked over her shoulder now. 'Patrick will be at university soon.' She skewed right round. 'When does the term actually start, Patrick?'

'October.'

'Oh, you've got a few weeks yet,' she smiled.

'Yeah.' He ran a hand through his hair. The thought had been worrying him a bit; he'd found a list of books he was supposed to be reading in the tracksuit bottoms he'd put on earlier. 'I think I ought to flip over to Cambridge tomorrow morning and make sure there're no messages or anything for me.'

Tanya clamped a hand on Kim's shoulder. 'You're not going with him. You owe me a day so don't get any ideas.'

Kim shoved her off, and she began tormenting him by tugging at his hair. Under cover of their horseplay, Leah said quietly, 'You will come back to us, won't you?'

Patrick nodded, staring at her, frustrated at having her within a few feet of him but not being able to touch her.

'I thought we might go out for the day on Sunday,' she said, louder, picking up Jo-jo and swinging him into the air. 'All of us. We could go to the coast, have lunch out.'

They were still lounging at the table. Tanya had cooked the meal tonight. It had been a delicious seafood pasta served with olives, tiny cherry tomatoes and mangetout peas, none of which Patrick had ever tried before. Then she'd made them a whipped-up confection with ice cream, chocolate mousse and ground nuts. Patrick had thanked her and said how nice it was, and she'd retorted, 'I'll let you do the washing up then.'

He was gathering up the plates when Leah

made her suggestion about going out on Sunday.

'Yes, all right,' said Tanya. She gave Kim a shove. 'Help Patrick.'

'Fuck off,' he said irritably.

Leah frowned but said nothing. Tanya gave Kim a final slap, then went off to watch the television. Leah followed her.

'Leave that, we'll do it after *Coronation Street*,' said Kim.

'I don't want to watch it,' said Patrick, disappointed that Leah hadn't offered to help him.

'Please yourself.' Kim mockingly draped a tea towel over Patrick's shoulder and went off with the others.

When Patrick went through to the sitting room, Tanya and Kim had an armchair each, and Leah was lying full length on the sofa with Jo-jo. Patrick hesitated a moment then went and perched on the arm of Kim's chair. Leah looked up. 'Come and sit with me,' she said, drawing her legs up beneath her. 'He'll only torment you.'

Kim immediately toppled him down on to his lap. 'No, I've got him now,' he said giving Patrick a noisy kiss on the cheek.

Patrick braced his hands on the arms of the chair, struggling to free himself as Kim gripped him round the waist. Through the soft material of the tracksuit he could feel the hard stub of Kim's cock. Leah laughed, and Patrick forced a laugh too, though he felt more like hitting Kim. He contented himself with a sharp elbow in Kim's ribs. Kim yelped and let him go, and he went and squeezed onto the end of the sofa, growing immediately hard himself on contact with Leah's bare feet and the sight of her smooth brown legs tucked up beside him.

The programme came to a finish; they watched on regardless, all except Leah who nestled against Jo-jo and closed her eyes, stretching her legs so that the sole of one foot was pressed against Patrick's thigh. He tried concentrating on the screen, making his own remarks about the programme along with Kim and Tanya. He even tried reading the inscriptions on the row of pewter mugs lined up on the mantelpiece. He could just make out the largest print: 'Presented to Auberon Carew on the...' Leah's toes wriggled against his leg and he enclosed them in his hand, hidden from the others by the mound of her hips. He would go to Cambridge early tomorrow and come back before Kim and Tanya got home from the shop. Plans unfolded in his head, driven by his desire to be with her like this, to sit with her in daylight, downstairs. To be able to kiss her, be with her in an ordinary way apart from the sex. His hand tightened round her foot, his forefinger grazing her sole. Instantly she jerked away, stifling laughter in a cough. Nobody took any notice, and he held onto her ankle, then ran his hand up her calf, coming to rest behind her knee. She tilted her leg a fraction, exposing the curve of her thigh. If only Kim and Tanya would disappear. He imagined what it would be like tomorrow, in this same position, free to do as they liked.

A burst of laughter, then applause came from the television. Kim and Tanya laughed too. Patrick kept watch, stroking soft circles against Leah's flesh, his fingers drawn irresistibly on beneath her skirt. Jo-jo had fallen sleep, and she lay there gazing down at him as though she was completely absorbed in the contours of his little face. By degrees, Patrick reached the bunched cotton of her pants, bulging at the groin like a tiny soft cushion, and more arousing even than her naked flesh. It was deliriously exciting to rub a finger against her. Within seconds she grew damp. He felt compelled to look at her, but her glazed expression was torture for him. In aching desperation he drew his hand away, and after a moment or two she sat up.

'Jo-jo asleep?' said Tanya, glancing round.

'Mmm.'

Tanya frowned. 'For God's sake pull your skirt down, Leah. You'll have poor Patrick getting hot flushes.'

Kim looked round now, and Leah jumped up from the sofa. 'Oh, shut up, you stupid bitch,' she said, and without another word she bundled Jo-jo up in her arms and marched out of the room.

'Big mouth,' said Kim, turning back to the television.

Patrick wanted to follow her but knew he mustn't. He'd never heard her snap at Tanya like that; she must be upset. He shouldn't have touched her in front of them—and with the baby asleep beside her. He was suddenly convinced it was the most shameful thing he'd ever done.

She'd think he didn't have any respect for her, and that all he wanted was sex. He sat there suffering torments of guilt until Kim suggested they go and play snooker.

But once in the games room Kim spread out the things they'd got from New Moon Dream Products and proposed they make a start on planning adverts.

'We can list a few items with a short explanation of what they do, and a few lines from these tests,' he said.

'Do you realise how much advertising costs?' said Patrick, but Kim was engrossed in reading.

'Listen to this,' he said, holding up one of the copies they'd been given. 'The woman says, "I felt far stronger vaginal sensations and experienced a very intense orgasm." And the man, "The effect hit me after fifteen minutes. I attained bigger erections than ever before." We might have to tone down the wording a bit.' He laughed and rubbed his hands together, clicking the rings. 'It's giving me a hard-on just reading about it. We're going to make a fortune out of this.'

Patrick didn't answer.

'What's up? Do you want a game first?'

'Just one, I'm shattered.' He was suddenly sick to death of Kim and his crude remarks; fed up with the whole day. But most of all he wanted to be with Leah, apologise for what he'd done. The more he thought about it, the worse it seemed.

'Do you want a drink before we start?'

'No, not tonight.' The thought of alcohol also

sickened him. He played one half-hearted game and then went off to bed.

Going past Leah's door, he stopped and listened, wanting to go in and make sure she would come to him. There wasn't a sound. Perhaps she had fallen asleep and forgotten him. He went on to his own room, feeling desperately miserable and lonely.

It was past midnight when she came. He was sitting on the edge of the bed fully dressed.

'What's the matter? Why aren't you in bed?' She went and turned on the bedside lamp then came and knelt on the floor in front of him, her hands on his knees. 'What is it?' she said softly, reaching up to push the hair from his forehead.

'I feel bad about...' He broke off and caught her wrists. 'You think this is only sex, don't you? You think that's all there is between us.'

She shook her head very slowly. 'Not as far as I'm concerned, it's not.'

He stared down at her. 'I wish I hadn't done what I did earlier.'

'So that's it.' Her voice dropped to a whisper. 'Why did you then, Patrick? Tell me why.'

'Because...because I love you so much, I always want to touch you.' He still gripped her wrists, and she leant over and kissed his knuckles.

'Then it's all right. Nothing's wrong if you love someone.'

'But do you love me?' He slid down on the carpet with her, holding her between his legs. 'Tell me the truth, do you really love me?'

259

'Are you testing me before you let me in bed with you?' she teased.

'Don't joke about it, I need to know.' As usual she wore only the scarlet kimono, and he wrapped it tight round her. 'You only say it when...'

'When I'm coming?' she finished for him. 'You still have a few hang-ups, don't you? Little things you won't say, or things you do and then regret.' She leant forward and brushed her lips very gently against his. 'But that's part of why I like you so much.'

'Like me? Is that it?'

'You're so troubled tonight.' She kissed him again. 'No, of course that's not it. I do like you, and I care about you like I care about Jo-jo and Kim. And,' she ducked her head down to look up into his face, 'I'm mad about you, completely and utterly crazy about you.'

He could only bury his head against her, sighing with relief somewhere between laughter and tears as though the greatest problem of his whole life had miraculously been solved.

'Better now?' she whispered.

It felt like the most special moment since he'd met her; the closest they'd ever been, and he wanted to wipe out anything that could spoil it.

'I've done things today that I didn't really want to.'

'With Kim?'

'Yeah, but he doesn't want me to tell anyone.'

'It's all right. He'll tell me in his own good time. Don't worry about it.' She looped her arms round his neck. 'Anything else?'

He hesitated, sorting through his mind for other things to tell her. 'I made my mother cry again before I came here,' he said finally.

'She'll forgive you. Mothers always do.'

But there was one more thing. Why it felt the most important of all, he had no idea. They were still sitting on the floor. It felt right somehow, all tied up with creeping out of bed and doing things you shouldn't. He shifted to a more comfortable position. 'There's something else I want to tell you.'

She yawned and reached up to drag a pillow from the bed. 'Come and whisper it,' she said, stretching out to lay her head on it.

But Patrick remained where he was, his back against the bed. 'This morning, after you'd gone, Kim and I came up to your bedroom. He got out one of my father's suits and I put it on. He wanted me to look smart—it was because of where we were going. I'm not blaming him,' he added quickly. 'I could have said no. I did at first. Then I changed my mind and I wore it.'

'Is that all?'

'You're not angry?'

'Why should I be? Which one was it, the dark one?' Patrick nodded and she rolled on to her side looking away from him across the room. 'Justina bought that for him. He wore it at my wedding. He was very vain. Conceited sometimes.' There was a wistful, almost dreamy tone to her voice. 'Still, he won't ever grow old now.' She rolled back again to face him. 'I bet you looked incredibly handsome. I wish

261

I'd seen you.' She was smiling. 'It might have been the one he was wearing when he met your mother. You can have it if you want—wear it and show her.'

The idea both repelled and attracted him. He imagined himself walking in with it on, Ginny's expression slowly changing as she recognised it. 'She probably wouldn't remember,' he said.

'You always remember everything about your first love.'

He shook his head. 'I don't think I could do that to her.'

'Why? Things like that—doing things you think are taboo,' there was a cajoling edge to her voice, 'are the best way to get close to someone.' She patted the carpet, and he crawled down beside her, face to face but not touching. 'We've done things together that I've never done with Carew, and things I don't think you've done before, right?' He nodded. 'And do you think we're close? Do you think I understand you?'

'Yes,' he murmured. 'Better than anyone.'

She moved nearer to him, her lips just an inch away. 'Listen. We're not going to make love tonight. I think you're a bit overdosed on sex. I'll stay and talk for a while longer then I'm going.' She clamped her hand over his mouth as he went to protest. 'And you need some sleep.'

He knew she was right but being sensible wasn't part of all this.

'But I've been waiting all day for you,' he said, working his tongue and teeth against her palm.

'I know, I know, but I think you need to calm down a little, we don't want to make any mistakes, do we?' She knelt up and backed away from him on her knees. 'And no masturbating after I've gone.' He smiled, sheepish and disarmed by her, and she moved further away. 'But I'm not sure I can trust you,' she said sitting on her haunches. 'What do you think?'

'I think...' He lunged at her, galvanized by desire and happiness. 'I think I won't let you go.'

## Chapter 15

Halfway up the stairs to his room, Patrick heard someone call him. It was Bel, one of the girls from the ground-floor flat.

'We've shoved some messages under your door,' she said. 'Your mother's phoned you three times.'

'OK, thanks.'

'My mother's the same—she thinks I've been kidnapped if I don't call her every week.'

He smiled briefly down at her.

'Oh, and there's some mail for you.' Bel indicated the row of pigeonholes by the door.

'I'll get it on my way out.' He started off up the stairs again.

'Is this just a flying visit then?' she called. 'A couple of people have been round for you as well.'

263

'I'll probably be back early next week.' He was impatient to be off. 'Could you tell anyone else who wants me? Tuesday or Wednesday, I expect.'

'Sure.'

The messages were more or less the same —'Please contact your mother'—and all dated; she had phoned every day. The last call had come this morning and had an extra line: 'Have you forgotten the twins' birthday?'

'Oh, shit!' He sank down on the crumpled bed. It seemed hard and narrow compared to the one he'd spent the last three nights in. The whole room looked dismal and dowdy in comparison.

He gathered together a few clothes, gave the room a cursory tidy, and went back downstairs. The mail was all university stuff. He shoved it in the bag with his clothes and went to phone Ginny. There was no answer.

'Oh, shit!' he said again, leaning back against the wall, unsure what to do.

Bel poked her head out. 'I forgot. Your friend Ruth came round on Thursday.'

'What did she want?' he said, tapping out Ginny's number again.

'A lift home, I think. We told her you'd already gone.'

He twisted round, the receiver against his ear. 'What did she say?'

'She wasn't too delighted.'

There was still no answer, and now he remembered that he'd told Ruth he'd be going home this weekend and she could come back with him if she wanted to.

'Oh no!' He slammed down the receiver. 'I'm really in shit street now.'

'Do you want a coffee?' Bel grinned.

He shook his head, preoccupied with his problems.

'No, thank you, Bel,' she said loudly. 'Very nice of you to offer, Bel.'

He smiled. 'Sorry. Yeah, perhaps I will, thanks.' It would waste a bit of time and maybe by then Ginny would be back from shopping or wherever she'd gone.

The ground-floor flat that Bel shared with the two other girls was far superior to his room. Not only was it better decorated and had its own tiny kitchen, it had a year's accumulation of their belongings: posters and pictures on the walls, pot plants on the windowsill. And it had a spicy lived-in odour that his room lacked: the fragrance of three girls, cooked meals, and a whiff of late-night get-togethers. He didn't know much about them, only that Bel was a second-year student studying Renaissance and Baroque music. Not so long ago he might have been intrigued by her, even attracted to her. But stick-thin girls with witchy green eyes and spiky burgundy hair no longer held any appeal for him, and his thoughts were elsewhere again as he sat with her to drink the coffee.

'You can say we kidnapped you if you need an alibi.'

'What? Oh yeah,' he smiled as her words registered.

'Say we chained you to the bed and beat you,'

one of the others suggested.

Patrick's smile hardly widened. 'I've forgotten a birthday, that's all.'

'Not your mother's, I hope,' said Bel.

'No. I've got twin sisters and they're seven today.' He looked across the room, remembering last year when he'd bought them a pet rabbit each and made them a hutch in the garden. The delight on their faces when he'd put the balls of white fluff into their arms came back to him now.

'You'd better get down the toy shop post haste,' said Bel.

'I'd better get home,' he said quietly.

The noise of children's laughter and shouts greeted him as he went round to the back door. The birthday party was in full swing. Streamers and balloons were scattered across the lawn and there were a dozen or so little girls and boys holding hands in a circle while Larry stood in the middle. Ginny was in the kitchen, with a woman Patrick didn't know, putting the finishing touches to the tea.

She looked up as he came in, gave a measured smile, and said to the woman, 'This is my son Patrick. We never quite know when we're going to see him these days.'

'Oh, you're the one who's got to Cambridge,' said the woman. 'I've heard a lot about you. Congratulations.'

'Hi. Thanks. Gran not here?' he added, turning to Ginny.

'No, she's not.' He saw the corners of her

mouth tighten and knew what was coming. 'We were hoping you could pick her up. She doesn't like driving through London on a Saturday.'

'How was I to know? I'm not psychic.'

There was a little embarrassed silence; the woman finished loading a plate with sandwiches. 'I'll take these out, shall I?' she said.

'Yes please,' said Ginny. 'Can you ask Larry to get them all sitting down?' Her voice was uneven with forced cheerfulness. 'I'll be out in a minute.' She waited until the woman was out of earshot and turned back to Patrick. 'You would have known if you'd been there when I phoned you. I've called you every day.'

'I know, I know. I got all your messages this morning.'

'Where were you?'

'Staying with a friend.'

She carried on spearing pieces of cheese and tiny sausages with cocktail sticks, but he knew by the look on her face that she didn't believe him, and he felt compelled to add, 'What's up? Can't I stay with a friend without getting permission?'

'You're nearly nineteen, you can do exactly as you like.'

'Well, what are you in a huff about? I'm home now, aren't I?'

'I would have liked Gran to have been here as well.'

He let out an impatient sigh. 'I told you, I didn't know.'

'You knew about Ruth though.'

His mouth fell open.

'Yes, I know you let her down.' Ginny emptied a giant bag of potato crisps into a bowl. 'She got home under her own steam anyway. I saw her down the shops this morning.'

'I didn't promise her,' he said lamely.

'Well?' She picked up a tray of drinks. 'Are you staying for your sisters' party, or are you rushing off back to your friend?'

Her emphasis on the last word told him she knew, or had a very good idea, where he'd been. How much she knew, he couldn't be sure; or who had told her, Mansour or Ruth.

He turned on his heel and went outside, planning to give the twins the presents he'd bought them and then go. They came rushing up to him, and he crouched down, the parcels behind his back.

'Mummy said you wasn't coming,' said Heidi. He knew it was Heidi even though they were dressed identically, because she was wearing a little badge with her name on it. And whenever he hadn't seen them for a few days, the tiny differences between them seemed more obvious for some reason. They kissed him, arms round his neck, craning behind him to see what he held. He gave them the jigsaw puzzles he'd bought in a hurry and with not enough money to get anything better. The disappointment on their faces stung him.

'I'll get you something nicer next week,' he said.

'This *is* nice,' said Heidi, brought up to be grateful and kind.

'I like mine too,' said Emma.

268

Ginny came out with the tray and stopped to see what they'd got. To his surprise, she smiled over the presents, then at him.

'Are you going to stay?' she asked.

He shrugged, feeling suddenly dejected. 'I don't think I'm very welcome, am I?'

'Patrick,' she said almost scoldingly, 'you *are* welcome. We all want you to stay.'

Larry had the children sitting down on the lawn by now and Ginny ushered the twins over to them and began handing round the drinks. Patrick hung about on the sidelines for a while then made the excuse that he wanted to sort some of his things out to take back to Cambridge with him. He disappeared into the house and phoned the shop.

'I've had to come home, to London. I'm staying here the night.'

'Why?' It was Kim who'd answered. 'I thought you were just going to Cambridge. I thought we could go out together tonight.'

'I can't talk now. Can you tell your mother I'll be back tomorrow.'

'She won't worry.'

'Tell her all the same. Apologise to her for me.'

'I was looking forward to going out.'

Ginny came into the kitchen; he heard the clatter of plates and then she went back outside.

'I've got to go. I'll be back tomorrow.'

Up in his room, he raked through a couple of drawers but hadn't the enthusiasm for any sorting out, and after a few minutes he stretched on his bed with a book. But he couldn't concentrate on this either, and ended up staring at the ceiling, torn between the desire to go back to Norfolk and his obligation to stay here.

The children drifted indoors; he could hear them downstairs, their excited voices carrying through the house as they played some game or other. He remembered other parties, other years—the twins' fifth birthday when he and Mansour had devised a treasure hunt that none of them could follow, and last year—he smiled sleepily—when much to Ginny's disgust he'd spent the whole afternoon in front of the television with a girl friend. And summer days of long ago when he used to play alone and listen to other children in other back gardens.

He jerked awake as a car pulled away below his window, his heart racing, imagining he was driving himself and had fallen asleep at the wheel. It was past seven now. He'd slept two hours; wasted two hours when he'd planned to spend this whole afternoon with Leah.

Downstairs, Ginny was washing up while the twins scampered about on the lawn playing with the remnants of streamers and balloons.

'Larry's gone to take some of the children home. He'll pick up fish and chips on his way back.' She smiled over her shoulder at him. 'I expect you're starving as usual.'

He wasn't but he nodded. 'Yeah, thanks,' and began to dry up for her, aimlessly rubbing the tea towel over plates far too wet.

'I'll put a clean pillowcase on your bed in a minute.'

He nodded again and went over to the

window. The twins were still chasing about, throwing the last of the balloons into the air and shrieking with delight as gusts of wind took them higher and over into neighbouring gardens. The afternoon sunshine had disappeared; thick little clouds were gathering, swirling and uniting in a great dark mass. Patrick frowned. Trust the weather to change and spoil the day out tomorrow. Or maybe he wouldn't get back in time and they'd go without him.

'They miss you.'

'Pardon?' He turned, blank-faced.

'The twins. They were so disappointed when they thought you weren't coming for their party.'

'Oh...' He shrugged, helpless under the weight of emotion.

'We all miss you,' she added quietly.

'I'm sorry about Gran. I would have picked her up.'

'It's all right. Larry would have fetched her yesterday but she had a committee meeting for the WI or something that she wouldn't miss. It's partly her own fault.'

'I'll go and see her.' He perched on the edge of the table, picking idly at leftover food. 'I'll have to make my peace with Ruth as well.'

Ginny shook the suds from her hands and began to dry them. There was something too studied and deliberate about her movements. She folded the towel into a neat square instead of hanging it back on its peg by the sink.

'Ruth told me you're seeing a married woman,' she said quietly. She looked straight

271

at him now. 'I know who it is. That's where you've been staying, isn't it?'

'I've made friends with her son, that's all.'

'Do you have to lie to me, Patrick?'

He looked away from her, guilt and annoyance putting him on the defensive. 'You wouldn't believe me whatever I said.'

'I would if it was the truth.'

'Ruth seems to have told you everything, so why should I bother trying to explain?' He heard her give a short unhappy sigh, but wouldn't look at her.

'It's that Leah Carew, isn't it?'

'You don't pronounce it like that.'

'Never mind her name. Whatever is she doing playing about with someone your age?'

'You don't know anything about it.'

'I know you're neglecting everything else, and I know you're heading for trouble—especially with her.'

'You know nothing!' He was shaking now. 'You never bother to find out anything. If you'd bothered to find out more about my father, you'd know I was his only child. His wife couldn't have any. He would probably have welcomed me—if he'd had the chance.'

Ginny covered her face with her hands; her shoulders began to heave as she gave way to despairing sobs. It was almost too painful to watch her but he felt compelled to add one last punishing lash.

'You kept me away from him until it was too late. But you won't keep me away from the people who knew him.'

272

'They'll ruin your life, like he ruined mine.'

Larry came barging through the door, his arms full of newspaper-wrapped parcels. He dumped them on the table and went straight to Ginny.

'I won't have this, Patrick, do you hear? I won't have you always upsetting your mother over that bastard. I've tried not to interfere but—'

'Larry, please.' Ginny clutched at his arm. 'You'll only make it worse.'

He half shook her off. 'No, I'm going to have my say for once. He's determined to set him up as some kind of idol. Tell him.'

Patrick stared at him: the squarish plain features and the hint of ginger in his thinning fair hair. He wanted to sneer, wanted to tell him about Leah and the suit and so many other things that came crowding into his head. But none of it would make sense. 'You don't know anything about him,' he said, his voice breaking up. 'And even if you did, you're too boring to understand. You couldn't understand anything about any of them.' With that he slammed out in a blur of tears and anger, and sped off up the road, narrowly missing an ice-cream van.

It was past midnight when he got back to Norfolk. There had been heavy traffic right across London, and he'd run out of petrol the other side of Newmarket and had to walk three miles to a garage. Wind and rain lashed at his windscreen as he pulled up outside the house but he hardly noticed. He left the car in the road and crept round to the back garden,

273

careful to avoid walking on the noisy gravel and keeping well away from the kitchen. Zula had the run of the house at night but he knew she usually settled against the Aga, whatever the weather. Leah's window was closed, and he scooped up a handful of small stones and threw them up to hit the glass. It took a few goes before she heard and came peering over the sill.

'It's me,' he called as loudly as he dared.

She leant out, framed in a glow of pale light. 'Kim said you weren't coming back tonight. Couldn't you stay away?'

'No.' He stretched his arms up against the wall as though he could reach her. She laughed, dangling her own arms down to him.

'You're getting soaked,' she said. 'Go round to the front door and I'll go and get hold of Zula.'

On the last lap of the drive, he'd imagined this moment: Leah in the doorway with arms wide open for him. It wasn't quite like that—she stood there gripping Zula's collar, the other hand tight round the dog's muzzle—but it was near enough. He went carefully in and patted Zula until her huge tail began to wag.

'I'll put her in the kitchen. She'll be all right now she knows it's only you.'

Patrick watched as Leah came back to him. She had on a blue satin nightdress he hadn't seen before.

'Come on,' she said, heading for the stairs.

He followed and caught her round the waist on the third stair. She slid round in his arms, slippery in the blue satin, her head level with his for a change.

'Kim sulked when he knew you weren't coming back. I had to pretend I wasn't bothered.'

'But you were, weren't you?'

'Only a tiny bit,' she whispered laughingly.

'I went home. They wanted me to stay.' He didn't feel like explaining any more.

'But you didn't.'

'No,' he said, taking hold of her arms and wrapping them round his neck. 'This is the only place I want to be.'

## Chapter 16

They drove north the next day in a blaze of blue sky and high spirits. There had been a violent storm in the night but the rain had stopped before dawn. Patrick had fallen asleep to the sound of a dripping gutter outside his window. Thoughts of home and images of tear-streaked and disappointed faces had vanished, and he saw only Leah, illuminated by flashes of lightning, her eyes big and startled as they waited together for the next great roll of thunder.

Kim was surprised to see him there at breakfast. 'How did you get in?' he asked when he discovered that Patrick had returned in the middle of the night.

Leah was sitting there sipping tea. She raised

275

her eyes enough to say be careful, and Patrick hesitated a moment before answering, not sure whether he should tell Kim that she had let him in. 'I climbed in the kitchen window,' he said finally.

'Breaking and entering,' Kim laughed. 'There's hope for you yet.'

Tanya was ironing, and she swivelled round. 'And Zula let you in?'

'Yeah, no problem, we're friends,' Patrick replied confidently, tossing his bacon rind towards the back door where Zula lay watching them as usual.

'You must be.' Tanya eyed him for a moment, then came over and gave Leah the dress she'd just ironed.

It was the one Leah had been wearing the first time he'd seen her, and as they were loading up the car he whispered as much to her. She seemed delighted that he remembered, pursing her lips to blow him a secret kiss.

They went in Patrick's car—it was the only one big enough for them all—and Leah suggested she and Tanya buy lunch to make up for the petrol. Patrick was grateful to her, knowing it was her way of saving him the embarrassment of embarking on the day out with very little money.

They stopped at a country pub for lunch, sitting out in the beer garden amongst other families in a hum of chatter and the tinkle of glasses and plates. Patrick found himself thinking of that day in Cambridge again when they'd sat by the river with Ruth and Carl, and how he'd imagined Leah and himself as a couple. It was different today, he couldn't show any particular interest in her, but this was better, much better because tonight they would be in bed together. Hardly an hour passed that he didn't think about it. There was only one drawback to all this, he thought smiling to himself, chin in hands, his eyelids growing heavy with the combination of warmth and the meal settling in his stomach, the lack of sleep.

'Wakey, wakey,' said Tanya, flicking a beer mat at him. He jolted upright, grinned and stretched, remembering that he had fallen asleep that day in Cambridge too. 'Is the bed in our guest room that uncomfortable?' she asked.

'What?' he said, beginning to yawn.

'You always look half asleep.'

'So would you if you'd been studying for exams for months on end,' said Leah. 'Don't take any notice of her, Patrick.' She smiled across at him, starting to yawn herself. 'Oh, it's catching,' she said.

'It's Kim keeping me up late. You'd better have a word with him,' said Patrick, wallowing in the risks of this carefree chatter.

'I never kept you up last night,' said Kim. 'Anyway, I'm not responsible for what you do once you're in bed,' he added loudly.

Tanya picked up the beer mat and threw it at Kim now. 'Why is it that you have to turn every conversation round to your favourite hobby?'

Kim laughed but Leah frowned at him. 'Shh, stop it,' she said.

'Yes, stop it, Kim,' mimicked Tanya. 'Or she'll swap you for Patrick.'

'We'll come without these two next time,' Leah said jokingly, leaning across to Patrick.

'Good idea,' he replied.

Kim laughed again and sent the beer mat flying towards Tanya. It missed and landed on a neighbouring table.

'I think we'd better go,' said Tanya in a singsong voice while she smiled a mock apology at the people sitting there.

The weather was warm enough for them to go swimming. They took it in turns with two of them staying with Jo-jo and their belongings. The day took on the quality of a summer holiday, running from the sea with goose-fleshed skin and dripping hair, kicking a ball barefoot to score goals between two rolled-up towels, gritty sand sticking to feet that had never looked so clean. When they flopped down to eat ice creams that Tanya had fetched from a nearby kiosk, Patrick had a flashback to a day like this when he was about six or seven. It stuck in his memory because Larry had been with them. He'd only just arrived on the scene, and Patrick remembered wishing he wasn't there because Ginny no longer wanted to play with him. He'd sat on his own, patiently building sandcastle after sandcastle. There had been another family close by with a crowd of children all older than he was. After a while, their boisterous games had begun to absorb him more than the sandcastles, and the mother had beckoned him over. He'd gone to her side and one of the children had come up and shown him a dead crab. But within minutes he'd been called and told not to be a nuisance. The woman had given him a hug, 'I can't imagine you ever being a nuisance,' then she'd looked across at Ginny. 'Your little lad's going to break a few hearts when he grows up,' she'd said.

It had stayed as a moment of high pleasure in his childhood memories: the woman's large soft bosom pressed against his cheek, and the vague and puzzling thrill of her thinking Ginny was his mother.

'Shall we go and get some tea or something?' said Kim.

'In a minute,' said Tanya. 'Can't you just sit still and relax for a change?'

They'd finished the ice creams. Patrick and Kim were lying face down on towels. A couple of feet in front of them, Leah and Tanya sat on a pair of canvas folding chairs with Jo-jo in his pushchair between them. Tanya was reading a magazine; she folded it over and held it towards Leah.

'This is the sort of stuff I want for the shop,' she said.

'"A return to decadent beauty,"' Leah read out loud. '"New romantics nineties style." Show it to Patrick, he knows all about them.'

Patrick raised his head to look. It was a double-page spread of a group of men and women dressed in Byronic frilled shirts and black leather boots. All had pale faces and moody expressions; the men's hair fell carelessly to their shoulders, while the women's was scraped dramatically back and held with big velvet bows.

'I like the boots,' he said.

'The whole lot would suit you,' said Tanya. 'You just need to grow your hair a bit.'

'I couldn't afford clothes like that.'

'Never mind, when I get my shop stocked up, I'll give you a discount.' She smiled down at him. 'Do you want some sun cream on your back?' Leah had just covered Jo-jo's legs with it and she tossed it to Tanya.

'Watch out, she's going to get her hands on you at last,' said Kim, kicking a spray of sand into the space between them.

'You mind your own business, little boy.' Tanya dropped the magazine over Kim's head and crouched down beside Patrick. 'Have I got permission to put my hands on you?' she said.

'Yeah, anytime,' Patrick replied with a smile, resting his head on his arms.

She squeezed a long line of the cream down his spine, then spread it carefully over his whole back. When she'd finished, Leah threw her down a brush. 'Here, brush the salt out of his hair.'

Patrick sat up and Tanya knelt behind him, a hand on his shoulder while she brushed his hair. 'There,' she said, leaning forward to smooth a fringe down over his forehead. 'Isn't he a doll, Leah?' And when Leah answered in a soft, considered tone, 'Yes, I think he is,' Patrick smiled happily, and joked, 'I don't get this sort of treatment very often.'

'Are we going to go and get some tea, or

are you going to ponce about with him all afternoon?' said Kim.

Tanya pointed a thumb in Kim's direction and said to Leah, 'Your son's getting jealous.'

'Bored,' Leah corrected.

They pulled clothes on over sun-dried costumes and made their way up through the town. The good weather had brought a flush of late holidaymakers and there were still plenty of places open. They chose a cafe right on the seafront and ordered crab sandwiches and a pot of tea which Tanya paid for, waving away Patrick's offer.

'Payment for helping in the shop.' She got up to go to the cash desk, stopping suddenly to hook an arm round his neck. 'If you smile at me again like that, I shall eat you up,' she hissed against his ear.

He felt a moment's embarrassment, then Leah laughed across the table. Jo-jo was on her lap and she rested a cheek against his head and said happily, 'We must do this again.'

They wandered round the shops on their way back to the car, and, down a side turning, came across a trendy-looking boutique, the single window display remarkably like the picture in the magazine.

'Look at this,' said Tanya. 'Just what I want. I must go and have a look inside.'

There were three steps up to the narrow doorway so Leah stayed outside with the pushchair, but Kim followed Tanya into the shop. Patrick seized this opportunity. 'I'll go and get us some sweets for the journey home,' he said, racing off to a newsagent's across the road. In less than a minute he was back with Leah.

She was leaning against the wall, a leg bent so that her foot was flat against it. Without a word he unwrapped a chocolate and put it in her mouth. She smiled up at him, the sunlight picking out silver flecks of salt in her lashes and eyebrows.

'Enjoying yourself?' she said.

To say yes was simply not enough, and he went and stood close by her, sliding his fingers down her arm until he clasped her hand. He opened his mouth to speak but closed it again, fearful of being interrupted because there was so much he wanted to say to her.

A group of people walked by, stopping to look in the shop window, but he hardly noticed them. He had his eyes fixed on Leah's other hand as it rocked the pushchair, the bright gold band of her wedding ring glinting in the sun. He moved his fingers up to caress the inside of her wrist, and with a little sigh pulled her arm against his side. 'I want you to leave him,' he whispered.

She glanced up. 'What?' Her face was expectant, alert, but he knew she hadn't heard, and in those confusing few seconds, he saw Tanya come through the shop door and look straight at them. Kim followed a few paces behind, and by then he had let go of Leah and moved away.

That evening Patrick felt as though he walked a high wire, unsure whether Tanya had actually seen them or not. She had given no indication that she was suspicious, although it was difficult to tell with her; the slightest remark could bring that sly, knowing look spreading across her face.

'All the stuff comes from a place in Bethnal Green.' She was busy telling Leah about the information she'd got from the woman who owned the boutique. 'I might go up there tomorrow. I'll probably stay overnight. Do you fancy coming?' Patrick's heart sank; he tried to catch Leah's eye but Tanya was looking round at him. 'You'll be here to help Kim in the shop, won't you?'

Leah answered first. 'No, I don't want to come, it's too much travelling for Jo-jo two days in a row.'

Tanya looked sideways at her. 'Shall I take Patrick instead?'

'No,' said Kim loudly. 'I'm not stopping in that shop all day on my own on a Monday, it's too boring. Anyway,' he rubbed his hands together, 'Patrick and I have important things to do.'

'I was only joking,' said Tanya with a smile that said maybe she was, maybe she wasn't. 'I'll go on my own.'

Patrick had still said nothing. They were in the sitting room surrounded by the remains of a late supper which they'd eaten in front of the television. Jo-jo had been put to bed as soon as they got home and Leah was in her usual place, feet tucked up on the sofa. Kim sat on the floor in front of her. She was trying to unsnarl his hair which the sea and sun had turned into a

283

mass of tangled dreadlocks.

'Ouch!' He let out a yell.

'You'll have to go and rinse it through,' said Leah.

'Just tie it all back so it's out of my way to play snooker.'

Patrick watched her reach up and begin to undo the silk scarf which held her own hair back. There was something uniquely feminine in the action: the angle of her arms, the soft curve of flesh between elbow and armpit and the movement of her breasts as her fingers tugged at the knot.

'Here, let me do it.' He was up on his feet standing behind the sofa and wiggling a slim forefinger under the knot. Her hair stayed in a tight bunch for a moment, then fell around her shoulders as she turned to thank him. He stood there, pretending to watch what she was doing. She glanced round again and met his eyes.

'Why don't you come and play snooker with us?' he said, resting his arms on the back of the sofa.

'I can't play.'

'We can teach you.'

She finished tying the scarf round Kim's hair. 'I don't want to pry into what you two do in there.'

Kim twisted round now but Patrick ignored him. 'You wouldn't be, we—'

'Don't keep on,' Kim interrupted. 'She hates it in the games room.'

A flash of unreasonable anger hit Patrick, made worse because he couldn't give in to it.

'What about darts?' he said, still ignoring Kim.

Leah got up and began gathering up the plates. 'I'll see,' she said, crouching down with her back to him.

Tanya got up as well but made no attempt to help her which was unusual; she seemed to do most of the jobs around the house while Leah did little apart from look after the baby.

'Why don't you have a game with us as well?' Patrick said, more to annoy Kim than anything.

'Not tonight,' said Tanya. 'I have to go and check my bank statement—see what I can afford for the shop. Leah'll play with you.'

Patrick hung over the sofa, watching from the corner of his eye as Tanya waltzed off, humming something that he knew but couldn't quite place, and wondering if he'd imagined the innuendo in her last remark.

Halfway through their first game, Leah came to join them, bringing cans of lager, ice-cold from the fridge.

'Well then,' she said. 'Who's going to turn me into a second Hurricane what's-his-name?'

Kim laughed. 'You're a bit out of date, Mother.' Then he chalked his cue for her and set up a couple of easy shots. Patrick stayed in the background; he was beginning to realise that Kim was happy as long as he had the limelight.

Once Leah had learnt the rules, they practised, taking it in turns to try and pot balls. Between shots, Kim sat in a corner with his guitar and strummed away to a Dire Straits tape he'd put on. His hoarse, chant-like imitation was surprisingly good, his guitar playing, pitched just a little louder than the tape, accomplished. Patrick was a fan of the group—he didn't like much of the stuff that filled the current charts—and listening to 'Romeo and Juliet', the sexy timbre of Kim's voice crackling like static from the shadows, pumped up a feeling of excitement in him.

The tape came to an end. Kim finished his third lager and put on a new one, turning up the volume. 'Right, let's play a proper game,' he said. 'You two against me.'

'You're very confident,' said Leah.

'Not really,' he shrugged, lips pursed. 'Two against one, I might even lose.'

It was stupid but Patrick felt his earlier anger rekindled, especially when Kim began to laugh.

'What's he laughing for?' said Leah. She looked puzzled for only a moment before the penny dropped. 'Oh, I'll be a liability—that's it, isn't it?' She laughed too, leaning against Patrick, a hand on his shoulder.

He hugged her casually, as he might have done anyone, but the action gave him a juvenile sense of triumph. 'We'll show him,' he said.

Kim pulled easily ahead but Patrick couldn't have cared less. Each faltering shot of Leah's gave him an opportunity to encircle her in his arms and make out he was helping her. The desire to win was the last thing on his mind as once again he took hold of her arm in the guise of helping her aim the cue. By some miracle

286

she potted a red and left the cue ball perfectly placed to pot the black.

'I can do this one myself,' she said, smiling up at him. He let go of her and she hit it too hard and sent it hurtling off the table.

'Try it again,' he said, replacing the ball and coming up behind her. 'Move round this way a bit, you're not in line.' He put his hand on her waist and bent his head close to her.

'Take your hands off my mother.' Kim's voice suddenly rose above the music.

Patrick peered round at him. 'Do what?'

'You heard me. Get your hands off her.'

Leah freed herself and took a step towards him. 'Don't be silly, Kim, he's just showing me—'

'Showing you what, eh?' Kim broke in.

'Don't be childish. He's just teaching me how to play.'

'Teaching you!' Kim burst out. 'He can't even fucking play himself.'

Patrick lunged forward and grabbed the end of Kim's cue, nearly pulling it from his hand. 'Don't speak to her like that.' He jabbed the cue away from him now, jerking Kim's arm sharply back. 'Apologise.'

Kim went rigid, only his eyes moved, darting from one to the other of them like a cornered animal. 'Kim,' Leah said gently, 'just calm down.' She tried to get hold of him, but he shouted, 'Don't touch me!' and wrenched the cue from Patrick's grasp. For a second he held it above his head. Then, with a choking cry of

287

anger he flung it across the table, and ran from the room.

'It's only to get your attention,' said Patrick.

'But I don't want you two to fall out.' She looked stricken as though it was the worst thing that could possibly happen. 'I'll have to go and talk to him.'

'Why? It's his fault. I'd never swear at my mother like that.'

'He doesn't mean it. He'll calm down if I go and talk to him.' She was standing with her back against the table. Patrick put an arm either side of her and tried to kiss her but she twisted away from him. 'Be sensible, Patrick. We've only got a couple of days left.'

He kept her imprisoned, gripping the curve of polished mahogany, but her words had completely deflated him. 'Then what?' he said flatly. 'Have I got to bow down to him just so I can carry on seeing you?'

'I want the two of you to be friends.' Her eyes became shiny; her mouth turned down. 'I thought you liked him.'

'I do most of the time.' He wasn't sure if it was true or not, but it made everything seem suddenly impossible. 'Can't we tell him?'

'No! Don't you dare. Swear to me, Patrick,' she punched a fist against his chest, 'swear to me you won't.' He remained stubbornly silent but she hit him again. 'Say it. Say you won't.'

He stared down at her. 'All right. I won't, I promise.'

'I have to go and talk to him. He'll be so upset. He doesn't mean to lose his temper. He's got problems—you don't understand.'

'No, I don't,' he muttered after her.

When she didn't come back after half an hour, his anger became hard to contain. All the plans he'd had of repeating what he'd said to her outside the boutique were wrecked. How could he bring such an important thing up now? He sprawled on the white leather sofa, his feet hooked over the arm. The tape that had been playing all this time came to an end, making a whirring sound as though something was stuck. He got up and switched it off, jabbing at the controls. Kim's snooker cue was still on the table where he'd thrown it. Patrick strode over and snatched it up. He gripped it with both hands, wanting to break it, but contented himself by hurling it across the room. It landed in front of the television, inches short of smashing into the screen. He picked up one of the balls, wishing he had the courage to aim it at something breakable. Never in his life had he smashed up anything, never even thought about it; now the idea grew more tempting with every minute he waited. When the door opened, he nearly leapt out of his skin.

'I'm sorry.' Kim had come back on his own. 'I'm sorry, OK?'

Patrick gripped the ball he was toying with and sent it spinning across the table. Kim went and picked up his cue from the floor. 'I fuck up everything. I know I do it.' He went and slumped down on the sofa, poking at the carpet with the end of the cue. 'I get people I really like and I go and fuck it up.'

289

'It's OK,' muttered Patrick.

'I jump to the wrong conclusions—I can't help it, I try not to.'

'I said it's OK.' Patrick's anger was fast fading; a worm of guilt had come to replace it. 'Forget it,' he added, going to sit at the other end of the sofa. Silence hung between them. Where's your mother? Patrick wanted to ask, but couldn't in this brittle atmosphere. 'Has your mother gone to bed?' he mumbled finally.

Kim nodded and cleared his throat. 'I bet she was talking about me, wasn't she?' It was obvious that he'd been crying and looked about to start again. 'I bet she told you not to trust me. I bet she told you about Carew.'

'What about him?'

'I hit him.' He paused, prodding away with the cue. 'With a candlestick.'

Patrick was mildly shocked, but somehow, not surprised. 'Why?' he said very quietly.

'I thought he'd hurt her. I did it to stop him.'

'What? Carew hurt your mother?'

'Yeah, I really thought he had. I heard all this screaming going on one night. It was just after we came back here, soon after they were married. I ran to their bedroom and there was blood everywhere. All over my mother and all over the bed. I just grabbed the candlestick. You would have done the same.'

'What had he done to her?' Patrick half whispered.

'It wasn't him. It was her dog. Diz. It used

to sleep in her bedroom.'

'The terrier?' Patrick remembered what Leah had told him that day in Cambridge.

'No, another Alsatian. Bigger than Zula. Carew said it was him the dog had gone for, but my mother was in the way. She's still got the scar.'

Patrick caught his breath. He'd seen that scar for the first time last night: a purple crescent on Leah's hip. In the dim light, he'd thought it was a tattoo, but Leah had laughed and said, no, they were teeth marks. Then she'd tilted her hip towards him and added, 'I'm very tasty,' and he'd forgotten to ask how she got it.

'I was fed up with people hurting my mother. Justina was always hitting her. Even your father...' Kim began rubbing at his face, frantically wiping away a mixture of tears and snot. 'Once I saw him, in here. He was holding her against the wall with a snooker cue. I was only small, I didn't know he was playing about. I thought, one day—'

'Kim, it's OK.' Patrick pushed a gentle elbow at him. 'It's in the past. Let's forget it.'

'But now I've had a go at you. I bet you'll piss off tomorrow, won't you?'

'No, I won't. Go and get us some more lager. We'll have another game.'

But when Kim came back with the cans, Patrick didn't feel like playing. He kept thinking of what Kim had said about Cody. It stirred up a confusion of feeling and brought back his earlier anger against Kim; everything he did seemed designed to get

291

attention. He sat there gulping down the lager, and when Kim tentatively suggested they do some of the catalogue he said he didn't feel like that either. They sat there in silence again until Patrick announced he was going to bed.

'No, don't go yet,' said Kim. He quickly passed Patrick another can. 'I remember your father playing snooker in here.'

Patrick rolled the can between his palms, not sure how to deal with this obvious ploy to keep him here. But he couldn't resist the bait.

'Yeah?' he said casually. 'When was that?'

'When I was little. I remember once—I must have been on my way to bed because I was supposed to kiss him goodnight—he lifted me up and stood me on the table. I played around kicking the balls into the pockets. Then I got carried away and started kicking them onto the floor.' He paused. 'We often watched him play. He used to sing to us as well.'

Patrick stared across the room to where the circle of light caught the scatter of coloured balls, the black, glossy and poised as though it still waited for that shot they'd abandoned. 'You don't have to invent things about him to please me,' he said.

'I'm not.' Kim swung round to face him. 'I'm not. I do remember all that. I was reminded of it when my mother knocked the ball on the floor.'

Kim sounded too earnest to be lying. And

292

as Patrick forced down this last lager which he didn't really want, he was beset with images of Kim prancing about on the table. And of those two who watched him, and of all the connections so achingly confused and complicated. Kim went and put another tape on. Outside it was pitch black. The room felt adrift from the rest of the house and charged with things Patrick would never know but wanted to so very much; memories that should be his, not Kim's. He glanced sideways; Kim was watching him, his eyes shiny with tears, just the way Leah's had been. He thought of that song that always made her cry.

'If he'd known about you, he might have wanted you here,' said Kim, brightening with every sentence. 'I bet he would have done.'

'Yeah,' said Patrick, getting up. He squashed the can up like a concertina, unable to rid himself of the picture of Kim placing a goodnight kiss on that face he'd never see. 'That would have pleased his wife.' He swung round and pounced on Kim, pushing him flat on the sofa and holding him down by the throat. 'Now remember next time you feel like causing trouble, pick on someone smaller, because I shall throttle you.'

Kim pretended to choke, then laughingly struggled to get free. And after a few blank and ugly seconds when he couldn't decide whether he meant to hurt Kim or not, Patrick let him go.

# Chapter 17

Monday dragged. Kim was soon back to his normal self, acting as though the row had never happened. But Patrick could concentrate on nothing. He felt as though a volcano simmered away inside him. Last night, Leah had soothed him to sleep with one of her little songs, but he had not slept for long, and the first thing he heard when he woke was the phone ringing.

He watched Kim serve a lone customer, then fold the ten pound note he'd taken and put it in his pocket.

'It's to get a bottle of something for tonight,' Kim said with a wink.

'If you must nick the takings, you ought to spend it on all this advertising you're planning,' said Patrick. 'I don't think you realise how much it's going to cost you.'

'Course I do. What's up with you today? You keep picking fault with everything.'

'Yeah, because you'll never make any money the way you go about things.' He picked up a sheet of paper which Kim had written out earlier and read it aloud. '"Impotence is a thing of the past, said Mr B of Coventry. Libido Star has made a new man of me and brightened up my retirement no end." You can't put out crap like this.'

'What's wrong with it?' Kim grinned. 'I think

294

it sounds brilliant. You've got to appeal to all ages. The old ones are the ones with the money.'

'You've got to be careful what you say. You have to be able to back up these claims. I don't want to end up in court with my name all over the papers.'

'Don't worry about it, everything will be in my name,' Kim said. 'If anybody asks, we can give them phone numbers to call. I'm sure we can sort out enough people willing to back up what we say. You, for instance.' He wiggled his shoulders, laughing to himself as he ran a finger down the page. 'You can be—'

'Well, let's use your number,' Patrick broke in. 'You can get Carew to speak to them. He could answer for Mr B.'

Kim looked up, his face serious for a second before breaking into a contemptuous smile. 'Very funny. The telephone code doesn't match.'

Patrick had expected more of a reaction; the only reason he'd said it was to annoy Kim.

'I've got to keep on good terms with Carew, anyway,' said Kim. 'He'll be supplying the cash I need.'

'I thought you said he didn't like you doing this?'

Kim rubbed his hands together. 'I shan't tell him what I want the money for. I'm not that stupid.'

'Won't your mother lend you some?'

'She hasn't got any.'

'Oh. None at all?' said Patrick. The question of their finances bothered him. He'd been thinking about it a lot, wondering how important Carew's money was to Leah, and wondering if she'd be prepared to live without it. At night, he was so sure of her. Then the following day, watching how carelessly she treated material things, how she'd leave her belongings lying about on the floor, or toss half a packet of chocolate biscuits to the dog without a second thought, he couldn't imagine how she'd ever adapt to being careful with money. He looked at Kim, not sure whether he'd answered. 'I'd better go and clear off those shelves for Tanya,' he said, knowing that he was in danger of picking a row with Kim.

'OK.' Kim was engrossed in siphoning something from a demijohn. 'Just sling everything in a box and we'll take it home. Most of it came from there anyway.'

Tanya had asked them to clear all the back shelves to make way for a new display unit and clothes rails she'd ordered. There were mostly books, some quite old, and tattered loose spines came away in Patrick's hand as he pulled them out. There was a section of poetry: Tennyson, Keats, Browning. He dropped them carelessly into a box on top of some broken crockery, deriving a certain masochistic pleasure from ill-treating them this way.

One shelf was full of children's books. Many he'd read himself. *Swallows and Amazons, Gulliver's Travels*. He had his back to the window blocking out the light, and as he turned the pages, struggling to make out the words, he was reminded of how he used to read by torchlight beneath the sheets. Why that had been necessary he couldn't remember because he'd always been encouraged to read. Thinking of bed, he yawned, and the words danced a little before his eyes. It wasn't surprising that these books hadn't sold, they were too well used. Many of the pages had little crayon drawings beside the text; goblins and dragons crept along the lines, and felt-tipped monsters decorated chapter headings. He smiled to himself, remembering how he had often wanted to illustrate his own books in this way but hadn't dared. The drawings all had a distinctive similarity about them, and Patrick turned to the fly leaf, knowing that the owner's name would be written there—the only thing he was allowed to write in his.

"Happy Birthday, Kim, with love from Cody." "Happy Christmas, Kim, with love from Cody." Every one was decorated with a string of kisses. Each had the year written in. Patrick looked at others. There was a series of Filmgoer Annuals all inscribed in the same way. Long after Cody had gone, he had kept on sending Kim these presents. Patrick was flooded with jealousy; his hands shook with the intensity of it. Kim had stolen his father.

There was a noise behind him. Patrick looked round to see Kim standing in the doorway. 'Shall we close up and go home?' he said.

Patrick dropped the books into the box with the others. 'Yeah, if you like.'

Later that evening, they sat together in the

games room taking turns sipping directly from the bottle of Southern Comfort that Kim had bought on the way home.

They had played snooker, just the two of them, and now they sat as they had last night, talking and making plans about the catalogue. Music droned away in the background: Dire Straits again, which Patrick had put on because it suited his mood, the lonely twang of the guitars and all that deceptive monotony. Kim was taking two swigs to his one now. Patrick waited as patiently as he could while Kim got drunker and drunker.

'I'm going to bed,' he said finally, watching for a response because Kim's eyes had been closed for the last five minutes.

They flicked open, closed and opened again. 'Shit, this stuff is lethal,' said Kim.

'That's because you've drunk so much.'

'Have I?' Kim got to his feet. 'Shall we have another game?'

Patrick let him stagger to the table, then went and hooked up one of his arms. 'Come on, let's get you upstairs.'

He'd never been in Kim's bedroom. It was twice as big as his own room at home, and ten times as untidy. But there was something luxurious about it as well: deep pile, faded pink carpeting and frilled curtains that matched the bedding and the lampshades.

'Have you always had this room?' Patrick asked, pulling back the duvet and tipping Kim on to the bed.

'Yep.'

'Even when Justina and Cody were here?'

'Yep,' repeated Kim, curling into a ball and patting the space beside him. 'Get in here,' he murmured sleepily.

'Like hell,' smiled Patrick, leaning over to drag off Kim's trainers. 'Do you know where I'm going to sleep tonight?' There was no answer. He pulled off Kim's socks and covered him with the duvet. 'Shall I tell you?' There was still no answer, just the sound of Kim's breathing already settling into the heavy, slow rhythm of sleep. 'I want you to know.' Patrick waited, staring down at Kim's face, watching as his lips parted and the noise of his breathing deepened into a grunting snore. 'With your mother,' he whispered.

He backed slowly out of the room and crept along the landing. Past Tanya's empty room, then the bathroom, and then he was at Leah's door.

She was over by the window and jumped with fright when she heard him.

'You scared me,' she said, a hand against her chest. 'I was watching the lightning. I think we're going to have another storm.' There were two lamps lit in the room and she went and switched one off. 'I'll be along in a minute.'

'I want to stay here.'

'I'd rather you didn't.'

'Why? There's no one to hear us.'

'Jo-jo might wake.'

'You said he never does. And what would it matter if he did?'

She shrugged and went to look out of the

window again. 'I don't have a key to this door.'

'It doesn't matter. Kim's out for the count.' He pushed her against the wall, hands on her shoulders. 'You're just making excuses.' She tried to prise herself free but he held on to her. 'I'm going to stay here. I want to sleep with you all night. I want to wake up with you in the morning.' He was aware that he was holding her by the arms now, gripping her with unnecessary force because she had stopped trying to get free. 'I'm going to stay.' He trapped her against the wall with his body, twisted his hands in her hair and dragged her head back. Still she offered no resistance and he held her there, unsure why he was doing this or what he would do next. He tugged her head back further until her throat arched towards him, knowing that if she made even the slightest protest he would let her go. But she just stared up at him, her eyes blank and slightly out of focus as though she looked at something beyond him. He shook her, released his hold a little, worried that he had hurt her. 'Leah,' he murmured and put his hand against her throat. She shivered and closed her eyes, and he felt her swallow. Her lips parted and her expression became submissive, voluptuous in a way he didn't understand.

'Don't,' he said, but had no idea why he said it, or why he tore open her nightdress and squeezed her breasts and sucked and bit at her skin.

He slid down on his knees in front of her, hid his face in her stomach, sought her with

300

his fingers, aware only of an anguished need to penetrate her and to be in control. He was vaguely aware that she did try to stop him now, but it was nothing more than a feeble struggle only half meant. He ground his face against her and pushed his fingers deeper into her, suddenly wanting her to fight him. But when finally she let out a little cry, he let her go, panting, and frightened of the way he felt.

They moved to the bed. The quilt became tangled beneath them. Sometimes he was above her, sometimes beneath her, and there were other ways, positions she guided him to that he'd never imagined, and contortions that she drove him to in her demands for more.

Somewhere in the middle of the night, she got up and went to the bathroom. She came back with a damp sponge and wiped his face with it. He shivered as cold drops slid down his chest, and she bundled up the quilt, which had fallen to the floor, and wrapped it round him.

He caught her wrist because water was dripping all over the bed. 'Are you glad I stayed?' he said.

She nodded. In the dim light, he could see a bruise on her upper arm and a livid red mark at the top of her breast. He wanted to apologise but couldn't think of words to say what he meant. Instead he leant over and kissed her very gently on the cheek. But she immediately hooked an arm round his neck and kissed him on the mouth, so hard that her teeth scraped against his. For a split second he wanted to push her away, tell her he was exhausted, but as he crumpled back on the pillows she started to masturbate him.

Several times the pleasure rose to an intense pitch, then left him. Maddened with frustration, he rolled over on top of her. It took longer than ever before. He slid his hands under her buttocks, pulling her tight up against him, and she sighed and caught at his fingers. In a blur of exhaustion, he heard her murmur something and felt her fingers digging into his. She whispered louder, the words caught on an anguished little sigh.

'Hurt me, Patrick,' she was saying.

He stopped, heaved himself up on his arms to look down into her face. She said it again, eyes closed, her head tossing from side to side.

'No. No, I don't want to hurt you.' The whole night seemed to cave in on him. He sank back down on her, his heart pounding. 'You're making me do things I don't want to.'

She was still and quiet now, no longer holding him, and he was seized with a miserable wash of guilt and confusion.

'You don't really love me, do you?' He raised his head to look at her again. 'I know you don't.'

He saw her smile and then she took his face between her hands and made him kiss her. 'You know I do. I love you more all the time.' Then she hugged him close and soon he was sobbing out a final prolonged orgasm, his face pressed into her neck.

He woke to find her feeding Jo-jo. The bed was

straightened and she had a different nightdress on. He didn't sit up but lay there with his cheek against her hip, listening to the sounds of Jo-jo sucking. It wasn't until she propped Jo-jo against her shoulder to rub his back that she looked down and saw he was awake. Her smile was brief, almost cold.

'Don't watch me,' she said. 'You know I hate it.'

He turned over without a word, and after a few seconds she said, 'Carew will be phoning soon.'

'So you want me to clear off.' His voice was hoarse, his throat dry from sleep. 'You're kicking me out—is that what you're trying to say?'

'It might be best if you go.'

'Best for who?'

'Patrick,' she said gently. 'Listen to me. I don't want you to be unhappy.'

He hunched away from her and she laid Jo-jo down and came to lean over his shoulder, resting her cheek against his. 'I'm making you unhappy, aren't I? What can I do to make you happy?' she whispered when he didn't reply.

'Leave him.' He rolled over to face her. 'I want you to leave him.'

'How can I?' She stroked his forehead but he pushed her hand away.

'You could if you wanted. I'll get a job.'

She shook her head. 'No, you've got your whole future ahead of you. I'd spoil your life.'

'My life will be spoilt if I can't be with you.'

'We can still see each other. Whenever Carew

303

goes away, you can stay here. He does other lecture tours, and quite often he goes to London for a weekend. I'll think of an excuse not to go with him. Now that you and Kim are such friends...'

'You'll have to tell him the truth. He'll want a divorce.'

'I'm not ready for that.' She looked startled. 'I've got Jo-jo to think of, and Kim.'

'You won't have any choice. He'll guess.' He flicked back the neck of her nightdress. 'Unless he's blind.'

She buttoned it up. 'He won't see. I don't sleep naked with him.'

'That's what you tell me. I don't know what to believe. I never know what to believe with you. How serious you are about me—about anything.'

'You're only saying that to upset me. You're trying to make me cry. You want to make me cry so Carew will hear.' She looked anxious and as he watched, her eyes were already filling with tears.

'Go on then, cry,' he said, feeling his heart screw up as the tears streamed down her face.

Jo-jo began to cry as well, his eyes fixed on them and his arms in the air to be picked up. And amidst all this, the phone began to ring.

It would have been so easy to betray her, make a noise, a cough perhaps so that Carew would ask who was there. Or even snatch the receiver from her and say, I'm here with your wife and I've been with her all night. But he couldn't do it; the look on her face, the silent plea for him to keep quiet, was enough to stop him. And as she began to speak, rubbing away the tears, he was even bothered by a niggle of guilt.

'Yes, of course I'm all right,' he heard her say. 'No, no, you didn't wake me, I've been feeding Jo-jo... Yes, of course... Tomorrow?... Oh good.' She smiled into the phone, absorbed and happy looking, answering Carew's questions. Patrick's feeling of guilt slid away. He went and sat close by her and took hold of her free hand. She tried to wriggle it free while still speaking but he squeezed it tighter. 'I'd better go,' she said. 'Jo-jo's getting fidgety.'

'Give him a kiss for me.' Patrick was so close to her, he could hear Carew's voice. 'I'll save all the ones I've got for you until I get home. I'll give them to you all in one go. We'll make up for lost time—for all the lost time.' There was silence as though he was waiting for an answer, then he said, 'Darling, are you sure everything's all right?'

'Yes, I told you.' Leah wrenched her hand away.

'I won't go on any more of these tours, I miss you too much.' He paused. 'I probably love you too much, that's the trouble.'

Patrick slumped back down on the bed, accidentally knocking Jo-jo who had been busy trying to get his foot into his mouth. The bump knocked Jo-jo's hand and it pinged back and hit him in the face and he burst out crying again. Patrick lifted him up and lay back on the pillow

with him. Leah said a hasty goodbye and turned
on him.

'Why did you do that?'

'I couldn't help it.'

'Give him to me.'

'No, he's all right.' He cuddled Jo-jo against
his chest. 'You didn't have to cut him off. Call
him back. You didn't tell him how much you
loved him.'

'Stop it.'

'Bet you can't wait for him to get back—all
that lost time to make up for.' He carried on
cuddling Jo-jo and began kissing his cheek, his
eyes defiantly on Leah. 'And all those kisses.
Go on, start crying again,' he said, swallowing
back his own misery. He passed Jo-jo to her
and jumped up from the bed.

'Where are you going?'

He shrugged, already half dressed. 'I don't
know. Anywhere.' He began to search for his
socks. When he found them and sat on the bed
to put them on, she came up behind him and
put her arms round his neck.

'Patrick,' she said quietly.

'What?' He tried to shrug her off.

'I love you.'

Tears stung his eyes. 'But not enough to
leave him.'

'If it makes you feel any better, I haven't...'
She broke off. 'Turn round, I can't talk properly
with your back to me.'

Half of him wanted to resist but he couldn't,
and he swivelled round to face her.

'Since that day when I first came to you

306

at Cambridge,' she began, slipping her arms round him again, 'I haven't let Carew make love to me.'

'I don't believe you,' he muttered.

'Come back to bed for a while.'

'No,' he said, but crawled back in with her fully dressed.

Pistons were jabbing against his chest, pounding away like a train gathering speed. Patrick opened his eyes and stared straight into Jo-jo's face. It was immediately wreathed in smiles, and his little legs began kicking away faster than ever. Patrick captured the baby's warm feet and held them cupped in his hands.

The room was filled with sunlight, its rays so brilliant that they turned the curtains transparent. Through the open window came a whole choir of birdsong. As he listened, it rose to a crescendo of sound then faded away for a few seconds as though the birds had paused for breath. Jo-jo gurgled happily, blowing out a froth of bubbles as he tried to free his legs. Leah slept on, curled in a ball with her back to them.

Patrick imagined what it would be like to wake up every morning like this, to have these past few days repeated over and over. It was what he wanted, exactly what he wanted. And he couldn't have it. Jo-jo was hiccupping loudly. A little explosion of vomit came from his lips and ran down his cheek, dribbling on to both the pillowcase and Patrick's shirt. Patrick sat him upright to pat his back and the movement woke Leah.

She rolled over, smiling and yawning and he wanted to say, don't move, don't get up, don't start this day that's going to be our last. But all that came out was, 'Jo-jo's been sick.'

She sat up, looking first at the baby then across towards the window. 'Whatever's the time?'

'I don't know.'

There was the sound of water running through the pipes. She flung herself sideways to see the clock on the bedside table. 'Quick, you'd better go. Kim sometimes brings me tea if he's up first.'

'I've been awake ages, I would have heard him.'

'Patrick, please do as I say.'

'What about tonight?' He made no move to go, just twisted his head towards her. 'What are your plans? Are you going to throw me out at dawn in case your husband gets home early.'

'Please. I don't want Kim to find you here. Please, please go.' She was kneeling on the edge of the bed, dishevelled and creased from sleep. 'Please, I'm begging you, Patrick, please go.'

He waited as long as he could bear to defy her, and only just made it because a few steps along the landing he heard Kim come up the stairs.

'Oh, you're up. I was going to bring you tea in bed.' Kim stood there, hunched and grimacing, a loaded tray in his hands. 'I've got the worst fucking headache I've ever had. I went down for some aspirin.' He yawned and shivered, setting the cups rattling. 'You don't look so hot yourself. Your shirt's covered in spew.'

Patrick glanced down at himself. 'I was just going for a piss.'

'Open my mum's door for me first. You can come and get your tea when you've done.'

He did as Kim asked, then went straight to the bathroom. Through the wall, he could hear the faint hum of them talking. Kim would be looking for sympathy, perhaps cuddling up to his mother, or stretching out on the bed, his head in her lap while she massaged his scalp. That was just the sort of thing she'd do. He wondered if she'd cleared up all the evidence of their lovemaking; normally he would do that, standing as he was now, watching the swirl of water flush away down the toilet bowl.

He washed the vomit from his shirt but had to take it off because he'd made it too wet. It stank, and so did he, but he couldn't be bothered with a shower. A deathly pale face stared back at him from the mirror. He scooped the hair from his forehead and ran impatient fingers round his chin but didn't feel like shaving either.

Kim's hoarse laughter came through the wall. Patrick stood very still, listening, imagining again the scene next door. Tomorrow they would all be here together and he would be back at Cambridge. The thought was unbearable. To carry on with his life as he'd planned would be unbearable: long days cooped up in lecture rooms, hours of studying, schedules and meetings—and perhaps the odd day when she might come and see him but never another time like this. He picked up the soap and began to lather it between his palms, and the next minute Kim was banging on the wall and shouting to him to hurry up. Patrick quickly splashed his face with water, hooked his shirt over his shoulder and went back to Leah's bedroom. The door was open a fraction and he tapped his knuckles against it.

'Come in,' she called.

Kim was sitting cross-legged at the foot of the bed while Leah sat propped on the pillows with Jo-jo.

She smiled at him. 'Come and have a cup of tea, Patrick, before it's cold.'

Patrick went and stood behind Kim, looking at her across the top of his head but she wouldn't meet his eyes.

'Are we going to the shop?' he said as Kim handed him the cup. 'As you feel so rough, I mean.'

'Yes, you are,' said Leah firmly before Kim could say anything.

'I'm ill,' complained Kim.

'You've got a hangover,' corrected Leah. 'And you have to go because Tanya's relying on you.'

Patrick felt as though he'd explode—all this chitchat about tea and the shop. He gulped down the lukewarm tea and put his cup back on the tray, then leant across to click his fingers at Jo-jo. Leah glanced up at him and he could see she felt uncomfortable with him so close. She must be thinking of last night—how could she not be? He moved a bit closer, let Jo-jo grip his finger and take it to his mouth. The desire to demonstrate how far he dared go became irresistible and he sank carefully on to the edge of the bed. Jo-jo's hard little gums chewed away at his fingertip.

Leah suddenly clapped her hands. 'Come on, you two, get moving or you'll be late.'

Kim gave a theatrical groan. 'You're so cruel, Mother.'

'You'll feel better once you've had a wash.' She clapped her hands again. 'Come on, shift. You look like a couple of tramps instead of my beautiful boys.'

Kim spluttered with croaky laughter and looped joined hands over Patrick from behind. 'Beautiful boys, are we?' he laughed, dragging Patrick backwards in a wrestling hug. 'I think my mother wants to adopt you, Patrick.'

'I wouldn't mind,' said Patrick. The word 'beautiful' rang in his head, reminding him of other things she'd said to him. He stared at her, imagined Carew lying there beside her in those maroon pyjamas, falling asleep over a paper, his bulk like a slumbering mountain, taking most of the bed. He heard Carew's voice again, almost pleading, 'We'll make up for lost time, for all the lost time,' and he felt suddenly sure of himself, aware of his youth and his good looks in a way he had never been before. 'No, I wouldn't mind that,' he said, lazing back against Kim's chest. 'Then I could stay here for ever.'

'And be my big brother,' laughed Kim, clasping him tight round the neck.

Patrick fought him off and dragged him to the floor, arrogant with excitement and wanting to show off his superior strength, sure that Leah must be comparing him with Carew.

'That's enough,' she shouted as they rolled about together. 'Out of here, the pair of you.'

Patrick held Kim down, and Leah picked up the milk jug and emptied it over them.

'Mum!' yelled Kim, catching most of it in his face. Patrick let him go, and Kim sat up rubbing the dribbles of milk from his eyes. 'You wouldn't like her as a mother,' he said. 'She's got a vicious streak.'

'Out!' yelled Leah, picking up the teapot.

With a whoop of laughter, Kim made for the door. Patrick followed but turned back at the last moment. 'I'll take the tray,' he said. But instead of picking up the tray, he snatched up her hand. He gripped it tightly, holding her bunched fingers while she struggled and pulled faces of protest, her eyes on Kim's retreating back. 'I'll see you tonight,' he said in a normal voice, adding a whispered, 'In here,' before letting her go.

## Chapter 18

By midday Kim's hangover had vanished, cured by some dreadful-looking mixture he'd been sipping. All morning he'd drifted in and out of the back room wearing dark glasses and a pained expression, leaving Patrick to serve the customers. But the last time he'd emerged, going straight out to turn round the open sign, he was grinning like a clown, and suggested they go to the pub for a wet lunch. Patrick agreed immediately. A dose of alcohol seemed as good a way as any of getting through the rest of the day.

They drove a little way out of town and sat in a smoky bar until closing time, Kim high on something more than the lager they were drinking. Patrick, too, began to feel light-headed; he had eaten nothing since yesterday and Kim's mood was infectious. The fact that he would probably be over the limit when they left the pub, and that one of them would have to take charge in the shop, ceased to matter.

When the second 'Time, gentlemen, please' was called, they were in the middle of a loud and crude discussion about how they would recruit volunteers to try out the products in the catalogue. As the landlord's voiced boomed out, Kim stopped mid-sentence and slumped back against the seat. 'I wish you didn't have to go back to Cambridge,' he said, his tone a niggling plea like that of a child trying to get its own way.

'So do I,' said Patrick without thinking.

'Don't you want to then?' Kim's face lit up. 'What about your degree and everything?'

Patrick shrugged, cautious because he was approaching the stage where words slipped out too easily. 'I'm not sure what I want to do. Not now.' The sentence hung between them. 'Now that I've met you lot.' Patrick drained his glass, gulping down the stupidity of the words.

313

Kim threw an arm round his shoulders. 'Yeah, I suppose it's fate,' he said, cuddling him like a lover.

There were two girls sitting across the bar from them. Kim had eyed them as they came in and made the odd loud remark to catch their attention. As other people started to leave, the girls lingered as though they hoped things would develop. Now they got up, and one made a detour on her way to the door.

'Have a nice afternoon together,' she said, adding an exaggerated, 'Darlings,' as she wheeled round to follow her giggling friend.

'Fuck off,' Kim called after them.

'Shh,' said Patrick, standing up and pulling Kim with him as the landlord came over to them with a brusque, 'Come on, you two.'

They passed the girls a little way along the road and Kim immediately wound down the car window and let out a shrill whistle, then leant across and kissed Patrick on the cheek.

'Leave off, Kim,' said Patrick, shoving him away.

'Well, girls are so paranoid about male friendships.' Kim skewed round to wave both hands at them. 'Even Tanya hates us being friends.'

'Does she? Why?'

'She's jealous. She can be a really jealous person. She's like Justina. My mother's the best of all of them.'

Yeah, Patrick wanted to say, don't I know it, but he had to content himself with an innocent nod of agreement.

Back in the shop, Kim began to harp on again about Patrick staying. They had been quite busy at one stage, with one customer after another and a little crowd of holidaymakers who lingered for ages over a box of T-shirts with mildly obscene slogans. Kim had grown irritable, moaning that they'd never finish the catalogue if they kept being interrupted.

'Yeah, we will,' soothed Patrick, warmed with alcohol and the countdown of hours before they went home to Leah.

'I shan't feel the same doing it without you,' Kim said. 'You're the only one who takes me seriously. I wish you could stay.' It was the umpteenth time he'd said it.

Patrick hoisted himself onto the worktop where Kim was lining up empty bottles, arranging and rearranging them like an army of little glass soldiers.

'I've got things to do, meetings and...' Patrick shrugged, the thought of it tiring and a bit worrying.

'Couldn't you stay until the term starts?'

'I can't just,' he shrugged again, 'stay on at your place.'

'Yes you can.' Kim's face was too eager. 'I'll ask my mother.'

'I'd have to sort something out with my room.' Patrick reached across and carefully moved one of the bottles to a new position as though he was playing a game of chess. 'I suppose you could mention it to your mother...' He took a breath. 'See what she says.'

'I know she'll say yes, she really likes you.'

315

'But your mother's nice to everyone.'

'It's not that. You know the other night when I blew my top at you?' Kim looked round as though someone might be listening. 'Well, she was really angry with me. She told me what a hard time you'd had with your own mother keeping everything secret from you. She said if there was one thing that Cody would have wanted, it was for me and you to be friends.'

'But he didn't even know about me.'

'That's the point,' said Kim, slapping him on the knee. 'You missed out. All the time he was playing with me and treating me like a son, it should have been you.'

Patrick swallowed and nodded, thinking of all those messages—to Kim with love.

'I think she wants to make it all up to you. My mum's like that.' Kim stared up into Patrick's face. 'I do as well. I've never had a friend I've liked as much as you.' For the first time since they'd met, Patrick was invaded with guilt about the deceit he was practising on Kim. He looked away, his eyes coming to rest on a giant demijohn. Flickering light from a faulty bulb made its contents sparkle a bright lurid green, and for a fleeting second he had the feeling that he should extricate himself from all this and get back to Cambridge.

'What about Carew?' he said carefully, his heart speeding a little. 'He won't want me around when he comes home, will he?'

It was Kim's turn to shrug off an answer. 'There's not much he can say if you're already there.'

There was another silence, then Patrick said, 'Perhaps we could come to some arrangement. Perhaps I could pay for my keep.'

'Yeah, that might be an idea. You could give it to my mother. She only gets what he hands out.' Kim's face brightened. 'Once we start earning money, we could even get a place of our own. A flat or something.' He rubbed his hands together, the rings clicking dully. 'We're going to make a fortune, you wait and see. You'll be too busy for degrees and all that crap.' The old-fashioned bell on the shop door began to jangle. Kim pointed a finger at him. 'You go. I want to make a phone call.'

Patrick slid from the worktop, shaky from lack of food and too much lager. A whole family were poking around in the box of printed T-shirts, the children dragging them out one by one and holding them up with sniggers and giggles. The slogans seemed to get progressively worse, and the mother suddenly snatched them all away and stuffed them back into the box, shepherding her offspring out with a curt thank you.

Kim was still on the phone, his tone argumentative in a private sort of way. Patrick leant against the counter, caught in a vacuum, unable to focus his mind clearly on anything.

'She wants to speak to you,' Kim called round the doorway.

'Who?'

'My mother.' Kim had a hand covering the mouthpiece and an impatient look on his face. 'I called to ask her about you staying. Quick, come and talk to her,' he said as Patrick stood there with his mouth half open.

In a daze he took the receiver.

'Can Kim hear?' Leah said very quietly.

'No.' Kim had gone to serve another customer.

'Was this your idea?' Her voice was still very low but filled with anger.

'Partly.'

'What are you trying to do to me?'

He wanted to apologise but with Kim liable to appear any moment he could only mutter a meaningless, 'Nothing.'

'You've been drinking as well, haven't you?'

'Yeah.'

'You'd better not stay here tonight,' she said. 'Do you hear?'

'Yeah.'

The line went dead.

'All right. Goodbye,' he mumbled into the hum of the receiver because Kim had his head round the door.

'She's not too happy, is she?' said Kim.

Patrick shook his head. He couldn't trust himself to speak to Kim with the storm of disappointment boiling away inside him.

'Don't worry.' Kim slapped his arm. 'We'll talk her round. I think she's a bit jittery about Carew finding out what I'm up to. I didn't think she knew so much—I expect that cow Tanya's been opening her big mouth.'

'What did she say to you?' said Patrick, stony-faced.

'Oh, just that I was trying to influence you and ruin your future. Come on, I've got something to cheer us up.' He whizzed through to the back room, unlocked a drawer marked *nux vomica,* and took out an old tobacco tin. 'This is something Tanya doesn't know about,' he said with a little grin, holding it carefully against his chest and levering up the lid. 'This is just for you and me.'

'I don't want the fucking stuff,' said Patrick, lounging irritably against the door frame, arms folded tightly across his chest.

'You don't have to smoke it, you can—'

'I don't care what you do with it. It's a load of crap like the rest of the stuff in here.'

Kim stood there blinking, his expression a mixture of confusion and hurt. 'But I thought... I thought you were beginning to get interested. I thought we were going to do this together. Don't you want to stay now?'

'I don't know,' Patrick said through gritted teeth.

'I'll persuade my mother, don't worry about that. We'll say you're just going to stay until the term starts. Why have you changed your mind?'

'I haven't. Now, can we drop it? I've got a splitting headache.' He quickly put up a hand. 'And I don't want any of your fucking cures.'

Kim shut the tobacco tin and pushed it into the back pocket of his jeans. 'You're still mad at me about Sunday night, aren't you?'

'No.' Patrick said with forced patience, closing his eyes because his head really was killing him.

'Then what the fuck have I done?'

'Nothing.'

Kim threw him a wounded look and went to lean on the worktop. He took out the tin again and played idly with its contents. 'You're a moody fucker, Patrick,' he said. 'I can't think why we all like you so much.'

'No, it's a mystery to me as well.' Patrick stared across at him, perfectly straight-faced, but a current of some kind seemed to run back and forth between them. At that moment, the bell in the shop began to clang. 'I'll go,' he said.

When he came back, Kim was busy mixing up something in a marble bowl, pouring carelessly measured amounts from a number of bottles and phials. There were splashes of liquid and trails of powder all over the worktop.

'I'm going to convince you once and for all,' he said. 'If we're going to do this together, you've got to believe in it. I want you to believe in it.' He looked up. His pupils were dilated so that his eyes looked darker and bigger than ever. 'You know what I'm making, don't you?'

Patrick shook his head, though he knew very well.

'Yes you do,' Kim laughed. 'Look at the colour, you know it.' He stuck a miniature funnel into the neck of one of his little blue bottles, and decanted the liquid into it. With the funnel still in place, he added a few white crystals, pinching them in as though he was adding salt to a meal. 'Nearly forgot that,' he said, licking his fingers clean.

Patrick watched, mesmerised, wondering once

320

more how he could ever have chanced giving this stuff to Leah.

'We'll go out tonight,' said Kim, forcing a tiny cork into the bottle. 'Pick up a couple of girls. Take them for a drink.' He smiled. 'Then you'll see.'

'Kim, I can't, not tonight. I'm too pumped up with all that lager. And my head.'

'Tomorrow then. It keeps.'

'I might not be here tomorrow.'

'You will be. I'll persuade her, don't worry.'

Leah had set the table on the terrace with a cloth and a vase full of bright orange marigolds. She'd even taken the trouble to put out folded napkins instead of the box of Kleenex she usually dumped in the middle of the table when they began eating.

Zula lay on the lawn, a bone between her paws. As they approached, her tail began to wag but at the same time a deep warning growl came from her throat. Kim aimed a teasing kick at her and sniffed the air. 'Something smells good.' He smiled at Patrick over his shoulder. 'Cheer up. She wouldn't have done all this if she was still mad at us.'

They went through to the kitchen. Jo-jo was in his baby chair and Leah was sitting in front of him spooning something sloppy-looking into his mouth. Most of it was oozing out again as he gurgled and jigged with excitement.

Kim went straight over and kissed her, then pulled up a chair close beside her. 'What's that cooking?'

'Chicken.' She looked at him very seriously for a moment, then her face broke into a smile. 'And roast potatoes.' She also smiled round at Patrick. It was as though the phone call had never happened.

'Tanya's not home yet then?' said Kim.

'No, but she shouldn't be long. We'll eat when she gets here.' She carried on feeding Jo-jo, and Kim leant closer to her and dipped his finger in the bowl.

'Don't, Kim.' She pushed him away. 'You smell like a brewery.'

'I've only had a couple. We went to the pub for our lunch.'

'You weren't supposed to close the shop. You know that.'

Patrick slid onto a chair the other side of the table and stared across the room. Time was slipping by again, wasted seconds and minutes. Soon it would run out completely and he could do nothing about it. Leah eased another spoonful into Jo-jo's mouth, gently scraping the dribbles from his chin. It seemed to take ages.

Kim got up to go searching in the fridge for something to eat, and Patrick looked quickly towards her but she was busy wiping Jo-jo's face. He thought of that afternoon last week when she'd reached for him across the table as soon as Tanya's back was turned. Now she barely acknowledged his presence.

'Perhaps I'd better go up and pack my things,' he said in a bleak attempt to get some reaction from her.

Kim straightened up, a hunk of cheese in his

hand. 'Mum,' he whined in protest. 'Can't he just stay for another week?'

Leah got up, moving so abruptly that she dropped the baby's spoon and sent it spinning across the floor.

'Mum,' Kim repeated. 'He doesn't have to be back—'

She wheeled round. 'Don't start, Kim, just don't start.' She was holding the bowl in front of her as though she was about to throw it at him. He flinched back from her. 'Don't think I wouldn't,' she shouted at him, then marched off towards the sink.

Kim looked at Patrick and pulled a face. 'Later,' he mouthed, a wary eye on his mother.

Patrick stared down at the scrubbed wood of the table, its surface patterned with the rings of hundreds of too-hot cups and pans.

'Want some cheese?' muttered Kim.

Patrick shook his head, then scrambled to his feet and rushed off upstairs.

He began packing his things, stuffing them any old how into his holdall. The next thing he knew, the door was opening, then clicking quietly closed. He knew it was Leah but wouldn't look up.

'Patrick, I'm sorry.' She came up behind him and put her arms round his waist. 'I don't want you to go away unhappy.'

He made a feeble attempt to pull her off but she hugged him tighter.

'I don't think you believe how serious I am about you,' he said, dragging the zip across so furiously that it ripped a protruding shirt sleeve.

'I do,' she murmured, pressing her cheek against his back. 'But how do you think I'd feel if you were here when Carew came home? Can't you imagine how unbearable it would be, for both of us?' He let her turn him round and take his hands between hers, manipulating him like a dummy. 'We'll see each other again soon. I'll come to Cambridge.'

'I might not be there,' he said dully.

'Patrick, please be sensible. You have to do your degree. You mustn't wreck your future—I don't want that on my conscience.'

'I'd give it all up for you.' He came to life, gripping her arms. 'Can't you understand? I don't want the future without you.'

'This isn't the end, Patrick. I don't want it to finish any more than you do.'

'Then let me stay tonight. I'll go early tomorrow. Just let me stay tonight,' he repeated. He tried to kiss her, but a car door banged down below, and she held him off and ran to the window.

'It's Tanya. Now be very careful what you say in front of her. She's already suspicious.'

'Is she? Kim's not.'

'No, I know he isn't.' She smiled. 'But in his own way I think Kim's a little in love with you himself.' Zula had begun to bark and whine in a high-pitched welcome. 'I'd better go down.'

'What about tonight?'

She hesitated. 'I don't know. But you definitely can't spend the night in my room. Imagine if he came home early. Look, I'll have to go. We'll talk later.'

They were all out on the terrace drinking tea when Patrick went down. As soon as he appeared, Leah got up, saying she would put Jo-jo to bed before she served the dinner.

'She's got over it now,' Kim said as Patrick pulled out a chair. 'I haven't seen her blow her top like that for ages.'

Tanya looked up. She was surrounded by large floppy cardboard boxes tied with thin string. 'What's been going on?'

'Oh, just Mum,' Kim said. 'Getting a bit wild.'

'I thought her adrenalin must be running high.' Tanya flicked a finger at the marigolds which had drooped nearly in half, their petals already closing for the night. 'Flowers on the table, roast chicken—what's been happening?'

'Nothing,' said Kim with a little scowl. 'She's cooked chicken before.'

'What have you got there?' asked Patrick in a bid to change the subject.

Tanya opened one of the boxes and with a little flourish held up a white cotton shirt almost identical to the ones they'd seen in the boutique on their day out.

'Wow,' said Kim. 'Very fancy.'

'It's not fancy, it's romantic,' she said, smoothing down the creased frills on the neck. 'Looks like I'll have to iron them all. Here.' She held it towards Patrick. 'Try it on.'

He shook his head. 'Not now.'

'Go on,' urged Kim.

'Are you deaf? I said no.'

Tanya's eyebrows shot up. 'What's up with

you? Hard day in the shop?'

Kim laughed. 'You have to tread a bit carefully with him today.'

'Getting a bit wild too, is he?'

Patrick poured himself some tea, steeling himself to ignore them.

'I suppose you'll have to be my model then.' Tanya tossed the shirt on to Kim's lap.

Kim was soon parading about in the shirt, a burgundy velvet jacket and matching leather boots.

'Mmm, you'd look quite fanciable if you were a few inches taller,' Tanya smiled.

'And if I had black hair and big blue eyes,' teased Kim. 'Come on, Patrick, try something on, just for Tanya.'

'Yeah, just for me,' said Tanya. She came up behind him, reached over and quickly pulled his T-shirt out of his jeans. 'Come on, Patrick,' she mocked. 'Get your clothes off.'

It wasn't a joke. He caught her expression as he twisted away from her, and knew it was done spitefully.

'You're as stupid as him,' he said, tucking his T-shirt back in.

'Stupid I am not,' she said pointedly, roughing up his hair.

He ducked away from her. 'Piss off.'

'Pa-te-rrick,' scolded Kim. 'Show a bit more interest than that when a lady tries to undress you—specially Tanya, she's desperate.'

Tanya smiled pleasantly, she even put out a hand and gently smoothed down Patrick's ruffled hair. 'He's only interested in one person,

326

Kim, and that's your mother.'

A lopsided smile came and went on Kim's face, the corner of his lip rising and falling as though he wasn't quite sure what he'd heard. Tanya bent down to gather up the boxes, feigning indifference, like someone who has planted a bomb and then walks calmly away before it explodes.

'What are you on about?' Kim's smile had vanished. 'What are you fucking on about, Tanya?'

Patrick dropped his head to stare at the grey flags of the terrace.

'Ask him,' said Tanya.

'I'm asking you, you fucking liar.'

'Don't you swear at me.' She jumped to her feet. 'What do you think he's here for, eh? Eh?' she repeated louder.

'He's my friend. That's why he's here. You're just jealous.' He fired the words out in short bursts. 'You're always fucking jealous.'

Tanya stared at him, her eyes narrowed. 'Oh yeah? Ask him. It's days with you and nights with your mother. If you don't believe me, ask her where she was all night when we went to London last week.'

Patrick looked up now. He spread apologetic hands, began to speak, but the words were lost as Kim came charging at him like a mad bull and butted him in the face. Patrick went sprawling. Zigzags of silvery light flashed across his vision and the ground billowed beneath him. He could hear Zula barking madly in the background but couldn't make out a word

327

of what Kim was shouting at him only a few feet away. He tried to get up but had barely raised his head when he felt a hard kick in the mouth; then more kicks, over and over into his ribs until everything spiralled into darkness.

Shapes appeared in front of him. Someone was hauling him up, and he found himself sitting against the rough stone wall of the terrace. Zula was howling from somewhere far off, and directly in front of him Leah was crying hysterically. He blinked a few times to get her into focus, and could see Tanya was crouched beside her.

'It's OK,' he managed. 'I'm all right.'

'Can you see?' asked Tanya.

He nodded and put a hand to his mouth. It was sticky with blood, and his lips and tongue felt peculiar. Tanya reached out and touched his left temple. 'I don't think it's too deep. Are you sure you can see all right?'

Patrick nodded again and closed his eyes because his head was spinning.

'Why did you have to tell him?' sobbed Leah.

'Don't try and put the blame on me. It's your fault. This is all your bloody fault.'

'You don't understand,' Leah wailed. 'Nobody understands.'

'Oh no?' said Tanya. 'I understand perfectly. I bet the minute you laid eyes on him...' She broke off and glared at Leah. 'You just couldn't resist him, could you?'

'It wasn't like that.'

'I'm not a fool, Leah. And neither is Carew,

so stop bawling and let me think what we're going to do. Where's Kim?'

'Gone indoors,' sobbed Leah.

'Stop bawling,' shouted Tanya. 'Go and get the first aid box and some water. We'll try and patch him up ourselves.'

'I'll be OK.' Patrick struggled to stand up, levering his elbows on top of the wall.

Tanya pushed on his shoulders. 'Stay where you are until I can see what damage he's done.' She prodded careful fingers against his ribs. 'How does that feel?'

It felt extremely painful but he took a breath, also painful, and said, 'Not too bad.'

'He's probably cracked a rib or two. How are your teeth?'

He ran a tentative finger inside his mouth. His lips hurt like hell but all his teeth seemed to be intact.

'Oh, shit.' Tanya stood up as shouting and screaming came from the house. Leah appeared at the French doors. She had a bowl in her hands and Kim was close behind her. He was crying and trying to stop her. Water splashed from the bowl as he caught her arm, and she suddenly turned and flung the lot at him, screaming that she'd never ever forgive him.

Tanya went tearing over to them, and Kim ran off yelling that he was going to kill them all. Patrick made a supreme effort to get up, preparing to defend himself if Kim attacked him again. He managed to get himself on to one of the chairs just as Tanya came hurrying back to him.

'For God's sake pull yourself together,' she shrieked at Leah. 'Go and get some more water. And bring a cloth so I can wipe all this blood up.'

When Leah came back with another bowl of water, it was Tanya who took charge again. She washed the cut over Patrick's eye and stuck a large plaster on it, then dabbed the blood from his mouth and where it had run down his face and neck.

'Does he need any stitches?' asked Leah. She was shaking, a sob breaking out as she spoke.

'I don't think so.' Tanya peeled up the plaster for another look. Patrick sat there clutching the sides of the chair, worried that he was going to pass out and fall off it.

'We'll have to get him home,' said Tanya.

'He can't go like this,' said Leah. 'He'll have to stay here tonight.'

'Don't be bloody stupid. We've got to get him out of here as soon as possible.'

Leah fell silent, shivering as though she was freezing cold.

'You'd better go and try to talk some sense into that son of yours,' Tanya said irritably. 'Enlighten him about what will happen if Carew ends up divorcing you. Ask him if he fancies working for his living!'

'I'll tell Carew myself. I'll explain everything to him.'

'Don't push your luck. You won't keep him drooling over what you've got between your legs forever, you know.'

'I hate you,' said Leah, breaking down in

330

tears again, then running off indoors.

'And sometimes, sister darling, I hate you,' Tanya called after her.

Patrick put his hands to his head. 'Stop it, stop it. It's not her fault.'

'It *is* her fault. And don't be taken in by all that crying. She can turn on the tears to order—always has done.' Tanya began scrubbing away at the blood-spattered flagstones. 'Sing me a song and make me cry,' she mimicked in a childish voice. 'Look at my eyes and see the tears.' With a last angry wipe she got up and emptied the bowl of bloody water into a flowerpot. 'Now sit tight a minute while I go and make sure she's not sending Kim into hysterics again.'

Patrick got shakily to his feet, a hand against his ribs, and took a few testing steps. It wasn't too bad as long as he didn't breathe too deeply. Everywhere was silent now; even Zula had stopped her dreadful howling. At the bottom of the lawn, dusk was already settling. This time last night he'd been feverish with excitement, watching Kim drink himself into oblivion while he waited to go to Leah. Now everything was in ruins.

He walked a few paces more, and then a few more until he was at the end of the terrace. For a moment, seeing the figure standing at the corner of the house, half hidden in shadow, he thought he was hallucinating. It moved, took shape, the long tangled hair blown black, caught in the draught between the house and the garage.

'Kim?' he said tentatively, wincing as fresh blood seeped from his lip.

Kim jerked his head away and leant back against the wall, arms crossed. Patrick walked towards him, bracing himself. All he planned to do was hold him off; he hadn't the slightest urge to hurt Kim, either in self-defence or revenge.

'Kim,' he said again, stopping a few feet away.

In answer, Kim held something towards him. 'It was for her, wasn't it?'

Patrick didn't need to look; he knew what it was.

'You gave it to my mother, didn't you?'

Patrick shook his head; blood came trickling down his face. 'No, I didn't. I told you, I didn't give it to anyone.' He looked now, and saw the little blue bottle.

'You liar.' Kim's lips twisted together; his face was streaked with tears and misery. 'You gave it to her at that party. Then you came to our house.'

'Kim, listen. Your mother and me—it's nothing to do with your potions.'

Kim stepped forward and thrust the bottle in his face. 'Here, you drink it. You drink it like you gave it to my mother.'

'Look, don't be silly, I've got to drive home. I'm in enough of a state as it is, thanks to you.'

'You're shit, that's what you are. You used me. All you wanted was my mother—and this.' He dangled the bottle from his fingertips.

'No, Kim. I asked you for it to please you...make out I believed you, that's all.'

You liar. You fucking liar.'

I've had a good time with you,' Patrick said in desperation. 'I didn't use you, and I didn't want your potions.'

Kim leant back against the wall again. His eyes sparkled with tears in the dim light. 'I know you gave it to my mother,' he said. 'She wouldn't have looked at you otherwise. She was happy as she was. She doesn't need any fuckers like you.'

'It's crap, Kim, and you know it.'

Kim held the bottle towards him again, his arm outstretched, his face sullen. 'Scared?' he said.

Patrick snatched it. 'What do I have to do to bring you to your senses?' He pulled out the cork, tilted his head back and shook the contents of the bottle down his throat, careful to avoid touching his lips. In one swallow it was all gone. It had barely any taste, just faintly metallic and slightly heating against the back of his tongue. He remembered how he'd poured the lot into Leah's coffee and how she'd complained about the taste. He stared at Kim. 'Satisfied?'

'You wait. You'll find out.' Kim swung round as Leah appeared at the far end of the terrace. She stood there, calling for Patrick, and Kim stepped quickly back behind the garage.

There was something lost and childlike about Leah as she came running across the flagstones.

Patrick wanted to hold out his arms, gather her up and drive off with her. Perhaps they could do that; perhaps she would come with him. The illusion lasted for the few seconds it took to imagine it, then Tanya came marching up behind her, carrying his holdall. He looked round but Kim had disappeared.

'Just say goodbye to him, Leah, then let him go,' commanded Tanya. 'I'll go and search for Kim.' She handed Patrick his holdall. 'Are you fit to drive?'

'Yeah, I'll be fine,' Patrick nodded.

Leah put her arms round his waist. 'I'll phone you tomorrow,' she said, then covered her face with her hands and sobbed. 'I don't know what to do, I don't know what to do.' He stroked her hair; he couldn't do much more; every breath hurt and his lips had swollen so much that he could see them when he looked down.

Tanya was walking away but after a few steps she turned back and yelled, 'Leah! Let him go and get indoors.'

And like an echo, Kim bellowed from behind the garage, 'I'll give you ten seconds to get out of here.'

Patrick half turned and saw Tanya go running over to him. Leah pulled away. 'I'm sorry, Patrick, I have to go.'

'Just make sure you phone me,' he called after her. 'Or come to Cambridge.' But his words were drowned out by Kim's shouting and the awful noise of Zula beginning to howl once more.

334

# Chapter 19

An urgent desire to vomit woke him but as he sat upright every nerve in his body screamed in protest. It took him several seconds of careful breathing to gather enough strength to get out of the car and stagger clear. In one agonising heave, his stomach emptied itself of all the lunchtime lager. He wiped a sleeve across his mouth without thinking, and was immediately in more pain.

It was pitch dark. He remembered pulling into the layby but couldn't recall where it was or how far he was from Cambridge. Shivering so violently his teeth were chattering, he crawled back into the car and drove on. It was difficult to drive; he felt sick and dizzy and could only see out of one eye because the left one had swollen closed. A couple of times he lost his concentration and nearly skidded off the road, dragging the wheel round just in time. Luckily there was little other traffic about, and after what seemed like hours and hours, he found himself back at Cambridge.

The house was quiet—everyone obviously in bed—and Patrick did his best to creep in unheard. But as he turned his key in the lock, the door swung open before he was ready, and he went with it, flying into the hallway head first. He landed against the wall, knocking over a bicycle that was propped there.

All three girls came out of the ground-floor flat. Bel rushed to kneel beside him.

'Jesus Christ! What the hell's happened to you?'

'A fight,' he groaned. 'I've been in a fight.' She peered closer, leaning over him, a hand on his forehead. Her face looked distorted, stretched and curving like the reflection in a trick mirror, and her fingers felt cold and sharp as chips of ice. He struggled to get to his feet; Bel caught his arm to help.

'We ought to take you to casualty.'

'No, I'm OK. Honest, I'll be OK.'

'What happened? Come in with us for a minute.'

He shook his head and pulled away from her, grabbing hold of the banisters to heave himself up the stairs. All three of them followed, trying to help him. But he wanted only to be on his own, and at his door he muttered that he'd see them in the morning, and disappeared inside.

But by morning he was feeling too wretched to see anyone. When Bel came tapping at his door, he called out a muffled, 'I'll see you later,' and buried his head in the pillow once more. He'd spent the whole night vomiting and shivering, crawling to the washbasin and back in a daze of pain. Towards dawn, retching once more on a sore and empty stomach, he cursed Kim, spluttering the worst obscenities he could think of, while he clung to the hard, cold porcelain of the bowl.

And when finally he slept, it was like being

pitched into an alien world, a swirling desert of heat from which he woke tearing at the sweat-soaked clothes that he'd been too weak to remove. But as soon as he took off his jeans, he was shivering again. He crawled back under the duvet and tried to concentrate his thoughts on the highlights of the last few days so that when he fell back to sleep he would dream beautiful dreams of Leah. But it didn't work; there *was* a woman in his dreams but she had no identity. She slid into bed with him and pressed herself down on him with the force and detachment of a rapist. The sensation had him writhing with nightmarish arousal. He floated upon surge after surge of excitement only to wake sweating with disappointment. Almost at once he drifted back to sleep, and found her there again. It seemed to go on and on. She became violent, sucking his split lip into her mouth, and he was launched on a roller coaster of spontaneous orgasm. After this, he fell into a deep and dreamless sleep until late afternoon when Bel came knocking again.

'Patrick, are you all right?'

'Yeah,' he called weakly.

'Come to the door,' she demanded. 'We've been knocking for you all day.'

All day? It meant something but he couldn't quite think what. 'Hang on,' he called, suddenly remembering. He staggered to the door and opened it a fraction. 'There hasn't been a phone call for me, has there?' he said.

'No, 'fraid not.'

He was about to close the door but Bel

337

stuck her hand against it. 'Is there anything you want?'

He shook his head.

'You do look a sight.' She smiled gently, ignoring his lack of gratitude. 'You ought to get some of that blood washed off. Do you want me to help you?'

A ball of self-pity rose in his throat; he imagined himself lying with his head in her lap while she washed his face and offered sympathy.

'No, I'm OK now, I can do it myself. You will give me a shout if there's a call for me, won't you?'

'Of course I will. Sure you're all right then?'

'Yeah, I just need to sleep,' he mumbled, closing the door before he made a fool of himself.

And sleep he did. Through the evening and all night and part of the following day, waking only once to have a long drowsy pee in the washbasin. And if it hadn't been for Bel knocking once more, he would have slept on even longer. He thought it was part of a dream where he'd been having sex on the white sofa in the games room, and someone came banging on the door. They wouldn't go away, and when finally he'd gone to open it, he found his father standing there. He jolted upright, rigid with shock.

'Open the door, Patrick, or we'll go and get a key off the landlord.' It was Bel, shouting and hammering on the door. 'Patrick! Open up, your mother's here.'

'OK, OK, I'm coming.' He looked desperately round the room, trying to focus on the shambles that surrounded him. When he finally stumbled across to open the door, pulling on his jeans as he went, he heard Bel say, 'Here he comes.'

Ginny stepped forward. He put the back of his hand to his mouth in an attempt to hide his face, and stood aside to let her in.

'I'll leave you to it then,' said Bel, closing the door behind them.

Patrick leant back against it and closed his eyes for a moment.

'She phoned me,' began Ginny. 'Leah Carew.' Her voice was pitched very low and she had her eyes fixed on his chest.

'When?'

'Yesterday. She told me that her son had attacked you, that's all.'

Patrick gave a long sigh and turned his head away from her. 'I'm all right,' he said. 'You needn't have come all this way.'

'I am your mother. I do care.' She broke off and looked round the room. 'What a mess,' she said, her voice choked with tears.

It seemed to emphasise the lack of communication between them. The need for sympathy ballooned inside him again. He shivered and wrapped his arms round his chest, then went to sit on the bed, head in his hands.

Ginny began to tidy up. He heard her wash out the basin, running the hot tap until steam drifted across the room.

'Hold your head up.' She was standing over him with a wet towel. He did as she said, and with careful little dabs she cleaned the dried blood from his face, then eased up the plaster on his temple. Without a word she fetched her bag, took out a tube of antiseptic cream, and smoothed a thick layer over the cut. 'I'm not sure if you don't need a stitch in that. What did he hit you with?'

'Just his head. It'll be all right.'

'Are your teeth okay?'

He nodded, and she gave a brief little smile. 'That's lucky. You always had such good teeth.'

She carried on cleaning him up in the matter-of-fact way she dealt with the twins, ordering him to lift up his arms so that she could pull his T-shirt over his head.

'You're covered in bruises,' she said in the same calm way. She sat down on the bed, folding the blood-spattered T-shirt into a neat little square as though it had just come fresh from the wash. He watched her pat and smooth it, then suddenly she held it to her face and began to cry. 'I can't bear to see you like this,' she sobbed.

He felt like crying too. He wanted to comfort her, cry with her, but he couldn't make that first move, and after a few seconds she got up and began removing the dirty linen from the bed.

'Have you got a clean pillowcase?' she asked, wiping away the tears as she spoke.

He sniffed back his own tears, and pointed towards a cupboard.

She changed the whole bed, and when it was done, he took off his jeans and lay down on the cool clean sheet. He watched her shake up the duvet, thumping it into shape before covering him with it.

'You look so pale,' she said, tucking it round him. He closed his eyes and felt the bed give as she sat down. 'It's all my fault,' she whispered, beginning to cry again.

He shook his head and muttered a barely audible, 'No, no it's not.'

'I should have told you.' She sounded as though she was trying to compose herself. 'I should have told you so you didn't go searching for him. I wish that's what I'd done. I wish I'd explained everything—told you why I didn't want any contact with him.'

Patrick waited, an odd little knot of anxiety tightening in his chest.

Ginny blew her nose, cleared her throat. 'It's so difficult to talk about.'

It was all so difficult. He stared up at the ceiling; it looked very grey and distant seen through only one eye. So very difficult. He thought of that day he'd worn his father's suit, and Leah's suggestion that he should wear it in front of Ginny. 'Please tell me about him,' he said. He heard her take a deep breath, and felt her shift position as though to get comfortable before she began. It reminded him of waiting for a bedtime story; Ginny had always been the one who read them to him.

'I was only fifteen when I first saw him. He was playing in a group of Irish musicians in a pub where we used to go.' She spoke in a flat monotone, looking down at her hands. 'I wasn't supposed to go there—you can imagine what trouble I'd have been in if Mum had known about it. But I had a friend who was a couple of years older than me, and I was tall for my age—maybe I looked older, I don't know. I was sort of going out with her brother, David, but he was more interested in being with his mates, and I got left on my own a lot. I didn't care though, I'd just sit in a corner of the bar and listen to the music. And watch.' She turned her head a fraction. 'Gabriel Patrick Cody, that was his name. He had his initials on his mandolin case. My friend asked him what they stood for—I asked her to. Everyone knew I had a crush on him. I wasn't the only one, he was very, very good-looking. Still, you've seen his photo, you know that.' She paused and took another deep breath. 'One night, when I was sitting there on my own, he came and spoke to me. Just something like, all on your own again? I expect I blushed; I was very shy, and he was twice my age. Then he walked off to the bar. David was with his mates as usual, but he came to see if I wanted a drink. When he went to get it, Gabriel put his arm out to block David's way. He said, if you keep leaving that lovely little girl friend of yours on her own, someone is going to steal her from you.' Ginny smiled to herself. It was a half embarrassed smile but so full of the pleasure of old memories that it seemed very poignant. 'I remember his words very clearly; I went to sleep dreaming of them. David felt a fool, I suppose, because he swore at him to mind his own business. Gabriel got hold of him round the throat, quite viciously, and wouldn't let go until someone stopped him. I didn't care—I thought it was all because of me.' She came to a sudden halt. 'Is that tap water all right to drink?'

'Yeah. Or there's a can of cider in the cupboard.'

'Maybe I'll have just half of it. Do you want the rest?'

Patrick's stomach did a somersault at the thought of it. 'No thanks.'

There was an awkwardness about her as she went to get the cider, then searched for a glass. Her movements were jerky, puppet-like, making Patrick feel tense for her. He tried to think of something to say to make her relax, fearing she might not go on.

But when she came back with half a glass of the cider, she took only a few sips before starting again.

'After that,' she shrugged, 'things just developed, and a couple of weeks later he picked me up from school one afternoon. He took me back to a flat. I don't know where it was, I didn't even think about it.' She took another few mouthfuls of the cider. 'I would have done what he wanted. I hadn't done it before...but I would have, with him, willingly.' With the next pause, she gulped down all that remained in the glass. 'But that wasn't what he wanted—not a willing girl.'

Patrick sat up, partly to break the silence and partly to ease the pain of his ribs which seemed to have gained an extra ache. It was like a burning sensation, spreading in hot fingers across his chest.

'You ought to have an X-ray,' Ginny said.

'X-ray?' he repeated blankly, then realised he had both hands held against his chest. 'It's not so great discovering you're the product of a rape, if that's what you're trying to say.'

'More or less—that's how it ended up.' She started to cry again, and this time he leant forward and put an arm round her shoulders.

'I knew he had a lot of women—Leah told me that. I knew that right from the beginning.'

'I'm not surprised.' Ginny put down the glass and picked up his T-shirt from where she'd tossed it on the floor with the sheet and pillowcase. She stretched it out, then crumpled it up into a ball. 'He probably only saw them once—that would have been enough for any normal woman. He kept me there for three hours... I couldn't tell anyone, I just couldn't. They would have made me repeat it all... I just couldn't.'

He squeezed her shoulder and put his head against hers. 'Don't cry,' he said. 'It's not your fault.'

'And, Patrick... I want you to know, I wouldn't have got rid of you, I swear I wouldn't. They suggested that to me, but I wouldn't. I just wish I'd stood up to them about who brought you up. When I left home, when I got so depressed about everything... You see, I didn't have any say in it.' Her words were punctuated by weeping. 'When I came back, they'd taken over completely. They bought your clothes, they told you what to do and when to do it. I came back to a child who hardly knew me. And they said that was best,

344

but nobody thought about me.'

'Larry knows, doesn't he?' It was just one of the many questions he wanted to ask her, and he picked it for its safety, or so he thought.

'I had to tell him. After what happened, I had problems with certain things...in our marriage.' She smiled at him through pale wet lashes. 'See, I still can't explain it properly to you.'

'It's OK, I understand.'

'I want you to, Patrick,' she sighed. 'I used to dream that we'd become really close once you came to live with us. I thought I'd be able to tell you all this calmly and...' She paused. 'But somehow I couldn't, and then it was all too late. When I found out you'd gone to that house, I was devastated. And upset you hadn't told me.' Her voice had nearly died away but she gave a little cough and started again. 'I only went there because I was desperate. You'd just learnt to walk. I bought you some shoes but Mum said they were no good and she and Dad would buy some. It seems a small enough thing now but it felt so important at the time. We had a row about it, and she said that unless I could support you financially, I had better keep quiet. You know the way she can be.'

'Yeah,' he nodded.

'I had never wanted anything more to do with him...after that day. But when I saw that picture in the paper, I was so upset. I thought, why should he look so happy when I was so miserable? I think I was probably angry—I don't really remember. I suppose I imagined that if I went there and confronted

345

him, he'd do something to support you, and I could get you back from Mum and Dad. Don't forget I was only seventeen—things seem very black and white at that age.'

'So you went there.'

'It took me weeks to pluck up the courage, and when I saw that beautiful house, I nearly came away. But I'd already got this picture in my mind of you and me in a little flat somewhere, and that kept me going.' She was still fiddling with the T-shirt, weaving it in and out of her fingers. He wanted to take it from her and hold on to her hand, but knew that soon Leah's name would be mentioned, and because of that, he couldn't do it. It was something about the feel of one palm against another, the intimacy of it, a feeling that it would link them all together in some obscure way.

'Justina answered the door. I've told you about that and how she dragged hold of her sister, how she hit her. But I didn't tell you how she swore at me. She said, he's a fucking tom cat, he'll fuck anything that moves. Patrick, I'm not just saying this to be spiteful, but they were like animals, swearing and fighting. And they were dirty...that beautiful house, and they were so scruffy and wild looking.'

Patrick sat very still. He knew she was telling the truth.

'Leah... I have to tell you...' Ginny paused. 'She looked the worst because she had on all this awful make-up and a tight minidress, although she was clearly pregnant—and younger than me, I thought. And there was another girl

346

as well, much younger. She was in the front garden—barefoot like they all were—and as I left, she picked up a handful of gravel off the path and threw it at me. She shouted, go away, bitch. My shoes were full of little stones but I didn't dare stop. I'd gone all that way...and they'd dashed my hopes in a few minutes.'

'They're not like that now,' he said quietly.

'But that's how I thought of them. I've never forgotten that day, and when I found out where you were...'

'Leah's not a bit like that. She hardly ever wears make-up. And she doesn't swear.' They were trivial things, but it felt important to make Ginny understand—undo that awful picture she had of them.

'Maybe not, Patrick, but she's married, isn't she?' It wasn't an accusation, and coming after so much else, it even felt like an invitation to talk about her.

'She doesn't love him. He's much older than she is.'

'And she's much older than you are.' Very gently, Ginny took hold of his hand.

'It doesn't feel like it.'

'I remember she was very pretty. Ruth said she was as well.'

'That's not the reason that I...for the way I feel about her.'

'But she's got a young baby, hasn't she?'

He nodded but the urge to talk about Leah had left him, and he drew his hand from Ginny's; there was so much he couldn't discuss with her.

347

'I suppose her older son found out what was going on, was that it?'

'Yeah.'

'Has he told his father?'

'It's his stepfather. He's abroad.' He knew he'd slipped into a 'don't ask me any more' tone, but Ginny just sighed and rubbed the back of his hand.

'I left the twins in the car,' she said, going to look out of the window. She opened it to crane her head out. 'It looks as though that girl from downstairs has taken them in with her. She said she'd look after them.'

'Go and bring them up. I don't look too bad, do I?'

'Well, you do, but they'll have to get over it. Are you coming home with me for a few days?'

'I... I won't come back with you,' he said slowly. 'I'll drive up in a day or two.' His heart felt very heavy. It was as though she took it for granted that he wouldn't be going back to Leah. And for the time being, he couldn't. All he could do was wait for her to phone him. But there was a wider inference to all this. It felt like the aftermath of a storm when everything settles down again and the disturbance is over, finished.

'I'll go and get the twins.' Ginny looked almost bright again. She went and washed her face and flicked a comb through her hair, then came to straighten the bed, mopping up a little seepage of blood from his lip. 'I won't be long.' She hesitated, then suddenly bent and kissed

348

him on the top of his head.

While she was gone, he thought over everything she'd told him. He felt blasted by it; not shocked, but damaged, as though his mind had undergone the same kind of attack as his body. Some of it hadn't quite sunk in; there were things that didn't fit, or they fitted in a way that he didn't want to think about or believe.

Ginny came back carrying a tray of coffee and biscuits. 'Look what Bel's done for us. What a nice girl. The twins were having a whale of a time with her. Weren't you?' she added over her shoulder.

They crept in behind her; it was obvious she'd warned them something was wrong. 'Yes, she's got lots of hats,' said one of them, her eyes fixed on Patrick.

Ginny laughed and pushed them both forward, but they stopped halfway across the room, tightly holding on to each other's hands.

'Don't worry, he'll get better soon,' said Ginny.

They looked at her, then back at Patrick and finally at each other.

'Go and sit with him, but be careful because he's got lots of bruises.' She gave them a biscuit each and bustled them over. They climbed on the bed but sat well away from him.

'Come and see me then, it's not contagious,' Patrick said, holding his arms out to them. They smiled at last, knowing a big word meant it must be funny, and crawled very carefully up beside him. Every single movement hurt to some degree, but he cuddled them, soothed by the closeness of their little warm bodies and their simple displays of affection. Soon they were feeding him tiny pieces of biscuit through his swollen lips.

He saw Ginny looking at them. 'Why don't you come home and stay for a bit?' she said. 'Till you...till you feel better.'

'I will come home, I promise you, but not just yet.' He rested his cheek on one of the twins' heads, his eyes on Ginny, pleading with her to understand and not start questioning him.

'You're not going to do anything silly, are you?' she said very quietly. 'About university, I mean.'

'We saw the university,' piped up one of the twins.

'Yes, and Mummy said you have to be really, really clever to go there,' said the other one. 'Are you really clever, Patrick?'

He tried not to smile because of his lip, but couldn't help it. 'No, I'm really stupid.'

'He's teasing you,' said Ginny. 'He is clever, he just does stupid things sometimes. Everyone does.' Their eyes met above the twins' heads again, and she came and sat with them.

'Whatever I decide, I'll tell you, OK?' he said.

She nodded. This new closeness between them was fragile; Patrick could almost feel the frailty of it. But it also felt precious. He wanted it to grow stronger, though he was well aware that this would depend on a number of things. Most important as far as he was concerned was whether Ginny was prepared to understand about Leah. But he guessed the critical thing for Ginny would be the decision he made about his future. And the two things were inextricably woven together.

## Chapter 20

Bel brought him food that evening.

'Your mother asked me to,' she said, thrusting the boxed pizza into his hands as though he might refuse. 'She left some money with me.'

'I'm getting into debt to you,' he smiled through the half-opened door.

'Don't worry about it, I might be asking you for a favour soon.' She swung off down the stairs before he could ask what, but he called over the banisters.

'You will give me a shout if there's a call for me, won't you?'

He saw her smiling up at him from below, her slanting green eyes bright with amusement.

'Don't worry, I'll be up banging on your door again the minute she phones,' she said, disappearing down the hall.

'Thanks, Bel, you're brilliant,' he shouted after her.

He stayed another whole day in his room. The cut on his forehead looked as though it would heal without stitches, but he now had a full-blown black eye, and his lip was still painfully swollen and seeped blood when he tried to shave and clean his teeth. His ribs were tender, but improving. Mentally, he was in limbo, waiting for the call from Leah.

The next day, he decided to go for a walk and test his fitness for the trip home. He had decided to go. There was always the chance that she would phone there instead, but he would leave a message with Bel just in case. He had no doubts that Leah would eventually phone him. There could be all sorts of reasons why she hadn't done so already. It was hard waiting, but it was all he could do, and this breathing space might even turn out to be a blessing in disguise—she might find she missed him too much to stay with Carew. He clung to this idea, and over the past twenty-four hours when his mind and body had finally cleared of whatever noxious ingredients Kim had poured into that little blue bottle, he'd made countless plans about their future together.

Coming down the stairs, he remembered how he'd fallen through the front door on Tuesday night. It seemed ages ago; in fact it was hard to believe that it was less than two weeks ago when he had stood waiting outside Mansour's house for Leah on the night of the party. Harder still to believe how much had happened to him between then and now—and how much he'd changed.

He knocked at Bel's door. One of the other girls answered and invited him in.

'I only wanted to say I'm just off out and—'

352

'We'll take a message,' Bel interrupted, with a teasing smile. She was at her music stand, her violin propped under her chin. She put it down and came to have a look at him, turning his face to the light with her fingertip. 'You're going to have a scar,' she frowned, her thin plucked brows coming together like little arrows. 'You should have had it stitched.'

'It'll make me all the more interesting,' he said, smiling very gingerly and touching the back of his hand to his mouth to mop up the saliva that dribbled out whenever he spoke.

Bel patted his cheek. 'You'll still be the prettiest boy in Corpus Christi.'

'Who beat you up, her husband?' asked one of the others.

'Mind your own business,' said Bel. She pushed him through the door, following him into the hall. 'Your mother said you might be going home soon.'

'Yeah, I might.'

'Do you go past St Albans?'

'I could do. Why, do you want a lift?'

'If you don't mind. I haven't been home at all this holiday. They keep nagging me so I'd better show my face for a couple of days. Here.' She pulled a tissue from her pocket. 'You're dribbling like a baby.'

'Thanks.' He took the tissue and wandered out into the sunshine, feeling oddly exposed after all the hours spent in his room. The glare hurt his eyes. He lowered his head and bumped straight into someone coming round the corner. An apology was on his lips when he looked up to find Carew in front of him.

The apology died away; he was speechless.

'Were you off somewhere important?' Carew sounded perfectly calm, even friendly. 'Only I think we need to talk.'

'I was just going for a walk, but if you want to...' Patrick waved an arm towards the house.

'No, no, I'll walk with you.' His expression had become a little grim. 'It might be better.'

They fell into step. Patrick stared straight ahead, waiting for Carew to begin. A group of students came laughing down the road towards them, taking all the pavement. Patrick hopped off the kerb to avoid them but Carew marched on, dividing them with his bulk. As they came together again, Carew said, 'I know what happened, Leah has told me everything.' They had come to the end of the road; there was another interruption while they crossed, weaving between traffic. 'Come on, this is useless, we'll go for a beer,' said Carew as they reached the other side.

Patrick followed him blindly into the pub and headed straight for a secluded corner table while Carew went to get the drinks. The shadowy interior of the bar was a relief; the billows of smoke and hubbub of conversation welcome.

Carew came back with two foaming half pints and placed them carefully on the cardboard mats. 'Kim really had a go at you, didn't he?' he said, settling himself in the angle of the bench seat opposite. He took a long slow mouthful of his beer, then leant forward and rested his elbows on the table, staring at Patrick over clasped hands. 'I'm sorry about that, but you'll heal.' He began tapping his knuckles together. 'Young bodies soon mend. Everything mends easily when you're young.' The longer Carew remained composed, the worse Patrick felt. It wasn't remorse or even guilt, but a growing certainty that Carew may have been told everything but he actually understood nothing.

Patrick cleared his throat but the words still came out discordant and hoarse after such a long silence. 'Does she know you're here?'

Carew shook his head. 'I didn't think it was wise to tell her. I've had enough to contend with already. I came home to a house in complete turmoil—Leah in bed with the baby and refusing to speak or get up, and Kim locked in the games room which, I might add, he has completely wrecked. Tanya was acting relatively sanely—for her that is.' He looked across the table, brows raised a fraction. 'So you see, I'm not looking for more trouble.'

'I thought... I thought Kim would calm down once I'd gone.'

'Oh, come on, you've got to know him quite well, I believe. You must have realised he wasn't going to stop at just battering you.' For the first time Carew sounded annoyed; he gave an impatient sigh and slapped a hand on the table. 'But I haven't come here to discuss Kim. I've come here to talk about you and my wife.'

Patrick took an awkward gulp of the beer. He didn't want it to be happening this way. Carew calmly sitting there opposite him, his tone mildly lecturing, felt worse than Kim's

355

attack. To discuss Leah with him, to even try and explain the beauty and intensity of what he felt for her, would be tantamount to betrayal. But he still wanted Carew to know the truth. He wiped a careful finger across his lips. 'I love her,' he said. 'I'm serious about her and I love her.'

'I'm sure you do. But the problem is, so do I. You might have the idea that because I haven't come here ranting and raving at you that I intend to pat you on the head and say, carry on, you've got advantages I can't compete with, I won't stand in your way. But I'm afraid it's not like that.'

'I don't think that. I—'

'And there is no way on this earth that she will carry on seeing you while she's married to me.' Carew shifted noisily on the leather bench. 'I shall fight you with reason, Patrick. And maybe a few home truths. Let me start by being brutal, shall I? I understand perfectly why you imagine you love her. She has everything, hasn't she? She can be anything, anyone. Sweet and kind and loving,' he lowered his voice, 'and very passionate. And you think she's only like that for you.'

'You can say what you like, but it won't make any difference.'

'Listen, be realistic. Do you really think she's going to leave me for you? Do you think she'll put you before Kim or the baby? And make no mistake, I'll fight tooth and nail before I let Jonah be taken away and brought up in some shabby little room. Or are you blind enough to imagine she'd leave without him?'

'No, of course not.' A couple of heads turned. Patrick lifted his glass, his hands shaking so much that the beer slopped. 'Give me your phone number. Let me talk to her. If she says she doesn't want to see me any more, OK, but I have to hear it from her.'

Carew shook his head very slowly. 'I'm not going to make it easy for you.'

'I'll come to the house then.'

'Patrick, you've done enough damage already. It's not only my marriage you're wrecking.' He stopped abruptly and rubbed a hand across his chest as though it pained him. 'Kim hasn't had an outburst like that for five years.' He paused again and gave his chest a little pat. 'But I don't suppose any of them have told you about the dog, have they?'

'Kim told me himself.' Patrick felt a little surge of triumph as though in some roundabout way Kim confiding in him had made him closer to Leah. 'I know all about it. He only hit you because he thought you'd hurt her.'

Carew's eyes narrowed slightly. 'What are you talking about?'

'When he hit you with the candlestick.'

'Oh, that was nothing. Kim had fits of temper like that all the time when he was younger. He'd hit out at the slightest provocation. That's not what I meant.' Carew's tone had become deadly serious. 'Didn't you know he killed the dog? He took it outside and beat it to death with a hammer. He was twelve years old and it took Tanya and me all the strength we had

357

to drag him off it. You had a lucky escape, take it from me.'

The hum of voices in the bar seemed to grow louder. Patrick swallowed back the shock, trying not to let it get the better of him.

'Kim wasn't totally to blame,' Carew went on, letting out a long sigh. 'He hasn't had the easiest of lives. Neither has Leah, come to that. But I understand them—both of them. Leah and I were very happy before you came on the scene. We were planning to have more children—that's what she loves best.' He glanced up. 'Children cost money. So does Leah. She's never worked. She can be extremely idle. When she's upset she just stays in bed. If I'm away, Kim waits on her. Sometimes the bedroom's like a tip when I get home—chocolate in the bed and clothes all over the floor.' He was smiling to himself, lost in thoughts of her. 'Tanya does most of the housework, and the cooking.'

It all fitted; it was the same Leah as Ginny's description, a Leah he knew himself, he just saw her with different eyes. He saw her now, sitting amongst a heap of rumpled bedclothes. He saw her curled on a kitchen chair in the scarlet kimono, hair unbrushed, reading a paper or playing with Jo-jo. Why was Carew telling him this? To put him off her? To demonstrate that he didn't know her?

'I don't care,' Patrick said quietly. 'I don't care about anything you've told me. I love her.'

'What?' Carew looked at him, blinking as though he hadn't quite heard.

'Why don't you ask her how she feels about me?'

'She's promised me that she won't contact you. Doesn't that say it all? She's made her choice. It's over, Patrick, so please don't cause more trouble by trying to see her.' He rubbed at his chest again, sighed and finished his beer with greedy gulps, then placed the glass down heavily on the mat. 'Kim didn't kill the dog because it bit her, he killed it because she lavished affection on it, just as she's done to you. I'm sure you can work out what will happen if you try to see her again. And Leah won't thank you if anything happens to Kim. You're way down the scale, Patrick.'

'I'm above you.'

Carew's eyes opened wide. 'You think so, do you? Don't fool yourself. You're supposed to be extra bright, aren't you? Hasn't it dawned on you yet why she's risked so much to have this fling with you?'

Patrick got to his feet. He was bathed in sweat and could see nothing but Carew's face shrunk to the size of a coin. 'Lies. It's all lies. You're just frightened of losing her. That's why you're saying all this.' The words bubbled from his swollen lips. He wasn't sure if they were coming out as he meant them and stopped as Carew began flapping a hand at him.

'Sit down, Patrick, you just didn't realise what you were getting into. Now finish your drink and I'll walk back with you. You don't look in a fit state to go rushing off on your own.'

Patrick shook his head and stumbled backwards. His chair fell sideways against the table. He went to grab it but it crashed to the floor, and he left it and went rushing out of the bar, barging into people on the way.

The street outside seemed unbearably full of light and noise, and he tucked his head down and marched on as quickly as he could without running. He took turning after turning as though he was trying to shake off a pursuer. If only he'd gone home with Ginny, he'd have escaped all this. But it would have happened eventually; Carew might even have come to London to confront him. Leah was his wife, and he didn't want to lose her. That's why he'd said all those things. That was the only reason. He slowed down, panting with exertion. How he hated Carew. For a moment he almost choked with the force of his hatred. But beneath it all there was a feeling of bleak inevitability, and something else, too deeply upsetting even to think about.

The sun was directly in his face now. It made his eyes water, and he wiped at them impatiently until the tissue that Bel had given him disintegrated into fluffy damp shreds. He tossed it away. It was some minutes before he realised that he was crying. The tears slid down to sting his lip, and he licked them away. But they became a flood, and he had to slip into an alleyway out of sight. He stood there, his forehead against a rough brick wall, and cried uncontrollably.

When the flow of tears eased, he thrust his

hand into his trouser pocket to see if he had a handkerchief. They were trousers he hadn't worn for some time, dragged out from the back of the cupboard because he was short of clean clothes. His fingers encountered something small and soft stuffed right at the bottom of the pocket. He pulled it out, knowing before he saw it that it was Jo-jo's little sock that he'd taken all those weeks ago. A vague fragrance still lingered on it: soap, babies, warm skin... His nostrils were suddenly full of Leah; his head whirled with images of her: barefoot in the kitchen on that first day he had seen her, and in the tangle of her bed on that last frenzied night. He pressed the sock against his eyes, first one, then the other, and walked on down the alleyway. It was long and shady, the high walls dripping with yellow and mauve flowers, some sprouting straight out of the brickwork. He would think of her until he reached the end; then it had to stop. But there were more thoughts than time left, and he slowed down, not wanting to let go of a single one.

He came out of the alleyway. Perhaps she was thinking of him too. Perhaps if he tried hard enough their thoughts would connect. Kim probably had a potion that would make such a thing possible—or he'd invent one some day in the future. He wandered along on that same route they had walked to the river with Ruth and Carl, and finally sank down on the grass on the same spot where they had all sat that day.

It was nearly dark by the time he got back to

the house. Bel's door was open and he could see a crowd of people inside. Upstairs there was a note pinned to his door. 'Sorry, still no call for you. Drop down later if you need cheering up, Bel.'

But he didn't accept the invitation. I look too much of a mess, he told himself. But he knew it wasn't really that. If he couldn't be with Leah, he didn't want to be with anybody. And later, as he lay stretched on his bed, listening to the thump of music below, he panicked a little, wondering, what if I can't ever forget her?

When finally he slept, he dreamt of her, as he knew he would. It was a soothing and strangely beautiful dream. She came and knelt by his bed and whispered something to him. Her tears fell on his shoulder as she spoke, and what she told him made him stop loving her, and he was happy again. But when he woke, the dream slipped away in seconds and he could barely remember the details of it, only that she had called him by his father's name.

This Large Print Book for the Partially sighted, who cannot read normal print, is published under the auspices of

**THE ULVERSCROFT FOUNDATION**

## Other MAGNA Romance Titles
## In Large Print

**ROSE BOUCHERON**
The Massinghams

**VIRGINIA COFFMAN**
The Royles

**RUTH HAMILTON**
Nest Of Sorrows

**SHEILA JANSEN**
Mary Maddison

**NANCY LIVINGSTON**
Never Were Such Times

**GENEVIEVE LYONS**
The Palucci Vendetta

**MARY MINTON**
Every Street